Duchess from Wyoming

Richard E Graglia

Copyright © 2022

All rights reserved.

ISBN: 9798824784985

For Kay

TABLE OF CONTENTS

Table of Contents, continued

Duchess from Wyoming

In 1880 Wyoming Territory, girls had guns.

One of these young ladies was out to get even with the man who murdered her father--just before last Christmas.   This man was a Sheriff who gunned down her father instead of bringing him to justice.   So she shot the sheriff.   After Arlene shot the sheriff she escaped. Arlene jumped on a train and headed east. She ended up in New York City.   Not good enough.   Arlene then got on an ocean liner and ended up in London.   Her first job was as a jockey who rode a thoroughbred in the 100th running of the Epsom Derby in 1880.   That same day Arlene met all four of Queen Victoria's sons. Three were unmarried.   She taught them how to smoke Cuban cigars.   Arlene then moved into a large house across the wall from Buckingham Palace, and across the street from Harrods Department Store.   She brought a bottle of good scotch (Macallan 1855) when Arlene was invited to meet Her Majesty, Queen Victoria.   Then the story gets interesting.   Did Arlene ever have to stand trial for the murder of the sheriff she shot? Happily for you, that question gets answered in this book.   (Yes, she did.)

CHAPTER 1

Colorado, May of 1880

Torrential rain turned the dirt roads in Fort Collins into foot deep mud. Roofs were leaking. The Cache-LaPoudre River was overflowing its banks. It was night. This was the worst storm since the outbreak of the Civil War twenty years ago. An occasional crack of lightning made this evening more entertaining. It lit up the town. Fort Collins, Colorado, had no street lamps, gas or electric. (New York City had gas street lamps in 1823. London had gas street lamps in the year 1417.)

On the front porch of a wooden house right on the main unimproved dirt road of Fort Collins sat a man enjoying the downpour. Rain was rare. Colorado east of the Rockies was part of the Great American Desert.

A horse with rider clopped down the crest of this street, avoiding the deep mud near the wooden plank side-walks on either side, and stopped her horse. The rider, a young female, took out her .32 caliber Smith & Wesson pistol, aimed carefully at the man sitting in his chair watching the rain. She shot once. The man slumped over. The young female rider took off north, toward Wyoming Territory, in the driving rain. The rain was coming up from Texas. This made riding north easier. The lady shooter had the rain and wind to her back all the way to Wyoming.

Nobody was outside, it was raining too hard and sideways. Winds were 20 miles an hour, gusts were easily 45 miles an hour.

She rode for what seemed an hour and slowed down to give her horse a rest. "Always rest your horse, Arlene," cautioned her father. "You kill your horse, you could die cause you can't (he said cain't) go nowhere. You listenin' girl?" The young woman had a hard time paying attention, especially if something could kill you. "Yeah, yeah, I know that," she said to her father years ago. She always agreed with him just to shut him up. She used to argue. That only prolonged the lecture and sometimes end in a beating. A well-deserved beating, according to her mother.

Hours later it was still raining hard. She was still riding. It was still dark. She couldn't see yet she kept moving north to Wyoming territory and home.

What's that? she wondered. Something smelled wonderful. An overpowering aroma of chili! Chili? There must be an Indian encampment, but which tribe. Some tribes were still openly hostile to whites (wasichu). Some tribes take women and make them tribal members. She saw light from a fire. Indians don't make big fires. Or hang a lantern on a pole. She was four or five hours from Cheyenne, maybe more due to mud and flooding. The hell with it, she thought. Arlene rode toward the chili.

Arlene approached the campsite cautiously. Renegade everything was out here. Lots of angry Rebels with guns and no skills, still angry at Jeff Davis and Bobbie Lee for failing the Confederacy fifteen years ago. Angry at God for letting the Confederacy fail. Angry Indians for letting the Great Spirit allow Wasi'chu and Long Knives to come to this land and take it over. All this land with wide open spaces to farm, ranch, mine, hunt, with lots of unemployed, shiftless angry white people who can't figure out what in God's name to do. Forget that. There's chili!

Now Arlene was close enough to the campfire to see an enclosed carriage, two horses and a white man. Everything she saw was safe and dry under a large canvas tarp. Even the ground they were on was bone dry. And the man was reading a book by lamplight. There was a large iron pot hanging on a hook over the campfire. The powerful aroma of chili was taunting Arlene.

Arlene dismounted and walked her horse over to the campfire with one hand on her .32 caliber pistol resting in her holster. The possible murder weapon if the man she shot was dead.

She stopped at the border between soaking wet and dry. She didn't know what to say other than she shot a guy dead down at Fort Collins.

"You want some chili?" said the young man sitting in a chair reading a book.

Arlene tied her horse up to a long tent pole. One of the several poles which helped hold up the huge tarp, but the man indicated to tie her horse under the canopy, out of the rain to dry off.

The man then got a couple of horse blankets, took off her horses saddle, put blankets on it. Then came up with a wooden bowl filled with oats. The horse ate.

Arlene nodded thanks'. The man brought a second wooden chair from somewhere and put it at his 3 foot square highly polished walnut table which sat flat on the ground. Nothing, not a hunk of fresh-baked cornbread, would accidentally roll of this table.

He filled a big, deep bowl of his chili at her place setting. And put down a large silver soup spoon and a couple of cloth napkins. Then a graniteware coffee mug. He picked up a coffee pot sitting on a flat iron surface also over the fire. He put a couple of logs on the fire.

"Hot coffee," said the man, looking about 27 or 28 years old, faint beard stubble from not shaving for maybe a couple of days, and standing about six feet something.   Arlene had no time to listen to the menu and specials, she was sitting on her comfortable chair, eating chili from the large ceramic bowl, and drinkng the best-tasting coffee she ever had in her life. Young life. Young sheriff-shooting life. She also had a plate of fresh-baked cornbread and a little bowl of fresh country butter.

She had chili all over her face and was about to wipe her face with the sleeve of her oil cloth jacket when the man lifted a cloth napkin and handed it to her—too late. The man sat with the napkin and demonstrated how to use this piece of cloth. Arlene kept eating like she hadn't had a meal in a month.   The man put the napkin, refolded, on the beautiful polished walnut table.

On the opposite side of the walnut table was a pile of napkins. They did not blow away in the wind gusts because they were held in place by a brand new Colt .44 Peacemaker hand gun. Its weight, when loaded, was enough to hold the cloth napkin pile firmly in place.

"Not a lot of people are out for a ride tonight," was the man's attempt at small talk.

Arlene kept eating.

Under another cloth, also resting on the small walnut table was a fresh-baked pie. Arlene knew this because Edward showed her the pie.

"Do you eat apple pie?"

Only eating, not talking, Arlene's eyes lit up. The power of her facial expression forced Edward to immediately cut a large piece of pie. Arlene nodded with delight. He put the large triangular piece of apple pie on a plate and placed it at the upper right of her large, and almost empty, bowl of chili.   He put a fork to the left of the pie plate, as decorum dictated.

"My name is Edward." announced the man who set up the camp, made the chili and even baked an apple pie.

Arlene was eating like she just discovered food. She looked at Edward when he said his name.

"I am on holiday from England."   Again, nothing from the silent, but well fed, young rider.

"Sir, do you live in Cheyenne?" wondered Edward obviously not being able to tell Arlene's sex. She wore a large poncho, flat brimmed cowboy hat, and her long stringy hair could be worn by half the population, boy or girl.

Arlene emptied the bowl of chili, picked up the bowl and handed it to Edward and with her chin, motioned to the cast iron pot of chili simmering over the campfire. Edward dutifully put more chili in Arlene's bowl.

Do you speak English?" wondered Edward.

While Edward was ladeling chili into Arlene's bowl, Arlene picked up the wedge of apple pie and took a large bite out of it. She smiled and nodded and took another bite.   The fork remained untouched next to the pie plate.

"I ain't a 'sir'. I'm a girl." said the rider.

"I apologize, young lady. And I assure you, my name is Edward."

"You look like a Jack." said Arlene with certainty.

"Well, my mistake, your ladyship. I assumed my name was Edward Clarence Augustus George Hanover. I like 'Jack' a lot better. I sincerely thank you, ma'am."

"Don't call me ma'am, Jack."

Do you always go out for a ride on nights like this?" wondered Jack.

"Good grub. Jack."

"Why thank you—by 'grub' you must mean your dinner.?" asked Jack.

"I'm tired," said Arlene.

"Then by all means, please sleep in my carriage. I shall sleep on the ground.   The doors in the carriage lock; you'll be safe," assured Jack in a serious tone indicating there would be no funny business.

"Do I need a lock?" accosted Arlene with her right hand patting the handle of her Smith & Wesson .32 caliber pistol.

"Again, I do apologise. I was just assuring your safety out here on the open plains."

"You ain't no trouble."

"Are there wild Indians about?"

"If you git scared, Jack, scream and I'll protect you," cautioned Arlene.

"Have you actually shot anyone, with that thing, Miss?" Edward said that not realizing women out west, especially in Wyoming, carry guns to shoot men they don't trust. Women trust their intuition, their instincts. That means Wyoming women shoot first.

" 'Bout an hour ago."

That little remark wiped the patronizing smirk off Edward's face. He didn't know if the young lady were joking or not. Her tone, plus the fact of her riding up to his camp late at night in inclement weather, not fearing him, and having the confidence of ten men, suggested that she shot someone 'bout an hour ago.'

Arlene sat on the step of the enclosed Coach and motioned for Jack to help take her boots off. When he did, lots of water poured out. Her wool socks were soaked and dirty.

"You want me to dry your boots and socks over the fire?" said Edward.

"Git my pie." said Arlene with authority.

Edward put Arlene's boots on iron rods that held up cross bars over the fire which held the chili pot. He strung her wet, dirty socks over the crossbar, away from the fire but not the heat.

"See you in the morning, Miss." Edward made sure her boots were secure.   He turned around, expecting a 'good night' from

Arlene, but she was already in the coach. Edward did not hear her lock the door. He also did not go near his own carriage.

Edward walked to the back of the enclosed carriage where there was an attached smaller trailer with wheels, opened it and took out a couple of blankets. He returned to his chair, ladled more chili, finished the cornbread, poured coffee, ate and read his book whilst enjoying the melodic sound of the steady downpour. He was afraid to look at his own carriage for fear that he'd be shot for being a peeping tom. Or a peeping Jack.

CHAPTER 2

Cheyenne, Wyoming Territory

Cheyenne, in 1880, had a population of 3,456, mostly whites. Lots of families up from the Lost Cause (Confederate South) who didn't want to mix with Yankees pouring south during 'reconstruction.' Also a rough mixture of failed gold and silver seekers from California and Nevada who were too humiliated to return to Ohio, Illinois, and wherever else, for not living up to their guarantees of untold fortunes. And not able to pay back everyone who lent them money, on the come. So these souls ended up in Wyoming Territory looking for ways to survive.

Edward, the day after he had homemade chili with a young lady at his campsite, in the pouring rain, had returned to Cheyenne. He checked back into his hotel room to bathe, shave, get properly dressed, then enjoy a filling American late luncheon in the hotel's dining room.

Meanwhile, Arlene was back home south of Cheyenne. After that, she went for a ride in downtown Cheyenne mostly to establish an alibi for last night—to be seen by the townsfolk. Arlene then spotted something she saw last night. The fancy enclosed carriage that belonged to Jack. The one she slept in last night. It was parked outside the biggest hotel in town. A couple of men were detaching the two-wheeled wooden trailer from the carriage and pulling it toward the train station, less than a block away.

Arlene, late teens, rode over to the hotel. Cheyenne was a railroad stop along the Union Pacific Rail Road, part of the transcontinental railroad which opened in May, 1869. Four years ago in June, 1876, the entire 3,000 mile transcontinental railroad track was cleared so that a special Transcontinental Express train could race from New York to San Francisco to celebrate America's 100th year of independence. The Express flew past Cheyenne going 63 miles an hour (!) three o'clock in the morning, and arrived in San Francisco (Oakland, actually) 83 hours and 39 minutes after leaving New York (Jersey City, New Jersey, actually).

That's 3 ½ days to cross the American continent! That set a cross-country speed record that wouldn't be broken until the next century.

That was the fastest any train, or any person in any conveyance, had ever crossed America. Ever.

Cheyenne was a major cattle and sheep shipping hub. Ranchers drove thousands of head of cows from western Kansas, Nebraska, Dakota Territory and Colorado, to ship them east to Chicago and Kansas City meatpacking houses (Armour and Swift), to add to the growing American demand for fresh beef. Most sheep were shorn (not slaughtered) and their wool was shipped to eastern knitting mills.

Arlene figured Jack might be in the hotel's dining room, so she headed that way.

The hotel's restaurant was a good sized room with twenty tables with white cotton tablecloths. Only three tables had diners. Two tables had multiple people eating luncheon. One table had one person, a young man, but he was well dressed in a dark blue jacket, tan vest, tan pants, white shirt and dark blue cravat. He was eating and looking around the room and stopped cold when he spotted the young lady in her buckskin outfit. He stopped eating. He smiled. Arlene smiled back and walked over to him. She got within speaking distance and happily remarked "Hey, Jack!"

He stood up and pulled out a chair at his table and gestured her to sit. She did. 'Jack' pushed her chair in and he moved over to his chair and continued standing. A tall, distinguished gentleman, dressed for a night at the opera, approached 'Jack' and pushed the chair in for Edward to sit down. Edward sat. The young lady thought that whole episode was theatrical and a waste of time. Guys don't have some other guy push their chair in.

"You leavin' town?" she asked.

"I refuse to answer any questions until you tell me your name. Call me 'Jack' all you like, but if you don't give me a name, real or fictitious, I shall call you Henrietta."

"I don't like Henrietta, so my name's Lindy. Lindy Mae Long," said Arlene Dross, who needed a new name because she shot a guy last night and he might be dead and she might be the killer. Who'll be hanged if caught.

"Yes, miss Lindy, I'm going to New York, then off to England shortly thereafter," said Edward with a bit of an English accent. "Would you like some luncheon. Or are you still contented from last night's supper?"

"If you're buyin', I'm eatin'."

Edward nodded and the tall, elegantly dressed man standing behind him walked over and summoned a waitress. Lindy put in her order: scrambled eggs, beefsteak, roasted potatoes, flapjacks and milk.

"How'd you find me?" wondered Edward.

"Saw your carriage," remarked Lindy drinking a glass of fresh Pasteurized milk, brought to her by the waitress.

"Had you a chance to shoot my Peacemaker?" wondered Edward referring to the brand new Colt .44 Peacemaker revolver he put on top of a pile of linen napkins yesterday to keep the napkins from blowing away.

Early this morning Lindy was gone, with cornbread and apple pie. Also, Edward's brand new Colt .44 six-shooter and leather holster were gone and replaced by a 2 pound rock which kept the napkins from blowing all over Wyoming territory. Very thoughtful.

"I didn't know how much to leave." lied Lindy.

"I think it's 14 American dollars." said Edward non-judgmentally.

Outside, down by the railroad tracks, a train whistle blew. An announcement was made in the hotel restaurant by a man with a naturally loud voice: "Listen up, gentlemen, the UP train to St Louis has arrived. This train does not stop in Chicago. Now boarding for St Louis, Cincinnati, Pittsburgh, Philadelphia, New York City."

"You best git goin' Jack," chirped Lindy.

"That isn't my train. Lindy," said Edward almost calling her Henrietta.

Jack had been reading the Cheyenne Laramie County *Leader* newspaper whose headline screamed 'Colorado Sheriff Shot Dead'

"Did you see this?" queried Jack, showing Lindy the headline. Lindy grabbed the paper and looked at the first paragraph: 'Ross Armitage, Sheriff of Larimer County, was gunned down in a

hail of bullets last night at his home in Fort Collins, Colorado. Deputies are looking for the killer, or killers in Colorado, Wyoming Territory and Western Kansas. Newly appointed sheriff, Kees Van Der Hoff, a former Deputy, said that there were several witnesses.'

" 'Hail of bullets'? I only shot once," confessed Lindy, a little too loudly if you asked Jack.

"Shhh. Why not announce it to everyone in town?" said Jack, scolding young Lindy. Jack also learned that she could read. Jack assumed that because Lindy cussed a lot and said 'ain't', she was illiterate. Not a lot of literate people in the wild west at the time.

"Did you see any witnesses?" wondered Jack.

"I could hardly see that sheriff on his front porch. If anyone seed me, they don't know who I am," reported Lindy with almost no confidence.

Lindy Mae Long's steak and eggs lunch showed up on three plates. Lindy Mae is maybe 5'4" and about 90 pounds with her boots, holster and stolen Colt .44 Peacemaker six-cylinder revolver strapped on. And soaking wet. She shoveled in her flapjacks, scrambled eggs, quarter pound of ribeye steak, diced and browned potatoes with onions, all smeared with fresh country butter and dark amber maple syrup imported from Vermont by way of Chicago via the Union Pacific Rail Road.

After eating-chewing-swallowing for 10 minutes, Lindy came up for air saying "You ain't gonna snitch on me, are y'all?"

"I won't have to if you keep volunteering that you shot this man."

"I only shot once!" protested Lindy.

"Once is enough to hang you. That's what they do out here," said Jack, shocked that hanging was very popular in the wild west. Jack added, "What'd you do with your .32?"

"It's home," assured Lindy.

"Dispose of it," insisted Jack.

Lindy furrowed her brow not understanding 'dispose'.

"Get rid of it. Bury it! It's evidence. Keep my .44 and never shoot it," suggested Jack.

Lindy, worried, finished her late luncheon and used her napkin to wash the remaining debris of steak and eggs from her mouth and chin.

"Will you do me the honour of escorting me to the train?" wondered Edward.

"Well, it is on my way home," shrugged Lindy Mae Long.

The Union Pacific five car train, heading east toward St Louis, blew its whistle and left town chugging clouds of thick white smoke into the air.

Another train, nine cars plus coal car, pulled by a large steam locomotive with 'New York Central RR' written on the coal car, pulled up in front of Edward, Lindy and the three stiff, over-dressed men standing three paces behind him.

The locomotive pulled the nine cars past Edward and continued until it got to the last car when it stopped. The last car had a balcony with an overhanging roof, to keep the intense western sun or pouring rain off anyone venturing out on the ample balcony during the trip.

A man appeared out of this last train car, came down the stairs and bowed gracefully to Edward. The man said "Welcome aboard sir."

Two sheriff's deputies from Colorado looking at everyone like they shot their sheriff, came over to Edward and his party because they were boarding a train and might possibly be the killer or killers who were fleeing the area. The deputies rode their horses over.

"We're sheriff's deputies from Colorado. Where were you last night?"

Edward spoke, "We, sir, were all in the hotel dining room enjoying dinner and staying out of the terrible rain storm. Anyone out in that storm has to be mentally impaired."

"Is anyone in your party armed?" wondered one of the deputies.

"No sir, none of us," said Edward.

"I am," said Lindy, who took out her .44, borrowed from Jack, and safely handed it to a deputy. The deputy sniffed the barrel, opened the cylinder and withdrew six bullets. Checking to see if they were all live bullets. They were.

The deputy nodded at Lindy, who was wearing clean and dry cowboy boots, leather pants and jacket. She changed at home.

"You can board. You have a good trip," said a deputy as the two deputies went looking for more murder suspects.

"I'm goin' with you, Jack." Lindy was cock-sure.

Edward looked at her and nodded assuringly.

"Is there room for my horse?" asked Lindy.

"We'll make room," assured Edward/Jack.

Lindy was about to climb aboard but this new guy, also dressed formally, who was standing inside the train car, blocked Lindy's ascension, allowing Edward to go up the three steel stair steps first.

After Edward walked into the train car then this man allowed Lindy to ascend and enter the train car.

Lindy was in the Lounge Car. A beautifully decorated car with a thick Persian Bijar Kilim carpet, comfortable-looking wingback chairs, end tables, a mahogany table for possible dining, overhead lighting and walls covered in intricate Jacquard silk weaving.

Behind Lindy came the three men who were Edward's traveling companions. Two of the three left by walking forward and exiting the Lounge Car and entering another car. The remaining man, an Under Butler, immediately made sure Edward was comfortable.

Edward sat down in a butter soft leather wingback chair. Lindy was looking at the interior of the car and nodding her approval.

"Would you like a refreshment?" wondered Edward, "a cup of tea, or coffee, or lemonade?"

"Lemonade." said Lindy who plopped down in a very comfortable wingback chair.

The Under Butler brought Lindy a glass of lemonade on a silver tray. The glass also contained two cubes of ice. She sipped and smiled. Very cold, tart and sweet at the same time.

Edward was brought a couple of pastries, fresh made by a pastry chef at work in the Kitchen Car of the train.

Lindy watched the Under Butler with curiosity then said, with the Under Butler standing right there, "That guy the conductor?"

Edward nearly choked on his pastry, chuckled and said, "No. Charles is my very efficient Under Butler. If you need anything on our voyage, please ask him. And don't forget to thank him," said Edward, with emphasis on thanking him. Lindy, thought Edward, must have heard of please

and thank you. But maybe mannerisms stopped at the border of Wyoming Territory.

Lindy looked at Charles the Under Butler and said, "Thank you, Mr Butler, for the lemonade. It's good."

"You are most welcome, your Ladyship."

The Executive Chef, Paris trained, had made the chili, simmered in red Bordeaux (claret), using fresh beef, onions, parsnips, garlic and several varieties of beans. Another chef, the pastry chef, had made the cornbread and two apple pies. Last night's campsite was set up by several Groundskeepers and the head Groomsman on Edward's estate in London. This information would eventually get to Lindy, hopefully before he had to cook something for her. Edward cannot cook. Anything. Edward cannot set up a campsite. Edward was an engineer. He designed systems and others built those systems.

Edward offered Lindy one of his pastries. She swooned.

"When'd you make these?" wondered Lindy, savoring the pastry filled with strawberry goodness and creamy white icing.

"I don't cook. I can't cook." admitted Edward.

"So who cooked last night?"

"I will introduce you to my kitchen staff as we get underway."

"Were you gonna keep this a secret?" challenged Lindy.

"Apparently everyone's got secrets," quipped Edward, looking at his Colt .44 now being worn by Lindy.

Lindy gulped. She sipped her lemonade and bit her pastry, as the train they were in moved out of the Cheyenne, Wyoming, train station and headed east toward New York.

The only thing on Lindy's (the former Arlene) mind was, 'can she get away with murder?'

CHAPTER 3

Escape!

The train Lindy and Jack were on left Cheyenne, Wyoming Territory, without an incident. The 2nd Footman came into the Lounge Car and handed Edward another copy of the Cheyenne *Laramie County Leader*, the same paper he'd left at the hotel's restaurant.

"Here, listen to this," said Jack, reading to Lindy: "The gunman or gunmen escaped unharmed in a terrific rain and lightning storm. A witness was unsure if they were the Berkinholt Gang, a group of devious bank robbers who live up in the foothills between Colorado and Wyoming Territory. Larimer County Sheriff's deputies are searching all the way down to Pueblo, Colorado, and up to Cheyenne, Wyoming Territory, for the murderer or murderers and are on the lookout for any members of the notorious Berkinholt Gang who have robbed banks in Denver, Golden, Fort Collins and Fort Morgan, Colorado, in recent years. Larimer County officials have posted a $500 reward for the capture of Sheriff Armitage's killer."

"Well, good. They ain't lookin' for me then."

"Who are the Berkinholt Gang, besides bank robbers?"

"My daddy's gang."

"Your real name is Arlene Berkinholt?"

"Naw. My daddy's name is Dross. That sheriff murdered my daddy five days before Christmas last year, when the gang was the Dross Devils Gang."

"Your father and the sheriff had a shoot out, like a duel?"

"A duel? Like face to face shootin' at each other?" wondered Lindy.

"Exactly." said Jack, excited about whether wild west stories were true.

"Hell no. Fuckin' sheriff murdered daddy. Fuckin' asshole shot daddy in the back six times!"

Jack was not as shocked by the sheriff's murderous ways as he was by Lindy's foul mouth. He wasn't used to language like that, from anyone, lest a young lady. Edward, a Cambridge man (Trinity College) with an undergraduate degree in the Classics, (he can read, write and speak Latin and Classical Greek as well as French), then went to America to earn a Master's Degree in Engineering from the Boston Institute of Technology (the future MIT) three years ago, was a cocooned (protected) English snob. With servants of course. Servants who were snootier than Edward (Jack). His trip to the American wild west was to 'unprotect' him from different classes of people. Like the sheriff--shooting Lindy who is wearing Jack's .44 caliber gun and using language fit for drunken, uneducated sailors. He wasn't sure he could get used to this 'lady'.

Edward, by the way, was making a mountain of money selling central heating to landlords of office buildings, apartment houses and government buildings in New York and Boston in America. London, Liverpool, Manchester, Sheffield, Edinburgh, Glasgow, Cardiff, Bristol, all of Britain's industrial cities. His company, Standard Central Heating, Ltd., was moving into Philadelphia, Baltimore and Washington City now, May of 1880, to provide heat and hot water before the upcoming winter.

Edward was having a very enjoyable time traveling through the American west on a private train he leased from one of the Vanderbilt sons, currently president of the New York Central Rail Road.

"Does the west have a system of jurisprudence? A court system? Or do sheriffs have the power to be judge, jury and executioner?" wondered Englishman Jack.

"Huh?"

"Did your father stand trial for anything?"

"No. He was just walking' down the street when the sheriff come up behind him and blasted away," argued Lindy with angst, anger and pain in her voice.

"What'd your daddy do to deserve to die?

"Nothin!"

"Do lawmen usually shoot innocent men in the back out west? Before Christmas?"

"This fat fuckin' coward did. Shot daddy dead."

"For no good reason." queried Edward, suspecting Lindy was skirting around the reason because whatever it was, her father was up to no good.

"The sheriff decided he didn't like how daddy made a livin'." revealed Lindy, getting agitated.

"Your daddy was a politician."cajoled Edward.

"Naw. He hated politicians."

"Good. Was your daddy a lawyer?"

"Naw. He hated them worse."

"I like your daddy. I'm on your side, no matter what he did, so long as he wasn't a politician or a lawyer." smiled Edward.

"Daddy might've been stickin' up banks. But that don't give that sumbitch no right to gun down my pa," said Lindy without a smattering of justification.

"Your father robbed a bank?"

"Lotsa banks," said Lindy, proudly, correcting 'Jack' adding, "That were his job," reported Lindy as though his father were a blacksmith or cordwainer, "it's how we et (ate)."

That was the end of their conversation until the 2nd Footman announced their train had crossed into the state of Nebraska.

Edward was fascinated by this young woman and her sense of justice. Her father did nothing wrong, according to Lindy, because he was feeding his family, with other people's bank deposits.

Later, at dinner, Edward seated Lindy at the elegantly set dinner table, in the Dining Car. A beautifully decorated room with heavy wool drapes that hung down to the floor. The dining table was circular and made of Indian Rosewood.

"You think you killed the sheriff?"

"I always hit what I aim at." cautioned Lindy.

"How many shots you fire?"

"Like I said a dozen fuckin' times: One."

"The paper said 'hail of bullets." reminded Jack.

Lindy laughed. "Paper's full of shit. Make everything sound worse than it happened. That's what daddy says," concluded Lindy Mae Long, aka Rleen Dross. (Her mother can't spell.)

"You must be a good shot to drop a man with a .32 caliber bullet," said Edward.

"I was lucky. I saw that murderer sittin' on his porch. I cocked my Smith and Wesson and it fired and he slumped over. I took off for home. I crossed the border and saw a fire. Yourn. I was gonna go 'round but I got a whiff of chili you pretended to make. I rode over, saw some scrawny-ass dude sittin' all proper at a table, and that high class stage coach, figured I'd eat and if you gave me trouble, I'd shoot you, too."

"How lucky for me that I'm an English gentleman." Edward thought that statement both ironic and amusing. Lindy didn't.

"I rode home, after I 'borrowed' your .44, and settled up with mother."

"So you're running. No one's looking for you." stated Edward.

"What would you do, Jack?"

"Run!"

"Maybe I'll get off at St Looie. You ain't gonna tell?"

"No, and neither are my staff members."

"Have you been to St Looie, Jack?"

"No. The train went through Chicago coming west. Have you?"

"Have I what?" wondered Lindy, not following Edward's train of thought.

"Been to Chicago. Or St Looie?"

"I ain't been out of the Territory 'cept for a couple trips to Colorado."

A 3rd Footman cleared their dishes as the 2nd Footman served dessert.

"Is your mother all alone now that your father is gone—and now you?"

"Mother's ornery as a rattler. She got a shotgun and a hair-trigger temper," announced Lindy.

Lindy was shown to her sleeping quarters by Jack.   The Sleeping Car had a narrow aisle going down the length of the car. There were four mahogany doors 15 feet apart running the length of the 80 foot car. That meant there were four sleeping compartments, equipped with a bed, dressing vanity, overstuffed chair, kerosene lamps and a separate room for a privy. There was also a clothes closet. There were window shades and drapes for further privacy. Lindy selected the sleeping compartment farthest down the hall.

"Do I need to lock my door, Jack?"
"Are you expecting bandits. Or the sheriff's posse?"
"I got a bigger gun."
"We'll be on the move all night. Cross Nebraska, down to Kansas by dawn, and to Kansas City by 9 or 10 in the morning," said Edward the travel agent.
"You know what I want to do now, Jack?" said Lindy.
"No, your ladyship," retorted Edward.
Lindy giggled and thought 'ladyship' sounded too uppity and preposterous, but liked being called a lady anyway.
"Stand out on your porch and stare at the land. I may not see this again." Lindy didn't sound sad or remorseful.
"Do you wish you had brought your mother with you?" asked Edward in a soft, endearing, impassioned manner.
"Hell no! You ever heard of stirrin' up a hornet's nest?"
"Indeed I have. I've stirred up several; it's why I remain happily on my own..."
"Then you'll be glad momma's back home where she belongs."
With that Lindy Mae Long got up and marched to the back of the train, opened the 'back door' and walked out to the covered platform she called the porch. Lindy took hold of the wrought iron railing and peered at the setting sun and watched the short grass plains roll by and felt free. The clickety-clack of the train rolling over the Union Pacific iron rails sounded comforting, mesmerizing. She smiled; smiled like she'd gotten away with something.

Traveling across Nebraska and snaking down Kansas, rumbling past wheat fields hour after hour, then all night long until 6 the next morning when the private train crossed the bridge that crossed the Missouri River into Kansas City, Missouri, gave Lindy time to think about her life. She was now far enough from Wyoming to hop off Jack's train and start a new life. Away from her mother and a long way from implications of murder.
Jack talked about St Louis. It was a large town on the other side of Missouri, with lots of opportunities for work. Legal or

otherwise.   Or, pointed out Jack, she could take another train to another part of America.

Chicago, for instance, had half a million residents. Chicago was coming back after the great fire of 1871.

St Louis was inhabited by 350,000 people. A very large city on the west side of the Mississippi River, reported Jack. The railroad bridge, the Eads Bridge, had been open since 1874. It was one of the first bridges across the mighty Mississippi River.

St Louis was more than 800 miles from Colorado where Lindy shot the sheriff. Good place to disappear.

They'd be in St. Louis later today.   Good time to make a decision.

CHAPTER 4

St Louis

Edward's train pulled into the new St Louis Union Depot at 4 o'clock in the afternoon. The train yards in St Louis were huge in scale with dozens of tracks and dozens of trains, mostly freight trains.

The freight trains were being taken apart and reassembled, car by car, so that the right cars would become part of a new train off in a new direction with its valuable, and expected, cargo.
Passenger trains came into the St Louis rail yard and stopped at the beautiful, new (opened in 1875) cathedral-like Union Depot at Tucker Boulevard.

Lindy was dressed in her buckskin trousers, fringed jacket and flat-brimmed hat. She had put her Colt .44 in a suitcase given to her by Jack, who also put some American money ($200) and three British gold sovereign coins, worth an estimated $1200, in gold by weight. Jack wrote Lindy a note wishing her good luck and God Speed in St Louis. Lindy was very intelligent and could figure everything out on her own.

Jack's note: 'Good luck to you Lindy. You'll do well in St Louis. P.S. If you like the sport of base-ball, St Louis has a team called the Brown Stockings. Good to have known you, Edward "Jack" Hanover, London.'

"Thanks for the stake, Jack. I'll pay you back, my word is good," said Lindy with confidence and authority, referring to the $50 cash Edward gave her at breakfast. That didn't include the gold sovereign and additional $200 cash Edward had put in her new suitcase.

Lindy opened the back door of the train, walked off the platform and set foot for the first time in Saint Louis, Missouri. Missouri had become the 24th state in 1821, and was the first state entirely on the west side of the Mississippi River. Lindy knew none of that.

The Union Depot was the largest building Lindy had ever seen. Then she walked inside and entered a magnificently large space with an arched ceiling nearly 50 feet high. The floors were made of smooth, polished stone. She was in an echo chamber. Lindy wasn't sure where to go so she headed for a door to get a look at St Louis.

St Louis had a population of 350,000 in 1880 and was the largest city out west, all the way to the Pacific Ocean. St Louis was the Gateway to the West. The next largest city was Kansas City (55,000), then Denver (35,600), then San Francisco (population of 234,000 since the 1849 gold rush).

St Louis was rife with tall buildings, five floors, because of the new steam powered Otis elevators with built-in no fail safety brakes. No more walking up four or more flights of stairs.

Edward promised Lindy there'd be plenty of jobs in St Louis. Factory jobs, farming, working on steamboats like Mark Twain. "You can ride a grain barge, a large boat filled with wheat or corn, all the way down to New Orleans on the Mississippi River! You'll have many adventures," promised Edward just half an hour ago as they finished breakfast in his Dining car.

There was an announcement for a train departing for Chicago, leaving from track 4. Then another announcement for a train departing for a place called Cincinnati on Track 7 in half an hour. The announcements were coming from a teenaged boy with a megaphone. Lindy couldn't tell time but wanted to hear more about this Cincinnati place and asked someone where track 7 was.

Lindy knew nothing of buying a ticket. All she knew was she got on a train and ended up in St Louis.

She walked over to track 7. There was a train on the track. Workmen in overalls were working on passenger train cars. A conductor saw her and smiled. She was young and beautiful and inquisitive.

"May I help you, young lady?" prayed the conductor.

"Do you go to Sin-Sin.ah…," Lindy was tongue-tied.

"Cincinnati. Yes, we leave in one hour," stated the conductor as he confirmed the departure with his pocket watch.

"Can I see inside the train a second?"

The conductor, always in a mood to help the occasional young, beautiful, curious woman who ventured past, nodded and boarded the train holding the door for Lindy.

Lindy walked into a passenger car and her heart sank. There was something wrong. Jack's Lounge car had a few big, comfortable seats, wingback chairs, overstuffed lounging chairs, small tables with lamps, beautiful carpeting on the floor, elegant wood paneling and drapes on the windows.

This car was row upon row of stiff wooden benches with thin padding, wooden floors and no drapes! The air looked dusty, because most of the windows were open and trains chugged out thick black smoke. And there were dozens of chugging locomotives all over the yard.

"May I see your Dining car?"

"Dining car? This train doesn't have a dining car," said the conductor.

"What about a sleeping car?"

"Well, passengers sleep in their seats."

"Well, I'll have to see your other trains to Chicago. Does that train have a Sleeper car?"

"All of our trains have these comfortable passenger cars."

"Really? I'm used to relaxing in the Lounge car, then being called to the dinner car, then, at night, going to sleep in my own room in a Sleeping car, so I thought that's how all trains are." Lindy was adamant.

The conductor laughed. "You are very delightful and are given to a fanciful, dancing imagination."

"I ain't imaginin' nothin', I just got off a train like 'gat!"

"Well if that's what you're used to, I'd go running back to that train before it takes off."

Which is exactly what a now-panicked Lindy must do. Only which way was Edward's fantasy train? Such a huge train depot. Oh my God, thought Lindy, what do I do?

Lindy recognized a statue in the depot and ran to a doorway she might have entered the train station through.

Out on the platform where Edward's gleaming train was parked was a different train. An old, tired locomotive and half a dozen dusty passenger cars, sat puffing. Lindy spotted a man in a uniform and asked, "Where'd that other train go?"

The man, a conductor, shrugged, looked at his pocket watch and muttered, "This train just arrived from Kansas City."

That didn't help. Lindy looked around the train yard and thought she saw the tail end of Edward's train leaving the yard. She wished she had her horse with her. Wait a minute, thought Lindy, I do have my horse with me and he's on Edward's train! She ran toward the train she thought might be Edward's. The blind optimism of youth.

Hanging onto her now-heavy suitcase, Lindy ran like an Olympic sprinter, slowly closing in on the train she thought might be Edward's. The train disappeared around the train yard behind a freight train being assembled from rolling stock coming in on different tracks. This could get confusing, and dangerous. Lots of moving train cars, on lots of tracks, with train cars being switched from one track to another, could kill an unsuspecting man. But what about a suspecting girl looking for a train that could be on its way to New York while she's trapped in the freight car assembling yard.

Lindy was now lost in the middle of this freight train assembling yard. Box cars and tanker cars and flat cars to her left and right. The train she thought was Edward's was a caboose with a back porch, like Edward's Lounge car.

Lindy was out of breath. She saw an opening to her right between fast-rolling box cars, hobbled across six sets of tracks and was back within 50 feet from the train station's platform. She threw her suitcase across the quarried stone floor and raced toward the platform. Welcome to St Louis, Rleen! thought Lindy, cop killer, girl who was on her way to New York on a private train with servants waiting on her hand and foot. Now she must gather her strength, find a place to stay, then look for a job.

After resting for a couple of minutes, Lindy stood up and looked for the entrance of the Union Depot. The place was getting crowded. More passenger trains were arriving. And more people were departing to parts unknown (to Lindy). Where could all these people be going wondered Lindy. She then figured out what she was going to do: work at the train station. Help the endless stream of passengers come and go; surely they need someone like that at the train station.

As Lindy opened the door to walk back into Union Depot she spotted, or thought she spotted, Edward's train. She hesitated, after all, she was away from Cheyenne and sheriff's deputies from Colorado. And New York is bigger, more crowded. She had pocket money and Edward's Colt .44 pistol. What more did she need?

She tightened the grip on her suitcase, headed inside the Depot when a clot of passengers, with belongings, pushed her back outside and nearly knocked her onto the railroad tracks, as the next train was pulling up.   Lindy caught her balance, jumped onto the tracks in front of the slowing Cincinnati, Indianapolis, St Louis & Chicago Railway train, and skipped toward the train car that looked like Edward's train.   It was.

Lindy bounded up the stairs on Jack's train's back platform. Lindy went out to the back porch, came back inside and opened the door to the Lounge car and came face to face with the serious Under Butler and 2nd Footman who were straightening the room.

"I beg your pardon, miss," said the very stiff Under Butler, annoyed that a commoner had witnessed him polishing furniture.

"Where's Jack? I mean, Edward."

"His Lordship is at the front of the train where the locomotive is located," said the 2nd Footman, also annoyed that this common girl—who should be cleaning and polishing—was not only intruding in pristine space, but is too familiar with Edward Clarence Augustus George in the first place.   And 'Jack'?   Whom does this obstreperous creature think she is?

Lindy put her suitcase down in an annoying part of the room (any part of the Lounge car would be an annoyance to these two starchy prigs) and raced out the back door, down the porch
steps and walked quickly to the locomotive to surprise Jack.   Or maybe he was expecting her.

At the massive locomotive there was no Edward.   There were three workmen toiling away with large wrenches, changing, or tightening, or doing something with the pistons that turn the large steel wheels.

"Hey, has any of you seen Edward.?"

The three men were covered in grease, their clothes needed to be burned, not given to some poor washer-woman to scrub clean. Two of the men continued working.

"Lindy!," said the third man who looked a lot like Edward (Jack) minus the grease, grime, dirt and filth.

"Jack?"

"Take that wrench and set it here on the crosshead wrist pin and hold tight while we turn the piston rod and reconnect it…"

Lindy took a larger-than-life (four feet in length) steel wrench with a fixed opening, slid it into a large steel bolt and held tight. Edward turned his wrench and the piston valve 'clicked' into place.

"Thanks," said Edward to Lindy.

"Now let's put the crank pins in and be off to New York. Are you joining us, Lindy?"

"Ahh," started Lindy, looking at the train station, the tall stone and brick buildings of St Louis, and then at this fellow she called Jack who isn't afraid to get dirty, unlike the starchy boys in the Lounge car.

"Yeah, I'm in. For now," cautioned Lindy.

Chapter 5

To New York

Several hours later, Lindy and Jack were at their dining table in the Dining car being waited on hand and foot by the Under Butler with the 2nd Footman standing at attention near the doorway to the Kitchen car.

Lindy and Edward were eating Delmonico's Beefsteak, prairie potato, green beans, tomatoes in olive oil with fresh oregano. And sipping French wine whilst moving at a 40 mile an hour clip across Indiana, heading toward Ohio and ultimately New York City.

"Will we go through Sin-Sin-someplace.?" wondered Lindy.

"Yes, Cincinnati was named after a 5th Century B.C. Roman Paladin who saved Rome," said Edward as though he were teaching a Cambridge class in pre-Christian Roman history, not knowing whether his student had any idea what he was talking about. Edward continued, "Are you planning on staying there?"

"How crowded is it?"

"About 250,000, but that's a hundred thousand less than St Louis."

"You know how big Cheyenne is?" asked Lindy, doing a comparative study.

"About 3,500,"much, much smaller."

"I know, I live there." said Lindy reacting as though his Lordship were lording his education over her. "And stop treating me like I'm stupid."

"Please, forgive me. I shan't do that again." guaranteed Edward.

"Shant? What the hell kind of word is that?"

"It's a British way of saying 'I shall not'."

"Could you not say that word again. Shan't. I'm goin' to the shanthouse to take a shan't."

Edward feigned embarrassment.

Back in the Lounge car, Lindy was sprawled across a seven foot wide velvet Davenport sofa, lying on her back, looking at the intricate ceiling, painted with a beautiful scene of garden flowers and highlighted by Tiffany kerosene lamps hanging every five feet.

"Please tell me about your father.   What was he like?" wondered Edward.

"I dunno," said Lindy, never having been asked such a question. "He loved momma and momma loved money."

"So the fastest way to get money was at the bank.?" replied Edward.

"Yeah," replied Lindy with a 'where else' tone in her voice.

"Did you know your father robbed banks?"

"Well..?" Recalled Lindy overhearing her parents talk openly about bank robbers for years.

"You said that sheriff shot your father before Christmas?"

"Who guns down your daddy before Christmas?" exclaimed Lindy.

Jack backed off.   Lindy, normally ice cold, was getting emotional. Something upper crust Englishmen were unfamiliar with.

"As soon as ma buried daddy, she bought a new go-to-town dress and went lookin' for a new man."

"You saw all this?" wondered Edward

"I was right there, Jack! Momma was planning her next move."

Edward might be an English gentleman, a member of the stiffest order of pampered, over-educated, extremely wealthy, entitled people on earth, but he grew up in a household where his mother was a money hungry social climber. Edward blamed his father's early, untimely death on his mother's never-ending blind ambition. Terrible parents, apparently, know no economic or class boundaries.

"Your mother was looking for a new husband?"

"She said, 'now it's your turn, duchess, to keep a roof over my head."

"'Duchess?'" wondered Edward.

"Momma called me duchess. Said I had my nose too high in the air."

"How were you supposed to keep a roof over your mother's head?" wondered Jack, "by using your .32 to rob banks?"

"Sell my body for money. How else?"

Jack was shocked. He altered the conversation:
"You loved your father," inquired Jack.
"I hated that sheriff."

The next morning Edward's private nine car train (Lounge car, Dining car, Sleeping car, Kitchen car; Staff Lounge & Dining car, Staff [males only] Sleeping car; two stock cars,"for horses and tack and another boxcar for carriages and extra luggage and gifts) pulled into the Cincinnati train station. Lindy was eating breakfast and looked out the window for a few seconds then continued with her sausages and flapjacks.   Out the window, the sous chef from Edward's train, ran to the depot over to a fruit seller's stand and bought a lot of fresh fruit, then ran back to the Kitchen car. Lindy observed some of this.   About a minute later the stiffer than usual Under Butler appeared with a glass of fresh-squeezed orange juice for Lindy and Edward.   Edward thanked his UnderButler, Lindy didn't.

"When do we get to New York?" wondered Lindy.

"Tomorrow night unless you want to get off at the next town, which is Pittsburgh in the Commonwealth of Pennsylvania. Or the stop after that on the other side of Pennsylvania in the city of Philadelphia which is the second largest city in America.   I like Philadelphia, great food."

Edward was brimming with knowledge because he'd been to these places and didn't just read about them. He walked their streets, ate their food, talked to their citizens, visited shops, museums and all sorts of other things which Lindy only imagined.

"When was you in this next town?"

"Three years ago. I was buying steel, which is hardened iron. All the railroad rails are now made of steel instead of iron. My boilers and furnaces are made of steel, for my central heating business." said Edward with enthusiasm (he was an engineer and loved to make things with this new product, steel), who stopped talking as Lindy was now staring out the window, not interested in steel.

About two hours out of Pittsburgh in the bucolic mid-Pennsylvania countryside Edward thought of something and stated with authority: "Lindy, you need to go clothes shopping in Philadelphia."

Lindy, staring at Pennsylvania's lush green countryside, much much different from the dry sage-infested plains with scraggly lilac bushes around Cheyenne, instead of all the stately elm, maple, oak and hickory trees out the window, heard Edward and shrugged, saying, 'uh-huh' without drawing her attention away from the view.

The finest, and largest, department store in Philadelphia was Wanamaker's at 13th and Market Streets. Wanamaker was the first department store electrically illuminated. Wanamaker was the first to install telephones, accept returns, have a completely ventilated building to keep shoppers comfortable. And Wanamaker's had a pneumatic tube system to quickly transport money and critical papers, forms and receipts, from check-out stations to the bookkeeping and accounting room on the top floor. In two years (1882) Wanamaker will have installed elevators.

Wanamaker opened a women's department three years ago, in 1877. Edward, visiting Wanamaker when he was heading out west a month ago, bought American suitings for himself and his key staff. (Edward later stopped in Kansas City at Kersey-Coates and bought denim dungarees sold by Levi Strauss.)

Edward's private train stopped in Philadelphia for the sole purpose of taking Lindy shopping at Wanamaker. Where Edward also wanted to go for things he wanted.   Edward and Lindy walked into the massive Wanamaker department store (with 129 counters and another first: price tags on all the goods) and Lindy gawked. Her jaw probably dropped but she controlled her emotions so that her mouth opened a tiny bit. Edward led her to the Women's department. He walked over to an accessories counter leaving Lindy alone with a Women's wear salesman. A man, thus salesman. Edward handed Lindy an envelope filled with American cash. Lindy looked inside and saw that Abe Lincoln was on the $100 bill. "That's Abe Lincoln? Holy shit," exclaimed Lindy. A couple of matronly ladies heard this obscenity and quickly moved away from the girl in the tight leather fringed pants.

Edward (Jack), in the meantime, noticed the Wanamaker Watch & Jewel Department. Jack was looking at Patek-Philippe pocket watches and then was comparing English dip pens exquisitely made by Joseph Gillott's Writing Instrument Company with Sir Josiah Mason's Dip Pen & Ink Mfg, Ltd. Edward couldn't decide so he bought both pens. He then wandered over to the Wanamaker Hat Department looking at straw summer hats.

Edward veered back to Women's Fashions to look for Lindy. A man carefully walking behind Edward was the 2nd Footman and he was carrying Edward's packages whilst Edward looked around the rows of daywear dresses. He did not find her. He looked in Women's Accessories and found her not. He didn't know what to do and went over to the Men's Fashions to see if she were looking for him. She was there, but not looking for Edward. She was trying on clothing in their Western America department. And Lindy found, and was wearing, an almost identical outfit of red-brown buckskin with fringe. "The only outfit left!" she said, excited, assuming the store was stocked with plenty of buckskin outfits with fringe. Edward smiled thinking 'she's never going to entertain the notion of wearing a dress.'

"Do you need a new hat? A summer hat?" wondered Edward.

"Summer hat? What's that?" (pronounced 'whassat')

Lindy walked out of Wanamaker wearing a light colored finely woven straw flat-brimmed summer hat from the Menswear department. Edward had his own straw summer hat on but his hat looked more English. The Under Butler, 2nd and 3rd Footmen were carrying a lot of packages which Lindy selected. Edward settled his account with British gold sovereign coins. He was saving his American money for dinner and amusements. Lindy took Edward by the arm and walked down Market Street with a big, broad happy-summer smile. Edward had not seen this side of her. He liked it. Where to next, he thought? Lindy answered his thoughts:

"Back to the train to try on all my new stuff!"

"You want dinner here?"

"How far's New York?"

"About 80 miles, or an hour and a half," stated Edward like a Keeper of the Timetable.

"Let's giddy-up outta here, Jack."

The last leg of their journey was through New Jersey to Jersey City where the train ride ended and a steam-powered ferry boat would glide Edward & Company to Manhattan across the Hudson River. The train, which Edward leased from the Vanderbilt family a month ago, had been paid for by Edward's representative at the Bank of New York.

Lindy walked into the Lounge car of Edward's train, waiting at the Philadelphia train station. She was followed by the Under Butler carrying too many beautifully wrapped packages from

Wanamaker.   The 2nd and 3rd Footmen placed the packages on available tables, then chairs and davenports. All supervised by Lindy who grabbed the biggest package and took it over to a corner, sat in an overstuffed chair, and shredded the paper, all to the annoyance of the Under Butler.

Their private train, operating on Pennsylvania Railroad track, left the Market and 32nd Street Station shortly after Edward nodded to the Under Butler, who told the engineer to head to New York City.

Out the window Edward looked at the brand new Broad Street Railroad Station under construction with its gothic and stunning architecture, which was borrowed from London's St. Pancras station. Edward's favorite train station.

Lindy, in the meantime, had torn open all of her packages like a kid at Christmas and had spread out all of her new possessions across the vast space of the 80 foot long Lounge car. Wanamakers 'Go West' department in their Men's Fashion section was a hit with Lindy Mae Long, gun slinging sheriff shooter from the real Wild West.   Lindy bought three pair of 'genuine' Sioux moccasins with colorful beadwork.   Two pair of 'Texas' riding boots, or cowboy boots. Several pair of buckskin and leather pants, called breaches, or britches.   Some had her seemingly favorite fringe, some didn't.   All pants had pockets.

"I see that you enjoy shopping," said Edward, while Lindy was tearing open packages.   He added, "New York's got a lot of department stores, along The Ladies' Mile.   A mile of stores for shopping, some restaurants, but mostly stores with clothes, jewelry, shoes."

"Ladies' Mile?" queried Lindy.

"Yes,   from 14th street to 23rd Street," stated Edward— information that fell on deaf ears.

"I can't shop there," said Lindy, suddenly disheartened.

Edward looked puzzled, baffled—"Why on earth not?"

"I ain't no fuckin' lady!"

Oh, yeah, that.   The dressing, and talking, like an uneducated boy.

Edward, having a domineering mother and a despotic, imperious, backstabbing older sister, did not try to convince Lindy that she was a lady. Never attempt to correct an attitude of a determined angry woman.   Edward learned that the hard way growing up.   It drove him out of England and into America. Apparently this 'disease' had spread in America, too.

Also, Lindy might not be allowed into stores such as Tiffany, B. Altman, Macy's, Arnold Constable, F.A.O. Schwarz, on Union Square, because she refused to wear a dress.

But those were Edward's concerns. New York City was 84 miles away and Lindy was busy opening her packages and having a wonderful time. This was the second time he had seen her smile. The first time was when she spotted the apple pie whilst eating her Texas chili under the tarp in that torrential rain storm just a couple of days ago.

Edward's private train stopped at a pier in the state of New Jersey, across the Hudson River from Manhattan.

Edward's staff, with the help of stevedores who worked the water front, loaded horses, carriages, tack, and all else aboard a private Vanderbilt-owned ferry. Lindy personally saw to her horse, L.C. (for Lost Colt). Lindy led L.C. to a compartment on the private ferry, also leased from Cornelius Vanderbilt II. A compartment built for race horses.

After inspecting every car of the private train, Edward sent a telegram to Cornelius Vanderbilt II thanking him for his generosity. Edward had the Bank of New York wire an additional $10,000 to Cornelius IInd upon returning the train perfectly spotless and in good working order.

CHAPTER 6

New York City

At long last all parties traveling with Edward Clarence Augustus George Hanover were settled in the Fifth Avenue Hotel in Manhattan. The Fifth Avenue Hotel took up an entire block of Fifth Avenue between 23rd and 24th Streets across from Madison Square, a beautifully landscaped park. Edward and his staff, including Lindy, took up twelve suites on the top two floors. Edward gave his staff three days off and handed each one a total of $100 in small bills of American money (£20 Sterling equalled $108 in 1880). Some staff immediately raced out of the hotel and disappeared into Manhattan. The remainder took hot baths in their private in-suite bathrooms, then caught up with their sleep.

A lot of worldly celebrities stayed at the Fifth Avenue Hotel. Amongst them were Albert, Prince of Wales, in October, 1860, one month before the presidential election that brought Abraham Lincoln to power. Commodore Vanderbilt was a regular; robber barons Jim Fisk, Jay Gould; the resolutely corrupt kingpin Boss Tweed; all gathered at the Fifth Avenue Hotel for shenanigans. Lawyer Chester A Arthur had a suite which he used as his office. Chester A Arthur was going to be elected Vice-President of the United States this November, serving under James Garfield in the 1880 election. Garfield would be assassinated and die in September 1881, which would ascend Chester A Arthur to the White House as the 21st President a year from now.

Lindy pulled a chair up to a window on the sixth floor of her four room suite at the Fifth Avenue Hotel and looked at the layout below. Edward, invited into Lindy's suite to answer questions about New York, explained why one street crossed another street at an odd angle. "Broadway crosses Fifth Avenue below us and crosses several other streets all the way uptown. It was a walking trail that meandered up Manhattan Island centuries ago. Are you hungry?"

"Apple pie!"

Shortly, Lindy and Edward were seated at a cafe near Union Square (14th Street to 17th Street, along Park Avenue South) where she was eating a piece of apple pie. Lined up and ready to be eaten were also a slice of blueberry pie, strawberry-rhubarb pie and huckleberry pie. Edward had a bowl of Manhattan Clam Chowder. He sipped his tea and would enjoy a piece of apple pie in a moment. Lindy was drinking coffee. Premium coffee from Ethiopia, not 'prairie' coffee like they have in Wyoming Territory. Out in Wyoming nobody knew what beans were used to make prairie coffee, but you loaded your cup with lots of sugar. Otherwise you drank beer, like Lindy's father.

Lindy was dressed in a new outfit. A light buckskin pair of pants and matching jacket with fringe.   She did not wear her sidearm. She had on her new shoes--half shoes, half boots with a riding heel. Her pockets were stuffed with all the money that Edward had given her including in her travel case. Next door to the apple pie cafe was Macy's Department Store on Sixth Avenue betwixt 13th and 14th Streets.

Macy's was the first store along the Ladies' Mile of department stores now serving upper middle class and ruling class women in the area, which included the City of Brooklyn, Manhattan and outlying parts of Long Island, Connecticut and New Jersey. Gilded Age shoppers were driven in their luxurious carriages up and down this Ladies' Mile of exclusive shops and cafes. Their servants carried packages and placed them carefully in compartments of their carriage, or a second carriage which trailed madame's custom built and upholstered enclosed or open carriage.

Mary Stilwell Edison, wife of Thomas, loved taking the ferry across the Hudson from West Orange, New Jersey, to Manhattan, to spend her husband's money on the finer things in life. And she found a lot of those things at Tiffany, Lord & Taylor (Broadway at 20th Street) and B. Altman (Sixth Avenue between 18th and 19th Streets).

European Royalty found its way to New York, stayed at the Fifth Avenue Hotel and its Queens (Royal and Consort) and Princesses lavished in taking their carriages along the Ladies' Mile with the local American monied class: Gilded Age, the second generation. The first generation were poor and entrepreneurial. The second generation was filthy rich. Many of the next generation would go broke from reckless spending. Thus shirtsleeves to shirtsleeves in three generations.

After spending all day along the Ladies' Mile, loading two carriages with purchases, Edward and Lindy came home to their separate suite of rooms. Lindy, by the way, had no trouble getting into any of the department stores, exclusive shops or cafes. She was with Edward, who dressed elegantly, who was also followed by three overly-stiff servants.   Lindy, it was assumed, must be a rich spoiled rotten brat, part of the Gilded Age.   Spoiled rotten brats were especially welcome at all these shops because their fathers happily spent fortunes to keep them quiet.

Several hours later, before dinner time, Edward knocked on Lindy's suite's door and announced, politely, "I am going to dine at the most famous steakhouse in America tonight, after my nap and bath--would you care to join me?"

"Hell yeah," rejoined Lindy Mae Long, girl who successfully shopped the entire Ladies' Mile, and is now famished.   Edward picked up the telephone in Lindy's suite and handed Lindy the In Suite Room Service Menu.   She ordered a bowl of chili with cornbread and apple pie. It was delivered posthaste. Edward gave Lindy a $5 bill to tip the room service gentleman.

"Why?" wondered Lindy about a 'tip'.

"He will remember the generous tip and the next time you order room service, it will come much faster, and hotter and better."

"So's a tip's a bribe?" Figured Lindy.

"A <u>big</u> $5 tip's a bribe," quipped Edward, "a ten cent tip isn't."

Delmonico's Restaurant in lower Manhattan had their own building. You entered past twin columns taken from Pompeii and announced yourself to the Maitre D'.   You were confronted by several choices of dining rooms. There were private dining rooms, dining rooms for unattended women, and large dining rooms for conventions. Dining rooms for celebrities and dining rooms for riff-raff.   The prices on Delmonico's menus were 'outrageous'. Delmonico's famous potato dish was 15¢! Delmonico's, opened in 1827 as a bakery, confectioner and cafe. By 1837 the two Delmonico brothers built an eight-story building at the corner of William and Beaver Street with their name set in stone above the doorway, bordered by those twin columns secured from the ruins of Pompeii, Italy.

How would Lindy Mae Long be able to get into Delmonico's dressed in fringed pants and a fringed jacket with her summer straw medium-brimmed hat? She would walk in with Edward who was wearing his black full dress suit, starched white shirt, white bowtie and top hat. The Maitre D', having recognized Edward from his several dining experiences before, shook hands. An attendant took Edward's hat.

"May I introduce a woman of royalty from out west. The grand-daughter of Major Stephen Long who made vast discoveries in Colorado country, Miss Lindy Mae Long. The Maitre D' Delmonico was impressed and bowed deeply. She smiled and bowed back. They were seated in the Celebrity dining area which was a civil distance—and walled off—from the walk-in trade dining area.

Delmonico's had introduced something new and bold in dining. A menu from which diners could make their own selections, called a la carte. The menus were also in French. Edward pointed to where the steak was on Lindy's menu.

"Why don't it say 'steak'?"

"Because it's in the French language."

"French?"

"So they can charge more money, because it's 'foreign'. Their cows come from Texas."

"Pretty sneaky," said Lindy with an approving smirk.

The waiter brought bottled water and opened the glass bottles, poured the New York Saratoga Springs sparkling water, took their orders with little trouble. Lindy didn't want green beans or other vegetables but gave in to the Delmonico potato with herbs and fresh country butter. She also learned that Delmonico's grew their own vegetables and fruit on acreage in the Williamsburg section of Brooklyn. So she also tried the green beans (haricot vert) floating in rich, creamery butter.

Whilst they ate, Edward noticed a couple enjoying themselves a few celebrity tables over. The man was Diamond Jim Brady, age 24, dining with a young beauty, new in town, who worked in theatre as an actress and singer. She was 19 year old Lillian Russell.

Both were carrying on, laughing and acting indiscreetly, oblivious to other patrons. They were wooing each other. Young Diamond Jim was single and planned on staying that way all his life, and Lillian was married and must have accidentally misplaced her husband this evening.

Eighteen months ago, in New York, Edward got into a card game with Diamond Jim and won $15,000 playing poker. Diamond Jim thought Edward was a stiff uppity Englishman who didn't know how to play poker and for sure didn't know how to bluff. That second part was true. Edward didn't know how to bluff. So when he acted like he had a Jack high straight flush, he did. And he won. He beat Diamond Jim's Ace high nothing. Edward took his winnings and went back to his hotel. Diamond Jim stayed and won $80,000 that night.

This evening got interesting when, without warning, Edward's Boston Tech roommate showed up alone at Delmonico's, spotted him and ingratiated himself at Edward's private table.

"Eddie!" came the warning shot, "At home in the Citadel."

(The Citadel was what regular patrons of Delmonico's called 'their' restaurant of choice.)

Edward winced, turned and there, unfortunately, was Roland H. Betthard, a seat-of-your-pants engineer who excelled at the Boston Institute of Technology, known as Boston Tech, and after 1916 known as M.I.T. It was Roland who watched Edward struggle with his central heating system, whether to use steam or hot water to vent through an office building or large housing complex. Roland took a look at Edward's cut-away engineering drawing of a six story office building and said, "steam" as he shoveled a roast beef sandwich into his mouth. That was years ago—the boys were in college.

Roland grabbed a chair from a table and sidled up to Edward's table as he gazed intently at Lindy Mae Long, drooling lasciviously, "Edward, whom have we here?"

Roland, according to Lindy Mae, reminded her of her father. No room for formality, says what he feels and does what he wants. Nothing formal or awkward or even polite about Roland. Lindy took a sudden interest in this roué.

"Why ain't I heard nothin' about this character, Jack?"

"Oh God," blurted out Roland, "You told her your name is Jack! Er, I mean, so, yes, dear old roomate, Jack!"

"Shut up, Rollie. Lindy told me I *look* like a Jack. So that's that. Besides, I do not deal in subterfuge." reminded Edward, a stiff way of speaking even in the late 19th Century.

"I need a drink and a steak." The difference betwixt Roland and Edward was hilariously obvious.

Roland ordered a gin and tonic with his Delmonico's steak and potato.

"Why are you in New York?" wondered Roland.

"I'm on my way back from holiday. I met Lindy out west in Wyoming."

"Are you two courting?" queried Roland.

"What's courting?" wondered Lindy.

"Be careful how you answer, Roland, she's got a gun and knows how to use it."

"I shot a sheriff in Colorado last week."

Roland's eyes grew wide and accepting. Wow! A dangerous girl from the wild west!

"You headed up to Boston?" wondered Roland, meaning is Edward going to Boston Tech for some reason.

"I'm going back to London."

"Are you going with Jack?" said Roland to Lindy, man killer.

"I don't know yet."

"I could show you a great time around here. I know New York all the way up to Inwood, take you to Central Park, see all the sights."

"When do you go, Jack?" wondered Lindy.

"Ah, the Britannic sails Monday." announced Edward.

"Where to?" wondered Lindy.

"Across the ocean to England, and my home in London."

"Will I ever see you again?" replied Lindy.

"I get back here every couple of years."

"And if I didn't happen by tonight would you've looked me up?" asked Roland.

"The last we talked you were going to move to Ohio," reminded Edward, "to Cleveland."

"So, you didn't go to Cleveland, or any other place in Ohio?"

"I passed through Ohio and wondered whether you'd be good company or annoying," conjectured Edward.

"And.?" wondered Roland still looking for an answer.

"I instructed the train operator to go as fast as he could through Ohio."

Lindy thought that was funny. She also liked having two rich men (boys in their late 20s who could afford steak) fighting over her.

Not a lot of that in Wyoming Territory. A lot of old drunks and poor cowboys fought over Lindy. One of the reasons she was armed.

After dinner Edward, Lindy and Roland walked back to the Fifth Avenue Hotel.   In the lobby, before they got to the elevators, Edward bade goodnight to Lindy and Roland and went up to his suite.   Roland, on the other hand asked Lindy if she'd like to see a live musical review at the Union Square Theatre. Lindy agreed. They went out and hailed a Hansom cab.

Tonight at the Union Square Theatre was an operetta featuring several new, young female singers as chorus. One of whom was Lillian Russell who had just eaten dinner with Diamond Jim Brady, notorious gambler, at Delmonico's. Diamond Jim was also a backer of this original operetta.

The play was *Boccaccio.* An Italian comic-operetta which takes place in Florence in 1348 as the spread of the Black Death sends citizens panicking.   The citizens, escaping Florence, stop to tell bawdy tales of unfaithful wives and philandering husbands with music. (Giovanni) Boccaccio meets a beautiful young lady named Fiametta, a ravashing unmarried blonde.   Fiametta is an assertive woman who does not shrink in the presence of men.   She is independent, confident, decisive. And self-assured.   Lindy didn't understand Italian but could easily understand Fiametta's attitude, personality and aggressiveness. And Lindy's blonde hair was real, not like Fiammetta's stage wig.   Lindy could even figure out what the stories were about: cheating! Lindy's mother accused her daddy of cheating and she didn't understand what her mother was talking about. (Stealing money from banks is obviously 'cheating', which her mother favored.)

When the operetta ended Lindy was the first to stand and applaud enthusiastically.   The rest of the audience applauded, too. But more politely, from their seats.   Roland jumped out of his seat and hooted, cheered and applauded loudly.

Five minutes later, Roland and Lindy walked through Union Square. The theatre was on 14th Street, so they walked north up to 23rd Street.

"Did you understand the story?" asked Roland. Unfortunately, his tone of voice was condescending.

"People are dying so they ended up gossiping and find out who's fucking who. And the main girl falls in love with the storyteller and ends up in a castle. Or didn't you think I'd figure it out?" wondered Lindy to an aghast Roland.

"I wasn't sure," said Roland, an engineer, which meant he probed every situation analytically concluding things as he saw them. Someone's feelings were never figured into his deliberations.

"So, 'cause I'm from Wyoming and don't dress like a lady and cuss up a storm, you figured my brain don't work like yourn."

"Yes.   I was trained at Boston Tech in engineering and mathematics.   So I'm obviously your better," reported Roland-the-robot.

Lindy stormed into the Fifth Avenue Hotel and was stopped by a hotelman in a crisp red uniform with two rows of polished brass buttons. He demanded to see her room key. Lindy took her opulent room key from her back buckskin pants pocket. The uniformed hotelman was taken aback when he saw her penthouse key. Penthouse apartments had at least four rooms and provided, if need be, servants, especially butlers and first footmen. The hotelman handed the penthouse key back to Lindy and said in a comforting, ingratiating tone, "Very good, your ladyship."

"Ladyship?!" snapped Lindy. Then, for once, she shut up and thought about the comment and saw that the hotelman was humbled (he was sweating) and not mocking her, like what's-his-name, Edward's college buddy.

"You're welcome my good man," replied Lindy, curtsying, then turned and headed to the bank of Otis elevators, strutting like the royal duchess which her mother despised. In the Fifth Avenue Hotel all women strutted like duchesses. The elevator operator elevated Lindy to her 6th floor suite.

There was someone loudly pounding on Edward's suite's thick rosewood door. The Under Butler opened the door to find Lindy in a huff. "Where's Jack." demanded Lindy, then rephrased her demand: "I need to talk to Edward. Pronto."

"His Lordship is unavailable madame,"   This statement fell on deaf ears as Lindy marched into Edward's penthouse suite. "Jack, get your ass out here!"

The Under Butler was distressed at the arrogance, insolence, crass comportment of this wretched cowgirl.

Edward, in a silk robe, came out from another room and looked concerned about Lindy's safety and well-being.

"I hate your Got-damned uppity friend, that sumbitch is insulting, thinks he's some kind of fuckin' genius. Are you like 'gat. Jack. Are you bettern' me?"

Edward's eyes widened and face paled. He sweated. Edward had long forgotten the breed of fellows with whom he was in school. Confident, arrogant, intelligent. conceited. If Edward knew the definition of a sociopath, he would have thought that, too.

"I apologize for Roland. He doesn't know, or care, if he hurts anyone's feelings. He's a very lonely man," is all Edward could manage.

"Next time I see him I'll shoot him."

"Is there anything I can do?" wondered Edward.

"Yeah, tell 'em what I just said."

"I've forgotten he was like that.." Edward had nothing to add to console Lindy and didn't even know if she were looking for consolation. He'd never met anyone like her. In fact, Edward felt safe walking around with Lindy in New York because she shot a sheriff (for good reason).

"I'll be out of your hair in the morning," said Lindy.

"Look, Lindy, let me show you around town until I go back home. See if you like New York enough to stay here if that's what you want.",

"You ain't gonna turn me in?"

"Of course not," said Edward truthfully.

"I don't trust you. I'm better off on my own. Always have been," stated Lindy walking out of his penthouse suite, down the hallway to her four room penthouse suite, with telephone, to call for room service, or any of the hotel's many other services available twenty-four hours a day in the year 1880. And then give a generous tip.

A knock, a gentle knock, on Lindy's door around ten o'clock the following morning, caused her to open it. Edward stood there and said, "would you like breakfast?"

Lindy's gracious reply was, "Yeah."

They had breakfast in Edward's suite's dining room which overlooked Madison Square, the park across Fifth Avenue, that bordered 23rd Street, up to 26th Street and Madison Avenue to the east.   Lindy found out she could have steak and eggs and grilled potatoes and bacon.   She ate like she'd always eaten, as though someone might steal food off her plate.

"How come your train was special?" announced Lindy, not looking up from shoveling in her breakfast.

"I paid to have my own train, for my staff and horses."

"When I showed my room key to that hotel boy, he called me 'your ladyship' like I was somebody. I take it my room was different from other rooms."

"You're right. These are luxury accommodations. Most hotel rooms are one room with a water closet down the hallway. You have a telephone and other luxuries like a private bathing salon."

"…On account of you're rich." concluded Lindy.

"Yes, I have the means to support such a standard of living."

Lindy laughed: "You take a long time to spit out 'I'm rich!'"

"I'm also over-educated. I can speak four languages. Two of which are quite dead, but they still teach them."

"So you think I can settle here?" wondered Lindy.

"Indeed, yes! You have innate intelligence, you know how to read people, you could work any number of situations, or even begin your own career."

"You're not lyin'?"

"How'd we meet? You were riding through a rain storm in the dark, came upon my camp and investigated. You didn't know me, if I were dangerous. You came in, looked the campsite over, decided that it was safe, sat down and ate, and ate more, slept, then got up and took off the next day. Most people, especially a girl, would not have stopped, not have trusted me, expected a confrontation. And missed out on a great meal of Texas chili, fresh baked cornbread and apple pie. Which was baked by my own chefs while other members of my staff set up camp."

"I wondered that myself. That tarp was too well set for just one man. Especially a tight-ass stiff like y'all." recalled Lindy.

"And you have another quality: observation. You see things others don't, or can't.   You'll get on very well in New York or anyplace else in America."

"How much for the breakfast, Jack?"

"It's on me," said Edward.

"I'm talking about tomorrow when I have to pay."

"I guess about fifty cents or so. Maybe a dollar," guessed Edward.

"That's a lot of money in Wyoming. Mama pays $3 a month to the land-lord for a two room house outside of town."

"Keep looking for work that you're good at and you'll make more money," was all Edward could muster.

"What's your job again?" asked Lindy, this time listening.

"I make heating systems for buildings—instead of fireplaces in every room, we've got iron radiators that heat up the whole room, no matter how big or small the room."

"You make them in New York?"

"Of course. But your boss would be Roland, and you said you want to shoot him."

"That's right," said Lindy cold-bloodily, pointing her finger like the barrel of a gun.

"Unfortunately, I need him alive."

"Oh." Then: "What about where you live? Got a place there I could work?"

"Yes, but what's wrong with New York?"

"Are you trying to get rid of me?" wondered Lindy, enjoying the free steak and egg breakfast, with bacon, fried potatoes, hot tea and lemonade with cubes of ice.

"Not at all. You were, as you would say, 'hell-bent' on getting off the train at Saint Louis. Then Cincinnati. Then Philadelphia. You're running out of land and the boat ride to England takes 9 days on the open ocean," reported Edward like a news-paper article.

Lindy had been putting two and two together for awhile and she figured that in London there was a pot of gold at the end of this rainbow. The private train, the four room hotel suite, dinner at the fancy restaurant. And all those stiff servants. This is the high life. And that play last night featured a character who lived in a European palace. Does Edward live in a palace? Why not find out?

"Do I have a job in your factory over there in London?"

"Yes, you do," assured Edward.

"Shake on it," demanded Lindy.

She shook Edward's hand and looked him square in the eye. Man to man.

"Will I be able to afford steak and eggs every day?"

"Not for awhile. As you get better at your job, and learn more about what I do, then you will be paid more money. And more money means better things, like steak and eggs for breakfast."

"If you're lying to me I'll shoot you, too."

"Let's take a carriage ride downtown," said Edward.

Their open Landau carriage with facing bench seats covered in leather, clip-clopped down to the corner of Broadway and 10th Street. Edward got out like the gentleman he is and Lindy jumped down like the pants-wearing cowgirl she is. They stood in front of Mathew Brady's photographic studio. Mathew Brady had documented the Civil War in photographs. Tens of thousands of photographs on thick glass plates. Hundreds of his glass plate photographs were now parts of greenhouses in private yards. Brady was deeply in debt for over-extending himself buying photographic equipment believing that he would make it all up selling picture books after the war. After the war everyone wanted to forget the carnage that touched virtually every family both north and south. So now Mathew Brady was open for business taking pictures of Civil War generals and those of the Carriage trade. Like Mrs Astor. And today, Her Ladyship Lindy Mae Long of the Wyoming Long's.

Brady took several portraits of Lindy—sitting in his famous chair which proves the photo was an authentic Brady. Standing. And standing with Edward Clarence Augustus George. All in her fringed buckskin outfit. With and without her summer hat. With a Sharp's carbine, a Spencer rifle and a Henry rifle. She looked tough. Tough and seductive.

"Now, we pack for England," said Edward, "unless you're afraid to take an ocean going ship."

"I ain't afraid," said Lindy with a twinge of fear in her voice.

CHAPTER 7

Aboard the SS Britannic

The Atlantic Ocean betwixt New York and Liverpool is 3,471 miles wide. The SS Britannic, traveling at 15 knots (28 miles an hour), took 9 days to make the crossing, usually. The trouble with trans-Atlantic crossings were the storms. Winds, rough seas and the occasional rogue wave smashing against the ship could make passenger life a living hell. The SS Britannic was 468 feet long, almost 40 feet wide (beam), and had a single propeller, driven by steam powered engines with an additional four masts, fully-rigged sails, to provide additional speed. Britannic was part sail boat, mostly steam ship.

The Britannic had room for 1720 passengers, but that was crossing east to west: Liverpool to New York. Going back to Liverpool, there were always fewer passengers. People (immigrants) were flocking to America, not the other way around. There were two classes of passenger. Saloon (First Class) and Steerage. First Class cabins were amidships, the most stable part of the ship as forward and aft took a pounding in rough seas. The 220 Saloon passengers were cordoned off from Steerage. Today's voyage from New York to Liverpool would be almost vacant of both classes of passengers. Saloon only had 39 passengers and Steerage was nearly empty. The only Steerage passengers were most likely criminals who were being deported back to England, Ireland and Scotland. And the usual small number of Welchmen. (cymro cythryblus)

Lindy was astounded. She had never imagined an ocean liner and now that she was standing on its wooden deck, she thought the 468 foot long ship was massive and as solid as her Rocky Mountains.

One of the Stewards showed Lindy her stateroom. It wasn't as large as her suite of rooms in the Fifth Avenue Hotel, but it would do.

Edward was walking around the ship when Lindy found him. "Why ain't you unpacking?" wondered Lindy.

"I'm all unpacked. Shall we have some tea?." and off they went.   It still didn't occur to Lindy that those stiff, starched people surrounding Edward did things like pack, unpack and see to it that Edward's life was trouble free.

The SS Britannic set sail at 2:30 in the afternoon on a beautiful clear and calm May afternoon, 1880.   The twin funnels chugged black smoke into the crisp New York air as Britannic cruised down the Hudson River past Bedloe's Island, future home of the Statue of Liberty, which would open to the public on October 28, 1886.

The skyline of Manhattan was flat. Most buildings were five or six stories tall from Battery Park to 30th Street. The tallest points were church steeples; the highest being Trinity Church's spire at 281 feet.

Lindy stood at the stern (back) of the ship awestruck at the size and complexity of New York City.   All those buildings and all those people crammed onto an island. All the river traffic. The big sailing ships, steamships mixed in with barges and ferry boats. However, nothing was taller, more massive and majestic than the Rocky Mountains right outside her west-facing window back home in Wyoming.   She missed her mountains.

The first day out was pleasant. The 468 foot long Britannic slipped smoothly through gentle seas and light breezes.   All four masts had sprouted full sails. Main sails, top gallants, top royals. And between the mizzen and aft masts were two tall funnels spilling out gray-black smoke over the passengers' heads as the SS Britannic sailed east by north east, from 41 degrees north latitude to 53 degrees north latitude, where Liverpool was located.

Edward thought that Lindy, who was raised in a land-locked part of America, might not acclimate to the sea.   Not an oversized lake, but a large, swelling, unpredictable, hostile, dangerous and deadly sea.

Their first dinner at sea was delightful. The Dining Saloon (First Class) was more than half empty. They had three waiters serving them and their dinner was beef for Lindy and lamb for Edward. Edward had a nice Pauillac, vintage 1855. He let Lindy try a small glass of his red wine. The sea was flat calm so there was no rocking, swaying, yawing.   They talked about the menu because Edward was familiar with the french names of each course and item.

  Then Lindy blurted out:

"How old are you, anyway?"

Edward, never having been asked such an impertinent question, kept a stiff upper lip and replied, "twenty-seven. And you?"

"A lady never reveals her secrets." Lindy took a bite of her rib roast, dipped it in gravy and while chewing, said to Edward, "So, Jack, why ain't you married?"

"Miss Long, are you being rude on purpose?"

"I dunno. What's 'rood' mean?"

"Rude means discourteous. Or even insolent. Disparaging. And uncivilised."

"Is that good or bad? All I asked was why ain't you married? You don't have to tell me; I can make up my own story." said Lindy taking a gulp of Edward's red wine because she liked the way it tasted.

"Well, maybe you're right. I'm surrounded by polite people, excluding immediately family, so: I *ain't* married because I don't have the time, the energy or force of will to alter my already industrious life. And what about you, why ain't you?" Edward paused because he was going to say 'betrothed' and stopped, fearing she wouldn't understand the word, then said, "married?"
Lindy reacted to Edward's slight hesitation, squinted at Edward, drank some more wine, then replied:

"I ain't ready to settle. Mamma spit me out when she was younger'n me. I was nothin' but trouble."

"How do you know that?" wondered Edward, a man raised by nannies and sent off to St. Paul's Academy then Trinity College, Cambridge, for a Classical education. Edward's mother and father saw him rarely, saw him when he was cleaned up. Then off to school at an early age and didn't show up again until he was 20 when he graduated from Cambridge. His father presented Edward with a pipe of port—145 gallons of port, stored in barrels at his birth and presented 20 or 21 years later upon graduation from college. A pipe of port is 7200 bottles of port wine. Enough for a lifetime.

"Mama and pa told me every day of my life how I ruined their lives. My pa said he was forced to rob banks on account of he had to feed me."

"How much were you eating?" joked Edward.

Lindy got the joke and laughed. "I din't know you was funny."

"I'm not. So you mother isn't going to miss you?"

"My mother will probably turn me in for shooting that murdering sheriff. So here I am."

They ate dessert, which included ice cream. Edward mentioned watching the sunset because he heard that it was especially beautiful because of all the colors in the sky.

Tonight's sunset was spectacular. The sky displayed impossible colorations neither Lindy nor Edward had ever seen. Dozens of hues of red, yellow, blue, purple, amber, gold, pink, green, and a color Lindy just called 'toreador rojo,"as she sat on her deck chair at the back of the ship sipping tea; Edward in his deck chair sipping vintage port. Thanks to the Industrial Revolution, hundreds of factory smokestacks were pumping tons of deadly toxins into the pristine atmosphere all over Brooklyn and New Jersey creating this impossibly spectacular colorful atmospheric display.

Lindy was thrown out of bed about four o'clock early the next morning when the mighty SS Britannic listed 25 degrees to port. Lindy did not strap herself into bed last night, which she could have. Lindy got up, dusted herself off and was thrown back toward her bed. The sea was boiling, white caps filled the entire visible ocean, yet the sky was starry and black. How could there be such a violent ocean if the weather was clear and starry?

Lindy walked down the hallway between her suite and Edward's, pounded on his door and when he opened it, she demanded, "What the fuck, Jack. What the fuck?"

Lindy stormed into Edward's suite. Edward was dressed in a silk burgundy robe, custom made leather slippers lined in sheer wool and did not look flustered. Edward motioned to a wingback chair.

"There was a storm two days ago in the mid-Atlantic and we're receiving the brunt of it."

"When's it gonna stop?"

"It's already slowing down. It'll be fully over by tea time."

"T-time? When's that?" Lindy was learning the English way.

"About four o'clock this afternoon.", reported Edward.

"I feel sick."

"Go back to your room and stay close to your commode."

Two days later Lindy and Edward were promenading around the Saloon Class deck, walking on the wide-plank polished and interlocked teak decking. The teak came from Southern Egypt. The teak logs were floated down the White Nile. Currently, May of 1880, Egypt belonged to the 580 year old Ottoman Empire who sold its teak to Britain and the Dutch at a handsome profit.

Lindy was asking focused questions about where she was going. Specifically, were there rattlesnakes, cattle and sheep ranches; farmers who tried to grow corn, wheat and beans. Did it ever rain. Were there mountains. How bad are your winters? Does the snow pile up over your rooftop? Are the roads paved, or like Cheyenne's— dirt in summer, axle deep mud in spring, frozen over all winter?

Edward's answers were simple, direct and boring. "There are no rattlesnakes. I have groundkeepers who use a cutting machine to trim my grass; no sheep. Farmers grow a variety of grains and vegetables including wheat, millett, corn for livestock, several varieties of green beans. My personal garden produces 31 kinds of vegetables and 11 kinds of fruits and berries. It rains once or twice a week. We do not have mountains like your Rocky Mountains, but we have a Scottish peak that's 2,000 feet high. We occasionally get snow which is usually less than a foot. Many of our city's roads, like London's, were paved by the Romans who invaded us in 43 B.C., about 1,900 years ago."

Lindy didn't know who the Romans were, or when 43BC was. But as long as the roads were paved, that's all she needed to know.

"What do you do for fun?" wondered Lindy who was falling asleep listening to Edward describe his life.

"There are cotillions, garden parties, cricket matches." said Edward as though he had to draw from distant memory.

"I said fun, Jack. Listenin' to crickets ain't fun."

"Well if you like to shoot, there are shooting parties to shoot pheasant, not people."

"All right! With a rifle?" wondered a now-excited Lindy.

"Shotgun. A rifle bullet might hit someone a mile away." cautioned Edward.

"I like to shoot my dinner." smirked Lindy. "Anything else?"

"There is horse racing."

Lindy exploded in joy. "Horse racing! You race horses!"

"You want to run in The Derby? The winner gets a few thousand pounds." said Edward, responding to Lindy's enthusiasm.

"A few thousand pounds of what?" wondered Lindy, not sure if she were being ribbed.

"Our money is called pounds.   Yours are called dollars. Currently, one of our pounds is worth five of your dollars.   That means 2,000 Pounds is $10,000."

$10,000 is bank robber money.   The kind of money Lindy's father was always talking about and not coming close to robbing.   A good bank holdup would net Lindy's father about $80 because it was split several ways.   There were five men in Lindy's father's gang. Sometimes. Most times there were three. One was usually in jail on a bar fight charge and another was usually drunk. Sometimes one of the drunkards would show up at the wrong bank and wait for the others, not taking the initiative to rob the bank while he was there. Other times, a drunk gang member would get arrested for public intoxication and argue with a sheriff, or deputy, get in a fist fight and end up back in jail.   The big banks were in Denver City. They were hard to rob because they had armed guards. The country banks had little or no money.   And the tellers were all armed and   trigger-happy.

"When's this race?"

"End of the month, about nine days from now. Is your horse a 3 year old?" wondered Edward, really excited to see Lindy excited about something.

"I don't know. How can you tell?"

"I've got a couple of three year old thoroughbreds in my stables, we'll find you one," said Edward with an English gentleman's assuredness.

"How you know I race?"

"I heard you riding up to my camp that night in the rain. In the dark. I thought it was an Indian on his paint, or a wild mustang running from the lightning."

"I was riding from the law, if you recall." reminded Lindy.

"Well, ride The Derby (pronounced darby by the English) like the sheriff's coming after you and you'll win your $10,000 prize," concluded Edward.

"When do I get my money?" said Lindy is 100% certitude. This excited Edward.

"You get the money, and a trophy, right after you win the Derby," guaranteed Edward, who'd entered The Derby the last four years in a row wherein his horses never finished in the top six. Also-rans.

"So, when I win this darby and get paid, forget about me working in your factory."

"I wouldn't think of you working there even if you didn't win The Derby. Anything else?"

"When do we get off this fuckin' boat?

CHAPTER 8

On To Jack's House

London and North Western Railway (LNWR) attached nine private cars plus a helper locomotive at Liverpool to accommodate Edward, his staff, his horses, Lindy's horse, and Lindy. She and Edward would take to the Lounge car which must do as the Luncheon car and a possible Afternoon Tea car. The trip from Liverpool to Euston Station, London, should take two-and-a-half hours, to possibly three-hours-forty-five, depending on rail freight traffic. There was a lot of rail freight from Liverpool to Manchester. The train trip took half an hour with an open track, but shipments of cotton coming from New Orleans, Charleston, Wilmington and Richmond choked Liverpool's harbor, which choked the railway to the textile mills in Lancashire, Cheshire and Derbyshire. But only Edward knew this. Lindy was staring out the window sipping tea and eating fresh baked scones slathered with thick, rich, delicious clotted cream made fresh near Tavistock Abbey, Devonshire.

Edward wound his gold Patek Philippe pocket watch and checked the time for the fourth time in two minutes.

"Hey, Jack. Time goes faster when you stop starin' at your clock." Lindy had a wad of clotted cream on her nose and a smile two axe handles wide. She was dipping a scone in her tea then slathering it with Devon cream like she'd been doing this all her life. She was glad to be on flat, hard, non-moving dry land. Like Wyoming, only in England land was green with lots of trees.

Shortly after their train went past Manchester a drizzle began. Lindy was awestruck at the green. Lush grass and endless trees in full bloom, mile after mile. She licked her thick, sweet Devonshire clotted cream, bit into her warm scone, sipped tea like a refined Englishwoman and marveled at where she was. In the Wyoming she'd dreamt of. If only there were a Rocky Mountain, or two, the scenery would be perfect.

A couple of hours later the land went from English countryside to the beginning of the Home Counties. The 19th Century suburbs of London. And finally, their train pulled into Euston Station, London, and stopped.

Lindy was staring hard at the citizenry ambling about. She had a curious expression.

"Is everybody a foreigner?" she wondered.

"A few are, but the rest are Britons, from England, Scotland, Wales and Ireland."

"They all look American," exclaimed Lindy.

Without missing a beat, Edward stated, "An overwhelming majority of Americans are Britons, from England, Scotland and Ireland. Even some Welsh landed in your Pennsylvania."

Lindy had heard the term 'foreigner' for years and it was always a negative reference. It was even a reference to the native population of Cheyenne, Arapahoe, Lakota, Dakota, Crow, Hunkpapa tribes. Lindy's imagination filled in the blanks so when she heard 'foreigners' she pictured creatures with odd-shaped heads, contorted faces, with face paint, bizarre hair styles, odd shaped clothing and all speaking in incomprehensible languages.

"We're home at last!" Edward was relieved, relaxed and he was smiling broadly.

"You mean you're home. I don't know wherein the Hell I am, Jack."

"Well, I'd like to think you could get used to England. You seem to like our delightful food and beverage." smiled Edward looking at Lindy's face, slathered in clotted (whipped) cream.

Jack did have a point, thought Lindy. This whole trip was Lindy's introduction to the finest restaurants, hotels, transportation, available only to upper station people. Upper, *upper* class. One night in a suite at the Fifth Avenue Hotel cost more than 99% of what America's working classes took home in a year. This was all unknown to Lindy, and the world's working classes.

The drizzle had slipped into rain, then back to drizzle and by the time their train got to London the skies had cleared and now the early afternoon turned sunny and blue.

Edward's personal staff, the Under Butler and Second Footman, had rounded up London & North Western Railway attendants to unload Edward's (and Lindy's) personal belongings.

The Under Butler had arranged for Edward's personal carriage with a well-trained team of four muscular Cleveland Bay horses.

Seated on the left-lead Bay horse was a Postilion, a jockey-sized gentleman in a uniform of red coat with brass buttons, black jodhpurs, black knee-length boots, white shirt with black cravat, black gloves. And a horse whip.

Edward's carriage was a large open Landau with two well-padded soft leather bench seats facing each other. The Under Butler held the door open and offered to help Lindy up the stairs of the custom built Landau carriage. Lindy didn't need any help, she was a cowgirl from Wyoming Territory who'd rather shoot you than accept help from a stiff foreigner. She stared the Under Butler down until he withdrew his helping hand and bowed. Edward, like Lindy, didn't need any help getting into the open (convertible) carriage because he was a man.

The four Cleveland Bay horses took off, pulling the Landau and its two passengers with grace and ease. The team of horses clip-clopped out of Euston station and under the magnificent Euston Arch which looked like the Brandenburg Gate with Doric columns. The Landau rode out onto Euston Road. The open Landau rode through downtown London and turned right toward Leicester Square, down to Piccadilly Circus and onto Piccadilly Road. (This was 1880. There were no motor cars.)

Behind Edward and Lindy's Landau were a parade of nine carriages belonging to Edward's party. All of his staff. All of their stuff. Plus Lindy's horse L.C. and L.C.'s tack. Lindy was facing front and didn't see the parade of Edward's fleet of custom built carriages behind her.

The Landau continued onto Piccadilly Road past the massive and walled grounds of Buckingham Palace, home of Her Majesty, Queen Victoria, and three of her four sons—Arthur, Alfred and Leopold. Her Majesty's elder son, Albert, Prince of Wales, was married to Alexandra, Princess of Wales, and they lived in Marlborough House with their five children—two boys and three girls. Their son, George Frederick Ernest Albert, would become King George V in May of 1910. Currently he was 15 years old and learning rugby.

Piccadilly Road bordered the grounds of Buckingham Palace. Edward's parade of carriages turned onto Knightsbridge Road which bordered Hyde Park to the south. There was an ivy covered wall along the south side of Knightsbridge Road. The parade of carriages clip clopped for half a mile then turned left onto Brompton Road heading toward a thirty foot tall black wrought iron double gate trimmed in 18 karat gold. The gate seemed to magically open (four security guards pulled the gate open out of sight from the street) and Edward's Landau entered and drove down a white crushed stone driveway. About half a mile down the drive was a massive three story building. To the left and right of the 20 foot wide crushed stone drive was a lawn greener than Ireland. Perfectly manicured.

Edward's Landau seemed to pick up speed. The four Cleveland bay horses seemed to recognize who they were and showed off in a prideful manner. Lindy got a sense of that watching the bays, trotting in perfect harmony, in step, clip-clopping as one.

The building was immense with stylized turrets and Lindy counted twelve fluted columns finished in Corinthian in the center of this massive structure. The front entrance of a hotel? As the Landau drew closer to this building, Lindy saw an unusual sight: there were people, 140 people, lined up outside the building.

"This your hotel?" she wondered.

"Yes," smiled Edward.

"Who're them people?"

"I am curious to find out," lied Edward.

"Which room is yourn?"

"The three windows on the third floor, left hand corner," stated Edward with confidence.

"Where's my room?"

"Ask the hotel keeper what's available and you can have it," said Edward in a comforting voice.

The landau pulled up to a break in the lineup of the 140 people standing at stiff English servant class attention. Seventy people in a semi-circle with a ten foot gap in the middle, and the other seventy people on the other side. The gap in the middle exposed the front entrance, granite stairs, outsized bronze front door set off by six granite fluted columns about sixty feet tall on each side of the deep, highly polished bronze front door.

Best looking hotel Lindy had ever seen, and she's seen at least three in her lifetime.

Edward stepped down from the Landau. The custom was to help a woman or child down from the carriage because he was first and foremost an English gentleman. However if he dare offer assistance to Lindy she might spit on his hand and jump down on her own.   Edward stepped aside   and nodded at his Butler and Housekeeper, the Number One and Two Heads of Household, and its vast staff.   He then turned toward Lindy who did something unexpected. She offered her hand toward Edward and looked him in the eye. Edward read her look as: 'don't worry, I ain't gonna spit in your eye.'

Edward offered his left hand and 'helped' Lindy, no delicate flower, down from the Landau carriage. There were gasps and muffled squeaks as the women servants reacted negatively to Lindy's buckskin breaches. With fringe. It's as though no woman had ever worn pants in public. None had.

Edward approached his Butler, Mr Harrison, and Housekeeper, Mrs Dahlgren, who've had the run of Ashfield Hall for many years.   They were hired more than fifteen years ago by Edward's late uncle Frederick, 2nd Duke of Sussex, grandson of King George III, nephew of King George IV, King William IV and first cousin of HM QueenVictoria, who left his entire estate to his nephew, Edward, now 3rd Duke of Sussex, who was invested as a royal duke. This was his style:

"Welcome home, your Royal Highness," said Mrs Dahlgren as she curtsied.

"Tis good to see you back, your Royal Highness," said Mr Harrison, as he bowed deeply.

"It's good to be home, Mr Harrison," remarked Edward Clarence Augustus George, 3rd Duke of Sussex; great-grandson of King George III.

Edward (Jack) inherited the house he is about to enter from his late uncle Prince Frederick Louis Arthur William. The house has a name: Ashfield Hall. Ashfield is 620,000 square feet of pomp and majesty.   Made of the finest building materials including Italian marble in half a dozen colors, granite in seven colors, mahogany, bronze, English elm timbers to span large rooms like grand ballrooms and the several royal dining rooms.

Prince Frederick Louis Arthur William was one of King George III grandsons. Prince Frederick died three months ago in February, 1880. Jack's uncle had no legitimate children. The house and Duchy should have gone to Jack's father, Prince Clarence, younger brother of uncle Frederick, but Jack's father died several years ago.   Jack was the only male heir, so through male primogeniture, Jack got all the land and the royal duchy and all that went with it. Including receiving £177,000 income each week in rent receipts from his inherited property located in the City of London. £177,000 each week. In London, Landlords collect rent once a week.

Edward, thus began receiving a detailed accounting of enterprises, financial institutions and retail shops sitting on real estate owned outright by Jack's grandfather, Prince Augustus. This land was taken by Royal Decree of King George IV and King William IV, who doted on their younger brother Prince Augustus, who was the sixth son of George III.

Augustus Frederick, a lovable, personable financial genius reminded his two older brothers, who would be kings, of their eminent domain that, as King, they owned all the land in the British Empire. And the most valuable land was around Buckingham Palace in the City of London.

Jack's grandfather, Augustus Frederick, was given this land, taken by King George IV, then added to by King William IV, in the City of London to collect the rent for the royal family. Augustus ended up with the Deeds of Trust for the land, a mile square in size. Augustus Frederick also owned his own house (Ashfield Hall), also sitting on land one mile square. Jack owns a total of land two miles square in the heart of London thanks to his grandfather Augustus and his uncle Frederick—both financial wonders, like the American JP Morgan.

Several of the Lessees who had buildings on this land included the Bank of England (on Threadneedle Street), Lloyd's of London, The Royal Mint, Cadbury, Trinity House, The London Gazette, Hoare's Bank, Coutt's Bank, Childs & Drummond's Bank, Barclays Bank, Twining's (N. 216 Strand), Fortnum & Mason, The Times, Rothschild's Bank, Josiah Wedgwood Pottery, Harrods Department Store—which lay conveniently across Brompton Road from Ashfield Hall's west gate.

Jack's late uncle Prince Frederick Louis had the weekly £177,000 divvied up amongst Hoare's, Barclay's, Coutt's, Childs & Drummond and Rothschild's banks, then had £40,000 delivered to Ashfield Hall in a delivery carriage marked 'Southwark Dairy' so as not to raise suspicion that large bills, gold coin (specie) and gold bullion was being transported across town. Royal Duke Edward has kept up this practice.

Jack was making money selling his central heating systems, both in Great Britain and in America, with his graduate school roomate and business partner Roland Betthard.   The sudden infusion of too much money was exhilarating. Jack paid his debts and expanded his business to sell central heating throughout Europe and the Republic of Ireland. His concern was working class and working poor who were dying of pneumonia and consumption due to horridly cold, drafty, dank homes and work places all winter. A sick worker is an unproductive worker, said Jack, who used that phrase to secure bank loans. Now that he'd secured a strong financial position, Jack still espoused that philosophy, only now he didn't have to tap dance for bankers. He built new factories and increased working class wages. He even gave everyone sick days with the caveat, 'Use them when you're sick, not hung over.'

Lindy Mae Long put her hand on Jack's arm and together they marched up the granite walkway, up seven pink granite steps as a uniformed valet, Thomas Westham, opened the six inch thick, 12 foot tall, 8 foot wide beautifully polished and gleaming bronze main entry door.

Lindy thought it was like the Fifth Avenue Hotel, but stuffier.

The entry foyer featured a 50 foot tall domed painted ceiling, black and white diamond-shaped marble floor, more mahogany panelling, a massive yet elegant fireplace and walls covered with paintings featuring family members including Kings George I, II, III, IV, King William IV, and HM Queen Victoria. Her Majesty was presented over the grand marble mantlepiece.

In front of Jack and Lindy was the Grand Staircase, about 20 feet wide with an easy slope up to the next floor, about 20 feet up. Lindy was staring at the Raphaelite paintings of angels on the ceiling peeking out from clouds and floating in a beautiful blue sky.

Edward, 3rd Duke of Sussex, paused by the fireplace with Lindy and waited for the house's two most important staff members to catch up.

"Will your royal highness be having afternoon tea?" wondered Mr Harrison, Butler.

"Let us get 'situated', Mr Harrison. I'm afraid I may not be available for dinner. I have a lot of catching up to do. All my correspondence. And I must meet with my accountant."

"Shall I have the Kitchen prepare a light supper and serve it in your office, sir?" wondered Mr Harrison.

"My deepest apologies, Mrs Dahlgren and Mr Harrison. My inattention back home is inexcusable. May I introduce a very important young woman from America. From western America, in the Wyoming Territory. Her Ladyship, Lindy Long. She is traveling with me and will be in need of a suite of apartments, Mrs Dahlgren," said Jack. Then, to Lindy, the royal duke said, "I sincerely apologize your Ladyship. Do you require refreshment? Hot tea, or a cold beverage? Some sweet cakes with fruit jams.? Please forgive my inattention."

"I'd like some tea, and sweet cakes and jam, if that's okay," said Lindy gently, respectfully, to Mrs Dahlgren. To Edward, 3rd Duke of Sussex, great-grandson of George III, King of Great Britain and Ireland, Lindy said, "Where's my room, Jack."

When Lindy called Edward Clarence Augustus George by the name 'Jack' just a moment ago, both Mr Harrison and Mrs Dahlgren furrowed their collective brows and wondered to themselves, 'did this wild west cowgirl just call his Royal Highness, a Royal Duke, great-grandson of King George IIIrd, 'Jack'?' Oh my.

Lindy's room was on the third floor, same as Jack's office. She was given a corner suite facing Harrods, exactly one half of a mile away and on the other side of the 30 foot high protective wall that Edward's grandfather had built surrounding his square mile of royal land. Jack's land was mostly an expansive great lawn, well watered with a sprinkler system (devised and installed by Jack before he inherited his late uncle Frederick's title and estate) and manicured by groundskeepers who used lawn mowers (developed and improved in 1859, 1868, 1870), instead of sheep. The sheep were shorn, their wool used for sweaters and woolen cricket uniforms.

Lindy's suite comprised four rooms including a water closet or bathing room. In the water closet was a flushable toilet, a claw-foot bath, a vanity basin. The washbasin and bath had hot and cold running water, thanks again to Jack, who installed his first central heating system in uncle Frederick's 620,000 square foot house more than three years ago. Each water closet also included one cast iron radiator providing much-needed radiant heat in those freezing British winters. The entire house's heating system, including boilers, water heaters, furnaces, radiators, miles of hot water pipes and cold water pipes, took 3 years to install.

There were 170 very large rooms in Ashfield Hall and 100 medium-sized rooms for the servants. There were 122 water closets (bathrooms) and a sewer system that linked into greater London's system. Greater London's sewer system was begun by the Romans whilst in London. The Romans named the city Londinium.

Mrs Dahlgren escorted Lindy to her suite of apartments. Lindy was shown how the individual devices in the bathroom functioned. When Mrs Dahlgren stopped up the drain in the bathing tub and turned on the hot and cold water, added liquid soap which made pink bubbles, and announced, "this is how to take a bubble bath, your Ladyship."

Lindy began disrobing. Mrs Dahlgren, blushing, turned away and said, "I shall have your hot tea and baked delights up to you quickly, your Ladyship."

"I plan to be in here awhile," said Lindy, very happy about her current circumstances.

"I serve at your pleasure your Ladyship. You relax as long as you please. Your tea shall be hot, your sweet cakes shall be fresh-baked, no matter how long you enjoy your bubble bath."

Mrs Dahlgren, a veteran Housekeeper, has seen upstart family members for twenty-two years and she hasn't seen anything new. Except for now. A girl who wears breaches right out in public. But Jack's friend seemed civil and not a spoiled rotten elitist. Mrs Dahlgren doesn't yet know about the dead sheriff back in the wild American west. Or her affinity for cussing like a sailor.

Lindy worked the hot water handle and the cold water handle to get the desired temperature. Lindy's 'tub' back home was an iron barrel, cut down. You fill up a bucket of water, heat it over the fire, then pour it over you. No bubbles, just water that was either too hot or too cold, especially during the long-ass Wyoming Territory winter. A steady below-zero breeze blew through their tiny two room hand-built house.

Today, Lindy Mae Long was taking her first bubble bath in a real bathing tub. Then enjoying hot tea and sweet cakes with fresh-made jam, placed on a table with a round marble top next to the bathing tub.   Lindy climbed into the tub with a mountain of pure white bubbles floating on top of the 90 degree water and soothed herself into a deep relaxation.

CHAPTER 9

The Derby

After Lindy's bath, and seeing that her bathwater was a little on the murky side, she refilled the bathing tub, re-soaped herself, scrubbed her hair two more times, then rinsed herself off with fresh clear, hot water, without new soap bubbles, and stepped out of the tub onto a thick white cotton bath mat, examined the water: clean! Then Lindy noticed a perfectly stacked pile of thick, soft white cotton towels on a white marble counter, also in her bathing room.

Lindy opened the bathing room door, looked to see if the coast were clear—it was—and walked into her suite's parlour. There was a round table that was set with a plate, tea cup, saucer, knife, fork, spoon, napkin, flowers and a note: 'Your Ladyship, please pull the red cord to ring me if you need anything. Thank you, [signed] Mrs Dahlgren.'

Lindy could read. Jack didn't think so. Lindy went to school until she was 11 but paid attention. Every day she read the Cheyenne *Daily Sun* to see whether her father might have made a withdrawal from a nearby bank, and to see if his name were mentioned. Which meant that a sheriff (or sheriffs) was looking for him. Lindy also kept up with the territorial events, especially four years ago, 1876, when the Lakota nations prevented the US Cavalry from murdering their women and children. The Lakota tribe handily wiped the 7th U.S. Cavalry and Lt. Col. George Custer off the face of the earth. Lindy read that and smiled. She didn't know her genealogy, but hoped she had a lot of Lakota blood in her. Warrior blood.

This first evening at Ashfield Hall in May of 1880, London, Middlesex County, England, United Kingdom, Lindy read the note Mrs Dahlgren had written, found the red pull-cord, pulled it, and in ten minutes Mrs Dahlgren knocked on Lindy's door and came in with two women. One woman carried a tray with a teapot, sugar bowl, sliced lemon arranged impeccably, all on fine china. The other woman carried a sterling silver tray with a considerable (unladylike) assortment of sweet cakes. Both trays had vases of local flowers selected with care from the estate's many flower gardens.

"Your Ladyship, this bowl contains strawberry preserves, this bowl contains gooseberry jam and this bowl contains blackberry jam.

Our pastry chef was trained in Vienna, worked in Paris for ten years and now makes the finest pastries for Ashfield Hall. Also, his Royal Highness, Edward, indicated he would like dinner around 6 o'clock. He would like to know whether that time suits you, your Ladyship?" said Mrs Dahlgren.

"Six? Suits me fine. Where's Jack? I mean Edward." wondered Lindy.

"His Royal Highness's apartments are at the other end of the hall. Last door on the left, your Ladyship," said Mrs Dahlgren.

The two women servers, dressed in kitchen whites, curtsied and left the room.

Mrs Dahlgren was not used to this Wyoming cowgirl calling a Royal Duke 'Jack'. How insulant. How disrespectful. How malapert. How American. That brazen hussy can take her breeches and migrate back to her wild west.

However, the look on Mrs Dahlgren's face was the usual British stoic non-disclosure of how she felt. She was born to be in service and this was her life. Now, as Housekeeper, she was as high as a woman could climb in service.

The head of the stables is called the Groomsman and his name is Chalmers. The 3rd Duke of Sussex, Edward, in riding boots up to his knees, wool jodhpurs, white cotton shirt, cravat, tan Harris tweed jacket, riding gloves, was walking Lindy's horse L.C. outside of the stables. The stables was a large stone and brick building with Greco-Roman features like a portico with six fluted marble columns, installed in 1776, the year in which Colonists in the Americas became displeased with their King and his government.

The Groomsman had a crew of 14 grooms who looked after Edward's English thoroughbred horses, two Morgan, a dozen Cleveland Bays, and four Hanoverian thoroughbreds.

The Groomsman bowed reverently (not sloppily or lazily) to Edward and said, "Good day your Royal Highness." Edward shook his Groomsman's hand and said, "Good day to you, Mr Chalmers.

What have you learned about the young lady's American horse, Elsie?"

"Elsie is about an eight year old *stallion* and something else that surprised me, your Lordship.   Elsie is a Hanoverian.   A thoroughbred! I believe he can race."

"Have you taken her for a run?" wondered Edward.

"No, your Lordship," replied Chalmers, reluctantly.

"Is there a problem?"

"Hanoverians are remarkably easy to train and are generally calm."

".But…" salted Edward.

"But he seems to be trained NOT to let anyone ride him, so I await her Ladyship."

Edward laughed expecting that sort of thing.

Walking toward the stables, about 200 yards from Ashfield Hall, came her Ladyship. She spotted Elsie and Elsie spotted Lindy, so Elsie trotted toward Lindy, happy to see each other. Elsie and Lindy head-butted. Elsie is a rich black Hanoverian thoroughbred, a breed originally from German royalty. Lindy's horse somehow ended up not only in America, but way out West. Most Hanoverians were show horses, dressage and show jumping.

Lindy handed Elsie a carrot. "Hey Jack, who's this?" wondered Lindy.

The Groomsman Chalmers was taken aback when she called the Royal Duke 'Jack'.

"This gentleman is the estate's Head Groomsman and he tells me Elsie is a Hanoverian thoroughbred. How did you come by Elsie?"

"I found him wandering on open range north of Cheyenne a couple of years ago. So I called him Elsie, 'Lost Colt.'"

Well, things got clearer for Edward and the Groomsman. A male horse with a girl's name now made sense. L.C. was just an orphaned four or five year old wandering around in a fenceless pasture in 1876. All of Wyoming Territory was a fenceless pasture. There were cattle ranchers with herds as large as 8,000 or 10,000 units (cow and calf), to wander aimlessly to eat all the grass they wanted to fatten them up, then at roundup in September, herd them onto cattle cars on the Union Pacific in Cheyenne, and ship the fattened cows to Chicago or Kansas City to turn them into steaks, chops, roasts, sausages at Swift, Morris and Armour packing houses. Small Wyoming farmers who were growing wheat, corn, beans, vegetables and fruit, were forced to put up barbed wire fences, at their expense, to keep the cows out. Farming was tough enough in a land that didn't get much rain, too much snow, and nonstop wind that drove people and animals mad.

The Lakota, Arapahoe and Northern Cheyenne Nations were now under control in 1880. But four years ago, June 1876, about 2000 warriors under the leadership of Sitting Bull, Crazy Horse, Two Moon and Gall had wiped out Lt Colonel Custer at the Battle of the Greasy Grass River. Some of Custer's cavalry had Hanoverian thoroughbred horses, like Lindy's horse. Lindy's lost horse was a riderless 7th Cavalry horse from the victorious Lakota battle against the tyrannical U.S. Cavalry set out to slaughter women and children so wasi'chu (Europeans/whites) could dig for gold in the Badlands of Dakota Territory. That land was sacred Lakota land.

"Can L.C. race?" taunted Edward.

Lindy snorted, jumped on L.C., who had no saddle (English or Western), took his reins (a hackamore not a bit), said "Git!!" and L.C. took off toward Harrods, which was about half a mile west on Edward's perfectly manicured lawn. A lawn that was one mile wide and one mile long had been established as Edward's yard with his 620,000 square foot house sitting in the center. His yard displayed one of the most stunning flower gardens, vegetable gardens, orchards, baroque garden, ferme, grand maze and parterre elegances in all of Europe and the British Isles. For winter months, an orangery and several elaborate, heated, outsized greenhouses fitted with quarter-inch thick glass panes. Because of the enclosed and heated greenhouses, fresh squeezed orange juice and lemonade were served all year. Limes were also grown in the greenhouses to accompany the gin & tonic, made with sugared quinine. Edward's uncle Frederick brought citrus orchards back from a visit to Spain.

L.C. was running full out and Lindy was guiding him down the right side of Edward's beautiful green lawn, then turned left at the west wall (where, across Brompton Road, Harrods Department Store stood silently, beckoning), along the protective west wall, then turned east along the south wall.

On the other side of the south wall was Buckingham Palace, home of Her Majesty Queen Victoria and several of her unwed adult children. Namely Princes Arthur, Alfred and Leopold. The queen's eldest son, Albert, was married to Alexandra. Albert and Alexandra were currently the Prince and Princess of Wales, but they didn't live in Cardiff, or anywhere near Wales. They lived around the corner from Buckingham Palace in Marlborough House. Portly Prince Albert could walk home to see his mother in 17 minutes, and the exercise would do him good. (It was a 9 minute walk for everyone else.) But listening to his mother continuously whine about her dead husband, consort Prince Albert, and blaming her son Albert for her husband's death, was too much for the Prince of Wales. Albert was waiting to become king. He was 39 years old but his mother was in great health. Albert didn't know he'd have to wait until January 22, 1901, to become king. Albert (Bertie) had also been married to Princess Alexandra (Alix), of Denmark, for 17 years, because his mother, The Queen, ordered him to settle down. When Bertie was 21 he entered into a politically advantageous marriage. But Bertie kept his girlfriends. By today, May, 1880, the happy couple had five children. Two boys and three girls. An heir, a spare, and three girls.

Whilst a large staff of servants tended to the Princess of Wales and her five charges, 39 year old Bertie tended to as many as fifty-five young ladies over a period of decades. Among whom were actress Lily Langtree, socialite Lady Randolph Churchill (Sir Winston's mother), actress Sarah Bernhardt, prostitute 'La Barucci' and wealthy humanitarian this, and wealthy party-goer that. Bertie was as faithless to his bride as many of the long line of Princes of Wales, as though it were part of their job requirements. The first Prince of Wales was created in 1301 (500 years ago), and would become King Edward II. Edward II did not whore around. He was in love with a man, and only one man. Edward II was a homosexual.

Bertie's father, Prince Consort Albert, tried to get through to his then 21 year old eldest son that whoring was not acceptable because Bertie's mother, as well as being Queen, was also Defender of the Faith, the Supreme Governor of the Church of England and Protector of the Sacredness of Marriage. Well, apparently that fell on deaf ears mainly because the next-in-line to the throne had a way of reminding everyone in earshot that he was the future king and didn't appreciate lectures on the consequences of philandering.

King William IV and his wife consort Queen Adelaide bore two daughters who died in infancy. However, King William IV had at least ten children out of wedlock with Dorothea Jordan, the king's companion for 20 years before he married Adelaide (who was the namesake of Adelaide, Australia.) Because William IV had no surviving legitimate children, his niece, Alexandrina Victoria, acceded to Queen. Victoria had no sense of humour about extramarital philanderings. HM had no sense of humour about most subjects.

All that Royal drama and trauma lay on the Queen's side of the stone wall that ran between Buckingham Palace and Ashfield Hall —Jack's estate—where Lindy was riding her horse.

Infidelity, intrigue, disappeared royal princes, Tower of London, beheadings, messy divorces, religious uprisings, Cromwell, world conquest, childless monarchs—that was the queen's side of this painful wall. Lindy knew nothing of that. Most of Her Majesty's subjects knew little of most of it.

On Jack's side of the wall, currently, not much excitement. Just an idealistic American girl who shot a sheriff half a world away in the rugged and wild, unpredictable west. That same girl was going to ride one of Jack's three year old thoroughbreds in next week's Epsom Derby.   So why does she continue to ride her Wyoming horse of questionable pedigree from an unknown sire and dam when she should be training and riding the registered and pedigreed thoroughbred?   One reason is because Jack, a confirmed passive-aggressive personality, is terrified of accosting Lindy. She's got a way of speaking that is direct and threatening. And she's got a Colt .44 and knows how to shoot.   And it's Jack's Colt .44! That's how passive he is.

Edward, dressed in white tie and starched shirt, led Lindy, dressed in tan buckskin, down several long halls, down marble staircases (covered in woolen carpeting to prevent slipping and causing a scene) and ended up someplace in the 620,000 square foot house, in one of the several dining rooms.   There was the Grand Ballroom, the Royal Dining room, the Petite Dining room and the Family Dining room.   Edward and Lindy headed for the Family Dining room. The room itself was forty feet by thirty feet with a twenty-five foot ceiling, four fireplaces and lots of polished marble. The table was a solid piece of Honduran mahogany four inches thick, four feet wide and twelve feet long. The family dining table. It was set for two. Lindy and Edward sat across from one another, four feet away, not twelve feet away.   Edward did not want the usual six course meal. He did not want to frighten Lindy with too much cutlery, too many stemmed glasses, too many dishes. They started with leek & cucumber soup; then hors d'oeuvres; then roast ribs of beouf, roast potatoes, asparagus with Hollandaise. A white French wine (Mersault) with the soup, Spanish sherry with the hors d'oeuvres; a St. Emilion red wine with the roast ribs of beouf. Then came dessert: chocolate mousse, pastries, ice cream, dessert wine; then, Edward was offered port and a humidor of Cuban cigars. Lindy grabbed a Cuban cigar, removed a box of matches from her pants pocket, lit her Cuban cigar like she'd been doing that for several years (she had) and watched Jack tenderly sip his port in a small, short-stemmed cut crystal glass. "This is port, it's from Portugal, a country south of here," said Jack.

"Why's your shirt so stiff, Jack?"

"It's been starched. It's what you wear to dinner if you're a man." is all Jack could fathom. It's how he grew up. The upper echelon men. The royal one-hundredth percent.

"You put the starch on?" wondered Lindy, poking at Jack's white cotton shirt loaded up with a lot of starch, painted on and ironed until it's so stiff the shirt can stand up on its own.

"No, no, the laundress puts the starch on," said Jack, not knowing what a long, hot, concentrated and hated job that starching a shirt was. At dinner parties with ten men, all shirts must be starched to perfection—no creases, no burn marks from the iron, no wet spots from uneven starching. Edward's shirt had been hanging in his closet for some months, since he inherited the house and grounds and threw an investiture/inheritance/accession party. Well, his mother arranged the party to size up her new home, last March, 1880. To meet the one-hundredth percenters in her husband's older brother's crowd. The other royalty—princes and dukes galore—and to introduce herself as her royal highness, Duchess Agatha, widow of Prince Clarence whose son Edward (Jack) is now the 3rd Duke of Sussex. And owner of the house Jack's mother was supposed to inherit through Jack's father. But no. Jack's father dropped dead in 1874, so Jack's mother was excluded from everything. No house, no additional royal family. No cozying up to the queen who lived conveniently right over the wall in Buckingham Palace.

HM Victoria did not attend Edward's party last March, but Alix, Princess of Wales, did attend and reported back to the Queen. The next day, Duchess Agatha, Edward's mother, who'd put on a wretchedly obscene display of social climbing and name dropping, received Letters Patent demoting her to a lowly non-royal Countess with no royal title, style and station.

The Princess of Wales, a Dane who was mocked by Edward's mother and Edward's Aunt Fanny—married to Edward's (Jack's) late uncle Frederick who was the 2nd Duke of Sussex and lived in

Ashfield Hall—were both demoted by Queen Victoria upon the death of Edward's uncle Frederick. Both women, Aunt Fanny and Edward's mother, Countess Agatha, were ordered to remove themselves from Ashfield Hall, giving the estate to its sole legal occupant: Edward (Jack).

HM also knew that her sons were good friends with Edward/ Jack. Edward's mother was ordered to return to her home in Mayfair where she lived with her late husband, Prince Clarence and their four children. Three girls and Edward.

Unmarried Edward, by the way, looked dashing in his starched white shirt. He met many eligible young ladies at this party, but took no interest in any of them.

"The big horserace is next Wednesday," remarked Jack watching Lindy enjoy her soup. She had picked up the correct spoon and was schlurping loudly. Edward/Jack, on the other hand, sat up board straight, dipped his soup spoon into his soup and moved the spoon away from him, raised the spoon up to his mouth and ate silently. Lindy was hunched over her soup bowl.

Her reply to Edward's remark was 'un-hun' between schlurps.

"I need you to ride one of my horses instead of yours."

Lindy stopped sucking up her soup for a second to take in this information, then continued schlurping.

She finished her soup by lifting her creme soup bowl, putting her head back, and letting the rest of the soup flow into her mouth. She wiped her mouth with her jacket's leather sleeve.

"Big table and no food, Jack!" said Lindy looking around for more grub.

From the kitchen came a sterling silver tray filled with finger food called hors d'oeuvres. A servant removed her creme soup service dish and bowl as another servant put a clean dish in its place. A third servant stood statue still holding the sterling silver tray filled with dessert-sized dishes and small bowls of delights featuring lamb, beef, bacon, roast vegetables. Lindy just took three or four plates saying, "Don't go nowheres with that tray."

The servant holding the tray looked at Prince Edward, Third Duke of Sussex, for a possible translation of Lindy's statement. Prince Edward, great-grandson of King George III and nephew of Aunt Queen Victoria, nodded and smiled at the servant who then placed the sterling silver tray on the massive solid mahogany table and walked downstairs to the kitchen—a large, organized, well-provisioned, state-of-the-art room—below stairs.

"Let's take a look at my horse, Noble Warrior, after supper. He's a three year old," said Edward with apprehension, still waiting for Lindy to rebuff his polite request.

"You want me to ride your horse at the big race next week?" said Lindy trying a lamb-based appetizer on a delicate mille feuille pastry. She liked it.

"Yes. Noble Warrior is already registered and I'd like you to take him for a ride tomorrow morning, after you meet him tonight."

"And if I win, how much do I get?"

"I will give you the whole purse, which is more than, ah, $30,000 in American money."

Edward wondered whether Lindy had any idea how much $30,000 was. In 1880 America, the average work week was 60 hours. A high paying job was $3.50 a day. Workers toiled away 10 hours a day, 6 days a week, then went to church on Sunday. The average annual salary was $1,092 ($21 a week for 52 weeks). Lindy would make 30 year's wages for less than 3 minutes of riding around a turf race course on a Wednesday afternoon in June. If she won.

"Thirty-thousand! All daddy wanted was $10,000. He said $10,000 would set us for life. Where's 'at horse?!"

Edward felt the weight of a three year old thoroughbred colt lifted from his shoulders.

"Tell me about your horse, L.C. What are those markings on his front left hoof?"

"Daddy says he's a cavalry horse who must've thrown his rider and rode off. I found him eating grass just north of Cheyenne about three or four year ago."

"I looked into those markings. L.C. is from the U.S. Army cavalry. The 7th Cavalry Regiment. Have you heard of Custer's Battle at the Big Horn?" tested Edward.

"I might've," remarked Lindy coyly.

"The Lakota Indians killed an entire regiment of US Cavalry in June of '76 up in Montana Territory and your L.C. was part of that battle."

"You know who won?" asked Lindy—who already knew.

"The Lakota. They killed all of Custer's men, including Custer. The Lakota were led by Sitting Bull, a chief; and Crazy Horse, another Lakota chief." reported Edward, an amateur historian who visited the site of Custer's Last Stand in Montana Territory before heading down to Cheyenne in Wyoming Territory to get back on his private train, on the Union Pacific tracks.

Lindy remembered her father was in an 'exaggerated and glorified state' when he heard the US Cavalry was 'wiped clean off the earth' by 'a bunch of injuns' a couple of years back. Now, Jack, over chocolate mousse, had confirmed her father's tale.

"Yes, Crazy Horse was a great Indian warrior, a great leader."

"I'm gonna name L.C. Crazy Horse," declared Lindy, eating chocolate mousse, smoking an El Presidente Corona, sipping 1822 Cockburn vintage port and smiling broadly, in pure delight. Right this minute, Lindy seemed less a threatening mountain lion and more a purring kitten to Jack.

"That would be a great honor for your horse, who was on the wrong side of the fight. I can have Crazy Horse officially registered in the Jockey Club of Britain and in the American Stud Book, which I have a copy of here at the house."

After their early supper, with plenty of late spring daylight left, Lindy and Jack went to the stables and met with Mr Chalmers, the Groomsman. Noble Warrior, Jack's beautiful, muscular, aggressive black Arabian Thoroughbred three year old colt, was saddled up and waiting for Lindy. She knew what to do. Lindy head-butted Nobel Warrior, forehead to forehead, then she kissed his nose, rubbed his neck, took his reins off, threw them on the ground, then walked him onto the great lawn while talking to him in a soothing voice. Lindy then fed him some carrots and a couple of cubes of sugar. Edward and Mr Chalmers looked on curiously. When's she gonna get on and ride? was what they were thinking.

Lindy opened Noble Warrior's mouth and demanded a hackamore. Minor groomsmen ran to produce the hackamore. Lindy slipped the bridle over Noble Warrior's head—nothing went in his mouth. Lindy fed Noble Warrior another carrot. It was easier to eat and enjoy. There was no steel bit weighing on Noble Warrior's tongue. Two steel roller pins on either side of the horse's tongue could not be comfortable.

Lindy let go of Noble Warrior's reins and the two of them walked off onto the great lawn. Lindy was having an inaudible conversation with Noble Warrior. Edward and Mr. Chalmers shrugged. Mr. Chalmers went back to his duties tending to 21 thoroughbreds in the immaculate stable 'pavilion', an interesting name for the large, cobblestone, heated, insulated, tile roofed barn.

At some point Lindy patted Noble Warrior on his hind quarters, took the reins and mounted him. She did not like the English saddle, shrugged, yelled "git!" and Noble Warrior took off heading west towards Harrods Department Store.

Duke Edward, standing by the stable pavilion, took notice and watched horse and rider full throttle moving as one. Edward had witnessed this only once and that was at the beginning of May in western Nebraska. Edward, with his party, saw a young Lakota scout on a white pinto paint running full out. The Lakota boy was no older than 14 and he was fearless. Where was he going in such a hurry? Out for a joyride (wowiyuski akayake) on his paint. Edward, 3rd Duke of Sussex, was impressed. If only such a jockey as this lived in Great Britain.

After a solid twenty minute workout galloping, trotting, cantering and walking, Lindy trotted Noble Warrior home to the stable, dismounted and walked him to a water trough. She spotted a large wooden bucket, gathered a brush, currycomb, hay wisp, sponge and cotton cloths.

Mr Chalmers came over holding something relatively new. A garden hose made of rubber, which replaced canvas and cotton hose material. Mr Chalmers, given instruction by Edward on how to deal with the 'Wyoming girl', brought a thoroughbred out of the stable and used the garden hose to wash the horse down. Of course Lindy watched, and of course she wanted in on the garden hose. But first, she was sponging Noble Warrior's sensitive nose, his eyes and eyelashes, checking his hooves for stones. She combed his tail and mane. Then buffed his hooves with some of the cotton cloth.

"When you're done, can I try that thing?" wondered Lindy, in a pleasant tone of voice. Not the usual command.

"Yes, your Ladyship. In England we call this a water hose." said the patient Mr Chalmers.

Lindy spent an hour on Noble Warrior. Then she took a hay wisp and used it to shine Noble Warrior's coat. The Arabian thoroughbred's coat radiated, drawing the attention of other barn rats—apprentice groomsmen who oooh'd and ahhh'd Noble Warrior.

Noble Warrior acted proudly, like he was the center of attention. He was.

Lindy walked her new buddy to his stall. Noble Warrior led the way. Lindy opened his stall's tall window on hinges which swung open like a door. Gave Warrior a headbutt on his forehead and walked down the stable's immaculately clean cobblestone walkway to visit her horse, L.C., now Crazy Horse.

Lindy took L.C. to the front of the stables, turned on the rubber horse hose and spent an hour with her horse, a former 7th Cavalry Regiment horse. "By the way, your new name is Crazy Horse." L.C. dipped his head, delighted in the news. Maybe Chief Crazy Horse (Ta'sunke Witco) personally killed L.C's rider, freeing the beautiful Hanoverian thoroughbred to find Lindy in southern Wyoming Territory. Battle of the Greasy Grass is the Lakota name for the same river the U.S. Army called the Little Big Horn.

Lindy brought a Hudson's Bay blanket she'd stored in Crazy Horse's saddle bags and bedded down in Noble Warrior's stall. That's where she slept until Wednesday, May 26th, the day of the Epsom Derby in Surrey, a section of London south of the Thames and 19 miles from Ashfield Hall. Lindy gave little thought to the race and had no idea how popular it was. She was thinking that it would be a race like they did back in Wyoming Territory: a couple of loudmouths on their ponies who thought they could beat Lindy because she was a girl. Lindy played that up big by pretending to not know how to get on her horse, how to ride, turn or stay on. Every time she raced, many times with the same idiots, she'd win twenty, thirty, fifty dollars. Every time. This 'darby' race had a prize of $30,090. Lindy was going to spend some of it at Harrods. Lindy was looking forward to teaching these foreigners (British) how to ride. Their saddles didn't have a horn and no place to strap on a scabbard for a Winchester, no place for a lariat, canteen, bedroll, saddle bags. These finicky foreigners look down their long noses at everyone. 'I'll teach them,' thought Lindy.

Jack, now settled in, began his work regimen: up by 9am, breakfast served in his office up on the third floor, northwest window overlooking the great lawn and beyond that, growing London. He could see the top floors of Harrods over Ashfield's 30 foot stone wall.   Also out these windows, the Royal Duke watched Lindy race, then trot, then walk, cantor and return to galloping, his three year old thoroughbred colt Noble Warrior.

Those were the only times when he saw Lindy. She was spending all of her time at the stables with Noble Warrior and Crazy Horse. All of her meals were brought to her. The dining staff had set up a table across from Noble Warrior's stall and made 'cowboy' cooking available.   Edward brought back from his trip to the American West, handwritten recipes from Montana Territory, Cheyenne, Dakota Territory, Nebraska and, of course, Delmonico's in New York. Lindy loved Delmonico's steaks served with butter and Hollandaise Sauce. With hash brown potatoes and a side of bacon.

Race Day

After eight days of training, Lindy was ready for The Derby, run at Epsom Downs, in the County of Surrey which is south of the Thames River. Lindy supervised Noble Warrior being walked into his specially designed horse wagon to transport him to a race track.

After a light breakfast, Edward and Lindy got into the estate's elaborate carriage, custom built by Henry Mulliner, who also personally built carriages, especially the Coronation Carriage, for Her Majesty Queen Victoria. Three other carriages carrying important household staff and the Groomsman's select staff, followed in the parade. The first two carriages where security staff, then Jack's royal carriage, then Noble Warrior's royal horse wagon, then six remaining carriages. The 20 mile ride to Epsom Downs took four hours. They were quartered in a private house owned by another member of the extended royal family.

Derby Day was a 10 day affair beginning the Saturday before the Wednesday Derby horse race. Hundreds of thousands of Londoners came for the entertainment. There were amusements galore: carnival events, shows, performers, fireworks—something going on all day and all night, drawing these massive crowds.

The horserace took place on Wednesday afternoon, May 26th, 1880. Most of the attendees (commoners) watched the race free of charge. There was a grandstand for nobility. And opposite the finish line was another grandstand for owners and the royal family.

Edward, 3rd Duke of Sussex, was both an owner and a member of the royal family. Her Majesty was not in attendance. She rarely left the grounds of Buckingham Palace since her husband, Consort Prince Albert, died of typhoid fever a week before Christmas, 1861, at the age of 42.

Instead, HRH Albert, Prince of Wales, Jack and Princes Alfred, Arthur and Leopold, sat in the Royal Box, right on the Finish line. Everyone had binoculars and everyone was very curious about Lindy, the 'wild cowgirl from Wyoming Territory'. Lindy had agreed to wear Jack's royal colours: yellow and royal blue. She had never worn silk. Once she held the blouse, felt real silk, she never wanted to take it off. This pleased Jack.

"What's this made of, Jack?" wondered Lindy.
"Silk, your Ladyship. Silk."
"I like silk."

Epsom Fair began 10 o'clock in the morning, Saturday, May 22, 1880. The crowds took time off from work. People worked 10 or 12 hours a day, six days a week. This Protestant nation took Sunday off. Half a million workers did not report back to work on Monday but stayed to enjoy the warm late spring air, the festivities and a chance to sleep in. Thank God for the Epsom Fair.

Even Parliament took the week off, as one famous member of Parliament (Disraeli) put it, "to reacquaint myself with my constituency.." Prime Minister Gladstone laughed at Benjamin Disraeli, former Prime Minister whom Gladstone beat last April, 1880. Disraeli was now just a conservative MP, who loved to drink and bet on the ponies. Like millions of other Londoners.

In 1880, the population of London hovered around 5 million. When as many as 500,000 people show up for the ten day festival of the Epsom Fair & Derby Day, there's not a lot employers can do. Except close shop and join the festivities. Working stiffs declared the Epsom Fair a national holiday. Unless you wanted several million workers to go on strike, it's wise to let workers take time off for the annual Fair. They're going to take time off anyway.

The royal box and nobility box seats were filled with overdressed, stuffy entitled personages. The royal box looked straight down the finish line, to see which horse finished first. The racecourse had been groomed to perfection. It was a flat track of turf—mowed lawn—that went slightly up hill, and ended going slightly downhill. The course was 1 mile, 4 furlongs and 6 yards. Four furlongs is 880 yards or one-half mile. So, the course was a left hand mile-and-a-half run. Winning times were coming in at 2 minutes and fifty seconds. The best time was 2:42, set in 1867. Last year, 1879, the winning time was 3:02. There were no reliable stop watches used before 1846 so nobody knew exactly how fast any horse was before then.

To determine the winner, judges stood at the finish line which was a rope tied onto two opposing poles, above the heads of the jockeys, that stretched across the finish line. There was no finish line photography in 1880.

Today, Wednesday May 26th, 1880, was the 100th running of The Derby. The richest race in British history began in 1780. At that time, the Royal Army and Navy were losing the war against the rebellious American Colonists who were British Subjects but no matter, the horserace was vastly more important. A hundred years ago, King George III, Queen Charlotte and many of their children (15 in all, including two future kings), were in attendance.

Today twenty-two 3-year old thoroughbreds were about to run for the richest purse in racing. And one of the jockeys was a girl. Lindy pulled her long hair back and tucked it under her silk cap, also in Jack's colours. Lindy didn't walk like a fainty-dainty girl whose gait screamed 'help me, help me, I'm a delicate thing.' She walked like a Newcastle coal miner, shoulders wide, back straight and stiff, and an unsmiling gaze that said she'd knock your block off if she felt like it. You are correct: Jack was terrified of Lindy.

A trumpet called the jockeys to mount up. There were two favorite horses: Robert the Devil and Bend Or. Lindy sized up each jockey and thought she could take them. She sized up their two thoroughbreds and thought this was going to be a race. The hardest race she'd ever run. A real race like the time two years ago that she had to outrun two Northern Cheyenne teenagers on mustangs shooting arrows at her. Lindy didn't know how to ride and shoot her .32 caliber six gun at the same time.

It took five or six minutes to line up the high-strung Derby thoroughbreds, numbered 1 through 22, at the starting line. A six inch wide white crushed chalk line which ran across the racecourse turf was the only restrictive barrier. The Official Starter stood at the chalk line and dropped his flag to start the race. About a hundred yards down the course was the Assistant Starter who would drop his flag to indicate a False Start. Or not, and let the racers thunder by.

When all 22 thoroughbreds were lined up and none stepped over the chalk line, the Official Starter dropped his flag.   The operator of the stop watch (a Louie Moinet compteur de tierces) which looked like a silver pocket watch, pressed the start button. The

Official Race Timer stood, of course, at the finish line.   In three minutes or less, there would be a winner.

The Race

A crowd estimated at 90,000 stretched along the white two-rail wooden fence surrounding the mile and a half racecourse. Epsom Downs was a public park so the fans watched for free.

The Epsom Grandstand was for nobility only and were sectioned off for the hierarchy of nobility: Duke, Duchess. Marquess, Marchioness.   Earl, Countess. Viscount, Viscountess. Baron, Baroness.

Royalty had its own exclusive stand: The Queen's Stand for Her Majesty, the Princes, Princesses.   Edward, 3rd Duke of Sussex, sat with Queen Victoria's four sons.   Edward and Albert had binoculars and their seats were in a direct line with the Finish line about twenty yards away, and fifteen feet up in the Queen's Stand, the premier private box, which is why it's good to be a nephew to the Queen and cousin to the Prince of Wales.

Lindy and Noble Warrior were wearing number 3. Number 1 and in position 1 was Robert the Devil. In position 2 was Bend Or. Then Lindy on Noble Warrior. And so on til number 22.

The official starter dropped his flag and the horses took off. Lindy had spent three days practicing the start.   And every day practicing the different aspects of the race.   The 3 furlong uphill climb.   The 5 furlong downhill end to the Wire. And the dreaded Tattenham Corner, a sharp left hand turn.   The racecourse, one and a half miles plus 6 yards, was not a closed loop. The Derby was U shaped.   And Edward had laid out the track on his one mile square lawn around his house.

The race started a hundred yards from the Royal Box seats and ended, of course, in front of the Royal Box seats.

Robert the Devil, a powerful Thoroughbred bay, the leading 3 year old colt in Europe, took an immediate six length lead. Bend Or blew past Lindy to take a weak second. Lindy did not panic because the horses were running up a slight hill. Lindy used to ride Crazy Horse up the Continental Divide, then down.   Riding hills in the Rocky Mountains, at altitude, for fun, got her used to situations.

As stated, The Epsom racecourse was reproduced at Edward's mile square acreage. All soft grass about three inches long. Lindy racing Crazy Horse, then Noble Warrior. Thoroughbreds run like hell for no reason, just because it's fun, is what Lindy believed watching Crazy Horse.

There are 8 furlongs in a mile thus 4 furlongs in a half mile. That's the race. The additional 6 yards must be so that the finish line is lined up with the Queen's throne or something, thought Lindy, getting a fix for all this royalty nonsense.

Lindy loved being called Your Ladyship by everyone, including Jack. Even more, she loved being waited on all day long. She wants breakfast served at the stables, someone cooks breakfast, someone else brings it to her, another person sets up a table, and yet another person pours the juice and tea. And when she's done someone else cleans it all up. And no one reminds her of how hard anyone worked to provide her with all these labour-intensive services. She's served afternoon tea and supper at the stables. She ate after she and Noble Warrior practice. Then after supper, Lindy washed and brushed her colt, all the time talking to him in a soothing voice. Never a harsh word, cuss word or rebuke. She saves those emotions for humans. Wretched humans.

As the left-hand turn approached, the racecourse dipped downward. Downhill! thought Lindy. Noble Warrior likes running downhill. Well, Warrior, let's show Robert the Devil what you got.

"Git!" yelled Lindy. Her yellow and blue wide vertical striped silk blouse tightened against her chest; she lifted up from her English saddle and leaned forward and let Warrior run after Robert the Devil. On her left, close to the rail, Lindy sensed Bend Or coming up fast. Lindy poked Noble Warrior slightly to encourage him to pick up more speed. Noble Warrior obliged Lindy.

Lindy blew by the Mile Marker (a mile to the finish line) as they made it around Tattenham Corner and headed downhill to the Finish line.

At the 5 furlong pole (5/8ths of a mile to go) Noble Warrior's senses kicked in. They'd been training from Furlong 5 to the finish the last four days. Robert the Devil was 5 lengths ahead and Bend Or was still creeping up on Lindy's left, drifting into the wooden rail. Noble Warrior lurched forward, pulling farther ahead of Bend Or. Within seconds Noble Warrior pulled closer to Robert the Devil. Four lengths, not five. Robert the Devil's jockey, Edward

Rossiter, whipped his colt. Fred Archer, crashing Bend Or into the wooden fence, was forced to raise his left leg onto Ben Or's neck. Rossiter turned to check on the racers and saw that Noble Warrior was close and that Bend Or had fallen back about eight lengths.

They entered the straightaway. Robert the Devil, then Nobel Warrior, then Bend Or. Two furlongs to go—440 yards or a quarter of a mile. Rossiter spurred Robert the Devil to make sure he'd win, needing to add four more lengths for good measure.

Lindy was in a similar fix a couple of months ago when her ego got the best of her and someone slipped ahead of Crazy Horse and nearly won. Lindy rubbed Noble Warriors neck and said, "Go get 'em, boy.." and she let Noble Warrior do his best.

Noble Warrior, with a hundred yards left, caught up to Robert the Devil and was half a head behind as they came down to the wire which was stretched above the horses (and jockeys). A wire stretched across the finish line so the Racing Official, on a stand above the horses, could have the best possible view of which horse, or horse's nose, finished first.

Lindy stared at the finish line. There were two tall white poles, 12 feet tall, at the Finish line, across the track, with a wire stretched between them above the horse's heads. Robert the Devil's head was ahead of Noble Warrior's and that wouldn't do. That would never do. Nobody beats Lindy. Lindy had a way with her horses. She'd taken jumpy, high strung ponies and turned them into focused racers.   She'd taken shy fillies and turned them into aggressive racers. And she turned Crazy Horse into a great racer.

Noble Warrior was a Thoroughbred, a royal horse, smart, well fed, well cared for. Lindy needed a horse that was angry. Noble Warrior was jealous of Crazy Horse. That's it! thought Lindy.

"Git moving, Crazy Horse, show me what you got!"

Noble Warrior snorted and took off. Anger, thought Lindy, the greatest emotion. The emotion that moves mountains. And race horses. Anger also shoots sheriffs. Now can this fancy pony who sleeps in a bigger room than most humans, beat The Devil. Fifty yards to go and we're closing and Robert the Devil's head is still in front. "Run Crazy Horse, run."

Noble Warrior's nostrils flared. Lindy felt Noble Warrior's muscular shoulders flex. He kicked up turf and charged forward in what Lindy thought was a rage. Robert the Devil was no fluke. Robert the Devil had won 9 of 11 races and was used to finishing first. And now he was less than 30 yards from the wire and moving all out for the win.

Lindy then did something she'd never done in a horserace. She took her horse whip and whipped Noble Warrior's right hind quarters. Noble Warrior unleashed the rest of his raging power. Now they were head to head with 12 yards to go.

Noble Warrior went ahead, then Robert the Devil was ahead by a nose with 2 yards, then 1 yard, then they raced under the wire and across the Finish line with a fury and intensity Lindy had never experienced. It was over. Who won?

Lindy and Edward Rossiter both slowed their ponies. Edward Rossiter tipped his cap to Lindy. She tipped hers to him. He thought Lindy was a young man with long hair pulled back and tied off neatly. Lindy, up til ten seconds ago, thought these foreigners were pasty-faced fops, a bunch of dandy boys with too much time on their soft, feminine hands to be able to race horses.

"Good run," said Edward Rossiter, on the back of Robert the Devil.

"I like running on grass," said Lindy.

"What's your name?" asked Rossiter.

"Lindy Long," she said.

"I'm Edward Rossiter, Lindy. What's your accent?" he wondered.

"Accent? I ain't got no accent."

"Where you from?"

"Wyoming. America."

"America? How'd you hear about the Derby?"

"My friend Jack. He lives in London," said Lindy.

"Good luck to you," said Edward Rossiter, who rode over to his owner, trainer and small entourage.

"And to you, Edward," said Lindy. (Lindy thought, 'now he looks like an Edward.')

The crowd, especially the few thousand who were near the finish line, went wild. Which caused the other 90,000 race goers to also go wild.

Lindy had no idea how she did, but out of 22 Thoroughbreds she'd come in at least second. And Jack said there was a 'substantial' purse for second place. Lindy thought that was good. She didn't like living off other people. She didn't like owing anybody anything. She did like getting even with people who owed her.

"We have a winner!" announced the Race Official.

Lindy and Edward Rossiter rode over to the Official standing between the Finish line and the Royal Box seats.

A circle had formed around two Derby Officials. Charles Brewer, Robert the Devil's owner, Charles Blanton, Robert the Devil's trainer; HRH Jack and Mr Chalmers; HRH Albert, Prince of Wales, Princes Alfred, Arthur and Leopold.

Fred Archer, jockey of Bend Or, rode up where the owner, 1st Duke of Westminster, Hugh Grosvenor, and Master of the Horse (1880-1885), joined the Prince of Wales and others to see who'd won the One Hundredth Running of The Derby.

"By a short head, the winner of the hundredth Derby is Noble Warrior."

The very stiff upper lipped, starched, stoic, imperturbable upper crust royals and nobles, jumped in the air and danced around like children. Lindy accepted a firm handshake from Edward Rossitor. Lindy dismounted and handed the reins of Noble Warrior to Mr Chalmers but Noble Warrior would have none of it. Noble Warrior grabbed Lindy's silk blouse and pulled her toward him. Lindy knocked her forehead against NobleWarrior's forehead and rubbed his head.

Edward/Jack offered his hand to Lindy and she shook it, saying "thanks, Jack."

Jack said, "Thank you, your Ladyship. You're the best jockey on two continents!"

Edward turned to the gentleman next to him and said to Lindy:

"May I introduce you, Lady Lindy Long, to his royal highness, Albert, Prince of Wales."

"Hi," said Lindy. The Prince of Wales did not offer his hand. Lindy nodded then talked to Jack.

"Now what, Jack?" she asked. The Prince of Wales responded quizzically to Lindy calling HRH Edward, 3rd Duke of Sussex, great-grandson of King George III, and a cousin to Albert, Prince of Wales, as 'Jack'. Did the Prince of Wales miss hear something? Was Jack one of Edward's string of family names? Or did he not tell her his real name when Edward went off to America a couple of months ago?

"Would you like to return home and rest. I'll get your winnings." reminded Jack.

The owner of Robert the Devil graciously bowed to Jack and left with his entourage. The 1st Duke of Westminster, Hugh Grosvenor, left with his family. Lindy shook hands (tight, like a man) with jockey Edward Rossiter and Fred Archer who rode Bend Or.

Lindy took the reins off Noble Warrior and walked him to his custom built horse wagon and said, "Good race, boy. See ya soon." She gave Noble Warrior another head butt on his forehead.

Lindy then got in Jack's carriage where she took off her boots and stretched out.

"What do you want for dinner?" wondered Jack.

"Delmonico's steak and a cold fuckin' beer."

CHAPTER 10

Speech to Staff

Ashfield Hall had a Grand Ballroom.   Today the Grand Ballroom in Jack's house was readied for 141 people. The room was 125 feet long by 65 feet wide with a 55 foot high ceiling. 60 crystal natural gas chandeliers, created and hand-blown by Waterford Crystal master glass blowers, hung from the ceiling. There were 22 Italian marble columns, fifty-five feel tall, standing proudly from floor to ceiling in the large ballroom. Columns finished in the Ionic.   The Grand Ballroom was indeed grand.

Staff members brought 141 carved mahogany chairs with thick, cushy padded seats, from the anteroom (storage room) off the ballroom. Also a couple of solid mahogany tables, 22 feet long (no leaves), were carried into the ballroom by ten strong men.

There was going to be a House Meeting called by Edward, 3rd Duke of Sussex—The Land Lord. His Royal Highness ordered all necessary staff to meet at 12:30.   There was no hint whether the meeting portended good or ill.

The kitchen staff was cooking luncheon for the house staff and grooms staff (groundskeepers and stable crew), which would be served at 11:00. What was left over was brought to Jack in his office and to Lindy, out in the stables.

The kitchen staff loved this total casualness. Jack's uncle, who owned Ashfield Hall, had a wife (Duchess Fanny) who invited many guests for luncheon, another crowd for afternoon tea, and yet more guests for dinner at 8. The kitchen staff worked from 6 in the morning straight through til 11 at night. Seven days a week.

When Jack inherited the estate from his uncle, his first meeting with the Butler, Housekeeper and Chef was short and simple: 'I am moving in alone, whatever you make for breakfast, lunch and dinner is fine with me. And I don't take tea. I do like pastries, beefsteak, hearty soups and cakes. So eat what you please, when you please. There will be no lavish parties with pretentious personages.'

There was great rejoicing, but in a low-key, subdued, polite English sort of way. No more working 12 hour days, seven days a week, as the late Duke's wife (Fanny) always wanted Ashfield Hall filled with jealous people eating and drinking excellent food and beverage. Jealous of Duchess Fanny and her lavish get-togethers.

At 12:30 post meridian Jack walked into the Great Ballroom, set up for 141 staff: 140 house staff and Mr Chalmers, Head Groomsman, who would report back to the stables where his staff included 58 groundskeepers and groomsmen who tended the grounds and the Thoroughbreds.

Edward was dressed casually, in Harris tweed. The carved mahogany chairs were set up in rows like a classroom. The two 22 foot long solid mahogany dining tables were set up opposite the chairs. At one of the tables were several bookkeepers with ledgers, dipping pens and money. At another table was one chair, for Jack, 3rd Duke of Sussex.

The staff were standing in front of the chairs.

"Good day!" said Jack, smiling. "Please be seated."

Servants were not allowed, by English law, to be seated in the presence of Royalty. Edward walked around to the other mahogany table and took his seat. When Jack sat, the Butler (Mister Harrison), still standing, nodded and the entire house staff took their seats.

"Thank you for coming. I have much needed **good** news. I went over your annual wages and I can't believe how cheap my uncle Frederick was. You are all getting a substantial raise in pay beginning today. Beginning this week, you are getting two days off each week. You are also getting reduced working hours. And you are all getting a paid one week holiday, aside from the holiday surrounding the Epsom Fair, which will also be paid time off. That's just the beginning. In the coming months your living quarters will be expanded and made more comfortable. You will also be given the option to move to town. I recently bought some apartments, rental in these apartments will be paid by me. And everyone will be given extra money for personal clothing, for education, to develop hobbies and avocations—for instance if you want to take up a musical instrument, I shall provide the instrument, the time and the teachers. If you wish to learn a language other than English, I shall provide the time and teachers and allow you time to practice your new language. If you wish to perfect your football skills or your cricket skills, you shall be given the time, the equipment and the playing field to accommodate those desires."

Jack stopped to take a sip of tea. The room was silent. As silent as Wyoming with no wind. A room of 141 staff members sitting breathlessly.

"Are there any questions?"

The silence remained unbroken because trained staff members could not respond to rhetoric.

Jack, still not used to the bureaucracy, detailed orderliness and decorum of staff organization, finally did what most would have done at the outset:

"Mr Harrison." retorted Edward.

The Butler, the general in charge of all house staff, stood and said, "Sir.?"

"Please ask any questions you feel your staff would like asked of me, Mr Harrison. That goes for Mrs Dahlgren, too." coaxed Jack.

"Sir," began Mr Harrison, "When you say 'reduced hours of service', does that mean less pay for the reduction in hours?"

"Great question," began Jack. "No. Everyone gets a **raise** in pay, double your current pay. And, instead of working 10 hours a day for 6 or even 7 days, no one works more than 8 hours, 5 days a week. With two days off. There will no longer be strangers entering my house for meals, or tea. I will live here by myself and the American girl. Far less work for everyone! Aunt Fanny is gone forever, now living in the west country, and no longer a royal duchess. The worse it could get is if my mother and my three sisters move in. But they will not be allowed to order lavish parties and meals. They are non-royals and will be temporary guests," concluded Jack.

Mrs Dahlgren, Head Housekeeper, spoke up on behalf of all the women staff, "Will your mother and sisters require chambermaids?"

"Thank you, Mrs Dahlgren," began Jack, "Mother, a non-royal countess, has her own chambermaid, as does my eldest sister Elsie. The other two don't need chambermaids."

Mrs Dahlgren asked, "Will we get the same two days off? And if so, who will do.."

Jack replied, "staff members will take their two days off at random times. The kitchen staff needs time off, and they will get fewer working hours immediately. If need be, I will hire additional staff to make sure meals are well prepared, taste delicious as usual, and served on time three times a day. Plus tea. Mrs Faucher, Head Chef will keep me apprised of her situation, as will Mr Harrison and of course, you, Mrs Dahlgren.   I expect to be informed of any and all staffing situations and solve them immediately. My wish is for our staff to be well paid, well rested, well fed and to enjoy your lives, and be respected by myself and family members or guests."

At this point Lindy opened one of the twenty-five foot tall mahogany French doors to the Grand Ballroom and stuck her head in, apparently looking for anyone. The whole house, except for the private security, was empty, and seated in the Grand Ballroom. Lindy came in which caused all staff members to stand—they weren't sure whether she were royalty, a crazy cousin, a bastard child of which there are many running around the Kingdom, or a member of the nobility. A peer at least.   Since Lindy was a friend of Jack, a royal duke, the staff, by law, must stand in her presence, not sure of her position but positive that she calls his royal highness 'Jack' for some particular reason unknown to everyone in the house.   Therefore she has a Power of Familiarity.

"What's goin' on, Jack?"

"I've announced the raises, time off and holidays for the staff who are overworked and underpaid," said Jack, quietly, now standing by his table because Lindy, a woman, is standing.

"May I continue addressing the staff?" said Jack, "Staff, please be seated. Lindy is not a royal," concluded Jack.

"Don't let me butt in." quipped Lindy.

"Now, kitchen staff, please come up to the table and collect your new pay. Line up according to your last name."

The kitchen staff immediately lined up at the bookkeeping table, according to their last name placards listing A-F, G-L, M-Q, P-Z on them.

"Thank you so much for all the hard work you perform so expertly, and patiently, every day," said Jack as he and Lindy walked out of the Grand Ballroom to let the staffers cheer, or boo, or let loose, based on what they'd just heard.

As Edward and Lindy left and closed the tall French door, 141 staff members got loud and happy. As one of the chefs received her raise, took the cash in hand, she shrieked with joy. Then another kitchen helper blurted out a joyful noise. The level of excitement and anticipatory squawking related to extra cash, the reality of shorter working hours, and two days off (they were told which two days) was realized by all the commotions of raucous jubilance.

Lindy, walking down one of the lengthy marble-floored, beautifully architected hallways, did the unthinkable: she stopped Jack and kissed him on the cheek. "They love you! They love what you did."

"They deserve it. Uncle Frederick's wife was very cruel to the servants."

"She still alive?" wondered Lindy.

"You can't kill Satan. Happily, Aunt Fanny is far away in the west country."

"Wait'll she finds out what you did." said Lindy with a peck of malevolence.

"Are you going to get on Crazy Horse and tell Aunt Fanny?" quipped Edward.

"No. Better. She will hear of it from a more reliable source," guaranteed Lindy.

Jack furrowed his brow and they marched down the hall. Jack went upstairs to his office, where he had biscuits, clotted cream (cream thicker and sweeter than whipping cream) and hot tea (he had a small cast iron stove powered by natural gas. The British first used natural gas in 1785 for street lights and homes). Lindy went outside and rode Crazy Horse over to Noble Warrior who was grazing on the great lawn.

CHAPTER 11

Jack's Mother Arrives

Countess Agatha was the second angriest woman in England. The angriest woman was the late Prince Frederick Louis Arthur William's widow, and Jack's Aunt Fanny: Duchess Fannie Marie. When Prince Frederick died, his entire estate went to Edward (Jack). Not Fanny, who never read up on Male Primogeniture (the eldest son gets everything).

Queen Victoria was so alarmed by Prince Frederick's death (they were first cousins) and its consequences, that Her Majesty immediately and personally ordered Prince Frederick's widow, Duchess Fanny, physically removed from Ashfield Hall including any family members and clinging friends of Fanny. Duchess Fanny and family were shipped to the west country and put up in a cramped 10,000 square foot cottage near Cardiff, Wales. Then Queen Victoria downgraded Duchess Fanny to a mere garden variety non-royal Countess. She was given a stipend of £1,000 a month (equivalent to $5,000 in 1880). And her style dropped from your Royal Highness to Lady Fanny. She was kicked out of the royal family. She was a non-royal nobody. She was mortified.

A week after Prince Frederick died in February 1880, when Duchess Fanny was downgraded to Countess Fanny, Jack's mother, the widow Duchess Agatha, was forced to turn in not only her royal title, but also her royal style of 'your royal highness'. Lady Agatha was also kicked out of the royal family.   B e c a u s e   P r i n c e Frederick was also the grandson of King George III, he had royal pulling power. When Jack's Uncle Frederick died last February, all that power disappeared from his power hungry wife. The only family member who benefitted from Prince Frederick's death was his nephew, and heir, Edward (Jack), who immediately inherited his Dukedom and became the 3rd Duke of Sussex with a large fully furnished house, 144 household staff, thoroughbred stables and £177,000 weekly income.

Jack's mother must also be downgraded to non-royal countess and styled as Lady because she could not outrank her sister-in-law, married to a royal duke. However, the downgraded Countess Agatha had been fuming in her house in Mayfair since her husband died in 1874. She had been waiting to inherit Ashfield Hall since she got married. In fact, that was the only reason she married Prince Clarence. She had ideas for redecorating Ashfield Hall, hire new servants, but especially to throw magnificent, majestic balls, cotillions and Christmas parties then tell Victoria that her house and grounds were larger and more magnificent than Buckingham Palace. Countess Agatha wanted to especially have grander, showier, excessive Christmas parties because Victoria's husband, consort Prince Albert, had died eleven days before Christmas, 1861 from typhoid fever. Victoria would never recover from Albert's death, thus she stopped throwing Christmas parties. And all parties. Even her children's birthday parties. Everybody in the household must suffer from Albert's untimely, tragic death.

Jack's mother planned on establishing big Christmas festivities when she took over Ashfield Hall, making sure to invite Victoria's litter of children, with or without their spouses in tow.

When Jack's mother read the news of Prince Frederick's death in *The Times,* she had her carriage hitched up and was quickly driven to Ashfield Hall. What she saw scared her: a sizeable contingent of the Queen's Life Guard (cavalry) and Queen's Guard (dismounted troops), ordered by Her Majesty, to enter Ashfield Hall and its grounds and secure house and grounds from looting. Especially from family members and other hooligans no longer part of the estate.

The next day, Jack's mother, Duchess Agatha, received Letters Patent from Her Majesty, divesting her royal duchy and title, revoking her style of Your Royal Highness, and invoking a new title, that of countess and a non-royal garden variety (weed) style of Lady.

Further, the Letters Patent instructed Jack's mother that she was not welcome at Ashfield Hall under any circumstance, especially the Yule Season.

If you wanted to anger Countess Agatha, go against any one of her social climbing schemes. No matter who you are. The countess bided her time, then pounced: upon her son, now a royal duke, living all alone in his inherited 620,000 square foot house, next door to Buckingham Palace.

Countess Agatha had bullied and manipulated her son all his life. Getting him into the right schools (Preparatory school at St Paul's Academy and university at Cambridge, Trinity College).
Jack broke free of his mother's domineering influence and escaped to America and entered Boston Tech to become an engineer.

Jack's mother's royal title was revoked in mid-February of 1880 and now it was the second week of June. Four months is long enough, thought Countess Agatha. The old woman (HM Victoria no doubt) would have long forgotten her order to keep me away from my inherited house, thought Lady Agatha.   'I hope the queen sees me and I give her apoplexy.'

Agatha and her husband Prince Clarence had four children. A boy and three girls. Jack was a middle child, born after two girls, Elsie and Harriet. (Yes, how appropriate, thought Jack upon meeting Elsie (L.C.), Lindy's horse. His sister Elsie had a long, sad horse face. The baby of the family was Nora.   Elsie, now 32, Harriet, now 30, Edward, 27 and Nora, 24.   All four children remain unmarried and Countess Agatha just figured something out:

Queen Victoria had three sons who are unmarried: Alfred age 36, Arthur age 30, and Leopold age 27. And five daughters: all married except for the baby, Princess Beatrice, age 23.

Countess Agatha must take her plans to Ashfield Hall posthaste whilst her three eligible daughters and her Royal Duke son, thanks to fate, are still unclaimed.

What a fitting set of circumstances, thought Countess Agatha. Her family merging with Queen Victoria's family. 'I'll pull that wall down betwixt Buckingham Palace and Ashfield Hall and I shall regain my rightful title, style and join the royal family as co-Queen. Styled Her Majesty.

Jack's mother, future co-queen, had plans which drove her husband Prince Clarence to drink, golf, cricket and a gentleman's club, with her constant nagging, scheming, manipulating and demanding that Clarence become more ambitious. He did. He took up horse racing, gambling and prostitutes. It turned out that there were well-heeled, well dressed, very young and beautiful prostitutes who frequented gentleman's clubs in London and area racecourses.

Prince Clarence (Jack's father) was asked to join a Gentleman's club in the St. James's district, Westminster, London. Prince Clarence joined Boodle's Club, founded 1762, which had a bar, a formal dining room, a library, a gymnasium, and private rooms for.privacy.   Prince Clarence spent as much time at Boodle's as possible, sipping cocktails made from Boodle's Gin.

In the meantime, Jack fled to America where he'd matriculated to the Boston Institute of Technology to study mathematics, engineering, electro-magnetism and physics.   Nine years ago, 1871, Edward was a freshman at Trinity College, Cambridge, studying a Classical Education.

At Boston Tech in 1874, Edward met Roland Betthard, an exceptional graduate student who understood mathematics, electromagnetism and physics, but who didn't understand women. He applied his engineering algorithms to women and usually ended up getting slapped, kicked, punched and thrown down flights of stairs.   Just ask Lindy, who, fortunately for Roland, was unarmed when she went out with him. But no matter, Jack and Roland built machinery to heat office buildings, factories, people's homes and created indoor plumbing: sinks in kitchens and sinks, bath tubs and toilets in bathrooms. These boys were ahead of their time.

Countess Agatha and her three daughters, Ladies Elsie, Harriet and Nora, were standing on the front portico of Ashfield Hall and knocking on the six inch thick solid bronze front door. There was a well polished and very loud bronze door knocker.

A few minutes later the door was opened by Thomas Westham, a valet (pronounced with the 't', this is not France), in a beautiful uniform—bright red jacket with polished brass buttons, black woollen slacks with a red stripe, highly polished ankle-high shoes, white gloves, who was large, muscular, intimidating.   As though Jack had hired him to specifically bar his mother, and other annoyances, from barging into his 620,000 square foot private home.

"I am Prince Edward's mother. I demand entry."

"His royal highness is unavailable, my Lady."

"I am used to being addressed as your royal highness," said the countess acidly.

"I'm sure you were, my Lady. I shall report your demand for entry to his royal highness at my earliest convenience," said Jack's valet, Thomas Westham.

Meanwhile, two other large, intimidating and impeccably uniformed men (not gentlemen, there was nothing gentle about any of these uniformed men) appeared and marched over to the Brogan custom built coach, pulled by eight magnificent horses, which brought Jack's mother and sisters and was parked in line with the front entry. One of these muscular, uniformed security men talked to both of Countess Agatha's coachmen, seated on the driver's bench, on the upper ledge seats of the tall carriage. The coachmen nodded in agreement. One of the coachmen stepped down from his 'shotgun' perch on the custom built carriage, and opened the passenger door.

Thomas Westham, Valet, inside the house, physically blocking the entry with his muscular frame, said to the countess, "My lady, your coachman has opened your carriage door. It is time to exit the premises out Brompton Road. I believe Harrods is currently open."

"When I'm co-Queen, I shall have your head on a pike." Countess Agatha thought she had destroyed this man's life with her threat. She turned and walked off the porch, down the seven pink granite steps, followed by her three unmarried daughters, and into her custom built Brogan carriage. The carriage then took off for her home in Mayfair. She was too upset, and possibly too broke, to stop at Harrods Department Store, across the street from Jack's West Gate.

Several hours later Jack was enjoying a seared steak dinner in his upstairs office, far away from the front entrance and his mother. As he sat at his mechanical drawing table, he read the entry door valet's note about his lovely mother demanding entrance. Jack opened a bottle of 1754 Hennessy cognac in his liquor cabinet, selected a cut crystal Waterford brandy balloon and poured his cognac nearly to the top. Jack was intimidated (whipped) by his mother.

Jack stared at the valet's note, written in a beautiful cursive and looked distraught. "HRH Edward: Lady Agatha arrived with her three daughters before tea this afternoon wanting urgently to see you about moving into Ashfield Hall. Lady Agatha & company, left without any further instruction.   Thomas Westham, Entry Valet. June 11, of the year One thousand eight hundred and eighty.

Jack took another healthy gulp of very good cognac. And a bit of perfectly grilled and seared steak. Lots of juice which went well with the roasted, sliced and seasoned potatoes. Jack drizzled some Hollandaise Sauce on his steak.

Without notice, or warning, Lindy bounced into Jack's office, stopped and saw him looking suicidal, holding a beautiful cut crystal brandy balloon in one hand and the valet's note in the other.

"Hey, Jack. You look like shit. Your girl dump you?"

"Worse," admitted Jack. "My mother showed up, angrier than usual, and demanded to move in."

"If your maw is as bad as mine, I'll shoot her for ya, no charge," smirked Lindy.

Jack chugged more Hennessy.

"Since everyone knows how evil she is, you'll be acquitted," declared Jack.

"A-quit? What's that?"

"Not guilty."

"Wow, you've got loads of money and this giant place yet your mother is a pain in your ass just like mine."

"She used to be a Duchess. Her title was recently reduced to Countess. She was an angry, vicious, vindictive Duchess. Now she's a ranting non-royal peer who can't go to any good parties."

"What the hell's wrong with you, Jack? Unless this ain't your place." All of Lindy's points were perfect. No matter what mother threw at Jack, Lindy was correct. Except for the fact that no matter how screwed up Lady Agatha was, she was family. The curse of all human relationships: Family.

"Wait'll she sees you! A girl in pants!" said Jack to Lindy.

"At least someone around here's wearing pants. What's that shit?" Lindy grabbed Jack's brandy balloon and took a sip. She liked it.

Jack squirmed every time Lindy used foul language, and shot back: "that's liquor, you'll get drunk." cautioned Jack.

Lindy looked at the label, screwed up her face: "1754? This's old."

"With wine and whiskey, the older the better," informed Jack. Lindy put the bottle in her mouth and took a long swig. Smiled, handed the bottle to Jack and said,

"Let's have some fun with your maw. Give her something else to be angry about." Lindy had lit up like a spoiled rotten child looking for trouble.

Jack, at first, didn't like any idea of throwing petrol on an out-of-control fire, but after a swig of Hennessy cognac, thought otherwise.

"She's moving in with my three sisters."

"They married?" wondered Lindy.

"No, in fact. Why?"

"Right next door in that palace are three wifeless princes," noted Lindy.

Jack now looked at Lindy in a new light. She's right! Jack's mother is the daughter of Satan. She's got to get her Duchy and style back. Of course! Why not move in next to Buckingham Palace and introduce my three sisters to Princes Alfred, Arthur and Leopold? A triple wedding! Edward's newly married sisters, newly-minted duchesses, will move out of Ashfield Hall and into the princes's new houses, and mom will move in with her youngest daughter (Nora). Then mom, with her title and Duchy restored, will spend the rest of her life visiting all her grandchildren and more importantly, will be out of Jack's house. Mother will drop over to Buckingham Palace, unannounced of course, with her daughters to visit with their joint granddaughters and all shall have a marvelous time. But the good news, thought Jack, mother will be out of my house with no reason to bother me again!

"What about you?" chimed in Lindy, sipping her cognac.

"I continue to enjoy my life," reported Edward with certainty.

"That ain't how I see it," pounced Lindy, who continued without taking a breath, "You ain't married. What're you, 30? 33?" interrogated Lindy, and without waiting for an answer (Jack did get out his age, "27!" but Lindy was too busy talking). "The queen's got one unmarried daughter, according to all the stable boys, and your mother's gunning for four weddings at the palace. You're the fourth, Jack. You're the fourth.." Lindy, quite proud of herself for telling a royal whatever who's supposed to have worldly knowledge, how mothers with a litter of unwed children finds a way to solve that 'problem.'

Jack grabbed the bottle of 1754 Hennessy cognac and poured more into his Waterford cut crystal brandy balloon and chugged. "You're right!"

"So what's worse, Jack. Me shooting a sheriff and hiding out in England. Or you, unmarried and doomed to marry the queen's last unsoiled daughter on account of your mother stickin' her nose where it don't belong?"

Jack stared out the window at the expansive manicured lawn in silence. Lindy wasn't silent. "You've got all this land, this house, hundreds of servants, piles of money, but no freedom 'cause your mommy is fixin' to take it from you. She'll live here **and** over at the palace. Maybe you should move to Wyoming, with your princess." Lindy smirked. Checkmate.

Jack put his drink down, got up, stretched and said, "I'm going for a ride." and walked out of his office.

Jack got on one of his thoroughbreds with an English saddle and clomped around his mile wide and mile long estate, mostly manicured lawn with ten profitable gardens and that imposing 620,000 square foot behemoth of a house in the middle of it all.

Ashfield Hall was originally built in 1701 for Lord Ashfield, and had been added onto until 1840. Ashfield House was bought by George III's sixth son, Prince Augustus Frederick in 1823, Jack's grandfather. Prince Augustus changed the name of Ashfield House to Ashfield Hall as its square footage increased from 150,000 square feet to 620,000 square feet. Not including the stables and other outbuildings.

In 1703, about a mile away, the foundation for Buckingham House was laid. In 1761, the first year of his reign, George III bought Buckingham House for his wife Queen Charlotte, and it became known as the Queen's House.

Victoria moved into Buckingham Palace in 1837 the year she acceded to the throne. Later, HM and her husband, consort Prince Albert, then raised their 9 children. Where today, June of 1880, three of her sons and one of Her Majesty's five daughters, remain carefree.

Jack called a meeting of his key staff: Mr Harrison, Butler; Mrs Dahlgren, Housekeeper; Mrs Faucher, Head Cook.

Mrs Faucher was a classically trained French executive chef. Jack's Uncle Frederick hired Mrs Faucher while on a trip to Paris with his wife, Fanny. Mrs Faucher was an executive chef at the one Parisian restaurant that Frederick's wife didn't loudly complain about. So Frederick, tired of his wife's incessant nagging and ruthless criticism, did the only thing he could do. Hire Mrs Faucher and insisted she bring only the kitchen staff Mrs Faucher desired. The restaurant went out of business three weeks later. The restaurant owner, Mrs Fachet's secret lover, shot himself. Unfortunately, he recovered.

When Jack inherited the Dukedom after Uncle Frederick died last February he also inherited his late uncle Frederick's entire staff.

Edward, looking apologetic, said this to his three chief staff members:

"My mother and three sisters are moving in next week. This might be bad news. My mother is a terrible human. So terrible that Her Majesty reduced my mother in rank from a Royal Duchess to a non-royal Countess with a non-royal style of Ladyship. So there will be no overcrowded stuffy dinners, cotillions, high teas, garden parties. As I stated, you will not be worked to death like you did when my Aunt Fanny presided over this house," said Jack with enthusiasm and a little bit of flare.

Jack thought he was through speaking; he felt he'd made his point about his mother. Mr Harrison's expression said Jack did a masterful job explaining his mother. But Mrs Dahlgren and Mrs Faucher thought not.

"Please," said Jack, "have you any questions?"

"Your royal highness," began Mrs Faucher, executive cook, "What happens when Lady Agatha orders us to make dinner for 30 guests the morning of her proposed dinner, sir?" Mrs Faucher, with her thick Loire Valley accent, suggested Jack had no idea what he was talking about.

"Mr Harrison will alert me in my office where I will instruct my mother that no such dinner is possible and that guests will be turned away at the front gate." said Jack, assured.

"What if those guests are the Prince and Princess of Wales and their children?"

"Come to me immediately where I will personally go to Marlborough House and warn off Princess Alexandra that no such invitation exists." said Jack completely unconvincingly.

Mr Harrison believed Edward. Mrs Dahlgren, Housekeeper, and Mrs Faucher, Executive Cook, glared at Jack. Both women have painful, exhaustive memories of Her Royal Highness Duchess Fanny, former head of Ashfield Hall, who ran amuck with too many guests invited to too many eating occasions. And cotillions. And royal balls. The household staff increased from 50 to the current 140. Feeding an extra 90 staff a day, plus the unknowing amount of guests without making the kitchen larger was a terror.

Jack then became not only the executive of his house, but a man. Although just a 27 year old 'man'.

"The rules of Royal Society are different. My mother, stripped of her Royal Rank is not allowed to, how you say, out-perform, royal families. Their parties can't overshadow the Queen's or the Princess of Wales. Or any royal family. Everyone knows Aunt Fanny and mother are no longer royals. If they dare try to show off, Her Majesty will send my mother to Australia, or worse, India. And living next door to Her Majesty, I can seek, and get, an audience with Her Majesty to ban all parties within earshot of Buckingham."

Well, Jack's attempt at Manhood had an effect on Mrs Faucher, but little on Mrs Dahlgren, who angrily said, "We'll see."

"Anything else?" wondered Jack.

Of course there was something else.

"That, that—how do you say—wild girl in trousers! What do we make of her? How long is she going to reside here?" wondered the Housekeeper, who is in charge of everyone who enters 'her house.' All 620,000 square feet of Ashfield Hall.

"Lady Lindy is visiting from America is all you need to know. She's a jockey and she spends all her time with the horses at the stables with Mr Chalmers. And, had you forgotten, she rode my horse, Noble Warrior, to victory at the 100th running of the Epsom Derby. So, unlike Mother and my three sisters, Lady Lindy has great accomplished skills."

"I'm to understand that she smokes cigars," said Mrs Dahlgren, Housekeeper.

"And so long as she wins horse races, she shall continue smoking cigars and drinking brandy," said Jack, who was now finished conversing. Except for this, "Yes, Mrs Dahlgren and Mrs Faucher, we shall see. Good day."

Agatha Arrives. With 3 Daughters.

Approximately 6:15am the beginning of a long line of large cargo wagons pulled up to the service entrance of Ashfield Hall. At the head of this parade was Lady Agatha, non-royal Countess of somewhere, expecting servants to appear and move her stuff in and do it quickly without scratching anything.

Mrs Dahlgren, the woman who runs the household with an iron fist, was notified that Edward's (Jack's) mother had arrived 'with her belongings'. Mrs. Dahlgren had been waiting for this moment so she could enjoy her breakfast a little more slowly than usual.

Jack's mother stewed at the side entrance of the 620,000 square foot house.

None of the 140 or so staff members was racing out of the house to aid Jack's mother.

Mrs Dahlgren sent her Head Housemaid to meet Lady Agatha. "Find out what she wants but don't let her set foot in my house." was Mrs Dahlgren's stern command.

Mrs Dahlgren was in charge of all the female staff and had little sway over the male staff. Mrs Dahlgren, therefore, couldn't command dozens of male staffers to move Lady Agatha's stuff inside and upstairs. That wasn't her problem. Neither was it the problem of Mr Harrison, Butler, who held command of all 145 inside staff. Mr Chalmers, Groomsman, was in charge of the 58 stable staff and groundskeepers. These would be the individuals who would move Lady Agatha's belongings. They could easily lift heavy furniture, if given the command.

The outdoor staff was an independent lot, full of vigor and aware of the freedom of their work. They did not dress formally. They did not have to watch their language. They did not have to be stiff, starched and disciplined. Thanks to Jack, they played football, rugby and cricket on perfectly groomed fields on the generous grounds of Ashfield Hall. The groomsmen helped train the thoroughbreds for races throughout Europe, Egypt and Persia.

They cleaned stalls, lifted bales of hay, oats and other edibles for the very particular Thoroughbred breeds. Carrying 150 pounds of horse feed was expected. Carrying two was preferred. And more manly.

The Butler was supposed to hold sway over the outdoor staff but the outdoor staff politely declined one day tying Mr Harrison to a donkey and letting him gallop over the grounds for a couple of hours. This was five years ago. This was before Jack inherited the estate. So, who was going to unload all of Jack's mother's stuff? The staff decided to let Jack, 3rd Duke of Sussex, great-grandson of George III, decide. And Jack didn't usually awaken until nine or nine-thirty. He hated mornings. He hated his family.

Lady Agatha, who moved in unannounced, expecting to be bowed to, to be swept into Ashfield Hall like the royal duchess she was just a few months ago, was left standing on a side entrance in front of a closed door.

Around 6:45am a string of different wagons clip-clopped up to the kitchen service entrance. These wagons were delivering victuals for today's breakfast, luncheon, dinner and afternoon tea. Jack took a lot of pressure off his kitchen staff by ordering foodstuffs from local London markets. Bakeries for pies, cakes, scones, biscuits, croissants, pastries; farmers' markets for fresh fruits and vegetables; eggs—brown and white—dairy, including milk, cream, ice cream, cheeses, butter; fish; beef, veal, lamb; squab, chickens, pheasant, turkey; nine kinds of flour, from all purpose to semolina.   The kitchen staff concentrated on creating exceptional meals and not spending hours gathering all the ingredients.

Lady Agatha, caring nothing about servants and deliveries, blocked the doorway until a strapping delivery boy, bringing sacks of flour into the kitchen, picked up Lady Agatha and put her in one of her cargo wagons and told the driver to make sure she stays out of everyone's way.

"The lady is a Countess," replied the driver of this wagon.

"Then she can count on a bloody nose you says to 'er," reminded the delivery boy, a cockney lad of quick-temper and Irish birth.

Jack got up around 9, 9:15, took his morning shower, (Edward stole the idea of a shower from classmates at Boston Tech) looked out one of his windows and saw a line of cargo wagons, shook his head and went downstairs to apologize to any and all as he sought out his mother.

Lady Agatha was not in the house, according to Mr Harrison, Butler, backed up by Mrs Dahlgren without further comment.

"She's outside?" wondered Jack.

"Yes, your royal highness," assured Mrs Dahlgren.

"She's not in the way is she?" queried Jack.

It was never a servant's place to offer an opinion regarding a family member. An outdoor staff member would offer a delightful opinion, 'A course the old woman's inna way, can'not ye do sumthin', your holiness?'

"Lady Agatha is waiting outside, your royal highness," is all he got from Mr Harrison, who has never wandered near the stables, nor far from the house, since his untimely and terrifying donkey ride.

The men who loaded and drove the wagons to Ashfield Hall finally, after three hours of waiting, carried Lady Agatha's belongings upstairs. Through the service entrance and back stairs.

Where to put countess Agatha's furnishings, as well as her three daughters', was up to Mrs Dahlgren, the iron-fisted Housekeeper.

Countress Agatha was given rooms in the remote off-the-beaten-path part of Ashfield Hall.

Mr Harrison, the Butler, saw how Jack's three sisters were whispering things to Jack. Jack called Mr Harrison over and suggested that his sisters would rather not be within earshot, or even gunshot, of their overpowering, conniving, social climbing mother. Mr Harrison had a sudden liking for Jack's three sisters, Elsie, Harriet and the baby, Nora, age 25.

Mrs Dahlgren showed the countess her apartments. Four rooms, a bathing room and a sensible number of closets. Lady Agatha needed more than a sensible number of clothes closets. She was told there was storage space in the basement. Lady Agatha offered a different opinion and huffed off to demand that her son tell the Housekeeper that this house belongs to he, Jack, and not the Housekeeper, and that you, Edward (Jack), demand I get what I was accustomed to: at least 40 rooms.

Jack wandered over to his mother's unacceptable apartment, its four tediously common rooms, and with the Housekeeper present said to his mother: "Mrs Dahlgren runs this entire house and these are the rooms she has carefully chosen for you. Either you accept where you are or return to Mayfair instantly. If you ever try and go behind Mrs Dahlgren's back again, you will be evicted from this place and will never pull off your current scheme. Next, until you are settled into your apartments, your meals shall be brought to you. The dining rooms, tea rooms, breakfast and luncheons rooms are off limits to you until you settle down and steer clear of the powers that be: Mr Harrison, Mrs Dahlgren and me. Her Majesty stripped your rank down to nearly a commoner for good reason. Be glad that you are here. Be happy you have a roof over your head. You forget, mother, I also own your house in Mayfair."

"Well!" huffed Agatha vehemently. But Jack wasn't finished:

"You may have a limited number of guests over for afternoon tea, no more than three. First you must give Mrs Dahlgren and the Luncheon Chef <u>two weeks' warning</u>. You will be billed for the tea and each staff member who participated will be paid 4 shillings and the executive cook will be paid a Crown. This is Mrs Dahlgren's house. She makes the rules. Good day, mother."

"I need more closets!" demanded, yes, demanded, Agatha.

"You've got closets aplenty in Mayfair. Bring what you need for a week here and return for a fresh supply of clothes next week," issued Jack with a tone of voice impersonating a man of power, might, and intimidation.

When Jack arrived home last month, Lady Agatha was about to order moving lorries for a one-way trip to her supposed new home at Ashfield Hall.   Forty-three rooms of furnishings, carpeting, pictures and miscellaneous fru-fru were to go to Ashfield Hall posthaste.   Then Jack's mother ran into the brick wall named Mrs Dahlgren. No move.

And now, Lady Agatha, with a tiny fraction of her belongings, was stuffed into four medium-sized rooms in her third floor apartment (no elevator) in the part of Ashfield Hall designated for friends of friends of lower peerage. Rooms which were cramped and appalling.
The servants had much better quarters.

Lady Agatha's rooms did not have pull down calling cords, nor call buttons, nor ringers of any sort. There was no way for Lady Agatha to summon housekeeping or the kitchen staff for assistance any time day or night. Lady Agatha was notorious for 'feeling like a beverage' at two in the morning. This was not possible at Ashfield Hall under Mrs Dahlgren's supervision.

These rooms were designed to create discomfort, misery and wretchedness so the tenant would wish to flee the estate posthaste. These apartments made sure 'friends' stayed a very short time.

Edward's sisters, Elsie, Harriet and Nora, had good news. They were given Royal Suites of seven rooms each, and all the conveniences of royalty in 1880. These suites were on the second floor, close to the dining rooms, sitting rooms, rooms with preferred views. And room service, breakfast in bed. Also, they would enjoy bubble baths, daily laundry services, and afternoon tea service. They also had their own Chambermaids.

Lady Agatha had to draw a map to find the dining room. Then she had to locate the kitchen below stairs. Then she had to introduce herself. Then she had to ask for something to eat. This went on for two days. Lady Agatha asked one of the servants, in a genial, friendly tone of voice, as opposed to her demeaning, insufferable, talk-down-to tone, where was her son's office.

Lady Agatha was finally shown Jack's office door. She burst in and uttered the following two words she'd never uttered before in her life, nor any previous lifetime: "You win."

Jack was sitting, having dinner, at a beautifully set dining table.   Adjacent to him was a ravaging beauty, under 20 years old, dressed like Annie Oakley. They stopped talking and looked askance at this interloper.

"What did I win, mother?" wondered Jack.

"I want.your permission to rejoin my family, to eat a meal together. Perhaps to have tea together. And, asking humbly, again with your permission, please, afford me the dignity of a small apartment on a lower floor in *your* abundant home. Your royal highness."

Lindy's look was curious as in, 'who the hell is this, Jack?'

Jack stood, approached his mother, bowed gracefully, offered his mother a seat at his and Lindy's table, which Lady Agatha gracefully accepted.

Jack pulled a sash cord and several minutes later an Underbutler knocked. Lady Agatha was given supper.

Several minutes after that, with great theatrics at table, Lady Agatha looked up and finally noticed Lindy. "My God, who are you, my dear? Edwazrd, did you adopt a child?"

"May I present an American, Lady Lindy Long; my guest. Lindy rode Noble Warrior to victory in the 100th Epsom Derby. Lindy won."

"How fascinating," replied Lady Agatha, "have you a title?"

"Yeah," said Lindy whilst chewing some of her dinner, "I'm a duchess. From Wyoming."

"What is your style, my dear?" taunted Lady Agatha.

"My style? I ride bareback or Western. Not on one of them sissy English saddles," answered Lindy.

"I see," affirmed Lady Agatha, adding, "Edward, you sure know how to choose your girl children."

"Jack didn't choose me. I chose him, lady."

"Getting serious for half a minute, Edward, did she just call you, a Royal Duke, whose style is Your Royal Highness, 'Jack'?"

"By the way, mother, in Wyoming, Lindy's style is Your Majesty. Now what's on your mind, except using your daughters to take over the Empire."

"I would like you to join us for dinner tomorrow evening in the family dining room and I humbly request that you dress accordingly."

"What time?"

"I should think seven," said Lady Agatha.

"See you at seven," answered Edward/Jack.

There was a pause. Edward thought his dialogue with his mother was over, so why is she still sitting at table? Here's why:

"My dear, I'm going to clue you in on how the Empire works. Your father was a Royal Prince and he had responsibilities to the Monarchy, even though he was not on course for the Throne. You also have responsibilities to the Monarch, and yet here you are, acting like a college boy with no responsibilities whatsoever. Her Majesty can do to you what she did to me and your aunt Fanny— strip you of your Royal title."

Edward laughed. In fact, he stood up, stretched, looked out his window and pointed to where the Monarchy is currently seated, on the other side of the 30 foot high wall betwixt Ashfield Hall property and Buckingham Palace property.   "Mother, I might move to America to get away from all this nonsense."

Lady Agatha swooned, grabbed a stool by Edward's mechanical drawing table to right herself,

"Nonsense!?" she spit venom at Edward, "The British Empire rules the world from across that wall. And you claim you want no part of it. You're mired in it, my boy. You grew up in it. You were educated by it. Do you think you just luckily got into the schools you did? You're best friends with the future king. Your two uncles were kings. Your aunt is Queen. Your grandfather had his two brothers claim land in the names of King George four and King William four, and now titles and deeds to that land and those weekly rent payments are in your vaults. You did nothing to earn it, yet you live very well on account of it. You are royalty and this household shall show it. You shall start having dinner parties. Your staff of 140 will start cooking and cleaning and serving again.   They haven't worked in months. You need to keep them fresh and alert.   I'm inviting the queen's sons to dinner in a month. In the meantime, I want your staff prepared for this night by performing their paid duties at least five times a week. Possibly more. When was the last time you served high tea?"

"I'm not a fan of high tea.   I'd rather have a beer," said Edward in a tone of voice that mocked his mother's tone of sincerity, cunningness and knife-twisting hedonism.

"We begin with planned dinners tomorrow. I want your staff to be tip-top sharp. I want them to look sharp and to know what they're doing. Complacency will not do. I don't know why your father kept you out of the military. You have no discipline, my boy. I shall now alert your Butler about our dinner arrangements. This is very important, Edward. Do not disappoint me."

If there's one thing no one's son ever wants to do is disappoint his mother. That's the worst sin of all. To fall short of a mother's expectation. Edward, according to his mother, has been a disappointment time and time again. And Edward took the brunt of those accusations to heart.

Edward, violating his aforementioned stance on his mother's dining arrangements, reversed course and told Mr Harrison, Butler, that there will be a formal dinner tomorrow at 7 for six. Lady Agatha and her four children. Plus Lady Lindy.

Tomorrow Night's Formal Dinner

Promptly at seven o'clock p.m., the UnderButler entered the family dining room carrying a silver tray with bowls of soup. Following the UnderButler was Mr Harrison who placed the soup dish and creme soup bowl squarely in front of Lady Agatha's place setting. Then Mr Harrison placed the next soup serving at Lady Elsie's place. And on until Edward's mother, three sisters, Lindy and Jack were served. The dining room was now full of people.

Jack's mother had given her speech to Mr Harrison and Company, especially the part about Jack's role as a member in good standing of the Royal Family, vis a vis his aunt Queen Victoria, and how Jack, 3rd Duke of Sussex, will host dinners for their Royal Highnesses the Prince and Princess of Wales; entertain Members of Parliament; take a more active role in his standing as a Royal Engineer, a title granted him by Queen Victoria for Jack's installation of a central heating system in Buckingham Palace just two years earlier. The Queen was impressed. And cozy all winter long.

The kitchen staff would come to order, begin cooking complicated, competitive dinners for a lucky few, as Jack's's mother kept just out of sight telling those in charge that Jack was finally taking his Dukedom and royal duties seriously.

For tonight's formal dinner, Jack and company enjoyed roast leg of lamb, vegetables in season and Mrs Faucher's chocolate Mousse. There was no fish course because this was Jack's house and he doesn't like fish. Except fish and chips, which was a lower class choice.

These arrangements of family dinners took the slack out of lackadaisical staff members and produced an enlivened household.

Now, to spring the trap carefully lain by Jack's power-hungry great white shark of a mother.

CHAPTER 12

The Sons of Victoria Get Falling Down Drunk.

Ashfield Hall didn't have a lot of entrances. Its main entrance faced north, toward Hyde Park. Lots of grandeur, tall Romanesque columns, pink and purple granite stairs, colorful Italian marble. Greco-Roman carvings, architecture—all designed to impress, elevate the senses, or to angry up the blood of the lesser nobility. Ashfield Hall was a royal palace, built before Buckingham Palace. And it was built for Frederick, Prince of Wales. Frederick was the eldest son of King George II. Frederick did not become King George III. Why not? Frederick, Prince of Wales, died in 1851 whilst his father, George II was still alive. King George III is the *grandson* of George II, not his son. Ashfield Hall was to be the future palace of King Frederick, not Buckingham House.

On the east side of Ashfield Hall was the happiest entrance. A modest entry door, often confused for a gardener's entrance, or a servant's household entrance, or a secret entrance should the Lord of the Manor return from a dalliance at the wee hours not wishing to disturb the household or his wife. It was a covered entry so one could get out of one's carriage and not get soaked. The rains come a couple of times a week over the British Isles.

There was a wide cobblestone road from the West Gate of Buckingham Palace that when opened went straight for Ashfield Hall's grand formal front entrance.

Forget that.

A small insignificant 'trail' curved quietly, imperceptibly, away from the cobblestone road and headed straight for this small, insignificant happy side entrance to Ashfield Hall.

That's the door you want if you were Victoria's adult male children and you wanted to sneak out of the Palace, away from your mother, loudly 'suffering' the death of her husband some twenty years ago. Victoria's grown male children were headed for Edward's private Gentleman's Club whose entrance was downplayed for a servant's door, lest they be discovered having fun.

Once again, Queen Victoria's grown children in 1880 were Albert, Prince of Wales, 39; Prince Alfred, 36; Prince Arthur, 30; Prince Leopold, 27.

The agreement amongst Edward (Jack) and Victoria's boys, was to show up several times a week, drive themselves over in a royal carriage and head through the small out-of-the-way door and enter the out-of-the-way private room and arrive anticipating a great evening at Jack's Gentleman's Club.

What on earth for? What's at Ashfield Hall that you can't get at Buckingham Palace?

Cuban cigars from fifteen world-famous manufacturers. A vast selection of French wines, cognac, sherry. Vintage port from Portugal. And for the faint-hearted or overly drunk: delicious bottled sparkling waters from deep pure effervescent springs across Europe and Iceland.

Also an assortment of edibles, crudités, hors d'oeuvres, fresh pastries, fresh baked baguettes upon which to pile on meats, cheeses and a variety of toppings incase your dinner was cold and dreadful because your mother was sobbing, demanding attention and you weren't allowed to start eating until Her Majesty lifted her fork. (Pick up your damned fork, old woman! thought her sons. Except Albert. He'd escaped to his own living Hell. By 1880 Bertie was married with 5 kids.)

After HM Victoria's ghastly theatrical nightly sorrowful display, everyone needed a drink.

Party time at Ashfield Hall began shortly after Edward moved in last March. Uncle Frederick was dead, Aunt Fanny was evicted and a 27 year old Edward who loved good wine and cigars, just moved in after several years in America, away from royalty, responsibility and his suffocating mother.

How long has this gentleman's club been in existence for Victoria's sons? Twenty-two years. Designed, built and stocked by Uncle Frederick. Perfectly hidden from his wife Fanny. He told her he was off to the Boodles Club and simply walked down to the basement (below stairs—no Lady, no Noble, no Royal would ever venture below stairs. If this information got out it would ruin lives, cause consternation, salacious gossip, and unfortunate women's names would be dragged through the muck. Probably.)

Edward was led to this room by Mr Harrison, the Butler. Mr Harrison didn't demand a raise in pay and duties—he expected something in return for this 'discovery.' Edward gave Mr Harrison

£10,000 cash, bought him a house in his favored Cornwall, a clothing account on Savile Row, quadrupled the size of his room at Ashfield, redecorated it.   And did the same for Mrs Dalhgren and the Executive Cook. , Mrs Faucher.   Their clothing account was at Harrods.

Mr Harrison was the only one who knew the real reason. Edward told Mrs Faucher and Mrs Dahlgren of his respect for all the hard work they do, and so on and so forth.   The two women knew all about the Gentleman's Club, yet went along with Edward's jabbering. They were shocked with all the goodies. Damn right they will not say a single word about Edward's boy's club in the basement. The two ladies love extra money and Harrods.   Since Edward's mother moved in, Mrs Dahlgren and Mrs Faucher have been doing extra shopping at Harrods to vent their frustration. It worked.

Four unmarried gentlemen (plus Bertie, Prince of Wales) and no one to stop them from enjoying their freedom.   The champagne cork was popped, the Cuban cigars were lit and so were Victoria's boys. Unmarried and unchaperoned.   Cousin Jack had come through and was a hero to all four of the queen's sons.

Edward shook everyone's hand and called them by their Christian names or nicknames.   Berty was, of course, Albert, Prince of Wales.   Alfie was Prince Alfred, Queen Victoria's favorite son; Artie was Prince Arthur, and Leo was Leopold.   Edward was either Edwardo or Eddie.

Bertie, future Kind Edward VII, was married but didn't act like it.   His wife and future queen, Alix, didn't mind, telling anyone who would listen,"I don't want that fat tub of lard lying on top of me. We've got enough children. Let him smother his whores."

"Where've you been, Edwardo?" wondered Arthur, "You get this nice house and take off for the American outback?"

"Jack went to Wyoming looking for trouble and found me." announced Lindy, the only woman ever to set foot in Jack's Gentleman's Club.   (Mrs Dahlgren, Housekeeper, and her female staff, were forbidden from entry. (On pain of losing her Harrods clothing account, etc.) Only the Butler was allowed to bring food, beverage. Two house boys cleaned the joint up. Edward rewarded these two young men with cigars and good rum. And a 'fiver' each (£5) to keep their mouths shut about the cigars and rum and the whereabouts of the Gentleman's Club.   You will be fired (sacked, dismissed, without references). These two young men were roomates in Jack's house and their rooms were around the corner of the Gentleman's Club in the basement. No one knew anything.

"Jack?!" The Prince of Wales sensed sexual shenanigans. "You sly dog.tell me all about it."

"As Lady Lindy would tell it, to her, I **look** like a Jack, therefore I am a Jack. Simple as that and no shenanigans, Bertie."

"In other words, dear brother," said Alfred, "Edwardo's the opposite of you." Alfred then looked at Lady Lindy, "Edwardo treats you with respect, dignity. The Prince of Wales would have treated you the opposite." Alfred thought he had saved Lindy's life. Lindy gave the Prince of Wales a look that was so thoroughly understood by Prince Albert, that he was immediately aroused and knew that their time together in the wild west would have been salacious, exhaustive and wicked.

"Gentlemen, this is Lady Lindy, from America's wild west. You met her at the Derby, she rode Noble Warrior to victory."

"Lady Lindy, I am Albert, Prince of Wales," said the larger-than-life prince, smiling and cupping Lindy's hands.

"Yeah, I know you. You're Berty and your wife's name is Alix," said Lindy putting a Cuban cigar in her mouth, bending over a candleabra in her very tight and snug-fitting fringed leather pants. Having lit her Cuban, she blew smoke into the room.   All the boys swooned. A girl smoking a cigar like she's done it before. A girl in skin tight leather pants was too much for the royal unwed trio. But not for Bertie.

Then Lindy opened Jack's glass liquor cabinet, looked at the bottles, grabbed a bottle of Macallan Scotch Whisky, vintage 1844, (bottled in its second year of existence) poured some into a crystal highball glass, tasted it, smiled, said to one of the other princes, "Who the hell are you?"

The protected, cocooned, ensconced princes swooned again. A girl, in pleasantly tight fringed pants, with a tan, is smoking and drinking and cussing like we do where mum can't hear or see us. Only she seems to do it when she wants without anyone's permission. This was all quite arousing. Quite.

An hour later all parties were deeply relaxed, seated in their overstuffed butter soft leather chairs, still smoking and still drinking and laughing. Bertie was pounding the table at some of the tales, tall or otherwise. Lindy was being Lindy, unfazed at the company, caring not a wit about royalty, titles, styles, or any other fairy tale nonsense. She liked the company.

"Now what about you, Edwardo, what's going on with you?"

"My mother moved in with my three sisters."

That shut everyone up. Like having the Queen suddenly open the door and saying, "Ah-Ha!"

"Tell 'em why she moved in, Jack. I dare ya." goaded Lindy.

"I should think you'd do a better job of it."

"All three of Jack's sisters are unmarried. And youse three are unmarried. Jack's mother's plan is to marry y'all off to her girls and then somehow become queen with your mother."   Lindy sat back and took another sip of her Macallan and watched the boys' faces.

Albert, Prince of Wales, exploded with laughter. Alfie, then Arthur, and finally Leo, also began tittering.

"Oh my God," declared Berty, "A palace coup!"

"Wait," said Arthur, "What about you, Edwardo, your mother has another unmarried wayward child. And we have an unmarried wayward sister: baby Beatrice. She's about 23 or something, is looking for someone suitable and you're it, old man," smugly smiled Arthur, Mum's third son.

More laughter and cheering until Bertie stood up and raised a glass to Edwardo/Jack and toasted: "To my cousin Edwardo, my future brother-in-law, a prince among men and a son-in-law to Her Majesty, our Mother. May I be your best man!"

"Of course," said Edward, standing and bowing, adding, "Your royal highness."

"So Lindy who are you to, ah, Jack?" wondered Leopold.

"His alibi," said Lindy.

The six kept drinking and smoking until two in the morning when a servant in a uniform knocked on the Gentleman's Club door.

"Open!" yelled Albert, future king.

The reluctant servant stuck his head in, saw Lindy and five males. When he spotted the Prince of Wales, the servant came all the way in the room, bowed deeply and handed Albert a note. Albert read it, crumpled it up and threw it on the floor.

"Note from mummy?" asked Alfred.

Lindy furrowed her brow.

"Mummy means Bertie's wife. We don't get notes from our Mum because she doesn't know where we are," reported Arthur.

"Well, there's no more food and little left to drink," said Bertie, "So I'm off."

"Why'd you tell Alex where you were, dammit," scolded Leo, "Now she'll tell Mum!"

After Bertie jumped in his private carriage and headed to Marlborough House, the palatial residence of the Prince and Princess of Wales and their five children, the rest of the gang piled in their borrowed Royal Carriage and drove drunk toward Buckingham Palace.

"You've got great friends, Jack. They're fun. And trapped. I can't wait to meet your sisters. Think they'll end up with the Queen's boys?"

"If my mother is pulling the strings, then yes," mused Jack.

"What'll she think of me?" wondered Lindy.

"She'll want you on the next boat to Wyoming. And never tell her you shot a sheriff. She'll call the new sheriff and turn you in."

"They can't come and take me, can they?"

"If that new sheriff has strong evidence, they might. But if my mother doesn't know, there's no problem."

Lindy felt assured so she hugged Jack. He liked that.

"So, what's your new wife like?" asked Lindy.

"Who? What?!" Jack was thrown for a loop. 'New wife' sobered Jack up like jumping into ice water. Jack be stunned and confused.

"That unmarried girl over at the queen's place," said Lindy.

Jack was amazed at Lindy's cognition. She drank more than anyone and she remembered tiny insignificant details of the conversation.

"That's Princess Beatrice, the baby of the family."

"What's she like?"

"I don't know. I haven't seen Beatrice since she was 10 or 11," reminisced Jack.

"Don't do anything stupid causing her to wear her bustle backwards," snorted Lindy.

"Huh?" Jack had no idea what she just said.

"Put her in the family way."

"What are you talking about? You sound drunk."

"Make her have a fucking baby!"

Jack's expression said he finally got it. And he was now scared. Knock up the Queen's youngest daughter, the one Her Majesty calls Baby, you could end up in the Tower of London.

CHAPTER 13

Back to Back Dinners

Jack was having dinner in the family dining room by himself at the unthinkable, unEnglish hour of 5:30 post meridian. He was thinking of the servants: it's easier for them to serve in the dining room, close to the kitchen, than in his office, a very long way, up on the third floor.

Whilst dining happily by himself, Jack was reading 'Black Beauty', a wonderful, life altering book published three years ago and written by an English author, Anna Sewell. 'Black Beauty' became an instant bestseller throughout the United Kingdom and North America. Jack was sitting under a gaslight chandelier for ease of reading.

The dining room door leading to the South Parlour opened and Lindy stuck her head in.

"Hey, Jack," said Lindy looking around noticing he was eating alone. Lindy spent most of her time outside since she enjoyed her horses more than people.

"What's for grub?" wondered Lindy.

"Tonight's grub: roasted beef, sauteed potatoes with cinnamon butter, asparagus with a buttery tart sauce from Holland, plus cream of mushroom soup. Then pastries."

"How do I git me some?"

Jack looked up at the First Footman, standing at attention for just such an occasion, nodded at the footman who disappeared through the Service entrance whilst several Footmen set a place for Lindy not far from Jack. Three forks on the left, one knife, two spoons, four stemmed crystal glasses (water, red wine, white wine, champagne), bread plate and knife, salt cellar, pepper cellar, personal short crystal vase with fresh cut blue fuscia flowers.

The First Footman arrived carrying a sterling silver tray with Lindy's dinner prepared on a large dinner plate, fresh baked French bread on the bread plate. A Second Footman put each beautifully presented dish at Lindy's pacesetting then returned to his post. A beverage server poured sparkling water and asked, "Would Your Ladyship wish wine or champagne?"

Lindy looked at Jack who nodded approval.

"Cham-pain if you don't mind." said Lindy in that Wyoming Territory way of hers, which annoyed Jack.

"May I suggest you simply say, 'champagne, please' when you're in England. Thank you," said Jack.

"You sound like my mother," said Lindy.

The Second Footman held a bottle of Laurant-Perrier champagne with the year 1856 printed on the label.

"*Please*, in whatever empty glass you're supposed to pour it." spoke Lindy.

The champagne went in the tall, thin, stemmed champagne flute.

Jack stage whispered to Lindy, "Thank you." As Lindy stared at Jack, he made a facial gesture toward the footman imploring her to follow the etiquette of the realm.

"Thank you, kind sir," said Lindy.

"You're welcome, your Ladyship," retorted the Second Footman.

The Footmen returned to their posts standing at attention, one stride in front of the back wall, staring straight ahead, and never at the diners.

"You want me to say 'please' and 'thank you' all the time?"

"I would prefer it and you'll notice that people will go out of their way to help you when you show common courtesy."

"That sheriff didn't say 'please' and 'thank you' when he shot my daddy in the back."

"Is that why you shot him? Because he wasn't gracious?" wondered Jack.

Lindy looked at the cover of the book Edward was reading. Black Beauty had an illustration of the head and neck of a beautiful horse.

"Whatcha readin'?"

Jack cheered up, sat up straight, picked up the book and said, "This is a perfect book for you. It's about a horse who goes through life with many different owners. In fact, one of the owners calls Black Beauty 'Jack.' The book is narrated by Black Beauty, the horse. Black Beauty reminds me of Crazy Horse. I would like you to read it," said the 27 year old Edward in a tone that sounded more like a 47 year old parent. She took it, flipped through the pages and put it down next to her.

"And this would be a good time to say..." said Jack-the-insistent-annoying-parent.

"Say?" wondered the etiuette-deaf Lindy.

"When someone hands you a gift, what do you say?"

"Thanks. My dinner's gettin' cold, so I'm gonna eat. So, Jack, *please,* let me eat!   And *Thank y'all* for gettin' the grub." which Lindy said to the two statues called Footmen.

[Lindy was born in Mobile, Alabama, in early 1865.   Her parents left for the wild west three years after the South lost their war, and settled in Wyoming Territory, in Laramie County. The wild west territory, about 100,000 square miles in size, had a population of less than 10,000 citizens. A mix of Native American tribes, former Confederates, former Union army, former gold and silver miners who went bust, cattle and sheep ranchers and the general riff-raff nobody likes but are always part of every population. Lindy's parents were that riff-raff.]

Jack and Lindy ate in silence for a minute or two, then the main dining room door opened and in walked three young ladies. Jack's sisters. Elsie, Harriet and Nora.

"Started without us?" wondered the eldest, Elsie, 32 years old, an unmarried woman dressed for a formal occasion.

"You're just gonna sit there? Aren't you going to help a lady take her seat?" crucified Elsie, still wondering why she wasn't married with six kids. She was 32!

"My humblest apologies." Jack got up and went over to his youngest sister, Nora, and seated her. Nora said "Thank you, your royal highness."

"You're welcome, Lady Nora."

"What about me?" wondered Elsie, dressed for a formal occasion.

"You said 'help a lady take her seat' and I did. Nora is a lady. You two are dissonant, cacophonous, duplicitous schemers," said Jack lightly, as though he'd said that dozens of times before.

"So, y'all are kin.." retorted Lindy, flipping through Black Beauty.

"Kin?" queried Elsie, "Is that a word?"

"Kin is from 13th Century Norse, meaning family. This is Lady Lindy. Where she is from she is a Duchess," reported Jack.

Elsie, the eldest, and Harriet, the second child and older than Jack by three years, sneered at Jack and did not give the time of day, nor even look, at Lindy.

Meanwhile, the dining room filled with footmen bringing dinners and selections of beverages to Jack's three sisters.

After all the dinners and drinks were served the only one to thank the footmen was Nora, who was Jack's favorite sibling.

"Lady Lindy, by the way, rode Noble Warrior to victory at the Derby a couple of weeks ago," interjected Jack.

That piece of information stunned the three sisters. Nora said, "Congratulations, your ladyship," and raised her champagne flute to Lindy. Lindy looked to Jack and he picked up his flute and repeated, "Congratulations Lady Lindy," said Jack, and sipped.

Elsie and Harriet were too busy eating to toast.

"So, when's y'alls weddin' to the queen's boys, ladies?" chirped Lindy, curiously, looking at all three sisters, sitting next to one another at the opposite end of the mahogany table.

That froze the sisters. The one thing hanging over all three sisters' heads was the highly improbable fact that all three would be happily married to the three unmarried sons of Her Majesty Queen Victoria. The one thing that was never discussed without the presence of their mother, Lady Agatha, was the weddings with the royal family. The fact that some fringe-wearing outsider who spoke a different language and dressed like a barbarian-heathen, even knew of these presumptive weddings, was an outrage. To the two elder sisters Lindy's question was an outright assault on their shaky standing in the Realm. Too old to find a suitable husband in general , let alone a royal prince.

Marrying a son of the Sovereign was the highest honour any woman could achieve. You are suddenly royalty, your title is at least a royal duchess and your style is Your Royal Highness. You get a fabulous house near Buckingham Palace, a country house, a staff. Your life is changed for the better, forever. Or so all the faerie tales affirm.

Unmarried elderly daughters of nobility didn't fit in the social scheme of things. They were kept out of family functions by becoming governesses—babysitters of their married siblings' spawn. The house staff (below stairs) scoffed at them, paid them no respect. Their family paid them even less respect. Elsie was 32, dowdy, overweight. And nasty. Nasty first, last and always.

Very defensive about her position, mediocre attractiveness, age and weight. And standing. She was the first born yet her silly, carefree, Americanized brother got the title, the land, the money and the 620,000 square foot house, fully furnished with priceless antiques from the 14th through the 19th centuries, and fully staffed. And one of his horses, whom he rarely had anything to do with, won the 100th running of the Epsom Derby. Jack, according to Elsie, went through life recklessly, without a plan, and his carefreeness got him everything anyone could dream of. If Elsie were a man, she would have all this abundance.

Jack loved it. Inwardly he was beaming. Jack did not especially like Elsie nor Harriet. He loved his 'little sister' Nora. Nora had spurned several advances by prominent suitors; all titled, all nobility, all wealthy. Not because she was holding out for a royal prince. She was in no hurry to marry and have children. Nora was 24, thin, attractive, fun and loved to have fun. Something frowned upon in Victorian England. By HM (Her Majesty) Victoria. Nora's suitors were all stiff boorish and inwardly unattractive. Outwardly, too. Nora was not a schemer, not conniving, not a shrill witch. Nora was a lot like Lindy, only brought up in Mayfair, privately tutored, and refined. Had Nora grown up in Wyoming Territory, she and Lindy would have been great friends. Or arch enemies. But each would be enjoying life as best she could. With loaded six guns and fast horses.

Elsie suddenly stood up and threw her Irish linen napkin down and stormed out of the family dining room. Harriet got up and followed Elsie out of the dining room. One of the valets moved to open the dining room door but Jack, 3rd Duke of Sussex, great-grandson of King George III, and nephew of Queen Victoria, waved the valet off and motioned him, with the nod of Jack's head, back to the waiting wall.

Elsie slammed the wormy chestnut dining room door. It popped back open. She slammed it again, louder.

"Use your fuckin' head," chirped Lindy.

Lindy, eating her roast beef with the fork in her right hand, sipping champagne at the same time, had fired a broadside at Elsie which knocked both ladies senseless. That was just not done.

Nora, youngest and funnest, burst into loud, approving laughter. Had she been sipping a drink, she would have spit it all over the table.

Elsie and Harriet were appalled at the directness of this assault from Lindy. Assault.

Interestingly, Harriet returned to the dining room. She'd decided that she wasn't appalled nor assaulted. She'd decided that this young, surly, fringed cowgirl knew things. Harriet wanted answers. And maybe the jockey who rode her brother's horse to win the Derby had important answers.

Harriet lifted Elsie's champagne tulip and guzzled its contents. Then she scraped Elsie's remaining dinner onto her plate, including the bread and butter. Then turned to the beverage valet and signaled her champagne tulip needs refreshing. The beverage valet poured more Laurent-Perrier champagne into Harriet's champagne flute. Jack wanted more. And so did Lindy.

"Tell me what you know about the weddings." cooed Harriet to Lindy.

"Y'all girls are gonna marry the Queen's boys cause your mama is a snake in the grass. I was wonderin' how y'alls gonna let them boys know what you're up to.?"

"Mother is working that out," admitted Harriet.

"That where momma is now?" wondered Lindy.

"She is meeting a friend for tea at Harrods," reluctantly offered Harriet.

"So which boy do you favor?" queried Lindy.

"I like Arthur. But he doesn't seem to want to talk to me," said Harriet with awkwardness.

"You just sit there and wait on him to talk to you?" interrogated Lindy with an astonished edge to her voice.

"Of course," admitted Harriet with a tone that suggested 'that's what's expected of me.'

"You get off your duff, sashay over to him, set yourself down and tell him what a big, strong handsome man he is. You smile like this. (showing a lot of teeth and batting her eyes) and you don't take your eyes off his, you hear me?" Lindy was assertive.

Harriet, never having heard anything like this looked to Jack for help. Jack was clue free.

"You want him to marry you, you'll do as I say. You want his heart to melt like pig fat in a hot skillet? You'll listen to me. You're young and pretty and that makes you what?" queried Lindy.

Harriet had no idea so she looked again to Jack for an answer.

"Don't look at Jack, he don't know shit. You're young and pretty and powerful! Yes, you got power. As long as you smile at him, he thinks you like him and guess what? Every boy wants a pretty girl to look at them, and *only* them, and smile."

"May I ask you a question, miss?" asked a very shy Nora the 24 year old baby of the family.

"..Course." said Lindy softly, seeing how shy she is.

"How can I get Leopold to like me?"

"Same's I told her. Go over to him, put your hand on his arm and smile and blush. Act all shy and weak. I call it play acting . But you go over to him and claim him as your knight.   Who's the other boy, Adolf?

"Alfred," said Jack.

"You sure?" challenged Lindy.

"I'm his cousin," huffed Jack.

Lindy shrugged and commanded: "Save him for the angry, bloated one. I like her. I can see her goin' up to ol' Freddy and slapping him hard across his face, grabbing him, then kissin' him square on his mouth. What's her name?"

"Elsie?" wondered Edward.

"Yeah—that's why I can't (cain't) remember her name. I got a horse named L.C." said Lindy.

Nora laughed so hard she actually spit champagne. Harriet squeaked and had to fan herself to keep from laughing aloud.

"Should we give Freddy to L.C.?" offered Lindy, "Or do you (looking at Harriet) want to try him out?"

"You mean if Arthur doesn't seem a fit, I can sit next to Alfred?" wondered Harriet.

"It's open season on the queen's boys. You're powerful cause y'all're beautiful, both of y'all". And men are lazy. To be with you all they have to do is take a buggy ride over here. Y'all're right next door. You ain't up in no fuckin' Scotland. So when momma invites them for dinner, they'll see how easy it is and…" said Lindy, suddenly interrupted.

"Invitation to dinner? Here? The three princes? When?" queried Harriet.

"Jack's mother hears somethin' she wants and she don't put much daylight between hearin' it and doin' it. I spect that's what she's doing tonight. Makin' a plan to seal the deal."

"What should I wear?" asked Harriet of Nora.

"Bright colors," said Lindy, dressed in her black leather pants and black leather fringed jacket. And since Derby Day, a silk blouse. "What's your favorite color?" asked Lindy of Harriet.

"Red, but mother would never."

"Red it is. And you?" asked Lindy of Nora.

"Purple."

"What about Angry L.C.?" wondered Lindy.

"Yellow, I think."

"Why all these different colors?" asked Jack.

"Yall's a wolf pack. Those pasty-faced boys are the sheep. Y'all are hunters only they don't know it. So you dress up to please them. You're wolves in sheep's clothing, get it?" Lindy was teaching the so-called elite.

"But first, we're going shoppin'. Jack's buyin'," commanded Lindy.

CHAPTER 14

Harrods

Lindy, Harriet and Nora set off for Harrods Department Store, which was conveniently waiting across the street from Ashfield Hall, fronting on Brompton Road. Before jumping in their carriage, Lindy had a brief chat with the absent, pouty, angry, terrible elder sister, Elsie, which went like this: "I'm taking your sisters to Harrods to buy something to wear to your dinner with the queen's boys. Wanna come?"

Elsie, suddenly in a chipper mood, got off her bed and put her cloak on.

"Your brother is buying." concluded Lindy, showing off a wad of £500 Bank of England notes—paper money. Lindy stuffed all the cash, about £7,500, in her black fringed leather pants front pocket.

Harrods had six floors of beautiful, exotic, luxurious goods. Over the past month, Lindy had been riding Crazy Horse or Noble Warrior over to Ashfield Hall's West Gate, dismounted to let them roam and eat grass, as she walked across Brompton Road and entered Harrods.. She headed for the 'silk shirt' department. She brought home beautiful, colorful 100% silk blouses, jackets and something they called 'accessories'.

To date, Lindy's been to Wanamakers in Philadelphia, then shopped along the entire Ladies' Mile of exquisite shops in New York City, from 14th Street to 24th Street. Shops which included Macy's, Tiffany, B. Altman and Lord & Taylor. Lindy had thus shopped big city department stores. And she liked living across the street from Harrods. So far, Harrods had everything she wanted: silk.

Cheyenne, Wyoming Territory, had a general store that had clothing for men and women. But she knew about Denver City and its big department store. She'd save up and hop on the Denver & Pacific Rail Road from Cheyenne. In a couple of hours she was in

Denver, walking through the Daniels & Fisher Department Store. She couldn't afford much, but she could dream.

And now Lindy was standing on the ground floor of Harrods, with three unmarried sisters, ready to spend hundreds or even thousands of Pounds Sterling on clothes for a dinner with three unmarried sons of Queen Victoria.

Lindy patted her front pants pocket making sure her wad of £7500 was secure.

"Mother will never approve," is the happy first comment Elsie made. The 32 year old, always-belligerent elder sister, never did anything without her mother's approval.

"That's why y'all ain't married. Anybody else need mommy's go-ahead?" condescended Lindy.

Nora and Harriet stood stunned that anyone could slap them across the face with the Truth as much as Lindy.

"Second floor, ladies: dresses, gowns and evening wear." announced Lindy with authority. Lindy knew what was on every floor, around every corner and in every nook and cranny of Harrods. The only point of confusion over here is they called the first floor the ground floor and the second floor the first floor. Lindy was not confused. England was.

At the Evening Dresses department, Elsie browsed the mother-approved gowns while Nora and Harriet were frothing at the mouth about all the new summer colours Harrods displayed.

Nora was looking at three dresses, all 'just in from gay Paree'. One dress was blush red, the next was medium rouge but the third evening gown was red hot red. Fire engine red. Have-sex-with-me-red.

Lindy took the two dull red dresses away from the salesman and put them back on the display rack.   Lindy handed the hot red gown to Nora.

"Make it fit tight," ordered Lindy to the salesman. She was done toying with these sisters and their deferential attitude.

Meanwhile, Elsie had chosen a beige dress that made her look 50. Lindy saw it and shook her head.

After two hours the ladies were recovering in Harrods Tea Salon. They had purchased several evening dresses and ball gowns, several pairs of shoes, accessories, perfumes, jewelry. The sisters were exhausted. They would have usually taken a month to decide on all these choices. Well, they never shopped with Lindy before. Lindy shopped like a man.   I need shoes, I go to the shoe department, I buy shoes. I don't dawdle. I don't go home and come back four or five times. Lindy had been window shopping in Denver for a long time. Now she's got cash. Window shopping days were over. Buying and taking home days had begun at Wanamakers.

"Why do you dress like a man?" wondered the naive-acting Nora, age 24.

"I pull on my britches, shirt, boots, hat and I jump on my horse. Takes you ladies two hours to git ready! For what? To sit your ass down for a cup of fuckin' tea?"

The sisters were eating a delicate meal of crustless cucumber sandwiches, scones and berries with tea. Lindy ordered a steak with a jacket potato topped with chili and cheese. In Wyoming Territory, a jacket potato is an unpeeled baked potato drenched in fresh churned butter. She drank lemonade.

Several of Jack's Footmen carried the ladies' purchases to an enclosed Clarence carriage which had the room to seat four adults with plenty of overhead. This carriage was designated packages only. The beautifully wrapped packages were neatly crammed into every square inch of space in the spacious, enclosed custom built carriage.

Lindy and the sisters got into their open Landau carriage and enjoyed the English summer sun as the Landeau clip-clopped across Brompton Road and through the massive gates of Ashfield Hall and drove down the half-mile long drive to their temporary quarters in Jack's 620,000 square foot house.

Everyone was overwhelmed and thrilled with their purchases, even Elsie. She had chosen items that were 'very appropriate' and very 'modest'. And added whenever she could, "mother will never approve of any of your poor choices and you'll have to take them all back."

Lindy held her tongue. For once. And for only a few minutes.

"I'm wearing one of my dresses to dinner tonight!" exclaimed Nora.

"Mother will order you out of the dining room," predicted Elsie.

"Your mom's coming to dinner tonight? Good," said a calm and mother-repellant Lindy Mae Long, winner of the 100th running of the Epsom Derby. "I can't wait to meet her and tell her how to get y'all married off. She's done a shitty job."

Elsie smirked knowing that meeting Mother would be like running through the whirring blades of a steel sawmill. Mother would cut this loud cowgirl down to size.

CHAPTER 15

Jack's Mother Meets the Cowgirl

Dinner before The Dinner with Victoria's unmarried boys was about to start. Jack, dressed in black tie, escorted his mother, Lady Agatha, into the family dining room. (Ashfield Hall has 4 other larger dining rooms and a Grand Ballroom sometimes used as a dining room for 200 members of royalty and nobility, usually on Christmas and New Year's Eve.)

Awaiting them and also comfortably seated were Jack's three sisters dressed in evening ware. Elsie wore navy, Harriet wore dark grey and Nora wore blinding sunshine yellow. Her dress lit up the room.

Also at table was Lindy Mae Long in black buckskin. Fringed tight pants and matching fringed jacket. Lindy wore a peach-colored silk blouse under her black leather fringed jacket. Harrods, of course. Jack's mother did not gaze, nor glare, at Lindy. Lindy yammered with everyone else, including the help.

Jack's mother's eyes went instantly to the bright noonday sun coming from where her youngest child, Nora, was sitting. Jack seated his mother to the right of Harriet and Nora. Mother was to the left of Elsie and Jack. Across the beautifully polished mahogany table from Lady Agatha sat that cowgirl & winning jockey, from the American wild west.

Jack nodded at the Butler and dinner was brought in by several Footmen. The soup course and beverages including sherry, champagne, bottled sparkling spring water from Evian, France. Lady Agatha and Elsie were served tea.

Before the last glass of champagne was poured the fun began:

"You'll remove yourself from my presence and change into something more civilized," said Lady Agatha who was looking down at her soup and nowhere else.

No one moved. All parties save Lady Agatha kept eating. Nora was enjoying her soup course in her lower class sunshine dress. As was Lindy in her wild west getup.

"Edward, is this your doing? Is this some sort of childish rebellion?" wondered mother.

"This is what I usually wear to dinner, mother," said Jack glibly. Lady Agatha was not amused.

Lady Agatha put her soup spoon down and slapped the mahogany table which also got no one's attention. Her four children were used to these theatrics.   Lindy's mother would wave a gun around, sometimes shooting it off, so Lindy continued to schlurp her soup like they do in the wild west and poor neighborhoods of London.

At tonight's dinner, the servants stood still, at attention, loving the drama. The servants, most of whom remained after Jack's uncle died, loved aunt Fanny's mood swings, venomous recriminations against 'beloved' guests and sudden explosions of temperament.   Now, as Jack inherited the house, title, land and servants, Agatha's meanness was more desperate. She had four children who were unmarried and only Elsie seemed to mind. Agatha was also a humiliated non-royal 'countess'.   Non-royal countesses don't count. And don't get invited to parties with royalty and nobility in attendance. No wonder she's desperate.

Lindy kept schlurping and dipping her fresh-baked French bread into the soup and drinking champagne like she lived in a desert.

Lindy signaled Mr. Harrison the Butler for additional French bread with sweet butter from Cornwall, wherever that was. "And could you get some strawberry jam. Please," continued Lindy.
When she said 'please' she looked to Jack hoping he'd heard her use one of the magic words, which had been absent from her lexicon since birth.

"I'm speaking here!" exploded Lady Agatha, glaring at Lindy.

"Don't quit y'alls yammering on account of me, old woman," offered Lindy, used to a drunk bank-robbing father and an angry cast iron pot throwing mother.

"Nora, take off that obscene dress immediately and put on something more suited to English civility."

"No, mother. I want more colour in my life. And thanks to Lindy who took me shopping at Harrods, I now own colourful dresses, blouses, jackets. And shoes!"

"Did you not know anything about this?" threatened mother glaring at Edward, 3rd Duke of Sussex, great-grandson of George III, and owner of 620,000 square foot Ashfield Hall, wherein his mother is but a temporary unwanted interloper.

"Lindy was gracious enough to take your beloved daughters to Harrods to buy a new wardrobe for your big dinner with Her Majesty's unmarried sons," clarified Edward/Jack.

Looking squarely at Elsie, Lady Agatha demanded, "And no one consulted me?"

"Don't pick on L.C. She weren't goin' on no part of our shopping trip. Except to buy some old woman clothes that no man in his right mind would want to be seen with," Lindy said this whilst buttering her slice of hot, steamy French bread, then spreading strawberry jam all over the melting fresh sweet country butter churned in the trouble-free County of Cornwall.

Elsie squeaked disapproval when she heard 'old woman clothes'. Mother, too, was taken aback.

"I've got a good mind to…" began Mother.

"You know why y'alls three pretty girls ain't married? Cause of y'all. Everything y'all them to do drives men away. Y'all forgot what a man wants," said Lindy in an even, quiet, reasonable, therapeutic tone, finally looking Lady Agatha right between her 'old woman' eyes.

All four of Lady Agatha's spawn were shocked, stunned into silence. No one, not even Jack's father, mousey Prince Clarence, talked to his wife like that.

Lindy dipped her wad of jam filled French bread into her still hot soup and took another bite, then washed it down with champagne. She looked up and motioned for the beverage Footman with a nod of her chin, holding up her champagne flute. More champagne, indicated Lindy, and the 3rd Footman filled it up to the top. Also, the dining room staff no longer looked to Jack for approval of Lindy's requests. Lindy was now family.

"Can you fathom who I am!' commanded Lady Agatha.

"Just some ordinary dame desperate to get back to royalty by scheming to marry off y'alls kin to the lady next door. Y'alls countin' on the queen to give your title back. But it ain't gonna work," remarked Lindy.

Lady Agatha, Jack's gold digging mother, gasped, held her breath and turned blue.

Elsie gasped, held her breath and turned blue.

Harriet gasped, held her breath and turned a pale shade of light purple.

Nora laughed her skinny white ass off in her sunshine yellow dress.

"Edward, who is this trollop and why is she at our table?" demanded mother.

"This is Duchess Lindy Long from Wyoming Territory in America, mother. Lindy is my guest and she is also the jockey who won the 100th running of the Epsom Derby."

"Listen cowgirl, you will not interfere in our lives," said mother, who turned to Nora and commanded, "And you, dear heart, return that hideous dress to-morrow."

Lindy looked at Harriet and Nora and asked a simple question, "Do y'alls really want to marry one of them queen's boys? Y'all live a life of rules with your mother harping at you for the rest of your lives, and the queen lording herself over y'alls for the rest of your miserable lives. If you still want that, then I'll show you how to make her boys fall in love with you. I s'pect mother wants L.C. to keep for herself to take care of her in her old age."

Mr Harrison, the Butler, ordered the soup course cleared as several women staff members did so, followed by two Footmen who brought in the main course.

"All right, if you refuse to vacate the dining room, then I shall go, I'll have the rest of my meal in my Drawing room," said mother to Mr Harrison, Butler.   A Footman helped mother arise from her hand-carved mahogany high-backed chair and opened one of the dining room doors for Lady Agatha to exit.

Elsie, who could stand to lose thirty pounds, stayed put. The main course was filet Ã la Beouf Wellington, a difficult beef dish to cook but a favourite of Jack's. Elsie, Harriet and Nora, all seated whilst mother huffed out. The 2nd Footman closed the dining room door lest mother slam it, upsetting the diners.

Elsie, whilst enjoying her Beouf Wellington, sipping Lafite Rothschild Pauillac, turned to Lindy, "How do you know so much about men? Are you a whore?"

"No, I'm still a fuckin' virgin. I know about men cause I tried dressing like y'alls—silly, frilly-dilly girly girls. That kept men away. Then I said the hell with it and put on britches. The tighter the trousers the more the men came. Baggy pants, no men. Tight britches, men came stormin' back." said professor Lindy.

"How do you know if he's reputable and not a cad..?" wondered Harriet.

Lindy didn't know what reputable meant but said, "All men want one thing: sex. All they want is to fuck you. And after they fuck you, they don't care about you in the same way. Until he wants to fuck you again. Then they come knockin' on your window three in the mornin'."

Elsie, Harriet, Edward were transfixed. They were frozen, staring in disbelief at Lindy. Nora agreed with Lindy. All the men who Nora had courted wanted sex. They made promises that they couldn't keep—if Nora agreed to have sex. Wanting sex in 1880 meant 'marry me' because a lady was brain washed into believing she must be a virgin on her wedding night.

"So the men I courted only wanted to marry me to have sex?" wondered Nora.

"That's it. To have sex and to keep y'all to hisself," staccatoed Lindy enjoying her filet of Wellington and Chateau Lafite red wine.

"Is that what love means to a man?" chimed in Elsie.

"Yup," concluded Lindy.

"That's absurd!" joined Harriet.

"No it ain't. Ask Jack. He gets 'urges' and there's only a couple a ways to satisfy them, ain't that right, Jack?"

The look on Jack's face screamed Leave me out of this!

The four women wouldn't let him out of it.

"There are some aspects of truth in what Lindy said. Especially in one's teen-aged years. But men do love women in ways other than sex," replied Jack, nervously.

"Name 'em," demanded Lindy.

"A man can love a woman for her beauty, her intelligence, her inquisitiveness, her personality." said Jack, regaining his confidence.

This made the three sisters feel slightly better.

"But first off, you just want to fuck us." said Lindy with total confidence.

Jack, nobody's fool, sipped his wine and kept his mouth shut.

"What do you want in a wife, Jack?" prodded Lindy.

The sisters sat up, shifted in their comfortable hand-carved mahogany deeply padded high-backed dining room chairs, folded their arms and stared at their brother, 3rd Duke of Sussex, great-grandson of George III and nephew of HM Aunt Victoria.

"Well, I obviously haven't given it a lot of thought. I've been working."

"Yeah, yeah, yeah, blah, blah, blah", chortled Lindy, "quit stallin'."

"I want a soft countenance. A gentle soul. A woman who's well read, well bred, one who fits in well no matter where I go. She can dance, she can have shocking opinions. She can be loving and warm. She can comfort. She can play a sport, even cricket! She can speak several languages. And she can even hold opinions which differ from mine." There, thought Jack, that will not only transfix them, stun them, but satisfy their hatred of men.

"So you want to marry the Virgin Fuckin' Mary," remarked Lindy.

The three sisters hooted.

"You're not fooling anybody," said Elsie.

"No such woman exists!" stated Jack. "What I want isn't possible. So I shall remain free from bondage. I refuse to enter into an arrangement wherein I pay for someone to boss me around, to nag, to pester, to suffocate my dreams, my projects, so I can attend some nonsensical garden party or sip tea with other badgering old women. My life is perfect, even in this ridiculously large house." Jack was now satisfied with this statement. The 3rd Duke of Sussex picked up a bottle of Lafite-Rothschild Pauillac (1852), poured some into his claret stem and drank a healthy gulp.

"To Jack!" shouted Lindy, "a man who knows what he wants and also knows that she don't exist! So why bother!"

Jack nodded at Lindy, surprised at her perceptual insights regarding matrimony.

"We ain't got to you three yet. Do you want to marry for love or for a title?" wondered Lindy of the three sisters.

"Definitely a royal title," smirked Nora. "And to make mom proud of me," concluded Nora, derisively.

"Are you being coy, or are you making light of the situation, Nora?" queried Harriet, middle daughter.

"I like Leopold. The youngest. He'll never be king and he seems like fun. And I want to have fun. I also want people to bow and curtsey and call me your royal highness. Then go shopping at Harrods," reasoned Nora, youngest and prettiest.

"Y'alls a good matchup, you and Leo," decided Lindy.

"You, Elsie. You're old, mean and cold as a Wyoming winter. That what a man wants?"   Lindy might as well have put a bullet between Elsie's eyes. Lindy had no idea that you never tell anyone the truth. It'll scar you for life. Their mother insists on telling the truth and look how her daughters turned out. And maybe why Jack's father died early. Did he die or did he escape?

"How should I act? All warm and subservient?" asked Elsie.

"Warm and kind and know how to cook. I don't know what that other word means but if it means pretending to bend to a man's demands, then yes. And just as soon as you seal the deal, you change back to old and mean and cold."

"You make it sound so simple." said Elsie and Harriet.

"It is simple! You sweet talk him. You smile instead of snarl. Snarlin's for angry dogs. You an angry dog? Or are you a happy, smilin' puppy, aiming to please? Dressed in bright, happy colors. Lots of rain and gray skies here. Bright colors makes you look bright and happy."

"Mother will not approve," surrendered Elsie.

"Perfect! Do the opposite of her and you'll be married by next month," predicted a very confident Lindy.

"I'd listen to Lindy," taunted Nora, the hot 24 year old dressed in blow torch yellow, "unless you want to end up a permanent governess to my children with Prince Leopold." Princess Nora said that as a matter of future fact.

Lindy swigged her champagne, stared at Mr Harrison and chirped, "Dessert for all!"

Jack had a look of horror on his face. Horror.

CHAPTER 16

Murder Suspect Located

After nearly two months investigating who shot and killed the Sheriff of Larimer County, Colorado, the new Sheriff (and former deputy) tracked down Lindy's mother who lived just south of Cheyenne, Wyoming Territory. Lindy's mother claimed that her daughter Rleen had 'vamoosed' the day after the Colorado sheriff was shot dead.

Lindy's mother, Irdine Dross, made a lot of noise about her missing daughter, filed a missing person's report at the Sheriff's office in Cheyenne, Wyoming Territory, about a week ago.

With her husband shot dead last Christmas and her daughter Lindy (real name Rleen) gone, no one was bringing in any money. When the food ran out, and Irdine digging up the last known hiding place of bank robbery money, Irdine took action. To somehow get reimbursed by the Territory for the money her Husband brought in.

Irdine wasn't liked by the Sheriff in Cheyenne. Irdine Dross was a short, wirey, fiesty, back-talking, threatening, armed, loud, foul-mouthed white woman from Alabama who got louder and more threatening when her husband and bread winner was shot dead by that no-good varmint sheriff from Colorado. Now as dead as her husband.

The new Colorado sheriff wasn't too happy with the Sheriff whose office was in Cheyenne, because the Wyoming sheriff did little to help solve the murder. "It took place in Larimer County, Colorado. I'm the Sheriff of *Laramie* County, Wyoming Territory. So why should I look for your suspect?"

Oddly, it took two months for that information of a missing daughter to travel 40 miles south to Fort Collins, Colorado. The Larimer County, Colorado, sheriff, Kees Van der Hoff, had heard two rumors going around Fort Collins, about the daughter of the dead bank robber having gone missing the day after the death of Sheriff Ross Armitage. Death by gunfire. And this girl lived just south of Cheyenne with her mother whose husband was murdered by Ross Armitage, the Colorado sheriff.

In Wyoming Territory women carried guns like a man, rode horses like a man, and shot dead threatening men, like a man. Range wars between farmers and ranchers were more cause for concern. Farmers had to fence their land to keep grazing cows out. Wyoming, according to ranchers, didn't need fences. Tens of thousands of acres of open, lush grassland. And not enough rain to grow trees or crops without irrigation. So ranchers tore down fences and got shot by farmers and their wives when they came near their barbed wire.

That kept the Wyoming Territory sheriff's departments busy most of the time. A missing girl, probably got kidnapped, or voluntarily ran to an Indian tribe on one of the reservations.

The only suspects of the Colorado sheriff's murder were Lindy's father's bank robber gang.
Each one of them had an alibi for the night in question. Mainly because it was raining hard and all the roads south to Fort Collins were two feet deep in mud. The gang only robbed banks on sunny days when the roads were dry so they could escape and not get stuck in mud. Plus no real man would ever be caught with a .32 caliber handgun. A girl's gun. A little boy's 'toy' gun.

Sheriff Van der Hoff, searching Irdine's modest home, found Lindy's .32 caliber handgun.
(It had been lying on the kitchen table since Lindy put it there two months ago.)
Irdine, Lindy's mother, handed the gun to Sheriff Van der Hoff, said that Rleen had been out in the rain all that night and returned soaking wet early the next morning that the Colorado sheriff had been shot and killed.
"What took you so long to come forward?" asked the Colorado sheriff.
"What took you so long to figure out where to look!?" shot back Iodine. "Sheriff kil't my husband before Christmas last and you finally figure out to git here? Dumb shit."
"Do you know the whereabouts of Arlene?"
"She come home that night and then she vanished the next mornin'. Maybe she run up Dakotas," mused Irdine.
"By the way, how did you find out our Sheriff had died?" gently interrogated Sheriff Van der Hoff, who spoke excellent English, "Did Arlene say she killed the Colorado sheriff?"

"Molly Jean told me. Said ol' Ross had been shot dead in that bad storm. Rleen had come home daylight the next day. I asked her where she been at and she told me to well, she used curses. She put her handgun down on the table. I asked her if she wanted somethin' to eat and you'll never believe what she had with her—fresh baked apple fuckin' pie!"

"Where'd she get an apple pie, ma'am" wondered Sheriff Van der Hoff.

"Damned if I know. Go back and ask Widow Armitage if someone stole a pie from her porch and you got your killer!" said Irdine Dross, Lindy's blathering mother. Widow Armitage is dead ex-Sheriff Ross Armitage's wife.

"What time of day, or night, did Rleen come in with the pie?"

"For the third time, it was rainin'. It twas next fuckin' mornin'," cursed Irdine.

"And was that the last time you saw Rleen?"

"That's the last I seed her. She changed clothes and rode off. Storm cleared out and she was riding up north to Cheyenne," said Irdine, filling in the blanks for the sheriff.

"You think she caught the train?"

"Train?! With what money?"

"Why'd she go to Cheyenne?" wondered the new Sheriff.

"Maybe she's got a feller up 'ere," which made sense to Irdine. "She dresses like a whore."

"Anything else?" wondered the Colorado sheriff.

"Yeah," began Irdine, "Best fuckin' pie I ever et."

"That's not what I asked, ma'am. Is it possible she took a train out of town?"

"Well, Hell's bells. How's she gonna get a horse on a train, sheriff?" Irdine was getting irritated. "She wasn't going nowhere without that cavalry horse."

"And she didn't send a telegram or send someone, this Molly you mentioned, to tell you where she is?" The Sheriff was closing in for the kill, or capture.

"I cain't read. Molly Jean's my friend, not Rleen's. Them two cross paths and hiss and spit like a couple of pit vipers," painted Irdine.

"Thank you, ma'am. If you hear from Arlene, notify your sheriff so he can alert me."

"You gon' ride back tonight?"

"Yeah, I've got a friend across the Colorado border who can cook. Got my bedroll, I'm all set," said Sheriff Kees Van der Hoff with a warm smile. First time he smiled all day.

Kees had his first strong lead in Sheriff Ross Armitage's killing: he had the murder weapon, a prime suspect, her motive, and a key witness.

Now all Sheriff Van der Hoff needs to do is find Arlene Dross who allegedly got on an eastbound train two months ago with or without her horse.. Or continued north up to the Dakotas or entered Canada. That narrowed everything down.

CHAPTER 17

Dinner With The Royal Princes

Jack was not invited to dinner in his own house, even though he was a royal duke, nephew of Queen Victoria and cousins to Her Majesty's children. Jack's mother (Agatha) learned of his drinking sessions which took place in a private room somewhere in the 620,000 square foot three-story house but could never interfere because she was a lady and ladies never barged into a room where gentlemen retired to talk business, politics, other sordid topics, whilst they drank something called port and smoked cigars made on a tropical isle called Cuba.

Back to reality, Agatha hunted for this drinking room every day. She thought it was an unused Drawing Room, Sitting Room, Library, Study or Picture Room on the main floor. Royal princes don't drink and smoke in the basement, thought Agatha.

Victoria's sons were a disgrace to the Crown because of the smoking and drinking. The Prince of Wales was a disgrace because of his debauchery with a lot of (55 and counting) younger married and much younger unmarried women. Lady Agatha believed her son was above promiscuity and it displeased her that Edward was complicit with smoking and drinking. Such were the dramatics of ladies of the Victorian era. Especially HM Victoria. Men were not amused.

Lady Lindy most assuredly was not invited to this esteemed dinner for reasons having to do with her youth, beauty, sassiness, ability to instantly arouse and her need to point things out that didn't need pointing out. Like Agatha'a Grand Plan to get her royal title back.

Tonight was Agatha's night. She sat at the head of the table. To her left were Elsie, Harriet and Nora. To her right were Princes Alfred, Arthur and Leopold.

The Petite Royal Dining Room was selected for its loftiness. A step up from the Family Dining Room. The Petite Royal Dining Room featured a taller ceiling (25 feet, not 15) finer cut of crystal chandelier, intricate architectural details, a more highly polished dark mahogany table, larger paintings hanging from the picture rail higher up on the walls, marble chair rail, the painted ceiling, two large fireplaces and a Housemaid (Keeper of the Flame) to tend each one. The dining chairs were from France with thick padding and arm rests. They were covered in silk cloth with an intricate pattern woven on Jacquard looms. These Jacquard patterns were exclusive to Ashfield Hall. Queen Victoria herself did not have these unique patterns. HM had her own unique Jacquard weavings.

The kitchen was alerted well ahead of time to this dinner and to its significance. That tonight, all three of Victoria's unwed sons would dine with Lady Agatha's unwed daughters for the sole purpose of triple weddings in the near future. And that should this miracle come about, it would elevate Countess Agatha to be reinstated as a Royal Duchess with a style of Royal Highness. Because her daughters had royal blood, and marry Royal Princes, they would qualify for the title Royal Duchess after their weddings had been secured. Seal the deal, girls.

Everything was at stake. Nothing could go wrong. Anyone who would hinder Lady Agatha's plan was kept away. The stage was set. Bring on the players.

The royal guests had just arrived. The carriage holding the three royal princes approached from Buckingham Palace's west gate which opened onto the east road of Ashfield Hall, which was Ashfield's east gate. (Jack's east gate didn't need security guards because Queen Victoria's west gate guards took care of security—it was the same gate.)

The three unmarried (happy, carefree, ebullient) sons would enter Ashfield Hall from its front door and not that seedy side entrance where the Queen's boys would go to drink and smoke cigars with Jack a couple of times a week to get away from the morbid gloom choking the fun out of living at Buckingham Palace.

There was one good reason why the boys should marry—to get out of the house where Queen Victoria was permanently, continuously, insufferably mourning her dead husband. Always wearing black and always reminding everyone of how miserable she was because her useless son, Albert, Prince of Wales, was the reason Victoria's beloved husband was dead in the first place. Just days before Christmas, 1861. It was Albert's rampant extramarital carryings-on that caused his father, Consort Prince Albert, in bad health, to go out into the cold, driving rain, to Cambridge University, to redress his fat, sexually wayward son. It obviously did no good. Albert, Prince of Wales, continued having sex with wayward women.

Bertie was bullied into marriage. Bertie continued defiling women at Marlborough House and his Gentleman's Clubs around London. But not Ashfield Hall. This is where you went to get away from nagging wives and demanding girlfriends. Thus the welcoming addition of free-spirited Lindy, the American who could drink and smoke everyone under the four inch thick solid mahogany table. All whilst being entertaining and not nagging. An impossible combination found in the fair sex, concluded the princes who attend Jack's Gentleman's Club.

The Royal Princes Three were greeted by Mr Harrison, Butler, and shown into the Petite Royal Dining Room. Had they come with the Queen, they would have been shown to a formal Drawing Room to rest and refresh before the five course meal. But Her Majesty was home loudly commiserating the loss, 20 years ago, of her beloved consort Prince Albert.

Countess Agatha greeted Prince Alfred, 35 years old, Prince Arthur, 30, and Prince Leopold, 27. The Countess curtsied as Mr Harrison, Butler, motioned for the three bachelors to enter the Petite Royal Dining Room which looked especially inviting tonight. The table, set for seven, was awash in color with early summer flowers set in low vases so guests could see each other across the table. The three candelabra were spaced perfectly on the polished mahogany table. Lady Agatha chose three candelabra and three floral vases for obvious reasons. The soft light of candles would make her daughters look radiant and a lot more attractive. This event is a high-powered sales job.

Jack, earlier, had peeked into the dining room, smirked at the set table and muttered 'the trap is lain.' and got the Hell out of there before a servant reported him to his mother.

Awaiting the royal princes were Elsie, 32, and Harriet, 30. Arriving a smidgen late was Nora, 24. Elsie and Harriet were wearing evening wear in the style, cut and colour chosen by their mother.   Nora snuck in from a side door broadcasting her audaciously bold, adventurous, foolhardy and reckless vividly explosive bright red dress. Elsie's eyes popped out of her head. She gasped for air. Had there been more people in attendance she would have theatrically fainted. Harriet blushed, not nearly as red as Nora's fire-engine red dress.

Nora sat down as though nothing out of the ordinary were going on. Nora smiled politely, victoriously, at her sisters who were seated next to her. Nora looked at the set up. Seven elegant chairs. The three sisters would sit to one side of mother. The three victims, er, royal princes, would sit on the other side of mother. How boring. Lindy told Nora, 'boy, girl, boy, girl, boy, girl. Let mama sit at the opposite end of y'alls.'

The First Footman stood behind Countess Agatha's chair, waiting to seat her. The three princes could seat themselves.

The protocol for this meal was in shambles. Royal Princes don't come to houses where the head of the household was a non-royal. Jack, Royal Duke and nephew of Victoria, must be present representing his duchy. 'To the Devil with Royal Custom,' vocalized Lady Agatha, 'those boys will marry my girls, so help me God.' Well, that certainly fixed Royal Custom & Protocol. Besides, the Royal Princes were happy to show up, get a meal, meet the new neighbors. Then smoke Cuban cigars and guzzle excellent vintage port with cousin Edwardo, Eddie, Jack or any new name now attached to him, after dinner.

Lady Agatha, escorted gingerly by Prince Alfred, took two steps into the Petite Royal Dining Room and was blinded by something obscenely red coming from the dining table. Lady Agatha swooned. Had she a lady's pistol, she would have shot Nora and then Nora's lady's maid.

How dare she ruin my dinner. This was a premeditated act of evil and subservience, thought Lady Agatha, who was seated, turned directly to Nora and glared. Then turned to the three princes seated to Agatha's right, and smiled genteelly, reverently, deferentially. Black widowly.

All princes looked past Lady Agatha, past Elsie, past Harriet and locked onto a brand new target. The young, fair, attractive brunette in the hot and quite daring prostitute red dress. Leopold, 27, gulped and smiled.

Nora blushed and smiled at all three boys equally. These royal princes, felt Nora, would have gotten into a messy, bloody fistfight over her then and there had an adult not been present.

Elsie was smiling and fuming at the same time. Harriet was half-smiling and fuming. Lady Agatha saw the lascivious looks on the royal princes' faces then suddenly thought, 'Jackpot! Why aren't Elsie and Harriet dressed like my seductress Nora?'

"May I introduce my daughters to your royal highnesses?" began Lady Agatha. Without waiting for a proper reply, "Lady Elsie," who smiled as the three unmarried princes nodded, "Lady Harriet," who also smiled and sat up straighter than normal, which was Royal Cadet straight in the first place. Again, the bachelor princes nodded. "And my baby, Lady Nora." who smiled suggestively, arousing all three horny royal princes who, at once, overlapping, clamoring for attention and approval, "You look radiant Lady Nora.", "You are a beacon of loveliness, my Lady," "Red is most inviting, Lady Nora!"

Nora was now in complete control of Victoria's three unmarried spawn and had them wrapped around her tight-ass and provocative red dress. Instead of sitting up straighter or becoming more subservient, Nora did the unthinkable: picked up a bottle of sherry and poured some for herself, then got up and walked over to the virgin boys with the sherry, chirping, "Let's have a toast to this dinner." and poured all three boys some sherry. Nora put the bottle down in front of Leopold and whispered something in his 27 year old ear: "I've always liked you, Leo."

Lindy Mae Long, shooter of sheriffs, manipulator of boys, didn't have to be there to know that Nora would put on the libidinous red dress, would have been fawned over by the three virgin princes, and would find any excuse to get up and show off her 24 year old body in her clinging revealing evening gown. Even though her Paris original went from bosom to floor, her gown's tightness showed off a body that screamed 'manhandle me boys. Manhandle me now.' It also showed off her milky white shoulders all the way down to the top of her soft, white, manipulating breasts.

Nora smiled coyly. The boys were about to explode.

Had any of the gentlemen gotten up, they would have shown everyone how glad they were to see Nora in her provocative whore's dress. So they remained seated and aroused.

The soup course was served. French onion soup served with champagne. Lady Agatha wanted alcohol to flow, low candle light and the air scented with perfume and the aroma of flowers, to wash over the three unmarried virgins causing them to lust after her daughters. Yes, Lady Agatha, seeing the princes come alive, and aroused, on account of Nora, threw out tradition and welcomed Nora's art of direct manipulation through seduction.

Well, one £49 bright red dress did the job faster and better than Agatha's staged and manipulated atmospherics. All the better to marry my middle-aged daughters off. Elsie was 32. In 1880 she should have had five or six children by now and could get on with her life. Even at 24, baby Nora was pushing it. Girls married before they were 18. Royalty had its own schedule because marriages were arranged. Alfred, the next son in line to the throne after his older brother Albert, Prince of Wales, was the spare heir. His arranged marriage fell through. His arranged wife, a German, married a Prussian Prince in direct line for their throne. Alfred was relieved. He didn't like her and didn't speak German. Now Alfred's gaze was locked onto the woman in I-want-sex-red. He wanted to lose his virginity to her. And not in six months on their wedding night, but shortly after dinner, tonight.

While enjoying his French onion soup, brother Arthur was also staring and smiling deliriously at Nora thinking the same thing as Alfred. Sex, tonight, Nora. Then we'll speak of marriage later.

Leopold was relaxed, at ease, giving sideways glances at Nora, the sudden love of his life, believing, for certain, he was going to have sex tonight. Leopold even started a conversation with Elsie and Harriet, who were only too delighted to finally get noticed.

As the fish course was being served (Jack was not at table, mother added the traditional fish course), Prince Arthur asked any of the ladies presents, "Had you attended The Derby this season?" attempting to find the sisters' interests. The sport of kings is also the sport of mere princes.

Harriet loved horses and horse racing and immediately perked up, "I've never missed a running, sir, and yes, I witnessed the 100th. I saw Edward from our seat across from the Royal Box. Brother Edward's three year old took the prize, of course. He was pleased, well, you know Eddie, when Noble Warrior crossed the finish line and everyone was cheering as though we'd just won a war,

Dear Edward simply nodded, smiled and said, 'well done,'" recalled Harriet with extra thick glee.

"Emotional Edwardo! That's our man," laughed Prince Arthur, "Has he always been so, how would you say, restrained?"

Arthur was talking to Elsie and Harriet about Edward.

Harriet recalled: "Our father, Prince Clarence, laid down a strict regimen of rules for Edward. First off, that his name is Edward and not any slight thereof. Second, he would attend St Paul's, then Trinity, Cambridge, then enter the Royal Navy."

"After Cambridge, Ol' Eddie took off for America," interjected Alfred, eldest prince at table, "And brought back that curious girl in fringe." Alfred smiled. This smile gave Lady Agatha concern and nearly a heart attack.

"She calls ol' Eddie 'Jack!'   A royal duke!" declared Leopold with too much enthusiasm for an 1880 dinner party with royalty.

"Nora, my dear," quickly interrupted Lady Agatha, "How are your piano recitals going?"

Cold water was thrown on the fish course.

"I am practicing Chopin's Nocturnes and am prepared for a recital at present." said Nora, quite satisfied in her killer Take All of Me red dress. Any mistakes will go unnoticed, she thought. She thought correctly.

"Your Royal Highnesses, this will assuage your curiosity regarding the Bosendorfer Opera Grand sitting in our humble dining quarters." offered Lady Agatha as Nora took the opportunity to seat herself at the keyboard. The Bosendorfer, acquired by Jack's uncle Frederick in 1861, was Serial Number 5555. Notable pianists had been invited to play. Among the greatest was Franz Liszt, in 1874 and again in 1877, In attendance both times were HM Victoria and HM Franz Joseph, Emperor of Austria, King of Hungary, Bohemia, Dalmatia and Croatia. No future kings were in attendance tonight.

Nora did not need sheet music, nor a candelabrum in which to illuminate her score.

The acoustics in the Petite Royal Dining Room were spectacular. The domed twenty-five foot ceiling, the furnishings, the woolen tapestries, the marble tiled floor, all worked in harmony to render Chopin's Nocture Opus 72 No. 1 in E minor into a lingering living, moving poem that added layers of depth to this gathering.

Lady Agatha insisted tonight must give new understanding of how important this soiree would mean to the three favored sons of Victoria.

Nora's recital was spectacular, emotional and brought out the depths of Chopin's ability to write the most heart-felt Nocturnes of any composer known to date.

"And Harriet, please inform their royal highnesses of your alacrity," said Lady Agatha.

"I draw and paint according to the plein air school; I have an assortment of landscapes from the West Country," began Harriet, adding, "I also study portraiture."

Jack had arranged for several Ashfield Hall staff to come into the dining room with Harriet's paintings. Framed.   And now exhibited on individual easels so the three princes can enjoy.

The staff members displayed twelve of her most colorful, elegant and story-telling works of art.

Her pièce de résistance were illustrations of the Royal Family. It began with a stunning charcoal sketch of Her Majesty during her early years on the Throne.   Followed by detailed individual sketches of adults Prince Alfred, Prince Arthur and Prince Leopold.   These sketches, in charcoal, pen and ink, some exhibiting a light dusting of color made from intricate dyes, mesmerized the boys.   They were awe-struck.

Harriet then presented each Prince with his own portrait, framed and resplendent, which could be propped up at table.

Lady Agatha was pleased.   She looked at each prince and when they caught Lady Agatha's eye, she smiled and nodded approval.

"And Elsie has several special gifts, among them, the gift of voice," announced Lady Agatha.

Lady Agatha saved the best for last.   Her eldest daughter, Elsie, sang three short, simple songs, accompanied by Nora on the Bosendorfer Opera Grand (which included the Liszt Octave). Elsie started with a popular Irish bar song with a voice so crisp, clear and projective, that the kitchen staff, below stairs, perked up and liked it. The princes were riveted, their toes were a-tappin'.   She then sang a patriotic marching song and closed with a beautiful, poignant Irish Ballad, *She is far from the land*, by Thomas Moore.   The dining room fell silent as Elsie sang from her heart.   The princes let the lyrics of a brave boy who died for his country sink in.   When Elsie finished there wasn't a dry eye in the house.   Even Mr Harrison needed a handkerchief.

Without any direction, all three gentlemen stood and applauded.   Elsie bowed gracefully and took her seat.

Lady Agatha relaxed. Exhaled victoriously. Her darlings had come through. Champagne was poured, the dessert course came in, there was toasting and carefree merriment.

After the dessert course the three princes arose in unison to thank Lady Agatha for a magnificent evening.

Each prince shook the hand of each sister, bowed, smiled and thanked each for their overwhelming contribution to a fabulous dinner.

The dinner continued with dessert and elated, enthusiastic bantering regarding the girls' talent, training and performances.

Dessert was cleared, Lady Agatha stood, thanked their royal highnesses, and left.

The boys said their farewells and Mr Harrison, Butler, escorted the princes out the front entrance into their awaiting enclosed carriage. The carriage clopped off and turned right toward Buckingham Palace.

Once the carriage was out of sight of the front entry and thirty foot tall windows of Ashfield Hall, it turned right again and headed for the side door of Ashfield where the boys went to get away from miserable mum and report to Jack's bar.

CHAPTER 18.

After Dinner

The three princes got out of their carriage and greeted Jack at the little-known side entry of Ashfield Hall.

When the boys entered Jack's mahogany panelled Gentlemen's Club they were delighted to see Lindy sitting in one of the very comfortable oxblood leather wingback chairs, feet up on the matching ottoman, sipping brandy and smoking a Romeo Y Julieta Belicoso Cuban cigar. She was wearing her black fringed outfit which comprised tight buckskin pants, black buckskin jacket and a black silk blouse. She wasn't wearing her cowgirl boots. She sported red woollen socks.

When the three royal princes arrived, Lindy hoisted her Waterford brandy balloon and said "set your asses down fellas."

The three princes took their usual seats as Jack put their favorite barware in front of the boys, as well as several bottles of vintage port, cognac, a bottle of Glenturret Scotch, vintage 1788, champagne and something new from America: Jack Daniel's Tennessee Sour Mash Whiskey. Founded 1866, fourteen years ago. Everything in America is always brand new.

There was also a selection of bottled natural spring water from Europe, Iceland, Scotland and Cornwall. Perrier and Evian from France were the two favorites.

Then Jack handed several humidors of Cuban cigars to the princes. Alfred favored Partagas Serie P Numero Duo and lit his cigar with a candelabrum then picked up his crystal short-stemmed port glass and sipped his 1866 Cockburn port. Arthur favored H. Upmann Reserva Cuban cigars, used the same candelabrum to light his, then enjoyed his crystal balloon of Louis Royer Cognac. Leopold loved Hoya de Monterrey Marevas Cuban cigars with his crystal snifter of Gautier cognac, 1818 Reserve.

Edward lit a Cuban cigar from Jose L Piedra, Habana, and sipped a 1723 Taylor Fladgate vintage port.

Uncle Frederick introduced Edward (Jack) to vintage port, cognac, French wines and Cuban cigars when Jack went off to St

Paul's Academy (a preparatory school founded in 1509).   Jack matriculated to Trinity College, Cambridge University, where he made friends through his plentiful supply of Cuban cigars, and cases of Bass Pale Ale and Whitbread Beer.

"Who's gettin' hitched?" wondered Lindy, puffing her H. Upmann Romeo Y Julieta and now sipping Jack Daniel's whiskey. Lindy had been drinking Jack Daniel's since she was about 9.

Nobody knew what 'hitched' meant.

"Married? You Leopold? Like Nora's stunning easy-on-the-eyes red dress?" continued Lindy.

Leopold blushed. And so did Alfred and Arthur.

"All three of you!?!" Wow, thought Lindy.

Alfred said, "I am smitten by Elsie's voice. She sang an Irish ballad and I was swept to tears."

All three princes seemed subdued.

"It's time I settled for a wife and your mother's presentment convinced me," said Arthur to Jack.

Lindy thought, 'Put a tight red dress on an average looking 24 year old and suddenly she heats up the room.'

Lindy got up and raced out of the Gentleman's Room, through an anti-mother-snooping-maze of crooked hallways, unlit corridors, very thick closed oak doorways, until she reached the dining room area.

Lindy burst into the Petite Royal Dining Room where Elsie and Harriet who were unsure how the dinner went. Nora felt really good because she looked really good.

Lindy, in her socks, slid to a halt on the polished marble dining room floor.

Announced Lindy, "those boys are ready to marry all three of y'all <u>tonight!</u>"

"How do you know that?" wondered Elsie.

"They're all drinkin' with Jack downstairs. Follow me!"

Jack and the boys were smoking and drinking away, feet up (no shoes, socks please) on the polished mahogany table.   Mr Harrison had brought in fresh baked sandwiches and pastries.

Lindy walked into the Gentlemen's Room, by herself. The boys and Jack immediately swiped their feet off the table, sat up straight and looked deliriously at Lindy. The usual scowl on her face was replaced by a very broad and seductive smile. Lindy stepped out of the way to let three stunning beauties enter the secret room.

The virgin princes were falling all over themselves to get up and offer beverages to the suddenly incredibly talented and beautiful women. Unchaperoned by their mother.

Elsie was standing confidently in her three inch Italian heels, swirling a brandy balloon half-filled with Hennessey. Harriet was holding Waterford barware with three fingers of Macallan 59 year old scotch whisky, as Alfred and Arthur had joined them. Leopold slid over to Nora who was a powerful red magnet. The boys had paired off. The boys were doing most of the talking which meant, according to Lindy, that they were very interested in the women.

Lindy wandered over and sat down next to Jack who raised his port glass and clinked it with Lindy's glass of Jack Daniels. "Very nice, Miss Wyoming," said Jack.

"Thanks, Jack."

"Is this what you did in America? Arrange guests at dinner parties?" wondered Jack.

"I'd train girls then fix 'em up for boys."

"'Train girls?" wondered Arthur.

"Make the hookers look like Hitterites and the Hitterites look like hookers. That draws boys to girls like flies to shit."

Well, that was visual. "You've got a lot of talent, Lindy," said Jack, sincerely.

Lindy did not know how to take a compliment. Maybe because she'd never gotten a sincere compliment. She suddenly got shy.

The gathering in the Gentlemen's Room was just getting started. The princes reported how well Nora played the piano, how Elsie sang like an angel and the boys showed Jack and Lindy their individual portraits, in pen and ink and colored in vibrant watercolors, all created expertly, lovingly, by Harriet.

"Get a piano in here, Jack!" ordered Lindy, "strike up the band!"

The four coddled man-boys raced out of the Gentleman's Room, went down the hall into one of the Music Rooms and pushed a nine foot Hamburg Steinway (on brass castors, of course) along the teak and marble floors and through the double doors of the Gentleman's Room. Lindy brought the padded stool.

Within seconds Nora was perched on her seat at the Hamburg Steinway and played a rollicking Irish bar song, to which all the boys knew the lyrics, which included sexual innuendos and foul language.   Elsie, joined by Harriet, who also took singing lessons, outsang the reserved boys' voices. The joint was jumping.

Leopold wanted to dance with piano-playing Nora.   Nora got up from the keyboard and was immediately replaced by Harriet. These sisters went to one of the finer finishing schools, yet had never put on a performance for any suitor. Mainly because they never went on a triple date at their brother's house where their mother had ironclad control of all the events.

Leopold and Nora were dancing to a rowdy Gaelic ballad when Prince Alfred took Elsie's hand and they began dancing. Elsie didn't stop singing. Well, Arthur shrugged and he and Harriet began dancing, too.

Jack, who had studied piano, took over. Jack knew a lot of drinking songs, and several tunes from across the Pond. Camptown Races, written by Stephen Foster in 1850 and published in Baltimore, was a favorite minstrel song, easy to dance to, especially when you've had a goodly amount to drink. So, too, were Dixie, Oh! Susanna, Turkey in the Straw and Yankee Doodle Dandy.

After an hour of dancing, happily exhausted, the three couples plunked down in their very comfortable seats.

Nora and Lindy smoked cigars whilst Elsie laughed. Elsie never laughed.   Elsie chided, scolded, reprimanded, lectured, hounded.   Tonight she took Alfred's Cuban and puffed on it. Choked, coughed, ate a pastry, then took another puff. Smiled.

Her sisters plus Lindy and Jack were stunned at Elsie's new mannerisms.

Before adjourning, the three Princes made plans with the sisters. Alfred with Elsie. Arthur with Harriet. Leopold with Nora.

Their first such outing would be a picnic far away from Buckingham Palace and Ashfield Hall where no one's mother could interfere, snoop or accidentally drop by. (Actually, Hyde Park, about 5 blocks up the road was the 'secret' picnic site.)

CHAPTER 19

By Command of Her Majesty Queen Victoria

After three weeks of being courted by His Royal Highness Prince Leopold, Nora was summoned by Queen Victoria for a face-to-face interrogation and inspection.

No royal family member could marry without permission from the Monarch. This was British Law created by the Royal Marriages Act of 1772, initiated by George III to void the marriage of his elder son George and 'that Catholic girl you illegally married.'

A son or daughter of a Sovereign couldn't marry another royal, member of the nobility, a peer, or especially a commoner, without approval from the Crown. Without Royal approval, no engagement, no wedding. There would be an annulment had a marriage taken place without the Sovereign's approval, or approval from the Privy Council.

There were additional details and oversights. Harriet and Elsie were over 25 years of age and they could legally challenge the edict. Victoria might want to know why they had not married at the 'acceptable' and 'normal' age. Around late teens to early twenties. Harriet, at 30, and Elsie at 32, were well over the age limit. The ladies had answers. Acceptable answers, garnered by their conniving, scheming, social climbing mother.

If HM rejected the young lady or ladies, the Prince or Princess would have to seek out another intended and go through the interrogation and inspection process again. And again. The Royal Marriages Act of 1772 guaranteed the quality of the consort so as to not taint the royal lineage with the 'wrong' religion. Lady Agatha and her spawn were Church of England. They were religiously solid gold. Victoria was Defender of the Faith and Head of the Church of England. The Church of England was founded by King Henry VIII so he could divorce one wife and take up with another and not need permission from the Pope in Rome. Always the best reason to found a religion: divorce for sexual gratification.

A formal invitation was hand delivered from The Palace, addressed to Edward, Third Duke of Sussex, and his sister, Lady

Nora Sussex. Edward (Jack) and his sister were to visit Her Majesty on Monday next at 10 o'clock that morning. Thus morning ware was appropriate dress. Not as dressy as High Tea or as formal as Dinner. And certainly nothing tight, breast enhancing or bright red.

Leopold had fallen uncontrollably in love with Nora. His younger sister Princess Beatrice, age 23, said he'd fallen in love with a tight red dress. Followed by a tight Safire blue dress, and then a knockout and even tighter prostitute purple dress. Lots of colourful dinners have followed since that first red dress made its stunning appearance.

Leopold protested Beatrice's truthful remarks, but not very loudly. Leopold also mentioned Nora's mastery of the piano and Beatrice countered that all girls who want to marry into the royal family had better play the piano masterfully. Leopold re-countered that Nora sang like an angel and Beatrice re-re-countered that all girls in tight red dresses sang like angels because it wasn't her singing, it was her tight red dress. Who is this Beatrice girl?

Princess Beatrice Mary Victoria Feodora was HM Victoria's baby daughter. Child number 9. Beatrice was called "baby" by her mother. As mentioned, Beatrice was 23 years old. Beatrice was also told she wasn't ever going to marry and run off leaving HM childless, alone in a large, empty house. Baby was not amused. She wanted to party, to meet eligible men, and to have sex. She was not counted among the Victorians with a Victorian sensibility. She was a victim of Victorianism.

Baby liked to lash out and state her unVictorian opinion whenever she felt the need. Beatrice was desperate to run off. With a man. Or perhaps men. But run off was top of mind.

Beatrice continuously mocked her three unmarried brothers for being mummy's boys, afraid to marry, leave the palace and procreate. That changed as soon as Elsie, Harriet and Nora took up with the boys, in Jack's convenient gentleman's lounge.

Leopold pointedly told Beatrice that he loved how Nora smoked a Cuban cigar and drank Scotch whisky 'like a sailor'. That shut Beatrice up. She was now jealous of Nora, her tight dazzling dresses and the fact that Nora was free to smoke and drink at her house whenever she pleased.

Beatrice was condemned to abstinence of all things pleasurable by her mother, the Queen. "Ask for her hand then," snorted Beatrice who stormed out of one of the many Drawing rooms at Buckingham Palace, leaving Leopold with no option but to ask Nora to marry him.   Which led to the upcoming Interrogation by Queen Victoria herself.

The Queen was tired of having the three most eligible bachelors in the British Empire unmarried. It was wearing on Her Majesty making her more testy and irritable. Her sons, three spares to the heir, were enjoying their freedom. The Queen wanted to move things along and issued a decree to bring this woman, and next door neighbor, to court, interrogate her, and if she passed the Queen's Examination, then she would give Leopold permission to marry this young woman in the tight yellow/purple/red dress. But don't wear your tight red dress to your interrogation.

Protocol dictated that Nora had to be escorted by the highest ranking family member. No consorts. That duty fell to Edward, 3rd Duke of Sussex and Nephew to Her Majesty.   The Queen and Edward had been in the same room at the same time only once or twice, which was years ago, and it was for a Christmas ceremony for Royal family members. Edward was twelve or thirteen.

The Queen was told who Edward's and Nora's mother was, that she was once a Duchess (consort) when married to Edward's father, Prince Clarence.   How did this twenty-seven year old Edward (Jack), 3rd Duke of Sussex, inherit his title? She was reminded that Edward's father predeceased his older brother, so that when Edward's uncle Frederick died, young Edward was next in line. Then Queen Victoria immediately remembered Prince Frederick's awful wife Duchess Fanny whom the Queen demoted to non-royal Countess then banished Fanny from the Home Counties; and also remembered young Duke Edward's awful mother, Duchess Agatha, and demoted her to Countess and took away her Royal Highness style but let her have her estate in Mayfair, which was owned by her only son Edward (Jack).

Today, Edward, 3rd Duke of Sussex, and his sister, Lady Nora, presented themselves at Buckingham Palace promptly at 9:45am for their 10am appointment with Her Majesty.

Nora was a nervous wreck. She was going to be interrogated by the most power woman on earth. Nora went squealing through Harrod's shoe department two days ago and was told she had to settle on only 20 pair of shoes, by Lindy. Whatever pairs Nora didn't like Lindy would receive. Well, Lindy learned about girls and their 'need' for shoes. Nora ended up with 40 pair.

"How are you?" Nora asked of Jack in the ante room, awaiting HM.

"I'm fine," reported Jack, cool, calm and dry. He wasn't getting interrogated.

Nora was angry. "How can you be so unconcerned?"

"Because I'm not getting questioned by the Queen to see if I'm good enough to join the Royal family. If I were you I'd jump out the window and marry a nice farmer," remarked Jack without regard to Nora's state of being.

Nora wished she could scream but that would count against her. If Nora knew what went on in the Palace daily, it's a miracle that everyone in the building isn't screaming and throwing things all the time. Instead of screaming, the live-at-home sons of Victoria venture over to Jack's Gentleman's Club and drink themselves into a happy, forgetful stupor. With the finest cigars.

At twenty after ten, Jack and Nora were summoned and walked down a seemingly mile long hallway and stopped at a pair of twenty foot tall doors. Nora took Jack's hand and Jack looked at his younger, radiant sister, dressed most conservatively, and smiled a reassuring smile.

Both doors suddenly, loudly, opened. Two Queen's Guards, dressed in bright red jackets with two rows of highly polished buttons, which featured a Crown above a stylized VR (Victoria Regina) on each and every Royal uniform button. The details surrounding Royal appearance were
endlessly overwhelming.

One of the Guards announced, loudly, clearly: "Your Majesty, by your Command, Edward, 3rd Duke of Sussex and his sister Lady Nora Sussex."

A gentleman dressed in black, matching HM Victoria's black outfit, stood next to the seated Queen and motioned Edward and Nora forward to stand in front of Queen Victoria, who was seated on a comfortable chair which doubled as her throne. She was not wearing her small crown. She wore a black ribbon in her hair. It looked like Her Majesty had not laughed, or even smiled, in twenty years, since the untimely and unfortunate passing of her beloved husband, Consort Prince Albert.

Edward and Nora approached then stopped. Edward bowed deeply at his waist.   Nora curtseyed deeply, bowing her head and scraping her left knee on the palace's Italian marble floor.   They both came upright and stood stiffly before Her Majesty and did not speak and did not look at her.

"Edward, you look very handsome. I've heard good things about you, young man," said Queen Victoria.

"Thank you, Your Majesty, that is very kind of you, ma'am."

"And Nora, all three of my sons are quite impressed and enamored of you. They all speak highly of your expertise at the piano and with song. It's rare that all of my sons would have something nice to say about anyone in particular. You impressed all of them, especially Leopold."

Nora blushed, smiled and bowed her head.   Nora was intimidated by Her Majesty.

All Edward could do was imagine how Lindy would react to meeting the queen. He broke his daydream off because he was afraid he was going to laugh out loud. This was serious. A good interview would mean Marriage No. 1 for the family.   One out of three, thought Edward.

"Where do you worship?" was the first question asked by the Queen.

"Church of England, your Majesty," replied Nora.

"How often do you attend services?" asked HM.

"Every Sunday, ma'am," said Nora.

"Have any spirits passed your lips?" wondered HM, regarding drinking alcohol.

"Father allowed us a small glass of wine at Christmas and I drank some, ma'am."

"Is this true Edward?" wondered the Queen.

"Yes, ma'am. Each of us had a taste of wine at Christmas," confirmed Edward.

"I see. And Edward, do you smoke?" asked the Queen.

"Yes I do ma'am. A Cuban cigar on occasion," said Edward.

"I detest the tobacco habit," contributed HM.

"Do you know Wordsworth?" challenged HM to Nora.

> "I wandered lonely as a Cloud
> That floats on high o'er Vales and Hills,
> When all at once I saw a crowd
> A host of dancing Daffodils;
> Along the Lake, beneath the trees,

Ten thousand dancing in the breeze." recited Nora from memory.

"Albert and I loved Wordsworth. I made him Poet Laureate in '43. After Albert passed away, I had Mr Wordsworth over to tea regularly. He would read me some of his writings."

"Where were you educated, my dear?" wondered Her Majesty.

"Queen's College, Westminster, ma'am," replied Nora.

The Queen made a facial gesture of surprise and delight, "very good, my dear, your father, Prince Clarence, was in favour of education for women. Leopold tells me you had a well rounded education in the musical arts, English literature and poetry. Have you anything to add?"

Nora stood straighter and without reservation reported, "I was allowed to take chemistry and mathematics, ma'am. I also studied objects too small to see by using a micro-scope. And I also studied botany, the French language, and peered at the stars through a tele-scope in a course of study called astronomy."

"I must ask: of my available sons, with whom are you interested, my dear?" wondered Queen Victoria.

"I am interested in Prince Leopold, ma'am. We enjoy a mutual understanding together. We appreciate the same subjects; we have a certain rhythm and move as though we were dancing through each occasion." lilted Nora.

"Edward," began HM, "have you witnessed these two together?"

"Yes ma'am. At table, together on a riding excursion; I've seen them walking the grounds holding hands. My resultant conclusion, ma'am, is that they are happy and well-placed together. Prince Leopold has told me of his favourable feeling for my sister. Ma'am." concluded Edward.

"Very good, then. You may go." The Queen shifted her gaze from Nora to her Appointments Secretary, possibly noticing how deeply Edward and Nora bowed and curtseyed.

Each one, Edward and Nora, backed out of the room almost to the giant 20 foot doorway. Each bowed or curtseyed deeply again, turned and got the hell out of there.

CHAPTER 20

Arrest the Murderess

Sheriff Friso Van der Hoff of Larimer County, Colorado, tracing the steps of Rleen Dross from the night she shot Sheriff Ross Armitage until she vanished, had uncovered the existence of a private train that left Cheyenne at 3:33 o'clock the following afternoon. The private train made stops at Cincinnati, Ohio; Pittsburgh and Philadelphia, Pennsylvania; and ended its journey at Jersey City, New Jersey. Sheriff Van der Hoff's investigation uncovered the name of the owner of this train: William H. Vanderbilt, of New York Central Rail Road, who leased the train to Edward C. Hanover, care of Ashfield Hall, Knightsbridge Road, London, England, United Kingdom. The lease cost Edward $11,000 for two months.

Did Rleen somehow stow away on this train?

Sheriff Van der Hoff wrote Edward Hanover a letter on Sheriff's Department letterhead seeking information regarding the whereabouts of Miss Rleen Dross and described her right down to her preference of clothing—leather fringed breeches and jacket. And her mannerisms—excessive use of profane language and other unladylike behavior. And also described her black Thoroughbred colt, L.C. which was also missing but had probably 'run off'.

Sheriff Van der Hoff got this information from the New York Central Rail Road saying that Edward Clarence Hanover, of London, England, had leased a nine-car train from William 'Billy' Vanderbilt, President and owner of the New York Central. That Edward had leased a locomotive, coal tender, and nine cars for eight weeks for £2,200 ($11,500) through Billy Vanderbilt, with rights of usage on the several rail lines from New York through Cheyenne, Wyoming, and back.

When Edward received the sheriff's letter he was shocked that someone from the wild west had the brain power to figure anything out. Edward showed the letter to Lindy who suggested he burn it.

Edward called on his law firm and summoned a barrister trained in international law: the United States and Canada.

Edward presented the Sheriff's letter and explained the circumstance: 'Arlene is accused of shooting and killing a Colorado sheriff, then escaping to England'. The barrister, Sir Eberhart Hibbard St. Clair, KCB, Esq., of the law firm Withers, Hunter, St Clair, gave Edward the following advice: "If Arlene is housed in Ashfield Hall, you would best notify this county sheriff. If Miss Dross did kill the Sheriff, you are already implicated as an accessory after the fact, which is a serious crime in America, with a possible prison sentence of up to 30 years."

"Can the sheriff come here and take her to America?" wondered Edward.

"Yes, indeed. America has always had extradition with the UK, since they were part of us from the outset," stated Sir Eberhart.

"But the letter wonders have I come in contact with Arlene. Well, no! She changed her name to Lindy Long, therefore I met an entirely different person. She originally got off the train in Cincinnati."

"Are you certain that Arlene actually killed the sheriff?"

"She said she shot him while he was sitting on his porch one night."

"From what distance and what caliber weapon" asked sir Eberhart.

"She said about forty feet. She had a .32 Smith and Wesson revolver."

"She must be an excellent shot. What time of day and what were the prevailing weather conditions?" Sir Eberhart had defended several members of the nobility and gotten several of them off.

"Well, it was raining hard all day and all night. She shot him at night. After she shot him, she took off north for her home when she saw my campfire. That's how I met her."

"So there was a driving rain storm, questionable visibility, a weapon with minimal killing power, and a scared girl running away. By the way, did she shoot from her horse, or did she carefully aim from the stability of the ground?" Sir Eberhart asked a substantive question.

"I, I don't know. She said she shot the sheriff because this sheriff murdered her father—shot her father six times in the back—cold bloodily."

"Get her in here and let's go over your options. Meanwhile, I will cable the pertinent local newspapers and get copies of them from the day of the shooting forward.   Next, I will summon investigators already in America. They're in Chicago. Isn't your business partner in America?

"Yeah, Roland, Roland Betthard is in New York. He has met and repelled Lindy."

"Maybe you do not involve this Roland individual. So, Miss Arlene's new name is Lindy?"

"Make sure your man telegraphs the Larimer County Express in Fort Collins, Colorado. And the Cheyenne, Wyoming, newspaper, the Cheyenne *Daily Sun*." said Edward.

A young man, Sir Eberhart's assistant, had been taking notes during this meeting.

"Should I pack for America?" wondered Edward.

"Not yet.   My investigators will go to Colorado and interrogate the Coroner, the decedant's widow, and will discover evidence and reveal witnesses. This will take time, possibly a month or so."

"Witnesses? It was a dark and stormy night," said Edward.

Sir Eberhart was unfazed: "There is always a bloody trail of witnesses and one of them is the murderer," exclaimed Eberhart.

Edward removed his business cheque book from his leather valise. His cheque book was the size of a large art book. Edward, in his elaborate and beautiful handwriting, wrote a cheque for £10,000.00 and tore it carefully from his cheque book and handed it to Sir Eberhart who handed it to his assistant without looking at the amount on the cheque.

"The investigators in America will be on tomorrow's train out to the Colorado territory," said Sir Eberhart, adding, "bring in the girl at your earliest convenience, your royal highness."

Lindy's earliest convenience was the following week. Lindy, accompanied by Jack, arrived at Sir Eberhart's offices sporting a cheerful countenance and her newest pair of fringed raiment. In a colour best described as muted tan, or desert sand.   And a dark purple silk blouse.

Lindy was introduced by Edward as Lindy Mae Long, of Wyoming Territory. Sir Eberhart asked her what her birth name was, and Lindy said straight out, "Arlene Dross," and her address in America, "Cheyenne, Laramie County, Wyoming Territory."

Sir Eberhart asked if she were a single woman, a married woman, a mother, a student, employed outside the home, or a housewife.

Lindy said, "I'm a gambler" and stopped talking.

"You're an unmarried woman." wondered Sir Eberhart.

"Yeah. Ain't that obvious?" countered Lindy.

"What sort of games of chance do you play?" asked Sir Eberhart.

Lindy looked a question at Edward, said, "What's he talking about, Jack?"

"What do you do to make money gambling," prompted Jack.

"Horse racing and high card," said Lindy with confidence.

"Edward reminded me you rode Noble Warrior to victory at the 100th," retorted Sir Eberhart, wondering, "what is 'high card'?"

"You got a deck of cards. You cut the deck and take a card. Pass the deck around to the other players, then bet to see who's got the high card. Aces are highest, jokers are usually lowest, unless you call jokers' wild..." This was the lengthiest explanation Lindy had ever given, as witnessed by Jack.

"Is this a profitable enterprise?" asked Sir Eberhart.

"Do I make money? Hell yeah. Ask Jack. He gave me thirty thousand pounds for winning the Darby." Lindy nodded at Jack and Jack smiled and nodded back.

"Did you make money in Wyoming?" asked Sir Eberhart.

"A course. Never lost a horse race and never lost at high card."

"Are you that talented at high card?" wondered Sir Eberhart.

"Talented?" wondered Lindy.

"You say you never lost at high card. That's pretty lucky," cajoled Sir Eberhart.

"Not luck. It's skill," countered Lindy.

"Cards are a game of chance," reminded Sir Eberhart.

"No they ain't," retorted Lindy haughtily.

"How can you randomly select the highest card out of a deck, time and again, and win every time?" Sir Eberhart was dying to know her secret.

"I cheat. And that takes talent." Lindy threw up her hands and looked askance both at Jack and Sir Eberhart.

"I see," said Sir Eberhart, curtly, who then looked askance at Edward.

"Edward, whom you call 'Jack', has alerted me to a motive for your shooting at Sheriff Armitage on the night in question." began Sir Eberhart.

"I didn't shoot at 'em. I shot em! I don't miss what I shoot at." boasted Lindy.

"I'll be sure to bring that up before the jury at the trial." cautioned Sir Eberhart.

"What fuckin' trial?" threatened Lindy.

"I've dispatched investigators to prove you Not Guilty of murder. When that evidence reaches this office, we shall, all of us, venture to Colorado. We will present our findings to the court in which case, according to United States Law, and Colorado State Law, will drop any charges. You are currently a 'Person of Interest' in the demise of Ross Armitage, late Sheriff of Laramie County, Colorado."

"You think I didn't kill the sheriff?" challenged Lindy.

"I do not," answered Sir Eberhart.

"I had 'em dead to rights," proclaimed Lindy. "And by the way, Mister lawyer, it ain't Laramie County, Colorado. It's Larimer County. I live in Laramie County, Wyoming. Colorado is Larimer. Best you write that down." rectified Lindy Mae Long.

"With a 25 year old Smith & Wesson thirty-two caliber pistol whose accuracy outside of fifteen feet is dubious. Add the fact that it was dark, you were outside in a drenching downpour, with a thirty mile an hour wind, on horseback, your vision blurred by rain blinding your sight, so the chance of your hitting the man in a vital organ was severely reduced."

"The newspapers said." argued Lindy.

"The unrestrained and sensational newspaper said the sheriff was shot down in a 'hail of bullets' when, in fact, you fired one bullet at the sheriff. Stop arguing for the hangman. The real murderer is on the loose and Sir Eberhart's men will find him," concluded Jack.

"So I didn't kill him?" wondered Lindy.

"No. My lawyer is sending investigators to find out what truly happened. When they conclude that you didn't kill anybody, you'll be free and clear." stated Jack.

"I'm free now," protested Lindy, gesturing that she was in England, not Wyoming.

"You'll be officially free. Legally free.   Now, you're on the run."

"What's that mean?"

"Right now they think you killed the sheriff. *You* think you killed the sheriff.   They could come over here from Colorado and arrest you, take you back, put you on trial and if you're found guilty, you'd be hanged."

"They can come here and git me? That ain't right," protested Lindy.

"It's the law.   Murder is a crime with no time limit.   You're wanted for the rest of your life.   So our investigators will question everyone surrounding the crime.   Starting with the Sheriff's body to see if your bullet hit a vital organ.   Then the list begins with the Sheriff's wife, deputies, your father's bank robbery gang, unknown enemies, even the doctor who pronounced the sheriff dead, plus nosey neighbors." said Sir Eberhart with authority.

"Nosey neighbors?" questioned Lindy.

"That's what I wondered.   Apparently, according to these investigators, in America, your neighbors are very interested in how you live your life, and will discuss what they think they know about you with others.   So maybe the investigators will discover information from the sheriff's neighbors," said Jack, whose closest neighbor was a mile away, over a thirty foot wall and was the most powerful woman on earth. With a palace full of unmarried adult children.

"So wait.   How'd they find me in the first place?"

Jack, talking to Lindy and his lawyer reported,: "I leased the train from a business partner, you met him, Roland Betthard. He's friends with Billy Vanderbilt, of the New York Central Rail Road. The record of the train at Cheyenne brought the Colorado Sheriff to me.   Your mother provided the rest of the information—your real name and the fact that you went missing the day after the shooting. And the sheriff's got your .32 caliber revolver."

"My mother snitched on me?   Maybe I need to shoot someone else." Lindy said that cold bloodedly.   It gave Jack the shivers.

"You ain't gonna turn me in, are you?" said Lindy in a threatening and worried way.

"I'm doing everything to prove you're innocence. If someone comes all the way here from the American west, you'll be safe here. I've got two other homes in the west country.   They'll never find you." said Jack.

"So they won't take me back in irons.?" asked Lindy, needing assurances.

"No," said Jack with finality.

"So why snoop around?" wondered Lindy, "If I'm not going back, why stir up trouble?"

"Because the odds you killed the sheriff are slim and when the investigators turn up proof of your innocence then my lawyer will go to Colorado to show the evidence and clear your name, officially, so no one will come looking for you ever again.   If you need to go home for any reason, you can return without a bounty on your head."

"I ain't going back," concluded Lindy.

"You won't have to," speculated Jack, trying to sound certain, as though his royal title would mean anything.

CHAPTER 21

Do You Wish To Be A Governess?

Sisters Elsie and Harriet were having breakfast with their mother. Nobody in or near this room was happy. It was dark and raining outside and dark and disappointing inside. Mother Agatha was distraught and angry. Her two unwed daughters were distraught and suicidal.

"Is that what you want? To be governesses? Teaching slobbering children who can't pay attention for two seconds? Guiding them on trips to the British Museum until you scream in horror? I've had it with you two." reported Countess Agatha, constantly aware that she used to be Your Royal Highness Duchess Agatha. "A lowly god-damned countess! Since when am I a bloody peasant!?" she'd mutter several times a day and night since she was downgraded by Her Majesty the Queen.

"Mother," said elder daughter Elsie, "we've followed your advice to the letter; we've done as you have instructed and we're still…" She didn't have to complete the awful thought.

"We were getting on with Alfred and Arthur quite well when you told us to stop," said Harriet, filled with angst and anger. "Nora ploughed ahead with Leo, always there, always with him, and she's engaged! She's planning the wedding!," continued Harriet.

"I told you to stop fawning over those boys lest they bed you before they wed you," threatened Agatha whose scheming guaranteed her daughters would remain unwed and unsoiled.

"Nora rejected your reasoned instruction for capturing a proper husband when that American girl Edward dragged here spoke to us about getting a man's attention." said Harriet, not giving up with Lindy's focused instruction to smile, charm, tell your man how important he is until you seal the deal, then return to normal.

"Yes, she took us to Harrods and bought Nora brightly coloured dresses and told us to smile more. Harriet and I, of course, rejected those dresses at once."

"And I told you to return those garments immediately because they made the wearer look like a harlot or a street urchin." countered the mostly-angry and always scheming Agatha, Countess.

Harriet got up, threw down her high thread count Irish linen napkin and swiftly exited the South Breakfast Room. Their one servant, a second or third Footman, opened the door to let Harriet pass.

Harriet went looking for the Wyoming girl and found her grooming Crazy Horse, her black Thoroughbred, by the stables.

Lindy took one look at Harriet and read the concern on her face, which caused Lindy to say, "Y'all ready to go back to Harrod's for duds to seal the deal?"

HARRODS SEAL THE DEAL DEPARTMENT.

Lindy: "It ain't just your dress. It's your attitude: King of the Hill.

Harriet, "You mean confidence?"

Elsie, "How'd you feel when Edward, er, Jack, asked you to ride Noble Warrior?"

Lindy, "I'd win!"

Elsie and Harriet couldn't help but swoon when they saw the victorious expression on Lindy's face. Her shoulders back, standing tall, immutable attitude told the girls that Lindy was an unstoppable force.

Elsie, now dressed in a red silk ballgown was trying to strut her stuff. Harriet had on an all dark purple ball gown, showing a lot of milky white shoulder. She, too, was trying to copy Lindy, in her trademark tight black leather jeans with lots of fringe, how to 'shake it'.   The salesman (a male of course) couldn't take his eyes off Lindy's ass in her too tight leather pants, which was disturbing to Elsie and Harriet.

Lindy grabbed the drooling salesman by the arm and offered him some advice. She took out a £10 note and gave it to the salesman and commanded, "Go out there and stare at them two girls like you want to marry them. And I see you staring at my ass I'll throw you down them fuckin' stairs. Got me?"

The 25 year old salesman 'got' Lindy and put the ten spot in his pocket. Ten Pounds was much more than his monthly salary, so he really got her.

Lindy strutted around with attitude. The sisters followed her. The salesman stared at the sisters, smiled and even applauded.

"Walk tall girls. Walk like you're the Queen. Walk tall your majesty!" ordered Lindy of Elsie, whose ballgown worked a miracle: it looked like Elsie had shed 30 pounds. (Lindy was unaware of the power of a tight, constricting internal organ rearranging corset.)

Elsie could hardly breathe, but when she saw herself in the full length mirror, she didn't recognize herself. She thought some skinny bitch was standing in front of her. That skinny bitch was Elsie.

The 25 year old salesman was drooling over Elsie. Lindy could tell he wasn't pretending because the guy couldn't keep his hands off her. Pretending to 'fit' her dress in several places across her voluptuous body. Lindy caught the eye of the salesman and she nodded her approval.

Harriet, not needing that tight of a corset, got one anyway. She how had a 25 inch waist. Harriet looked, well, according to Lindy: "You look very fuckable."

With their corsets in place, Elsie and Harriet were fitted with a dozen more dresses that highlighted waist and cleavage. Lots of bare shoulders and revealing backs. Long, swanlike necks.

"Very fuckable, indeed," approved Lindy, who handed the salesman a £100 bill for his tip.

CHAPTER 22

Jack Meets Baby

Edward, Third Duke of Sussex, Nephew to Her Majesty Victoria, Queen of the United Kingdom of Great Britain and Ireland, Empress of India, and mother of Prince Leopold, was Commanded by Her Majesty to show up at Buckingham Palace to meet and discuss the upcoming marriage of Leopold to Edward's youngest sister Nora, aged 24.

Leopold's fiancee, Nora, was approved by HM.   Next step, the Wedding.   This also needed approval by the Queen and the bride's father or guardian. Edward was deemed old enough and royal enough to provide those services as Lady Nora's Guardian.

Leopold was shy and therefore would love to elope. There will be no elopement whilst Victoria sits on the Throne of the British Empire.

Being escorted to the Queen's Chambers, Jack ran into Leopold and Arthur and their younger sister Princess Beatrice. Jack had never met any of Her Majesty's daughters. He wasn't interested in them. He was interested in smoking good cigars and drinking vintage port and telling stories one couldn't tell in mixed company. Stories teenaged boys heard, then mis-told, at their preparatory academies.

Edward smiled as he patted Leopold on the arm.   "I'm supposed to say something good about Nora, why she's good enough to be your wife. And I can't think of a thing!" joked Edward. Arthur laughed more than Leopold.

"And you are.?" wondered Princess Beatrice.

"Edward, your Royal Highness, your next door neighbor."

"Eddie lives in the house on the other side of the West Gate," chortled Arthur.   The daughters of Victoria had heard of their brothers piling into a Royal carriage and driving themselves next door for hours of fun, to get away from their mum, dressed in black, and who pandered and demanded consolement.   That's the job of daughters.

"So you are the cause of my brothers' drunkenness?" interrogated young Beatrice.

"Yes I am," boasted Edward with a great deal of pride.

"I heard there is a lewd and wild female amongst this troupe." griped Beatrice.

"Yes. Lindy. She dresses as she pleases. She says what she pleases. And she shoots people who displease her. She's from Wyoming, carries a six-gun, wears leather fringed breeches and does not ride side-saddle. She rode Noble Warrior to victory at the 100th," replied Edward as though he were reading Lindy's Curriculum Vitae.

"And she drank us all under the table!" hooted Arthur.

"Arthur's in love. Forbidden fruit," chirped Leopold.

"Mum would never approve her," said Arthur, saddened.

"Does mum have to approve your wife?" asked Beatrice of Edward.

"Yes, unfortunately, unless I return to America where I am out of the reach of Royal Proclamations, Duties, Obligations and the Royal Marriages Act."

"Can I come to one of your drinking parties?" wondred Beatrice. "I'm 24."

Edward looked to Arthur and Leopold, "You want your sister drinking with us? She's liable to tell Her Majesty and ruin it for all of you," threatened Edward.

"You think I like being locked up in this dreadful prison all my life?" complained Beatrice.

"Yes!!" said Arthur and Leopold simultaneously. "You tell mum you'll not get married and will be with her forever! You say it each night at dinner. It makes her feel wanted. You're a great, soothing agent, Bea," argued Arthur.

A well-dressed Dragoon, in uniform, approached Edward, bowed gracefully, as he must dozens of times a day, and issued Edward into the Queen's chambers.

Edward looked at Leopold and nodded in the affirmative, then nodded at Arthur and even gave Beatrice a nod before he disappeared into the Dungeon of Hell, so called by all Victoria's sons.

Beatrice, ruffled, threatened her two brothers, "I'm coming to your next drinking party."

CHAPTER 23

Red Thunder

Albert, Prince of Wales, Princes Alfred, Arthur, Leopold; Edward, Third Duke of Sussex, and Lindy, Duchess of Wyoming Territory, were all seated in their very comfortable overstuffed chairs covered in rich, butter-soft oxblood leather. And so, too, was Princess Beatrice.

The boys, and Lindy, were puffing their individual selections of the several Cuban cigar manufacturers. Around the large four inch thick, highly polished Honduran mahogany table there were several selections of Scotch whisky, Jack Daniels American whiskey and vintage port bottles. There was also a selection of ice cold lemonade, French and Italian carbonated water, African coffees, plus fresh-baked pastries, cakes and even tropical fruit. All provided by Jack, the host.

Jack understood Customer Service. He made his Gentleman's Club the place to be. Convenient, private, and the best bar in town— or the world, because it was free!

Jack's Aunt Fanny, who used to live in Ashfield Hall, now a former Royal Duchess, spent money almost as fast as it came in. To keep her husband happy, and drunk, Duchess Fanny bought cases of French wine, Portuguese Port, the finest of Scotland's Scotch and the Prince of Wales's favored Cuban cigars.

Albert, Prince of Wales, elder statesman and future King, looked a question at his baby sister, then announced, "If it pleases our Host and Hostess, the Royal Duke and American Duchess, may I present our sister, Beatrice. I heard that she is eager to join this group because she believes she can keep up with everyone. Everyone except our American Duchess, Lady Lindy from the great American territory of Wyoming."

There is applause. Even from Lindy.

"If y'all need help lightin' y'alls cigars, Leo will oblige you," offered Lindy to Princess Beatrice.

Beatrice smiled coyly, grabbed an H. Upmann cigar and a cigar cutter and cut off the mouth end like she'd been smoking since she was thirteen. She had. Leopold offered her a candle to light her Cuban cigar and Princess Beatrice sat back and blew blue-grey smoke into the mahogany panelled, richly carpeted room's atmosphere with a 12 foot ceiling. She smiled. No mother or Palace spy to tell on her. She was amongst confidants.

By the way, the last thing Beatrice said to brother Arthur this evening upon entering the royal carriage to come over from Buckingham was, "I'm gonna meet my husband tonight."

Prince Arthur looked oddly at Beatrice and uttered, "You haven't seen Lady Lindy have you. Otherwise you won't find your husband at Edwardo's."

"We'll see about that," countered Princess Beatrice, the only daughter of Queen Victoria who was not yet married. Or was even being courted, because the Queen did not want her youngest daughter, whom the Queen called Baby, married and running off, leaving Victoria 'abandoned' and all alone. HM Victoria having no husband, greatly feared all her children leaving home, abandoning the Queen, causing her to live by herself in an 'empty' 829,000 square foot palace.

Currently, all correspondence from prospective gentlemen callers was intercepted by the Queen's personal secretary (called an Equerry) diminishing Beatrice's chances of being courted. Assuring that HM would have the precious company of the young Princess Beatrice Mary Victoria Feodore all to herself.

Albert, Prince of Wales, asked Beatrice, "Are you old enough to be here?"

"I'm 24, Bertie. Does Alix know where you are?" taunted Beatrice speaking of Alexandra, Princess of Wales, and mother of Bertie's five children.

Beatrice knew of Prince Albert's liaisons with many (56) other women. Alix (Princess Alexandra of Denmark) was aware of these affairs and shrugged them off. Albert was very fat and Alix did not want a 'giant wildebeest' lying atop her. Besides, she had five children. An heir and four spares. Alix was done with sex; a great relief.

The brothers burst out laughing at Beatrice's impetuous response. Everyone in the Kingdom knew about Bertie's infidelity. He bragged about it in places like Jack's Gentleman's Club.

Beatrice blew smoke Bertie's way then took a sip of very old Scotch (1819 Balblair single malt), leaned back in her overstuffed, wonderfully comfortable wingback chair and smirked. Alix was home with her girlfriends playing cards and having a wonderful time without him. And his tedious stories.

"Always leave it to a girl to liven things up," said Lindy regarding Beatrice.

"The rumour around Bucky is that your sisters are supposed to marry my brothers," said Beatrice to Jack, revealing that Buckingham Palace had cute nicknames given by Her Majesty's issue.

"My mother cooked up plans for my sisters years ago. My father was supposed to inherit this house and title and mother would insinuate herself into Buckingham and drag my sisters with her." remarked Jack.

"And you, young lady," shot Beatrice, "Are you a real Duchess?"

"Might be. Maw calls me Duchess cause she says I hold my nose too high in the air."

"Your 'maw' certainly knows duchesses," jolted Beatrice, a Royal Princess who easily looks down on duchesses. And every other rank, file and position of nobility. The immediate Royal Family is the only place to be, was understood by all present.

The two young ladies were eyeballing each other closely. Neither blinked.

Albert (Bertie), Prince of Wales, always on guard to start trouble, got the ball rolling when he said, "Edwardo has failed to marry, lo these many years."

"You're not soft on Edward, Lindy?   He's a royal Duke. Thought you might be mated, cause of the Duchess thing." queried Beatrice.

"Jack came to Wyoming Territory at the right time and offered me an avenue of escape," said Lindy, sitting three chairs away from Jack and not next to him, or the other men.

"Why's she calling you Jack?" wondered Beatrice.

"Because he looks like a Jack," said Arthur and Leopold in unison.

Never missing an opportunity to start a brawl, Princess Beatrice glared at Lindy and dared: "What do I look like?"

Lindy studied Beatrice's face, blew Cuban smoke skyward and announced:

"Shappa suits you. Shappa is a Lakota Injun name for a strong woman full of sass, spit and snake venom. Shappa means Red Thunder. I name you Red Thunder." Lindy nodded.

Beatrice, expecting something insulting, thought about 'spit and snake venom' and 'Red Thunder', decided it was a magnificent complement, stood up and whooped like an Indian. "I am Red Thunder!"

"Red Thunder? No, no, no. Baby's already a handful!" cried Arthur, revealing Beatrice's nickname, by her mother, the Queen.

Red Thunder came to life. She whooped, stood up with her Waterford crystal glass of Scotch and declared, "I am Red Thunder, damn you all to Hell!"

Red Thunder walked around the beautiful mahogany table and gave Lindy a hug. The two clinked crystal barware and shouted "Red Thunder!"

The boys looked at one another and wondered what the hell just happened? We lost our private Gentlemen's Club.

"What about us? Have you monikers for us?" demanded Albert, Prince of Wales.

"If them's names, a'course I do."

"I am Red Thunder, you pathetic commoners!" cried Princess Red Thunder. Red Thunder fit Beatrice like a custom made outfit. It was though this girl from the wild American west, reached into Beatrice's soul and gave it a name.

Lindy pointed and called out their new names: "Y'alls Tex or Texas (Albert), Y'alls Buck (Arthur), we need a Bronco (Alfred) and y'alls Billy the Kid (Leopold), and a course, Ol' Jack here, y'alls Jack," concluded Lindy Mae Long, Duchess of Wyoming.

As the two ladies were celebrating Princess Red Thunder's new name, from across the table one of her brothers offered a toast: "Thanks to our beloved Duchess of Wyoming, from this day forward, my name is Tex!" announced Tex, Prince of Wales and Texas.

"You're about the size of Texas," hooted Arthur (Buck).

"You mean Tex-ass!" chortled Alfred (Bronco).

The gathering quickly elevated into a loud party and the party got livelier, thanks to the only non-royal, non-Brit, non-sheriff shooter in the room. Tex & Buck & Bronco & Billy the Kid & Jack & Red Thunder were out of their chairs, dancing around the room hooting their new names.

Lindy leaned back in her chair and put her feet—with moccasins—on the 150 year old four inch thick, forty-nine inch wide, fourteen foot long oval mahogany table, cut from the mahogany forests of Honduras, between the Hondo and Belize Rivers, in 1753.

Lindy smiled, puffed and sipped looking at these dancing fools—the future King and the Ruling class of the United Kingdom, Great Britain and half of the rest of the World.

During the naming festivities, Red Thunder sat down next to Lindy and congratulated her on winning the 100th Running of the Epsom Derby.

Lindy thanked Princess Thunder, adding, "Let's go riding tomorrow, I've got my pony here from Wyoming."

Red Thunder loved the idea and gave Lindy a kiss on the cheek.

CHAPTER 24

Yee-Ha!

Red Thunder rode a beautiful black Hanovarian Thoroughbred mare through the gate connecting Buckingham Palace with Ashfield Hall. Lindy, on Crazy Horse, saw her and rode over. Lindy, dressed in black leather with fringe rode up to Red Thunder who was delightfully dressed in red. Red Thunder was riding side-saddle. Lindy stared at the Princess and wondered where her legs were. Red Thunder stared at Lindy and said, "Have you another pair of leather pants for me?"

Half an hour later, both ladies, dressed in tight leather pants with fringe were riding full gallop on the mile long and mile wide lawns of Ashfield Hall. There were no mothers available to cast disapproval upon them.

Red Thunder and Lindy ended up at Jack's stables where his Thoroughbreds were. And where Crazy Horse and Noble Warrior were in stalls next to each other. Also, where Lindy had a bed for herself and a simple pine table upon which to dine. And be with her ponies, as she called them.

Red Thunder was relieved to see that Lindy was sleeping by herself and not Jack.

"What's it like growing up in that palace?"

"I wish I could escape," admitted Red Thunder.

"You mean jump on a train and be somewheres else?" taunted Lindy.

"Yes!" said a delighted Red Thunder. "Only…only they'd find me and drag me back."

"But you're a princess; you git to do what you want.?" wondered Lindy.

Red Thunder laughed out loud. "Wow, where'd you hear that shit? In a faerie tale?"

"A course." Lindy reacted favorably to Princess Beatrice swearing.

"Do you take naps out here?" said Red Thunder, looking at the made bed, table and one chair.

"I spend weeks out here with my ponies. Jack's and mine. My paw says cavalry soldiers 'marries' their horse. I thought he meant they fuck them, but nah, it's like they become kin. So I wash them, brush them, comb them, check their hooves. And bed down with them. Makes me feel good," reported Lindy.

"Your horse ever throw you?" wondered Red Thunder.

"Yeah, when I first got to know her. Then I took care of her every day, slept in the barn every night. Never got throw'd again."

"What's your father do? He raise Thoroughbreds?"

"Paw used to rob banks."

Beatrice laughed, "Bertie—shit—I mean Tex—says all bankers rob their customers."

"Paw tweren't no banker. He was a bank robber. And the fuckin' sheriff gunned him down in the street," reported Lindy, "shot him dead."

Beatrice looked horrified. "Is this true? It sounds like a wild west story, Lindy."

"Well, nobody was doin' nothing about it, so I shot the sheriff, then jumped on a train to get outta town, and that was Jack's train. And here I am."

"And you had the wherewithal to take Crazy Horse! I'm impressed."

"I'd never leave Crazy Horse behind. I spotted Jack's carriage being put on a train car so I put Crazy Horse in the same car. Asked some stiff where Jack was and I met him in the bar. Next thing you know, here I am."

"Are you still a virgin?" wondered Red Thunder.

"Did we fuck? No. He ain't interested," said Lindy.

Beatrice seemed satisfied with that answer.

"Shall we have tea?" quipped Red Thunder.

"Your place or mine?"

"Yours, of course. Mine's crowded with my mum."

Red Thunder and Lindy walked over to the big house where they were served tea and pastries in a comfortable drawing room not far from the kitchen.

CHAPTER 25

Mother and Daughter Have Tea

Beatrice (Red Thunder) was invited to Tea by her Mother. Beatrice begged off, again, because she had more important things to do. She was palling around with Lindy, who was teaching Red Thunder how to groom and take care of her Thoroughbred horse, Major-General, named after the featured song in Gilbert & Sullivan's 1879 hit play Pirates of Penzance.

The Queen's plans for Beatrice were to be the Queen's personal secretary. And confidant. Which is what Beatrice was doing until she got a whiff of what went on at Ashfield Hall, beginning in June when came back from America. Suddenly, Beatrice's brothers went riding off sober in a 'borrowed' carriage after dinners, and coming home drunk, happy and smelling of finely aged brandy and cigar smoke. Red Thunder wanted in.

No one at Buckingham Palace was allowed to be drunk and happy. Or sober and happy. Happy was out of the question since Consort Prince Albert died in December of 1861, of typhoid fever.

The unmarried brothers, Alfred, Arthur and Leopold (about to be married in October), were suddenly full of life since Edward inherited Ashfield Hall. And immediately invited Albert, Prince of Wales, and his brothers over for dinner, just the gentlemen of course, where they sat at table in the family dining room and carried on. They adjourned to the Gentleman's Room as soon as Edward was told by his Butler that such a room existed.

Beatrice tried to weasel her way into Ashfield Hall and it took until June, when she hornswaggled Edward as he was wandering around Buckingham Palace waiting to meet with the Queen. Red Thunder's entanglement with Edward was more beneficial to Red Thunder, of course.

Life had not only changed dramatically for Beatrice, it had improved exponentially. Red Thunder was born and her new best friend was Lindy Mae Long from way the hell out in the wild American West in a land called Wyoming. "What's the difference between a territory and a state?" wondered Red Thunder.

"You get a star on the flag when you're a state. Other'un that, I ain't got no idea," said Lindy.

Beatrice was corralled by several of her mother's chambermaids today and brought into the Queen's small dining room. Nothing fancy. An ordinary unvarnished plain pine table, pine chairs, ordinary cutlery, dishes and teacups. The chef prepared an easy-to-digest light tea. Tea with pastries, petite-fours, and the usual scones slathered with clotted cream from Devonshire, where HM had several dairy farms.

There were only two chairs at the table. The window looked out onto the courtyard three stories below, and not the beautiful, intricate gardens out front.

"Good afternoon, Baby," said the Queen.

"Mum." Beatrice then stood at attention, curtsied, and said, "Your Majesty." All Subjects show respect for the Sovereign, even if she's your suffocating mother and you are her insufferable youngest daughter.

"Where have you been and what have you been up to. You're never about." interrogated Her Majesty.

"I've got a new friend. She's lively. She rides, in fact, you know of her. She rode Edward's horse to win the Derby at Surrey."

"She? **She** rode Noble Warrior?" The Queen kept up with horse racing. Her son, Albert, Prince of Wales, the son who killed her beloved husband, Consort Prince Albert, had entered three year olds in the Epsom Derby several times, to no avail. Yet.

"She's quite stimulating," said Beatrice very perkily.

The Butler arrived and behind him were several kitchen staff who simultaneously poured tea, placed a basket of scones, a plate of delicate French and Viennese pastries, and left. The Butler remained to see whether Her Majesty or Princess Beatrice required anything else. Otherwise, tea had been served. Simple, tasty, hot, fresh brewed and fresh baked.

The Queen nodded and Mr. Harrison, the Butler, bowed then backed out of the room.

"I don't like your ambling about. You have duties you've been ignoring. Letters and other correspondence need writing, posting, filing. The Government doesn't stop because you want to play with a new friend. I don't like you going out on your own and not telling me where you are."

Her Majesty was distraught at Beatrice's irresponsible actions.

"Hire an assistant, mummy. They're plenty in London. I am finally having fun!" cried Beatrice.

"Fun? You're a member of the Royal Family. You have responsibilities and your first responsibility is to the Queen. I am your Queen first. Your mother second. And the Queen needs you by her side, not galavanting about the realm with someone other than the Queen."

"And I'm off to have fun with Lindy. Your Majesty. I may stay at her house tonight if you don't stop nagging me. And I'm going to marry Edward—his sister is marrying Leo in a couple of months. If I marry Edward, I'll live next door and I can come visit you anytime," said Red Thunder, who isn't a Baby, but a grown woman on a serious mission with an acid tongue.

Red Thunder got up, curtsied to her mother, very deeply and theatrically, then backed out of the small room (no one ever turns one's back on The Empire) then ran down the hallway and changed into her riding tight leather fringed riding pants, hopped on her black Thoroughbred Major-General, and rode out the west gate of Buckingham Palace onto the grounds of Ashfield Hall.
Red Thunder was on the move.

CHAPTER 26

Red Thunder invites Jack to Tea

Red Thunder was now spending a lot of time away from the Palace grounds, over at Jack's place. Mostly riding with Lindy. Her best times were at the Gentleman's Club. Smoking and drinking were forbidden by Her Majesty, even though the Queen was introduced to scotch by John Brown, a servant who took the Queen horseback riding and paid 'too much attention' to Her Majesty, according to jealous royals and house staff. Some of whom referred to HM as 'Mrs Brown.'

Red Thunder began dressing in tight red leather trousers to ride Major-General 'like a man', and headed off to ride with Lindy on the 640 acre (a mile square) grounds of Ashfield Hall.

Two days ago Red Thunder handed Lindy a sealed envelope to give to Jack. Lindy did so.

Mid-day was when Her Majesty would take long walks through the hallways of the Palace for exercise and to 'check on everyone' to see what her staff were doing during the day.

Today, Jack was invited to tea by Red Thunder at Bucky, at Mid-day.

Jack arrived and followed a palace Usher down the long hallways until he arrived at a small dining room set aside for the Queen's children. The term 'small' was set to palace standards. The room itself was forty feet by forty feet by forty feet high. There were two fireplaces opposite one another. The walls were painted a deep red with arctic white trim, and covered with paintings of the royal children, dating back to the portraits of the 9 children of William I, the Conqueror, around the year 1080, or 800 years ago.

The palace Usher, wearing a bright red tail-coat, advanced to the set tea table, pulled out a comfortable-looking chair and waited for Jack to stop staring around the room and take a seat.
Jack thanked the Usher who turned and left the room.

The table was set for two. There was no food or beverage in sight. Not a bread stick, not a glass of London's finest tap water.

A couple of minutes later, Princess Beatrice entered, wearing bright red and a huge smile. Jack arose and bowed his head—they were cousins yet Beatrice outranked him. Beatrice offered her delicate hand, Jack kissed it. Jack pulled out Beatrice's chair, seated her and himself.

Within seconds two chef's aides (waiters) appeared with a bounty of pastries, sandwiches, and tea.

Jack was searching for something nice to say when Beatrice announced: "I wanted to thank you for inviting me to your drinking club."

"You are a noteworthy addition to our Gentleman's club, Beatrice." is all Jack could produce. Stiffly but sincerely. He sounded like the Clerk of the Green Cloth calling a Board meeting to order.

"Beatrice is no longer my name, Jack." offering her only hint before she kicked Jack out of her house.

"My apologies, Red Thunder" said Jack.

"I've been riding with Lindy; she's pretty good." said Red Thunder, cooly.

"She won the 100th," reminded Jack, about the 100th time he's reminded everyone of Lindy's victory.

"That's right, Jack, Noble Warrior was your three year old."

"Bertie had a horse in the race and finished fourth, Desert Orchid," mentioned Jack.

"That's cause his name is Desert Orchid. Sounds like a foppish Bedoin who'd rather fuck boy horses," reported the very raw and raunchy Baby. Jack wasn't used to girls cursing like sailors. Now he knows two by name.

"Yeah, you certainly have been spending a lot of time around Lindy," quipped Jack.

"Why doesn't Lindy have a nickname?" wondered Red Thunder.

"She does: Duchess."

"So why don't you call her Duchess?" wondered Red Thunder.

"Actually, Lindy is her nickname. Her real name is Arlene. She had to change it when she left town." gossiped Jack.

"What'd she do, shoot someone?" laughed Red Thunder.

"Actually, yes. But I don't think she killed him," offered Jack.

Jack was about to explain the shooting when the children's dining room door opened and a man announced distinctively: "Her Majesty."

Into the room clomped five feet tall Queen Victoria dressed in her usual black.

Jack immediately stood up, faced Her Majesty and orchestrated a deep bow-at-the-waist without speaking. One doesn't speak to a Sovereign until the Sovereign recognizes her subject.

"Baby, why didn't you tell me you were having tea," announced the Queen of the United Kingdom and Empress of India and absolute ruler of a lot of other countries, territories and islands.

"I wanted to thank Edward for being of service to me on several occasions. And for introducing me to a wonderful young American woman. We go riding together, she and I."

"You look familiar. Do I know you, sir?" asked the Queen.

"Your Majesty, I am Edward, third Duke of Sussex of Ashfield Hall. I presented my sister, Lady Nora, to your Majesty a fortnight ago, regarding the wedding to His Royal Highness, Prince Leopold.

"Do you entertain my sons, on occasion, at your house?" prodded the Queen.

"Yes, ma'am."

"Do they drink wines and brandies?"

"Yes ma'am."

Do they smoke?"

"Yes ma'am."

"What in the name of God do they smoke?

"Cuban cigars, ma'am."

"Do you smoke and drink?"

"Of course, ma'am."

"Where do you accomplish this sordid, distasteful thing?"

"I have a room I call the Gentleman's Club. Ma'am."

"I'll bet you do," said Queen Victoria with attitude.

"Did you arrange this tet-a-tet?" accused Victoria of Edward regarding this tea.

"No, ma'am. I would have had the Princess come to my house."

"For what purpose?"

"Well, for starters, to avoid any interruptions, Ma'am."

Beatrice broke out laughing and couldn't stop. She needed a glass of water to calm down.

"Mother, that's why your sons, especially Albert, go to Jack's house. To get way from you so they can smoke and drink and laugh!"

"Is that true?"

"Boys need to get away from domineering women and secret ourselves away to enjoy the simple pleasures of manhood. Your Majesty," reported Edward, full of vim.

"How'd you meet Baby?" said the Queen looking only at Beatrice.

"I was summoned by Your Majesty to help select a location for the wedding of Prince Leopold and Lady Nora when I ran into Prince Arthur and Princess Beatrice in the hallway outside your offices," testified Edward.

"Were you and Arthur listening at my door?" wondered the Queen to Beatrice.

"Well, sure. Wouldn't you?   Then I saw Jack and I pounced on him!" gloated Red Thunder.

"Now who's this 'Jack'?"

"Edward here. I call him Jack and he calls me Red Thunder."

"Red Thunder? How awful. Sounds like the name of one of Bertie's horses," announced Victoria.

"Where did you come up with the name 'Red Thunder'?" continued Victoria.

"One of the members of our club suggested Red Thunder, it's from the Lakota Sioux Indian language in Western America, ma'am." offered Edward.

"It sounds dangerous.   I don't like it.   I like Baby," pronounced Victoria.   "But I assume I'm powerless to stop you, Baby."

"Completely powerless, mother," asserted Red Thunder.

"Is that why you dress in that awful red?"

"Yes, mum."

"Do you have designs on Baby, Edward?"

"No, ma'am.   Her Royal Highness is very nice to be with, I enjoy her company," said Edward.

"I don't want her married, do you understand?" announced Victoria, looking at both of them.

"I'll marry whom I choose, mother."

"What about you. Baby will need my approval to marry and she isn't getting it. You'll have to wait til I'm dead and buried to be betrothed. Do you understand me, Baby?"

"Yeah. Sure."

"And you, Edward?"

"Yes Your Majesty, I understand thoroughly, ma'am."

"Well, then, good-day. Those are an awful lot of pastries, Baby. You'll get fat, like Albert. Here, Edward, you look like you could put on some weight. Take these to your house before they get stale," retorted the Queen as she clomped out to continue her hall monitoring.

"Thank you, your Majesty," said Edward bowing deeply and theatrically.

A House Guard opened and closed the children's dining room door leaving Jack and Red Thunder alone.

"Mother just told you to fuck off," said Beatrice with a smile.

"Well, thank you for tea, Princess Red Thunder."

"And you can thank mum for throwing cold water on our supposed marriage. You do want to marry me?" wondered Red Thunder.

"We just met, your Royal Highness." cautioned Edward.

"Answer me one question and do not lie: have you fucked Lindy?"

"No."

"But you want to.?"

"Of course!" pronounced Edward.

"Now get out!" said Red Thunder, semi-kiddingly.

Edward bowed toward Red Thunder.

Beatrice walked over to Edward, grabbed him by his jacket's lapels, jerked him towards her, then kissed him deeply, slipping the tip of her tongue until it tickled Edward's tongue. No one had ever accosted Edward like that before. He loved it and wanted more.

"That's what I think of you, Jack. I'll be over for dinner tomorrow night. Know what we're having?"

Jack shrugged and suggested: "Tongue?"

"Don't be vulgar." said Red Thunder as she stuck her tongue out and flapped it creating a promiscuous gesture.

Edward, holding a tray of pastries, somehow managed not to spill them, smiled, turned and walked down the hallway hoping he might quickly exit the 829,000 square foot palace without further incident.

CHAPTER 27

Alfred and Elsie's Wedding Plans

Victoria, Queen of the most powerful, most globally situated, wealthiest, most feared Empire on earth, was in a frightful tizzy.

Out of the blue her favourite son, Prince Alfred, had asked Lady Elsie to marry him. So far Edward's mother's plan to marry all three daughters to the three unmarried sons of HM Victoria were on track. Things were unfolding fast at Buckingham Palace. Plans for the marriage of Prince Leopold and Lady Nora were finalized. Now suddenly a second wedding. St George's Chapel, at Windsor Castle, was booked for Prince Leopold and Lady Nora's wedding in October. The Royal wedding planner was in a fury for Victoria's second son's (Prince Alfred) wedding. The Holidays were fast arriving and the Royal Event Calendar was filling up fast.

However, something came to light that might eliminate the problem of future wedding date trauma:

Today, HM needed to see her second son, Alfred, posthaste. No one had seen him. Victoria told her staff to "look for Alfred in all his hiding places. I know you know where they all are. Fetch him."

Victoria watched her menservants bow in unison and back out of her room. As soon as they closed the door she opened her secret compartment, took out a bottle of Macallan Scotch (1855), poured herself a steadying shot, and knocked one back. She poured another.

Not long after that, Prince Alfred showed up, smiling and sunny. He walked up to his mum, kissed her on each cheek, took three steps back and bowed deeply and respectfully to HM, Queen of half the globe, saying sincerely, "Your Majesty."

Alfred's mother got right to the point:

"The Royal Physician, Dr. James J. Thomson, informed me that your fiancee, Lady Elsie of Sussex, is with child."

Alfred, second son of Victoria, stood there as though his mother just gave a report on today's weather. Sunny and happy. Alfred rarely paid attention when an adult was speaking, and this annoyed the Queen very much.

"Dr Thomson reports that you are definitely the father!" j'accused Her Majesty.

Alfred's cheery disposition then changed to one of disbelief, anger, disappointment and regret. He began looking for an exit. There weren't any.

"Thus, your nuptials shall be moved up to a few weeks from today because the poor girl shall start to show," calculated Her Majesty.

"A few weeks?!" retorted a stunned, shocked spare-to-the-throne.

"Your future wife reported to Dr Thomson, who examined her, that this untidiness we are experiencing was brought about by The Bottle and your drunkeness."

"Mummy, I'm sorry. I really am. I did not intend for this to happen." pled Alfred.

"We are the Royal Family and everything we do is examined and scrutinized maniacally by those horrid news-papers. And the blame will always fall upon Me. Parliament will be in an uproar. Gladstone will be all over the press saying how can I be the Queen and Empress of half the world when I can't even reign in my own family. And what do I tell him? That my second son has also abandoned morality? I am the head of the Church! Does not the sacredness of the Church of England mean anything to you?"

"The wedding of Leopold and what's-her-name is the bigger wedding. You're right to hide Elsie and my wedding under the carpet. We'll marry at Osborne House!" suggested Alfred, a brilliant boy whose brilliance will never be known, as the profligate Albert, Prince of Wales, will become king, always in the lime light, with and without his stable of whores.

"Bring your fiancee to me this week so we can now decide on a date and whereabouts of your wedding. And the two of you come up with a reason for this immediate consummation of vows. A reason that even the *Daily Telegraph* readers will understand!" ordered Her Majesty.

The wedding of Prince Alfred and his pregnant fiancee, Lady Elsie of Sussex, happened so quickly, so privately, so invisibly, that word around town was that Lady Elsie must be with child. And that word was supplied by many of the Palace's servants, the loose-lipped Princess Beatrice and the more powerful Alexandra, Princess of Wales, who sang to the news-papers to distract *The Times* and nine other news-papers from her husband's, Albert, Prince of Wales' incessant, non-stop philandering.   Alexandra (Alix to her husband and dear friends) mentioned, regarding Albert's philandering, that at least she knows where her husband is—lying atop his differing nightly filly with his 22 crushing stone (308 lbs) of weight.   Thank God he's not lying atop me!"

The agonizing weight of Royalty.   Few subjects of Victoria were sure how many offspring the Prince of Wales had spawned.   So when mention of the wedding of Alfred to someone he impregnated, was hidden in a small column on the Social Pages and not the Royal Report on the front page, for a bribe, meaning a medal of the Most Excellent Order of the British Empire,   usually the Third Class CBE (Commander of the British Empire)   for the Publisher of *The Times,* and a Fourth Class   OBE (Officer of the British Empire) for *The Time's* Editor.   Third, Fourth and Fifth Class medals do not award you the prefix title of Sir or Dame.   But you are elevated amongst your peers.   The reason for this sudden elevation is kept secret and away from the public and only prevailed in unreliable gossip circles.

This is how Royalty kept things as quiet as possible.   *The Times* was the newspaper trusted by the upper station citizens.   Including the House of Lords and Commons.   And those who spread 'true' gossip.   If it were in *The Times of London*, it must be true.

But how many Knighthoods would it take to control Queen Victoria's children whilst running amuck?

CHAPTER 28

The Marriage of
Prince Leopold & Lady Nora

The royal wedding of Prince Leopold, Duke of Albany, to Lady Nora, who will become Royal Duchess of Albany, was the cheerful, young and happy royal wedding. A large, select crowd filled St. George's Chapel at Windsor Castle.

Edward, Third Duke of Sussex, escorted his sister Lady Nora down the aisle.

Nora wore a spectacular ball gown shaped dress, in pure white, with a Honiton lace veil. Honiton lace is handmade in Devon, England, and is a favorite of HM.

Lady Nora's breathtaking dress featured a fitted bodice with a tight corset, a wide, flowing skirt, which was accomplished with stiff undying crinoline. Nora was cinched into a jealousy-inducing 17 inch waist.   She was alsoshowing off her wide child-bearing hips, especially to her future mother-in-law, The Queen. Nora selected the ball gown silhouette because it set an accepting Royal standard. Her wedding attire screamed that she belonged at Saint George's Chapel marrying a Royal Prince and fourth son of Queen Victoria.

As Nora and Edward walked down the aisle, approaching Prince Leopold, standing with his Man of Honour, Albert, Prince of Wales, Nora turned and gave her brother a kiss on his cheek. Edward shook Leopold's hand, turned and took his seat in the gallery in the same row as HM and the rest of the Queen's offspring and spouses. Lindy was not there. She accepted her invitation, sent by Edward and signed 'Jack' but she refused to put on a dress. "Dresses are for fuckin' sissies!" stated Lindy about ten years ago. Lindy was currently out riding Crazy Horse all over the square mile grounds of Jack's estate.

St George's Choir sang spiritual and matrimonial hymns. Then Queen Victoria's Poet Laureate, Alfred Lord Tennyson, read this verse: "In which we two were wont to meet. The field, the chamber and the street. For all is dark where thou are not."

Countess Agatha with Harriet, sat across the aisle from HM. Duchess Elsie, pregnant and showing, sat with her husband, Prince Alfred, Duke of Saxe-Coburg and Gotha, on the Queen's side of the Chapel. Now two of Agatha's girls were married. And Elsie was four months from giving birth to her baby, Agatha's first grandchild, and another grandchild for HM.

The wedding reception was tricky. The bride was supposed to provide the venue whilst the groom paid for the food, beverage and entertainment.   The boys who always ended up in Jack's Gentleman's Club pushed for the reception to be in Jack's Grand Ballroom, so the boys and Jack could easily disappear to cigars, port, champagne and cognac or whiskey called Jack Daniels from America. And, of course, Lindy, and now the unruly Red Thunder, would be happily in attendance. Dressed inappropriately of course.

Jack wanted the reception at his house. His mother, Countess Agatha (one wedding away from having her Duchess title and style returned) favored Buckingham Palace. To get HM used to seeing Countess Agatha when her married sons came over for dinner with Agatha's daughters.

HM solved the problem by sending a note to Edward, the only true royal at Ashfield Hall, telling him how delighted HM is that Edward chose his house to host the reception. HM didn't want Agatha anywhere near the Palace because the Queen detested Lady Agatha and all her drama.

Nora's first dance was with Jack. Leopold, as programmed, cut in and had his first dance with his beautiful wife in her jaw dropping wedding gown. Those gathered were well trained to appear at weddings and receptions watching the newlywed couple dance. In other words, there were no embarrassing Americans present. Just the usual upper station royals and nobles.

Not half an hour into the reception, complete with orchestra, distant cousins, nieces and nephews, enough humanity to fill the cavernous Grand Ballroom, did Jack; Albert, Prince of Wales; Alfred and Arthur, disappear to the Gentleman's Club downstairs. Leo was stuck with his wife whilst everyone else disappeared to have fun.

The boys opened the door and were greeted with a cloud of wonderful smelling Cuban cigars. Within this cloud were Lindy in tight sand-colored leather (with obligatory fringe) and Red Thunder, also dressed in tight leather, only red of course.   Red Thunder's leather pants and jacket were custom fitted from Harrods and delivered to Lindy at Ashfield Hall, lest The Queen or one of her spies, intercept this lewd and obscene package headed to Princess Beatrice Mary Victoria Feodore.

The girls were drinking Jack Daniels. They were smoking H. Upmann cigars. Beatrice headed straight for Jack and kissed him on his lips. Jack's immediate instincts were to look directly to Lindy to see how she felt about this not-necessarily-unwanted-trespass-upon-his-person. Lindy could not care less.

Jack therefore leaned into Red Thunder and brought her closer to him, whereupon she pushed him away.

"Please," cried Red Thunder, "I am not yours to possess." Then two seconds later, Red Thunder cooed, "Yet."

"Where is the Jack Daniels, Jack?" wondered Prince Alfred.

"How's my sister? Did you leave her all alone upstairs in her delicate condition?" smiled Jack talking to Prince Alfred, father-to-be and brand new husband of Elsie, woman who was now five months pregnant.

"Damn right.   Harriet is taking care of her.   I hope," responded Alfred. The boys were busy lighting cigars and pouring their favourite drinks.

Back upstairs at the reception in Jack's Grand Ballroom, Nora, the brand new bride, couldn't find Jack. Nora couldn't find her brand new husband, Prince Leopold. She thought 'damn!' Nora knew exactly where the boys were and what they were doing. And that American girl was there, smoking, drinking and showing herself off in those too-tight leather breeches! And Leopold's married not half an hour ago.

Nora, in a tizzy, needed to get to the hidden Gentlemen's Club to set the tone for Leo's marriage. There will be ground rules. There will be consequences. And her brother Jack will suffer, too.

Out of nowhere a man put his arms around Nora's waist, turned her around, lifted her off the Italian marble floor and kissed her! How shocking. How breathtaking. Who on earth was now kissing Nora so familiarly.

"Leopold! My darling!" sighed Nora.

"Where were you headed my dear?" asked Leopold.

"I couldn't find you." admitted Nora.

"So you thought I'd snuck off to Eddie's Pub.?"

"That thought did occur to me but you are my husband and I was ashamed to have such a wicked thought come to me. You'd never ever betray me like that." Nora actually said those words.

"Of course not my love. We must venture there together!" offered Leopold.

"Well, I'd feel unwelcome, my sweet," replied Nora.

"Yes, brother Albert would create a scene: 'No wives and no mothers! You know the rules, Leo', and he is the Prince of Wales," reminded youngest son Leo."

"What shall we do, husband?" demanded Nora, brand new wife of Royalty, waiting patiently for her royal title and style of Your Royal Highness.

"Make yourself known at the Palace—we call it Bucky. Have tea with mum," said Leopold trying to be as comforting as possible, whilst welcoming his new bride into the inner Royal Family as he kept open the door to his happy, fraternal debauchery (smoke and drink only) at Eddie's Club, now known as Jack's Club, now serving Jack Daniels.

Nora's clinging, all pervading mother slithered over to the newly wedded couple and reminded all within earshot of her daughter's new status: "Your Royal Highnesses, would you deign to cut the cake?" Non-royal Countess Agatha had an urge to remind everyone that her daughter was now, and forever more, a member of the Royal Family, and a close member at that.

When Agatha curtseyed and called Nora Your Royal Highness out loud at the reception in front of all attendees, Agatha felt great. Better than great. Accepted and powerful. She smiled more gleefully than usual. She, too, was impatiently awaiting her return as Royal Duchess with style of Your Royal Highness.

"Thank you, mother. I needed that," acknowledged almost Royal Duchess Nora.

CHAPTER 29

The Murder Trial

A pair of Colorado arresting officers had just arrived in London to retrieve the Prisoner (Arlene Dross, AKA Lindy Mae Long) for the murder of the Larimer County Sheriff, Ross Armitage, last May, 1880.

The Colorado lawmen had a list of rules regarding returning the prisoner to Colorado: Lindy must be shackled, hands and feet, at all times. Lindy had to travel 3rd class, (steerage), all the way to Larimer County, Colorado. Lindy must eat food in 'prisoner's portions'. Lindy was allowed only one 'bathroom' break per day. Lindy would sleep on a makeshift mattress. If Lindy attempted escape, she would be considered a fugitive, wanted dead or alive.

Edward took matters into his own hands and went to Parliament to seek council from the Lord High Chancellor, who presided over the House of Lords. And who had the power of creating Contracts and Obligations with Foreign Nations.

All of the Colorado Sheriff's requests were denied by the Office of the Lord High Chancellor, in the British House of Lords (or Upper House).   The agreement for the treatment of the Prisoner Lindy Mae Long was spelled out precisely in a Legally Binding International Contract:

"If you want Lindy to go back, then these are my demands," began Edward, Third Duke of Sussex, active member of the Royal Family, who is authorized to conduct legal business in the House of Lords because of his membership as a blood relative in the Royal Family.

Edward continued speaking to the Colorado lawmen: "You will sign this legal contract. If you renege on the agreement then, by Force of Law, Lindy will be released to me and she'll return to England where she is a nationalized subject of Her Majesty, the Queen. This will cause irreparable harm between the United States and the United Kingdom, and you will be blamed, charged, be put on trial and end up in an English prison yourselves."

Edward, along with Edward's Barrister, Edward's staff, Lindy and the two Colorado lawmen, boarded Edward's (Jack's) private train at St. Pancras Station, London. The train went to Liverpool, 220 miles north by northwest. The trip through the beautiful English countryside took four hours.

The Sheriff and his deputy enjoyed a Delmonico's steak, French wine, fresh baked French bread, Viennese pastries, then single-malt scotch, coffee or tea. They spent the rest of the trip napping.

They arrived in Liverpool with three hours to spare before the SS Britannic sailed for New York on the evening tide.

The Sheriff and his deputy had a cabin in Third Class. It was tiny, drafty and packed with immigrants heading to the Land of Opportunity. A rowdy bunch.

Edward arrived in steerage to inspect the Colorado lawmen's accommodations.

"Gentlemen, if you wish, I've acquired tickets for Saloon Class suites. Or you can remain here."

Jack, Lindy, Jack's staff and Barrister had cabins in Saloon (First) Class. And now, so did Sheriff Van Der Hoff and his Deputy. First Class to New York does not compare to steerage class in any way, shape or form. You arrive at New York at the same time, but those in steerage are in worse shape due to frequent Atlantic storms, being domiciled at the back of the ship, where the ship rolls, yaws and pitches more than the middle, where First Class is.

When Britannic arrived in New York eight and a half days later, the retinue took Jack's private train west to Chicago, then southwest to Omaha, then west to Cheyenne. There Jack's private train went due south and crossed into Colorado.

Jack's ten car train pulled into the railroad station in the small town (population 1,300) of Fort Collins, Colorado, in October, 1880, about five months after he and Lindy skedaddled. Actually, Jack just boarded his private train with his staff and left town in a civilized manner. Lindy skedaddled.

Lindy returned to the scene of the crime with no fanfare because Jack's train was unscheduled. Jack's private investigators, who'd arrived 7 weeks ago, had arranged for hotel rooms under his name and the name of Jack's barrister. The lead private investigator would meet Jack when his train arrived.

Jack and his staff would take a room at the Agricultural Hotel at the corner of Mountain and Mason Streets, close to the college in Fort Collins. Lindy would stay in the train. Jack's chef would tend to Lindy.

Jack presented himself at the sheriff's office the following morning making arrangements for Lindy.   He did not want Lindy jailed. He wanted the sheriff to look at her set up and said, "She's come 6,000 miles from a comfortable home in England to stand trial. She's innocent; she's here to clear her name. I want her to confine herself to my train. I fear if the citizens knew she were in a jail cell they might torch the building."

The sheriff enjoyed a good laugh and ordered Lindy locked up in jail cell number 2. Cell number one got filled up with drunks on Friday and Saturday. It was Tuesday and this week's inmates were being released into the custody of their angry wives and mothers who didn't have any control over their husbands' or sons' drinking and pugilism.

Jack's two American private investigators, Danny Maxwell lead investigator, and Oscar Sullivan, investigator, had been roaming around the area for the past seven weeks. They came up with some interesting facts about the case of who murdered Ross Armitage, Sheriff of Larimer County, Colorado. Sheriff for the past 17 years. The sheriff lived in Fort Collins, the County Seat of Larimer County, the reason Danny and Oscar were in Fort Collins. It was the site of the murder and the site of the County Court House.

Both Danny and Oscar came to Jack's hotel suite at the Agricultural Hotel. They were joined by Jack's lawyer, Sir Eberhart St. Clair. Eberhart referred to himself as Hart.

With a goodly amount of dinner and drink, they went over the evidence gathered betwixt Fort Collins, Colorado, and Cheyenne, Wyoming Territory, by the two investigators.

Danny and Oscar talked to over 250 citizens, both in Fort Collins, Colorado; Cheyenne, Wyoming Territory; and half a dozen small towns in the area. They talked to Lindy's mother. They talked to the dead sheriff's widow. They kept as low a profile as you can when you're a known outsider in a tiny community where everyone's got her nose in everyone's business.

They went above and beyond gathering information. Danny and Oscar made repairs on houses, including fitting windows and doors; they painted, repaired roofs, chopped firewood for the brutally cold upcoming winter.   Did they do this out of kindness? You may have thought so, but Jack paid them $1000 extra for these services, and an additional $2000 to pay for the lumber, shingles, roofing material, and cash for locals to cut and stack cords of firewood.

As they painted, put up wallpaper, built custom kitchen cabinetry and countertops, repaired holes in roofs, the wives would bring Danny and Oscar tea, sandwiches. And gossip. 'True' gossip. This gossip was part of the evidence collected about the case of the murdered sheriff, the late Ross Armitage, of Fort Collins, Colorado.

Jack went to the jail to escort Lindy to the courtroom to be arraigned: explain the charges against her, plead to those charges, set bail and get any further instructions for a capital crime of murder, and set a trial date.

Lindy's cell, by the way, had a blanket hanging between Cell 1 and Cell 2 that blocked the view of men behind bars wishing to catch a peek of Lindy. Jack brought a bed with a thick brand new mattress.

"Who's that for?" asked Lindy.

"Well, you," replied Jack.

"Yall're getting me out of here, Jack," stated Lindy firmly.

"When the judge asks how you plead you say 'not guilty', got it?"

"Yeah. Y'alls lawyers said if I accidentally say guilty, they can 'accidentally' hang me this afternoon." argued Lindy like saying not guilty was the wrong thing to do. Lindy added, "I fuckin' shot the fat asshole, he slumped over. I don't miss."

Jack made the international impersonation of a rope around his neck with his hand pulling up the invisible noose and his face looking hanged, with tongue out.

"The judge will accept your guilty plea and watch you hang this afternoon, before dinner."

In court, both Hart St Clair and Reno Sweetwater— prominent defense attorney from Denver City—were waiting at the Defendant's Table near the judge's bench.   Lindy and Jack walked in accompanied by a sheriff's deputy who took Lindy's handcuffs off in front of the judge.

Judge MacMillan was at his seat, signing documents and handing them to a Court Stenographer, a woman, who looked very efficient and imperious. As though she and the judge were the only two in the building who were not tainted and soiled with the shame of crime.

"Your Honor," stated Hart St Clair, "I am counsel who represents Miss Arlene Dross in the matter, People versus Miss Arlene Dross, for the capital crime of murder."

"Are you Arlene Dross?" asked the judge.

"Yeah." said Lindy. Hart nudged her and gave her a look. "Ah, yes sir, your honor," re-stated Lindy.

"You are charged with the shooting death of Sheriff Ross Armitage, on or about May 3rd, 1880, right here in Fort Collins, Colorado. Do you understand the charge against you?" asked the judge.

"Yes," said Lindy, suddenly nervous, possibly recognizing the seriousness of the charges.

"Then how do you plead. Guilty or not guilty?" demanded the judge.

Lindy looked back at Jack who was standing behind her in the empty courtroom.

Then she looked at her lawyer, who stood motionless, then at the judge. She sighed, exhaled and finally said, "Not guilty, sir."

"Note that the defendant pleads not guilty to the charge of murder," said the judge as though he were reading from a grocery list.

"To the question of bail or no bail, Miss Dross. Are you gonna high tail it out of here, run off to God knows where, to avoid the trial?" wondered the judge.

"I ain't running no where. I came back from England to clear my name, judge."

At this moment, the prosecuting attorney, Hays Randolf, ran into the court with his hat on and deeply apologized to the judge, took his hat off, and asked the judge, "Did I miss anything, your Honor?" Hays was out of breath. He must've run a marathon.

"In less than 1 minute you would have missed my charge of Contempt of Court, your $100 fine and your one week stay in our jail for being late, Mr Randolf," assured Judge MacMillan.

Hays Randolf, local prosecutor and man who lives three blocks away, gulped.

"Are you going to also arrive late for the trial, Mr Randolf? I'm about to set bail if that's all right with you? The defendant came all the way over from London, England, and she was on time. I expect the same of you. And before I forget, you are fined $10 for your tardiness. Do not come late to my court again, or a basement jail cell awaits you," reassured Judge MacMillan.

Ten dollars was more than most people made in a fortnight. That was a stiff fine.

"Now, Mr Randolf, what are your thoughts on bail for Miss Dross?" asked the judge.

"I plead for no bail because she's a runner, your Honor. She'll take off back to England, or Canada for all I know. Keep her in jail until the trial's over, your Honor," demanded Hays Randolf, prosecutor for Larimer County, Colorado.

Reno Sweetwater, up from Denver City, said, "Miss Dross accidentally ended up in England last May when she boarded a train belonging to this gentleman, Mr Edward Hanover, of London. Mr Hanover brought Miss Dross back from London solely for her to stand trial for murder, and to clear her name. Miss Dross is here, and is staying here because she knows this trial will prove her innocence. Therefore, I guarantee that Miss Dross will not flee this county for the duration of this trial. I recommend bail, your Honor."

"Miss Dross, I understand you live in Cheyenne, up in Wyoming Territory?" asked the judge.

"Yes, sir," said Lindy.

"If I set bail and you're out of jail, that means you can't wander off to Cheyenne, or set foot outside of Larimer County. In fact, you will stay in the town of Fort Collins during your trial. Is that understood?" The judge was adamant. And not afraid to throw a tardy person in jail.

"Yes, sir. I'll stay put. I got no where to go anyways," said Lindy unnecessarily.

"Your honor, as soon as she's released, she'll jump on someone's pony and gallop out of town and be gone forever!" said Hays Randolf.

"If I was gonna run away, I'd stay put at Jack's house in England! I left my horse there!" prickled Lindy to Hays Randolf, prosecutor.

"Maybe you thought that then. But if you lose the trial, you're gonna get hanged by the neck til you're dead. That's why you'll run," said Hays, convinced of her guilt.

"We got proof that I'm innocent, that's why I ain't running," concluded Lindy.

"I set bail at $500," instructed the judge.   "Trial starts tomorrow morning 10am.   Sharp. You got that, Mr Randolf?" ordered the judge.

Hays Randolf got it loud and expensive.

Lindy gave Jack a hug.   Jack walked over to the Court Stenographer and gave her a $500 bill. Paper money from the United States Treasury with an engraving of Civil War Major General Joseph King Mansfield on the front of the $500 bill.   Jack got the receipt and handed it to Hart St Clair. The Bailiff received the proof of purchase of a Bail Bond and put the document on the judge's bench.

The judge nodded at the group, got up and exited through his private door.

The trial was set for 10 o'clock, Thursday (tomorrow) morning, October 14th, 1880.

That night Jack, Lindy, Hart St. Clair, Reno Sweetwater, Danny Maxwell and Oscar Sullivan ate dinner in a Fort Collins restaurant that served large steaks.

Their table was off to the side, away from diners.

Danny Maxwell, lead private investigator, continued reporting 7 weeks of town gossip. Jack, Hart St Clair and Reno Sweetwater looked disinterested. Lindy was salivating. 'Gossip is gold' said her mother. Lindy learned that when you've got something on an enemy, you can use it any time to drive a stake through her heart.

This gossip was evidence:

"We figured the only way to get townsfolk to say anything meaningful about the late sheriff was to become beneficial to the town's ladies," reported Danny Maxwell.

Danny and Oscar each had notebooks, pocket sized, filled with information they checked out. A lot of gossip from different sources was true.

"Beneficial?" wondered Reno Sweetwater, thinking it meant sex.

We spent our time repairing their houses. Their men were useless. We repaired leaky roofs, did brickwork, wood work, yard work, stone work, repaired buckboards, took horses to get re-shoed and buggy wheels to get repaired. And had the town vet take a look at their horses and pets. We also redid their kitchens, re-dug water wells, and the women, all of them, fed us cookies and cakes and stories about who might've killed the sheriff."

"Might've" said Lindy outloud.

"So how many of these ladies, with new roofs and kitchens, mentioned Arlene Dross?" inquired Hart St Clair, English Barrister who graduated from The Oxford University Faculty of Law, founded in 1219 during the reign of King Henry III, which was 760 years ago.

"One lady mentioned Arlene, everyone else said your gun's a pea shooter, couldn't put a hole in a pie crust," interjected Danny Maxwell. "Any number of felons, gamblers, bushwackers, card sharks, highwaymen, had it in for the sheriff. Some took pot shots at him setting on his porch. And like Lindy, they all missed."

"Any names of murder suspects?" demanded Reno, who wanted names of known felons who committed crimes of violence and were apprehended by Ross Armitage and the Larimer County, Colorado, sheriff's department.

"There was a list of twelve or so suspects known to have a beef with the sheriff's department or made threats against Sheriff Armitage. New sheriff Van Der Hoff had a similar list, but only five suspects. The ladies seemed to know more about what's going on in town." stated Danny Maxwell.

"Why's that?" interrupted Edward.

"Cause those suspects were their troublesome kids," volunteered Danny Maxwell.

The attendees looked at Lindy, another troubled teen.

"Do these ladies call their own children 'troubled'?" wondered Hart St Clair.

"Hell no. Their own kids were little angels. Everybody else's kids were causing all the trouble," affirmed Oscar Sullivan.

"And who're the ladies' lead suspect?" asked Reno Sweetwater.

"We checked out all twelve names and every one of them is accounted for. They all had alibis. Right off, nine were already in jail, state prison, county jail. Two up in Wyoming. Four in Denver City and three here in Fort Collins, at the time of the killing," said Oscar Sullivan reading from his notebook.

Turns out that Lindy knew all 12 of these hellions. And had been making money off them for five years, since she was 12. She also thought that if it weren't for Jack's train, she might be in jail right now. Or hanged last May.

"Two fellas claimed to be drunk at the time, and the ladies took us aside and pointed out which two. We followed those boys around and they had no quarrel with Ross Armitage. The quarrel was with their mothers, who kept turning them into the sheriff for hooliganism and gambling—horse racing down College Avenue," accurately reported Oscar Sullivan.

Jack cast a knowing eyeball at Lindy and she let that accusation bounce off her and land harmlessly on the floor. Of course she was racing horses. Her Hanoverian Thoroughbred against untrained, partially broken ponies. It was highway robbery. But the boys liked to look at Lindy in her skin tight outfit. She, of course, knew exactly what she was doing 24 hours a day.

"What about the night that Lindy took a shot at the sheriff. Any witnesses?" asked Reno Sweetwater.

"It was raining hard. Lightning and thunder.all day. Lots of mud. Couldn't go out lest you want to get stuck." reminded Danny Maxwell.

"All these ladies heard the gossip about a bullet that hit the sheriff in his, ah, this bone, up here abouts." said Oscar Sullivan, pointing to his clavicle. "Nowhere near his heart."

"How'd they hear that?" inquired Hart St Clair and Reno.

"Coroner's wife, Gladys Hardee. She's got the inside story on all gruesome crimes. She said there are at least three versions of the Coroner's autopsy on Ross Armitage," reported Danny Maxwell.

"**Three** versions? Of the autopsy? Does the Coroner write several versions and have the prosecution vote on the one that will most likely convict? This certainly is the wild West," concluded Hart St Clair, Barrister who wanted a crack at a real live wild west American murder trial.

"So who, then, did these women think was the killer, or killers?" asked Reno Sweetwater, high powered Denver City lawyer.

"Speculation is the sheriff's widow could have had a romantic interest other than her husband." reported Danny Maxwell, reading from his notebook.

"Widow Armitage engaged a lover?" queried Hart St. Clair.

"So did she kill her husband?" asked Reno Sweetwater of the two investigators, Danny and Oscar.

"Inconclusive," said Hart St. Clair, "how'd she kill him and lift his immense body onto the porch swing that night?"

"She killed him while he was sitting on the porch swing!" speculated Oscar Sullivan.

"How?" wondered Edward.

"She hit him over the head with a cast iron skillet," guessed Oscar.

"Was there bleeding from the back of his head?

"Her boyfriend killed him then moved him to the porch swing," said Lindy, like this happens all the time where she comes from.

"So, who is her inamorato?" wondered Oxford educated Hart St. Clair.

"What?" wondered most.

"Her lover," clarified Cambridge educated Jack.

"What name did the gossip girls come up with?" asked Reno Sweetwater, educated at the Columbia College of Law in New York City.

"Two gentlemen were mentioned, a lot, by the ladies we talked to. These men, who separately squired the sheriff's wife around town, did so in broad daylight," began Danny Maxwell.

"They each were seen with her before she was a widow. Did her husband know that his wife had admirers? Several ladies said the sheriff did know." Oscar reported this piece of juicy news.

"And these mens' names are.?" asked Reno, losing patience with not getting answers:

"The new sheriff, Kees Van Der Hoff. And the mayor, Horton Armitage, the sheriff's younger brother!" said Danny Maxwell.

"The town mayor ain't married and is very friendly with the ladies—married or looking," stated Danny reading from his thick handwritten notebook, packed with seven weeks of investigative snooping.

"Any proof of shenanigans?" wondered Reno Sweetwater.

"Well, Horton, the mayor, had good reason to be over to his brother's house—for meals. Mrs Armitage is a good cook. Best homemade cakes, pies and brownies in Colorado, says everyone. Then Kees Van Der Hoff, at the time, the deputy sheriff, ha also had good reason to be at the sherif's house," stated Oscar Sullivan.

"Did anyone see the widow coming' out of a hotel, then ten minutes later the deputy or the mayor coming out of the same hotel with a big ol' smile on his face?" wondered Lindy.

"The word from the gossip girls was the mayor was tied up with several ladies, some married, some not, as I said," repeated Oscar Sullivan.

"We need the original autopsy report—if what the coroner's wife said is true," said Reno Sweetwater., adding, "since the bullet probably didn't kill him, something else did. And the Coroner knows what it was—if he's written more than one autopsy."

"Before we start calling the new sheriff or the mayor to the stand, let's make damned sure we can tie them to the widow with a motive to kill Ross Armitage.." said Reno Sweetwater.

When Lindy got back to her hotel room after their steak dinner, there was a package on her bed. An unopened package wrapped beautifully with Harrods exclusive gift-wrap. She, of course, tore it open. There was a note on top. Lindy smiled.

Day 1

The Bailiff ordered everyone "All rise." as Judge MacMillan entered the courtroom in his black robe. Pinned to the robe was a Christian cross. In his hand was his family Bible. The judge paused to look at the courtroom. The place was packed, mostly with men. There was a smattering of women, about 12, seated in the back, mainly because they were rowdy and opinionated. Behavior which IS annoying to men, but not the judge.

Hays Randolf, the County Prosecutor, was half an hour early. The Larimer County sheriff, Kees Van Der Hoff, sat behind the Prosecutor's Table, on the other side of the barrier (bar), where the gallery (audience) was seated.

Jack sat behind the Defendant's Table in the first row of gallery seating. At the Defendant's Table were Lindy's legal team including Hart St. Clair and Colorado Criminal Defense Attorney Reno Sweetwater, up from Arapahoe County's largest city, Denver.

The Larimer County Prosecutor, Hays Randolf, was ordered by the judge to give opening arguments to the seated jury of 12 men. The jurors had been selected this morning between 10 am and 10:44am by Hays Randolf and Reno Sweetwater. The trial was set to start now.

"Gentlemen of the jury. This is a case of cold-blooded murder. One Arlene Dross, from the Territory of Wyoming, did shoot to death, our beloved sheriff, Ross Armitage. Sheriff Armitage was home on a quiet May evening, sitting on his porch swing, when the prisoner, Miss Arlene Dross, crossed the Territorial Boundary, slunk across the border into the State of Colorado, and without warning, took aim and shot Ross Armitage to death. He didn't have a chance to defend himself. He was gunned down for no good reason. I declare you, our loyal jury, to immediately weigh the overwhelming evidence against her, find her guilty, and sentence her to be hanged by the neck until dead. This town will not be safe if she is allowed to wander its streets."

Jack had put a note on the Defendant's Table in front of Lindy. The note was written in large easy-to-ready letters. It said: DO NOT SAY ANYTHING. DO NOT CUSS. LOOK INNOCENT.

Hays Randolf sat down, satisfied with his opening remarks.

Rising for the defense was Reno Sweetwater, Lindy's other lawyer.

Reno: "Gentlemen of the jury. Everything the prosecutor said about Miss Dross was 100% true!"

Lindy, wishing she had her Colt .45 so she could have shot the prosecutor to death, stood up and shouted, "You're my fuckin' lawyer!"

Judge MacMillan lightly tapped his gavel. Judge MacMillan tolerates a lot of outbursts. He likes the drama. He invites the rowdy ladies who all have opinions and who all love to voice her opinions. The judge loves it. The best outburst was when a defendant couldn't remember the name of the girl he was cheating on his wife with. All 12 of the Rowdy Ladies of the Back Bench shouted, "Virginia Harper you cheating piece of shit!" in unison. The judge accepted that as Gospel. The judge declared the man divorced, told him to pay his wife $500 for undue suffering and mental cruelty, then thanked the Rowdy Ladies. That happened two months ago.

After Lindy's standing performance and vulgar utterance, there were gasps from the gallery. One juror was shocked.

But then, her lawyer, Reno Sweetwater, explained: "Arlene did set out to shoot your beloved Sheriff Armitage. She did so because one week before Christmas last, Sheriff Armitage gunned down Arlene's father, in cold blood, on Mason Street right here in town. And you remember it. Arlene's father had been accused of a crime, yet Sheriff Armitage took it upon himself to be judge, jury and executioner. He didn't give Arlene's father a chance to go to trial. Sheriff Armitage shot Arlene's daddy in the back six times. A week before Christmas, '79."

The gallery gasped. The Rowdy Ladies fake gasped. The late sheriff was a bully, an intimidator and a lousy law enforcer.

Reno Sweetwater continued: "Arlene set out to even the score. But first she approached Sheriff Armitage himself. The sheriff would not listen to Arlene even though everyone in town knew that Sheriff Armitage murdered Arlene's father in cold blood. Sheriff Armitage told Arlene to her face, 'why waste money on a trial, everyone knows your daddy's a criminal and deserved to die.'"

"Arlene got nowhere. Her father was murdered in cold blood and no one would help her. She, a juvenile in the eyes of the law, took matters into her own hands, just like Sheriff Armitage did. One night, last May, in a driving rain storm, Arlene rode down from Wyoming and found the sheriff's house. He was indeed sitting on the front porch. Arlene, on horseback, about forty feet away, took out her thirty-two caliber Smith & Wesson and fired one shot at the sheriff. She hit the sheriff in his left shoulder. This shot did not kill the sheriff. Because the sheriff (Reno Sweetwater paused two seconds for effect) **was already dead!"**

The courtroom exploded in a deafening uproar! Random comments of disbelief and other comments of 'I told you so!' Even the Rowdy Ladies were shocked. This was unexpected news.

Judge MacMillian rapped his gavel gently and called everyone to order. His tone of voice was conciliatory, not threatening.

When things settled down Reno Sweetwater addressed the jury again, "We will prove, beyond any doubt, that Arlene Dross is innocent of any crime, whatsoever. And not only that, we will expose the real murderer, which is what Sheriff Van Der Hoff is supposed to do."

Reno Sweetwater sat down next to Lindy (Arlene Dross) at the Defendant's Table. On Lindy's other side was Hart St. Clair, the London Barrister. Behind the Defendant's Table were Jack and private investigator Oscar Sullivan. Danny Maxwell, the other private investigator, was tying up loose ends outside the courthouse.

The Prosecutor, Hays Randolf, called his first witness, Marcus Hardee, the County Coroner.

The judge swore Marcus Hardee in and the coroner took a seat on the wooden Witness Chair.

Hays Randolf, "Mr Hardee, what is your job"
Dr Hardee: "I am the County Coroner for Larimer County."
Hays Randolf, "What are your qualifications?"
Dr Hardee: "I am a board certified Medical Doctor with training in Pathology and post mortem physiology."
Hays Randolf, "And what does that mean?"
Dr Hardee: "I can tell how, when, where and under what circumstances the victim died."
Hays Randolf, "Did you examine the body of the late Sheriff Ross Armitage?"
Dr Hardeer: "Yes."
Hays Randolf, "What were your findings?"
Dr Hardee: "I found that he died of a single gunshot wound above his heart."
Gasps in the courtroom.
Hays Randolf, "What caliber bullet was found?"
Dr Hardee: "One .32 caliber bullet.
Hays Randolf "Did the new sheriff, Sheriff Van Der Hoff, show you a .32 caliber pistol?"
Dr Hardee: "Yes he did."
Hays Randolf "Did Sheriff Van Der Hoff tell you who belonged to the .32 caliber pistol?"
Dr Hardee: "He said it belonged to Arlene Dross, sitting right over there."
The gallery went wild! The judge took a sip of tea, sat back and enjoyed the bewildered and astonished excitement. Then after he took a bite of some fresh-baked coffeecake, Judge MacMillan tapped his gavel until there was reasonable quiet.
"Your witness, Mr Sweetwater." said Hays Randolf, Prosecutor.

Lindy's first chair lawyer arose, nodded to Hays Randolf, and walked over to the witness, Dr. Marcus Hardee, MD, Larimer County Coroner, seated in the Witness Chair, next to the judge's bench.
"Good day, Doctor Hardee," said Reno Sweetwater to the Coroner.
Dr Hardee nodded.

"Your testimony about Sheriff Armitage's cause of death was interesting, sir," began Reno Sweetwater. "Interesting because of where that bullet struck, sir. Not in, or near his heart, but a foot away. The bullet hit his collar bone, did it not?" asserted Reno Sweetwater.

"I never wrote that the bullet hit the sheriff's heart. I said it hit near his heart." said the Coroner, a little jangled from the direct question.

"You are under oath, sir. How far from the sheriff's heart did that bullet hit?" pushed Reno Sweetwater.

"A couple of inches." The Coroner sounded rattled and unsure of himself.

"Under penalty of perjury and five years behind bars for each lie, sir, did that tiny .32 caliber bullet kill Sheriff Armitage?" Reno went in for the kill.

There was silence. The Coroner looked at the Prosecutor's Table for help. Hays Randolf glared at the Coroner in silence.

"According to my final autopsy report, it did." squeaked the Coroner.

"So how close to..wait… Your **final** autopsy report? How many autopsy reports did you write, sir?" asked Reno Sweetwater, jolted by the Coroner's bold, brash, revealing statement.

The gallery roared in protest, shock and anger.

"At first, the newspaper said he was shot in a hail of bullets. However, I only found one, but my first report I might have said 'multiple bullet wounds'." confessed Dr Hardee.

"Is it your habit, sir, to depend on unfounded newspaper reports to dictate how you determine the cause of death?" accosted Reno Sweetwater, Lindy's lawyer and Lindy's exit out of Colorado and safely back to England.

"I re-examined the body and wrote my revised autopsy report citing one bullet as the cause of death," reported Dr Hardee with hesitation.

"Did the bullet entry wound bleed, sir?" wondered Reno Sweetwater.

"Ah. No it did not," reported Dr Hardee with certitude.

"If a bullet wound near the heart did not bleed onto the sheriff's shirt, what did that tell you?" focused Reno Sweetwater.

"Well, that would indicate that the sheriff was probably already dead," cautioned Dr Hardee.

"*Probably* dead?" began Reno Sweetwater, adding, "How many autopsies in your career did you report where there was no bleeding from a wound and that wound was the cause of death?"

"As far as my 17 year career as a coroner is concerned, not one. The cause of death was somewhere else in the body." affirmed Dr Hardee.

"So if the sheriff's chest bullet wound did not bleed, then that wound was not the cause of death. So the bullet did not kill the sheriff, according to you and your 17 year career!"
Reno Sweetwater could not hold back his jubilation.

Dr Hardee had to think about it.

"What killed the sheriff, Dr Hardee. You just said it wasn't the measly little .32 caliber bullet." Reno had the coroner cornered.

"He was dead, there was a bullet in him so I assumed that the .32 caliber bullet killed him."

"**Assumed!?**   Did you check for another cause of death? Maybe he died of pneumonia! He was out in a rainstorm all day. According to the news-paper, three people died of pneumonia from that terrible storm.   And the three were all younger than Sheriff Armitage, God rest his soul."

"The bullet must've killed him," said Dr Hardee with zero confidence in his voice.

"I demand a new autopsy, your Honor," said Reno Sweetwater to the judge. Adding,
"And, no further questions until we see a new autopsy report where the Coroner actually looks for the real cause of death.". Reno Sweetwater walked back to the Defendant's Table wearing a victorious smirk and nodded positively at Lindy.

Hays Randolf, prosecutor, arose and said, "May I re-direct, your Honor?

"Will this take long, we're ready for luncheon," remarked Judge MacMillan.

"One question your Honor: Dr Hardee, according to your signed autopsy report, what was the cause of death for our beloved late sheriff Ross Armitage?"

"Gunshot wound to the chest," said Dr Hardee with more confidence.

The judge spoke, "Folks, it's time for luncheon. Be back here in one hour," as Judge MacMillan tapped his gavel, got up and disappeared through a hidden door to his left.

The gallery all exploded in hundred-mile-an-hour nonstop speculating. All this information had stripped certainty over the 'hail of bullets' typical sensationalist newspaper gossip of what really happened.

If Lindy didn't kill the sheriff, who did? And how?

Hays Randolf, prosecutor, did not look flustered. Hays smiled confidently at Hart St. Clair and Reno Sweetwater as Hays left for luncheon.   Hays's only concern was getting back in one hour.

Lindy, with her legal team including Oscar Sullivan, ate in the courtroom cafe. Lindy was not cheerful. The young and immature girl drew a question from Reno Sweetwater. "Why so glum, Arlene?"

"Cause I missed him."

"Why don't we pay the Coroner to say you shot the sheriff in his heart, killing him instantly. That way you'll feel better about your aim. And when they hang you today, you'll come to your senses, then your neck will snap and you'll be happy. Stop arguing for the hangman." Jack was getting fed up with this girl in particular and American stupidity in general.

"The Coroner is writing autopsy reports to please too many people. The mayor, who is the sheriff's younger brother. And, I say, a possible killer, who is someone with clout in this town. Find those other autopsy reports," delegated Reno Sweetwater, "look everywhere. Maybe they're hidden in the coroner's barn or buried in his backyard…!"

Back in Court, the Prosecutor, Hays Randolf, rose from his chair at the Prosecutor's Table and called his next witness.

"I call Irdine Jackson Dross to the witness chair," announced Hays Randolf.

The Bailiff repeated the call out in the Court's hallway, out of earshot of the proceedings for Lindy's mother, who was sitting in the hallway with other witnesses.

Irdine Jackson married Robert Dyce Dross in Mobile, Alabama, in 1862 during the War Between the States, whilst Irdine was 6 months pregnant with Arlene.   Irdine's Southern Baptist preacher had planned a shotgun wedding for Robert just as he got back from Havana, Cuba, on a successful blockade run aboard a sleek, fast steam-powered boat that carried cotton to the Havana safe harbor (couldn't be raided by the Union Navy) 633 miles south of Mobile Bay.

Robert Dross was Senior Navigator on a Blockade Runner, a steamboat packed with bales of cotton that headed out of Mobile Bay at high tide on moonless nights in order to slip past the United States Navy Western Blocking Squadron which set out to capture sleek, fast steam-powered ships like Robert's blockade runner. Robert's blockade runner was built at the Clydebank Shipyards in Scotland by practiced hands who knew the ship building trade from centuries of building ocean-going ships. Southerners didn't have the necessary shipbuilding skills to produce ocean going boats. Nor the money to pay for a fleet of blockade running boats to transport cotton to places like Havana, and bring back guns and ammunition for Confederate armies.

Robert was paid $1,000 in gold coin for running 500 pound cotton bales to Havana, Cuba. They'd return to Mobile Bay with a ship full of treasures. Why so much money for Robert Dross? Robert was an experienced navigator who knew how to avoid rocks and sandbars along Mobile Bay's jagged inlet. His knowledge was invaluable, guaranteeing an incident-free escape from Mobile Harbor with a cargo worth maybe eighty or ninety thousand dollars in gold. (Confederate money was worthless to Cuban, British and European traders. You trade in gold and silver.)

The Captain and First Officer of the steamboat were experienced British sea captains taking time off from the Royal Navy to make a lot of money. These captains were paid $2,500 and $2,000 in gold for sailing from Mobile Bay safely 633 miles south to Havana Harbor for the purpose of dropping off their cargo of bales of cotton, then loading the steamship,, specially built for outrunning U.S. Navy ships on the high seas, and returning to Mobile, Alabama, loaded with ammunition, guns, food, cannon, blankets to turn over to the Confederacy. There were also goods for the ladies: yards of French silks, shoes from Italy, hats from London, purses (called reticles in the mid-19th century) and dresses from Paris, plus perfumes, coats and gloves. The ladies' husbands paid cash at the dock when the blockade runners arrived, in the dead of night.

Robert returned safely, was paid his $1,000 gold. Ten minutes later Robert was confronted by Irdine's Southern Baptist pastor and told he was to marry Irdine Jackson immediately. Irdine took control of Robert's $1,000 in gold coins. Robert didn't know what hit him. His plans were for a boisterous drunken dinner at Mobile's best steakhouse (7 Seas Steaks) then four or five days of drunken whoring. Then rest and wait for his blockade runner to take off for Havana again.

After the War Between the States in 1865, Mr and Mrs Robert Dross moved from Mobile, Alabama, by train and ferry boat to St Louis, Missouri, then west to Kansas City, then farther west through the State of Kansas, then over to Cheyenne, which was in Dakota Territory. Their love-child, Rleen, was three-and-a-half. Robert and Irdine wanted out of the South where Yankees were flooding in. And out of the United States in general, to one of the Territories being settled before statehood.

Robert, with half his blockade running cash gone from partying, gambling and whoring in Alabama, arrived with his family in Cheyenne, Dakota Territory, just in time for winter. He built a cabin, furnished it and moved in just in time for the first snow: four feet. He bought a lot of firewood (5 full cords), canned food and blankets. Now his supply of gold was down to $150.   Robert Dyce Dross snowbound through the 1865-66 winter devised a scheme to make money starting in spring: robbery. Robert robbed stagecoaches, trains, travelers along the California, Oregon and Mormon trails. He also picked up things the travelers in the Conestoga wagons threw out—furniture, dishes and anything too cumbersome—and sold it to townsfolk in Cheyenne, or to travelers coming behind those who threw stuff out. He did okay. Irdine was pleased.

When the TransContinental Rail Road was finished in 1869, Robert concentrated on robbing banks. He formed a gang of Alabama Confederates and was successful until he was shot dead by Sheriff Ross Armitage last December 22nd, 1879. His daughter Rleen was 17, old enough to know how to get even.

"Do you swear by Almighty God to tell the truth, the whole truth, and nothing but the truth, so help you God?"

Irdine Dross replied, "A course I do, I'm a Southern Christian woman."

The entire courtroom thought her reply was truthful and respectful. So did Judge MacMillan.

Hays Randolph walked over to the Witness Chair, which was next to the judge's bench, and started his interrogation: "Mrs Dross, how are you related to the prisoner, Arlene Dross?"

Irdine, "I'm her mother."

"Did Arlene, the day after Sheriff Armitage was shot dead, tell you that she was the one who shot Sheriff Armitage?"

"In a way, yes."

The gallery gasped and lightly chatted 'I told you so's'.

"Well, did she say she shot Sheriff Armitage, yes or no?"

"Her gestures, her attitude and her ability to be as slippery as a snake sliding through oil said she did something illegal the night before."

The gallery laughed.

"Do you know who owns this gun?" asked Hays Randolf showing Lindy's .32 caliber Smith & Wesson handgun.

"Yeah, it's Rleen's."

"Did you know this .32 caliber Smith & Wesson was used to shoot Sheriff Armitage?"

"Yes."

"How'd you know that. Did Arlene tell you she shot Sheriff Armitage?"

"No, the new sheriff told me Rleen used it to shoot the old sheriff."

"Did you believe Sheriff Van Der Hoff when he told you?"

"A course. He had no reason to lie."

The ladies in the back of the courtroom hooted, booted and taunted Irdine.

"Why didn't you defend your daughter, Mrs Dross?" wondered Hays Randolf.

"Cause Rleen ain't nothing but trouble since she become a 'woman'."

"Could you explain that for the jury, please?"

"That means she went from a sweet, innocent little girl who helped around the house then turned into some kind of back-talkin', cussin', ill-mannered devil-child. Always up to no good. Sneaking' around. Always looking for trouble. When the new sheriff came by and saw Rleen's pistol, he looked inside and saw one bullet's fired. Sheriff Armitage was shot with only one bullet. From a .32. Rleen's .32. She done it. I know 'cause a mother always knows."

"Here's the one question I need to know the answer to Mrs Dross: why'd Arlene shoot the sheriff in the first place?" wondered Hays Randolf, Prosecutor.

"Cause the sheriff gunned down my husband in cold blood a week afore last Christmas. Gunned him down in the street, like shootin' a runaway slave."

"Why'd Sheriff Armitage shoot your husband?"

"He didn't just shoot him. He killed my husband in cold blood. For no good reason!"

Irdine's blood was up.

"Wasn't your husband a wanted criminal? Didn't your husband rob almost every bank in five Colorado counties and several counties across the border in Wyoming Territory?"

"You got no proof of that."

"So your 17 year old daughter took it upon herself to go after the sheriff and do to him what the sheriff did to your husband. Or did you send her out to get even?"

"Duchess was never home. She was running around with half the town's boys."

"Who is 'duchess', Mrs Dross?" wondered Hays Randolf?

"Sometimes I call Rleen 'duchess' cause she thinks her shit don't stink. Acts like she's some kinda fuckin' royalty."

The audience snickered at her accurate assessment.

"Answer the question Mrs Dross," insisted Judge MacMillan.

"What was the question?" asked Iodine.

"Did you send Arlene out to kill Sheriff Armitage?" reminded Judge MacMillan.

"Naw.   She done that on her own," said Irdine unconvincingly.

"Why do you say that, Mrs Dross?" asked Hays Randolf.

"Cause that sheriff murdered Robert right before Christmas and Arlene didn't do nothin' about it until May. Why she waited so longs to get even I'll never know."

"No further questions, your Honor," concluded Hays Randolf.

Irdine got up to go when the judge tapped his gavel and said, "Mrs Dross, go back to your Witness Chair, please."

"Why? He says he was done."

"Arlene's counselor might want to ask you some questions.," remarked Judge MacMillan.

"Good afternoon to you, Mrs Dross," said Hart St. Clair in his very distinct upper class English accent. An accent further refined at Oxford University Faculty of Law. Whilst studying Common and Civil Indigenous Law at Oxford, Hart also practiced Rhetoric. Hart also passed the American Bar and could practice in the several United States and its Trust Territories, like Wyoming, the Dakotas and Alaska, if need be.

"A mother does indeed always know, thank you for reminding us, your ladyship," chirped Hart St Clair knowing that American women melt at the sound of a foreign accent. Especially one they can understand.

"Did you not miss your daughter, Arlene, when she'd disappeared the day after Sheriff Armitage had died?"

"Had you been here and seed what I did for that brat, I rejoiced unto the Lord that she wasn't around."

"How long after the death of Sheriff Armitage did the new sheriff, Kees Van Der Hoff, arrive at your home?"

"Coupla weeks," stated Irdine Dross to the best of her ability.

"Did he not ask you about Arlene's whereabouts?" wondered Hart St. Clair.

"He asked straight out where she was and I tol' him she done run off," admitted Irdine.

"Did the sheriff ask where she might be?"

"I said, if she was smart, she'd be hidin' with them injuns," admitted Irdine.

"So you basically told the new sheriff that your daughter was a suspect?" concluded Hart St. Clair.

"Say that again, only in English."

There was audience laughter.

"Why did you tell the sheriff that Arlene should be in hiding?"

"Cause who else had a reason to kill the sheriff?"

"We have a list of seven other people," said Hart St. Clair with certainty, adding, "Your honor, I have concluded asking questions of this witness. Thank you Mrs Dross." announced Hart St Clair, bowing to her, as though she were Victoria herself.

Hart St. Clair smiled at her and Irdine smiled back.

Hays Randolf stood, then walked dramatically over to the jury and announced, "I call Sheriff Kees Van Der Hoff to the Witness Chair."

The man who replaced deceased Sheriff Ross Armitage pledged to tell the truth unto Almighty God and took a seat on the Witness Chair.

Hays Randolf: "How long after Sheriff Armitage was murdered did you knock on Irdine Dross's door in Cheyenne, Wyoming Territory?

"Ten days," said Sheriff Van Der Hoff.   His tone was staccato. He used precise language.

"Who were you looking for, Sheriff?"

"Arlene Dross, daughter of the late Robert Dyce Dross, a wanted bank robber and ex-convict.   A very dangerous criminal," concluded Sheriff Van Der Hoff.

"What took ten days to ride up to Cheyenne? Bad weather? Impassable roads?" wondered Hays Randolf.

"I needed permission from the Territorial Court to talk to any of its citizens. It took 5 days for the Wyoming Territorial Court to grant permission, and this was all by Western Union Telegraph. That gave Arlene five more days to escape," said Sheriff Van Der Hoff, calmly, without emotion.

"Who was home when you got there?" wondered Hays Randolf.

"Mrs Dross," stated Sheriff Van Der Hoff, just answering the question and not adding anything.

"Was Mrs Dross of any help, Sheriff?"

"She turned over the murder weapon, the Smith & Wesson thirty-two caliber six gun, and gave me the motive why Arlene shot Sheriff Armitage," stated Sheriff Van Der Hoff.

Hart St Clair said, "Objection, your Honor. The Smith & Wesson pistol has not been identified as a 'murder' weapon."

The judge sustained the motion saying to the jury, "Disregard that the .32 is a murder weapon until it's establish how Sheriff Armitage actually died."

"What did you do next?" asked Hays Randolf of witness Kees Van Der Hoff, Sheriff of Larimer County, Colorado.

"Sent telegrams out to sheriff's departments all over Wyoming and Dakota Territory and to the states of Nebraska, Kansas, Missouri, especially Kansas City and St. Louis. We had a likeness of Arlene drawn up by an artist at the Denver Post newspaper, and they printed a hundred of them and we mailed them to all the local news-papers.

"What did the wanted poster say?" asked Hays Randolph.

The sheriff had several copies of the poster with him. Large black type screamed 'ARLENE DROSS. WANTED FOR MURDER OF COLORADO SHERIFF ARMITAGE. $500 REWARD. Contact Larimer County Sheriff Dept., Fort Collins, Colorado.'

A very good likeness of Arlene, her name spelled correctly as Arlene Dross, Cheyenne, Wyoming Territory. 5'8", 'Dresses in pants, matching jacket with fringe, flat brim hat, rides a black thoroughbred called L.C.. VERY DANGEROUS'.

"How'd you track her down in London, England?"

"We got a telegram from." Sheriff Van Der Hoff reached in his jeans pocket and took out a notepad, opened it and found a name, "Some Countess Agatha Hanover in London," said Sheriff Van Der Hoff matter-of-factly.

Jack shot up like he was struck by lightning.   Lindy shot straight up, too.   She whipped around and glared at Jack who was sitting behind her, when she recognized Jack's mother's name.

Sheriff Van Der Hoff read the telegram, written like a missive, with no regard that each letter of the alphabet cost 5 shillings ($1 per letter!): "My son Edward brought your murderer, Arlene Dross, to my London home where she is to-day.   Come to Ashfield Hall on Brompton Road, Knightsbridge, London, United Kingdom, south of Hyde Park, next to Buckingham Palace, home of Her Majesty Victoria, Queen of the United Kingdom and Empress of India.   (Signed) Royal Countess Agatha Hanover, United Kingdom."

"This woman in England learnt that she was harboring a fugitive," stated Hays Randolf.

"Yes," replied Sheriff Van Der Hoff, witness.

"What did you do next?"

"I needed permission from the Governor of Colorado for Extradition Papers, then permission to travel to England, claim the suspect and bring her back to Colorado for trial.   I also needed the funds for travel, lodging and food."

"I see that you're back with the prisoner, Miss Dross.   Did she come willingly?"

"Yes she did.   The gentleman whose lodging she stayed in was admirably cooperative and supplied, at no cost to the sheriff's department, our own lodging accommodations, plus exemplary meals, travel by private train and saloon class accommodation on the SS Britannic steam ship when we crossed the Atlantic Ocean," said Sheriff Van Der Hoff in a mollifying and appreciative tone.

"Did you interrogate the prisoner?" asked Hays Randolf of the Sheriff.

"Of course."

"Did she confess to the killing?" inquired Hays Randolf.

"No she did not.   Her lawyer was present and told her not to say anything," said the Sheriff.

"Anything at all?" wondered Hays Randolf.

"The prisoner talked about horse racing," said the sheriff.

"Anything else?"

"That she won a horse race and that Mr Jack Hanover gave her the entire purse valued at 30,000 dollars, or Pounds, I can't remember which," reported Sheriff Van Der Hoff.

"No further questions at this time, Sheriff. Your witness." said Hays Randolf to Sir Eberhart St. Clair, Esquire.

Arlene's lawyer approached Sheriff Van Der Hoff and picked up the Smith & Wesson .32 caliber six gun from the evidence table in front of the judge's bench.

"You, Sheriff Van Der Hoff, are calling this gun the murder weapon?" stated Hart St. Clair.

"I am," repeated the sheriff.

"The bullet from this gun lodged in Sheriff Armitage's shoulder, did it not?" interrogated Hart St. Clair.

"Real close to his heart," asserted Sheriff Van Der Hoff.

"And that small singular .32 caliber bullet brought down a man who is 6'3" tall and weighed some 250 pounds. Everybody in town called Sheriff Armitage 'the Bear' because of his immense size. Nothing short of an elephant gun would bring him down. Yet that small bullet which lodged in his left shoulder, far away from any life-threatening blood vessels somehow killed him dead instantly. Nonsense. In fact, the Coroner, whom I shall recall, stated there was no blood emanating from the bullet shot into Sheriff Armitage's shoulder. No blood! Do you know what that means, sir?" Hart St. Clair was showing emotion and aggressiveness. Anti-English traits.

"Could mean anything," backhanded Sheriff Van Der Hoff.

"It could only mean one thing, sheriff. That Sheriff Armitage was already dead!"

Some gasped, most heard that he was already dead so this was old news.

"Someone other than the prisoner had killed the sheriff earlier in the day and seated the deceased sheriff on his front porch swing appearing to be asleep," concluded Hart St. Clair, who added, "I am through with the witness for the time being, your Honour."

Hays Randolf arose and called his next witness: "I re-call the Larimer County Coroner, Dr Marcus Hardee, back to the Witness Chair for re-direct, your honor."

The Coroner, a medical doctor, returned to the Witness Chair.

Judge MacMillan reminded Dr Hardee, MD, that he was still under Oath and that an Almighty Angry, Judgmental and Punishing God was watching him closely.

"Your Coroner's report concluded that Sheriff Ross Armitage's cause of death was due to a bullet fired from this pistol, is this not true?" Hays Randolf was is no mood for indecisiveness.

The Coroner looked queasy and hesitated.

"Do you need to refer to your Autopsy Report?" badgered Hays Randolf.

"That Autopsy Report was written in haste. I only examined the body looking for multiple bullet wounds. The newspaper reported the sheriff had died of multiple gunshot wounds. I only found the one. The .32 caliber lead bullet."

"And since you signed the Autopsy Report, then Sheriff Armitage must have died of a gunshot wound or many gunshot wounds." hotly demanded Hays Randolf.

Judge MacMillan chimed in: "Mr Randolf, you cannot put words in the witness's mouth. In Larimer County you ask witnesses questions, not draw your own conclusions."

"I'm sorry, your honor. Mr Coroner, does your signed Autopsy Report conclude that Cause of Death was due to a gunshot wound?" asked a less arrogant Hays Randolf.

"Yes, Sheriff Armitage died of a single gunshot wound."

"And what was the caliber of the bullet that killed Sheriff Armitage?" asked Hays Randolf.

"A thirty-two caliber bullet," replied the Coroner.

"We will put a bookmark in these proceedings. Court is adjourned til 10 o'clock tomorrow morning," announced Judge MacMillan.

"All rise," commanded the large Bailiff.

Immediately After Court

Lindy, dressed in her tight leather fringed outfit, grabbed Jack by the arm and headed outside and pushed him up against the courthouse's red brick wall.

"I'm killin' your fuckin' mother. Six shots to her thick, fat head. Don't try to stop me."

"I'll hold her still while you shoot," guaranteed Jack.

"I don't trust women. How could she turn me in? And who told her that I shot the fuckin' sheriff?"

"I believe that was you. You told a lot of people you shot the sheriff. You told me while you were eating chili five minutes after you rode into my camp, which was right after you shot the sheriff!" reminded Jack.

"You'd actually hold your mother still so I could shoot her?" threatened Lindy.

"You have my word on it, as a Royal Duke," proclaimed Jack.

"You ain't afraid I'll miss and hit you?" interrogated Lindy in an unusually caring voice.

"You shot the sheriff from 30 feet, at night, in the rain, on your horse, with a 40 mile an hour wind blowing. You won't miss the Countess from two feet away."

Lindy hugged Jack and said, "I love you Jack."

That Night.

Lindy, Jack, Hart St. Clair, Reno Sweetwater and Danny Maxwell had dinner brought to Jack's three room suite. The middle room was set up as their dining room.

Lindy sat next to Jack.

Hart St. Clair was relaxed and said, "the Coroner said, under oath, that 'his first autopsy report' written hastily, said the sheriff died of that single .32 wound. His *first* autopsy report? How many autopsy reports did he write to get it right for court?"

Reno chimed in, "We need to get one thing straight—was the sheriff already dead when Arlene shot him. If yes, we won. We go home."

"First of all, why so many autopsy reports?   It's like everyone's got a different opinion of how he died. Looks like Lindy solved a lot of problems by shooting the sheriff," said Reno Sweetwater, a man who grew up in the wild west."

"I think half the town knows what happened and don't care who gets hanged. The actual killer or Lindy," cautioned Hart St Clair.

"So if I didn't kill the sheriff, who did?" wondered Lindy.

Oddly, from Lindy's point of view, nobody seemed to care.

"The only thing that matters is you're not guilty," said Reno.

"Don't you wanna know who killed him? And if he was already a goner, who killed him and put him on that porch swing? His skinny-ass ghost wife? No fucking way. She had help."

"That's the sheriff's job. He'll be under pressure to find the killer or killers," replied Reno..

"What if the widow had a boyfriend and he killed the sheriff and lifted him on the porch swing. Then fucked the brand new widow." Lindy was upset that no one, not even Jack, cared who killed the sheriff.

"Why'd you call the widow a 'ghost wife'?" wondered Jack.

"You ever see her? It's the middle of the summer she looks white as a ghost. Why's she hiding in the house? She got a man under her bed?" Lindy was focused on a love affair when all the men were focused on clearing Lindy's name, getting paid then going home.

"Let's corner the Coroner. He's shaky as a leaf in a chinook. We need those 'extra' autopsy reports—namely the original report. That's the one that said what really happened," mentioned Reno Sweetwater.

"Me and Oscar will dig through the town dump and anywhere else the Coroner would get rid of those autopsy papers."

CHAPTER 30

Day 2

Hays Randolf called his final witness, Susan Armitage, the dead sheriff's widow. Susan Armitage married Ross Armitage right out of high school in Fort Collins. What Susan and Ross wanted more than anything were children and a good paying government job. In 1868 when they graduated from Auntie Stone's Classroom (an actual high school), they planned on moving to Kansas City, Missouri, or Topeka, Kansas, to work for the government. Good, steady pay, enough to raise a family.

Word got out in 1868 that Colorado Territory, which had applied for statehood seven years earlier, was up before the U.S. Senate for consideration to become a state. Susan and Ross Armitage stayed in Fort Collins. Ross joined the Larimer County Sheriff's Department and Susan worked for the Larimer County Tax Assessor's office as part of Colorado Territory.

And now, twelve years later, with no husband and no children, Susan Armitage seemed lost. And about to testify to see if this jury would recommend she receive more than a widow's pension for her tragic loss.

Susan swore to tell the truth, the whole truth and nothing but the truth, so help her God.

Hays Randolf, protecting her dead husband as the county prosecutor, asked gentle questions of Susan Armitage, Widow.

Susan appeared pale white. As though she never ventured outside in the summer sun.

"Do you miss your husband, Mrs Armitage?" was the obsequious, ingratiating and sniveling question Hays Randolf proffered to Widow Armitage.

She wept, of course. Lindy, sitting at the Defendant's Table, rolled her eyes.

"Do you want to see the murderer get justice?" asked Hays Randolf.

Mrs Armitage held her simple cotton handkerchief and wept theatrically, and nodded yes.

"Why would Arlene Dross murder your husband, ma'am?" wondered Hays Randolf.

"To get even because my husband rightly shot Arlene's father. Arlene's father had been robbing banks all up and down Colorado and Wyoming for ten years. Never been caught and everyone alive knew he was the gang leader. My husband, the Sheriff of Larimer County, put an end to Robert Dyce Dross's wicked ways."

From his gallery seat a foot behind Lindy, Edward put his hand on Lindy's shoulder as a reminder to keep her mouth shut, no outbursts, no remarks. It will anger the jury and you'll end up hanged. "You can't shoot my mother if you're hanged in Colorado," is all Jack had to say.

"Your witness," said Hays Randolph.

Hart St. Clair arose and kept his distance from Susan Armitage. He did not want to appear as a bully or intimidator. He wanted to appear as an English gentleman.

"Your ladyship," began the English barrister with his very refined Oxonian accent, "this is a very delicate question. Did you discover your husband in his final condition, or did someone else discover him?" asked an inquiring Hart St. Clair.

"I found him," said Susan less theatrically, sniffling, wiping tears away.

"When did you discover that he was not asleep in his porch chair?" wondered Hart St. Clair.

"It's a swing, not a chair, and I don't remember. I did say, 'Time for bed, Ross,' and he didn't respond," recalled Susan Armitage.

"What were you thinking when he didn't respond?" snaked Hart St. Clair.

"I thought I hope he's all right," said Susan.

"Why did you think that?" questioned Hart St. Clair.

"Well, he's the sheriff and a lot of people might want to harm him," revealed sSusan Armitage.

Hart St. Clair looked over at Hays Randolf who looked pained, closed his eyes at the Prosecutor's Table.

"So every time your husband sat on the front porch and fell asleep, you assumed he might be shot by any member of society?" gently asked Hart St. Clair.

"Objection, your Honor," said a testy Hays Randolf.

"On what Order of Cross-Examination do you object?" queried Judge MacMillan.

"Assuming facts not admitted in evidence," whiffed Hays Randolf.

"Mrs Armitage just admitted her fear of Sheriff Armitage getting harmed by unnamed suspects in the community." responded Hart St. Clair.

"I'll allow it, counselor. Mrs Armitage, please answer Mister St. Clair's question," ordered Judge Macmillan.

Fumbling for an answer Mrs Armitage said, "Well many times. He's the sheriff, he has to arrest people and throw them in jail. He has enemies," testified Susan.

"How many enemies, ma'am?" wondered Hart St. Clair.

"Well, several," said Susan.

"Several? Please give the Court a number. Ten, twenty, thirty enemies?" queried Hart St. Clair.

"About five or six," admitted Susan Armitage weakly, attempting to hold the number down.

"So, out of five or six enemies whom you believed would want to harm your husband for varying reasons, why did you pick on poor Miss Arlene Dross?" Hart St. Clair asked that question to the entire gallery.

"Miss Dross, please stand so we can see what a terrible threat you are to this community," asked Hart St Clair of Lindy.

Arlene (Lindy Mae Long) stood up.

The Courtroom murmured. Positive murmurs from men. Negative murmurs from women.

Lindy stood still in her fringed leather outfit with a contrasting silk blouse. Her face was pure innocence, with her blonde hair pulled back and her blue eyes. She didn't smile. But she was innocent beauty. She also did not wear her Colt .45 Peacemaker.

"Mrs Armitage, this is Arlene Dross. She is one of five or so 'dangerous' citizens whom you testified would want to harm your husband. What are the names of the rest?" demanded Hart St. Clair.

"She done it!" j'accused Susan Armitage in a voice that could be heard six blocks away.

"Did you see Miss Arlene 'do' it?"

"The new sheriff said she done it; that suits me."

"Thank you Mrs Armitage. No further questions at this time."

As Hart sat down next to Lindy, she said in a threatening whisper, "Why'd you let her off the hook? She only named me!?"

"The jury feels sorry for her. I did not want the jury to turn against you by bullying and intimidating the Widow. Right now, the jury is about to vote you not guilty," countered Hart.

Hart St Clair then noticed one of his investigators coming into court.

Oscar Sullivan entered the court on tippy-toes, and handed Danny Maxwell, lead private investigator, something wrapped in heavy paper, tied with string.

Hays Randolf jumped to his feet and immediately engaged Mrs Armitage in re-direct examination.

"Mrs Armitage, why did the sheriff say that Miss Arlene Dross shot and killed your husband?"

"Cause the sheriff found her gun at her house, and the coroner found the bullet in my husband and the coroner said Ross died of a gunshot wound."

"Why not Arlene's mother?" examined Hays Randolf.

"It was a downpour! A torrent of water from an angry God. No one in his right mind was out that night. Only a crazy, vengeful child would go out in a deluge like that and Arlene had good reason to go out. To get even with my husband for shooting her no-good bank-robbing father!" cried Susan Armitage, "and she admitted it! She said she shot my poor husband!"

Theatrical weeping, making sure everyone on the jury looked saddened.

Hart St. Clair, sitting next to Arlene at the Defendant's Table, gripped her hand and gestured to a large note printed on paper that said, 'Look innocent!' And Arlene showed childlike innocence. Which is good because all the jurors were staring at her. How could a defiant, troublesome young lady who wore tight leather pants, always argued with everyone, and always carried a sidearm, look so vulnerable and innocent. For starters, Crazy Horse was home in England. Just thinking of her horse put Arlene in a relaxed, homicide-free mood. She looked at peace to the jury.

"I rest my case, your honor," said Hays Randolf defiantly.

"Let's take a one hour break and return after luncheon." ordered Judge MacMillan.

He tapped his gavel and the Bailiff said "All rise".

After a luncheon of fried chicken, potato salad, cold cucumber salad and hot tea in Hart St. Clair's hotel suite out of sight of citizens in nearby restaurants, they did not discuss the case. The fried chicken and potato salad were delicious, the tea was sweet and hot.

"When's we gonna talk about the murder trial?" wondered Arlene, enjoying fried chicken.

Reno held up a large envelope and said, "Inside this envelope is our ticket back home. You'll be found innocent."

"All rise," said the Bailiff after luncheon.

"Mr. Saint Clair, it's your turn," informed Judge MacMillan.

Hart St Clair rose from his seat at the Defendant's Table and walked to the center of the courtroom and summoned the County Coroner, Dr. Marcus Hardee, MD, to take the Witness Chair.

Judge MacMillan reminded Doctor Hardee that he was still sworn in.

Hart St.Clair had a large paper envelope in his hand. Hart St. Clair removed an official document, in full view of the judge, jury and gallery. Hart placed the document taken from the envelope and placed it on Judge MacMillan's desk.

"Your Honor," reported Hart St.Clair in his full, eloquent, erudite Oxonian voice, "I enter into the Records, Doctor Hardee, County Coroner's **Original** Autopsy report."

The gallery gasped for air. Judge MacMillan looked a question at this document.

Prosecutor Hays Randolf jumped up and yelled out, "I protest, your Honor! What unscrupulous device has Defense Counsel unbounded now?"

"Come see for yourself," advised the judge.

Hays Randolph, miffed, got up and clomped hurriedly over to the Bench, took the document in question and studied it. Hart St. Clair stood by with an easy 'she's not guilty' smirk.

"Where'd this come from?" demanded Hays Randolf.

"You'll get your chance, Mr. Randolf. In the Law, we call it Cross Examination." chided Judge MacMillan, then gesturing the prosecutor back to his table.

"Is this a true document?" asked Judge MacMillan.

"Yes, your Honor. You have in your hand, the original autopsy report written and signed by Doctor Marcus Hardee, MD, the County Coroner. I shall reveal that this document was hidden from view, secreted away whilst a newer autopsy report was dreamed up," offered Hart St. Clair.

"Examine your witness, Mr. St. Clair."

"Thank you, your Honour."

"Are you, or are you not, the current County Coroner for Larimer County, Colorado?"
asked Hart St.Clair.

"Yes, I am," quietly stated the County Coroner, Marcus Hardee, MD.

Hart St.Clair handed the coroner the original signed autopsy report.

"First, is this an official Autopsy form for Larimer County?"

"Yes it is," said the coroner after reading each of the four pages, carefully.

"Is this your signature, Dr Hardee?" wondered Hart St. Clair.

"It looks like my signature," mumbled the coroner.

"Is this your signature, sir, yes or no," said Hart St. Clair with more emphasis.

"I believe so. Yes," admitted the coroner.

"You swear to it, doctor?" riveted Hart St. Clair.

"I, I do," admitted the coroner.

"Thank you, sir," said Hart St. Clair.

The gallery broke into astonished chatter. The easy-going judge let the courtroom express their new-found indignation and relief at this new revelation.

"What was the Cause of Death of the late Sheriff Ross Armitage as stated in your original Autopsy Report?" wondered Hart St Clair.

There was a pause as the coroner was looking over the Autopsy report, a document he's seen hundreds of time.

"Arsenic poisoning," determined the County Coroner.

The gallery gasped. More importantly, the jury gasped.

"Poisoning. And not a gunshot wound?" asked Hart St. Clair.

"Yes, the cause of death of the sheriff was poisoning by arsenic," declared the coroner.

"And not a gunshot wound?" added Hart St. Clair.

"No. The bullet hit the sheriff in his shoulder, near his clavicle—his collar bone," added the coroner, pointing to his own clavicle.

"Do you swear unto Almighty God that this Autopsy Report is the true Autopsy Report, so help you God?" said master Barrister Sir Eberhart Hibbard St. Clair, KCB, Esq.

(KCB is Knight Commander of the Most Honourable Order of the Bath, founded by King George I, May 18, 1725.)

The Larimer County Coroner paused, looked at the floor and said, "Yes, this is the true and original Autopsy report."

"Say again which of the many poisons did the sheriff die from?" wondered Hart St. Clair.

"Arsenic" said the coroner.

"The same arsenic as the sheriff's wife had several boxes of, in wafer form?"

The gallery, especially the ladies in the back, reacted with vocal wonderment, condemnation and a couple of shrieks.   The judge loved the outburst.

"The very same" replied the coroner.

The gallery gasped. One of the Rowdy Ladies yelled, "Susan poisoned her husband!"   Another Rowdy Lady shouted, "String her up!"

Judge MacMillan allowed the gallery to chant 'string her up' for a short time before he gently tapped his gavel and pointed to Hart St. Clair to continue. These courtroom outbursts allowed the judge to nibble on a pastry or two and drink his coffee. The judge could stand to lose a couple of pounds, but his mother-in-law, from Vienna, owned the Fort Collins bakery named Kirschtorte.

"Doctor Hardee, let us get to your Coroner's Report, which you also signed stating, firmly and clearly, that it was a gunshot wound from a .32 caliber Smith & Wesson that shot and killed the sheriff.   How did that come about when you knew the sheriff was poisoned with arsenic?"

"I was under pressure to say he died by gunfire because that's what the newspaper said," squeaked the coroner.

"Who put you up to this charade?" cudgeled Hart St. Clair.

"I'm not sure," lied the coroner.

"You are sure. Do not go to jail for perjury sir. Do not protect a murderer," cautioned Hart St Clair.

"He said he'd kill my wife, our baby. Even our dog! What was I supposed to do?" cried the coroner.

The gallery was aghast and angry.

"Tell us who threatened your family and your puppy. Tell us!" commanded Hart St. Clair.

"Sheriff Van Der Hoff, he made me change it.". said the shaky and vulnerable coroner.

"Thank you, sir," quipped Hart St. Clair.

Hays Randolf, prosecutor, flipped through notes, asked questions of his assistant counsel and thought for a second, stood and said, "No questions, your honor."

Hays Randolf wanted to see how the very aggressive new sheriff would deal with this. And let the Brit lawyer solve the murder.

The judge pointed to Hart St. Clair and said, "Where did you find the original autopsy report, counselor?"

"One of our investigators, Mr Daniel Maxwell, found it in the town's garbage dump, folded and stuffed in a milk bottle, your honour," confirmed Hart St. Clair.

Judge MacMillan finished sipping his coffee and ordered: "call your next witness counselor."

"I call Kees Van Der Hoff, Sheriff of Larimer County, Colorado," said Hart St. Clair in an accusative voice that Van Der Hoff must be guilty of something.

The sheriff was waiting in the hallway, like other witnesses, out of earshot of testimony. But he heard the commotion from the gallery, especially the most vocal ladies.

Sheriff Van Der Hoff walked to the Witness Chair expecting nothing but questions that would seal Lindy's fate.

Before the sheriff was sworn in, the Bailiff, a black man who was 6'7" and weighed about 270 pounds, took Sheriff Van Der Hoff's Colt .45 Peacemaker with his holster and kept it. The judge administered the Oath using his family Bible.

"Good day, sheriff," began Hart St. Clair, smiling as though nothing was the matter, "I have a couple of quick questions for you, sir," continued Hart St Clair: "Were you satisfied with the coroner's autopsy report?"

"Yes. Completely satisfied," happily replied Kees Van Der Hoff, sheriff.

"That, as the Autopsy revealed, Sheriff Armitage died of arsenic poisoning." proclaimed Hart St. Clair.

"Yes, ah. What? No!! Where'd you get 'poisoning'? Ross was shot dead by Arlene Dross," finalized Sheriff Van Der Hoff.

"We got arsenic poisoning from Dr Hardee's *original* Autopsy Report. A report that you saw and disagreed with because arsenic poisoning of Sheriff Armitage would have implicated his wife, Susan Armitage." exclaimed Hart St Clair. "Why, sir, would you need to protect Sheriff Armitage's wife?"

"I didn't protect her. The murderer is sitting right there. I'm protecting the town from Arlene, not Widow Armitage." cried Kees Van Der Hoff.

Hart St. Clair showed Sheriff Van Der Hoff the original autopsy report, crinkled, folded with wear and tear. Kees Van Der Hoff read it and shook his head.

"You'll notice the bullet lodged in the sheriff's collar bone, a long way from his heart. The coroner also found about three pounds of arsenic poison in the sheriff's body. Three pounds of poison, sir," dramatised Hart St Clair, English Barrister.

"The coroner's a liar!" said the sheriff.

"The bullet wound did not bleed, sheriff. That means Sheriff Armitage was already dead when he was shot. Already dead, sitting on the front porch swing. How did Widow Armitage lift her dead husband who weighed 250 pounds onto the porch swing, sir?" wondered Hart St. Clair.

"How should I know?" fenced Sheriff Van Der Hoff.

"Because you lifted the dead sheriff, sir," chided Hart St. Clair.

"What!?   That's absurd," said Sheriff Van Der Hoff nervously.

"Sheriff, you were seen squiring Susan Armitage around town for several months before the sheriff died of arsenic poisoning. We have a dozen qualified witnesses, including Horton Armitage, the sheriff's younger brother, and Mayor of Fort Collins," taunted Hart St. Clair.

"They're framing me!" said Sheriff Van Der Hoff.

"Nobody's framin' you. All of us seen you proudly sportin' Susan around, all smiley and full of yourself!" said one of the Rowdy Ladies on behalf of her 'sisterhood' the Rowdy Ladies of the Back Bench.

"I object, your honor," shouted Hays Randolf, prosecutor.

"I'll allow it," said Judge MacMillan, taking a bite of his mother-in-law's exceptional chocolate ganache.

"The County Coroner asserts that you ordered him to write a new Autopsy report. One in which states that a .32 caliber bullet, lodged in Sheriff Armitage's chest, near his heart and not his shoulder, killed him. Yet his original Autopsy Report said that his body was, and I quote from his Autopsy Report, that the late sheriff's body was 'soaked in arsenic poison' and that is the cause of his death. Further, the bullet that hit the sheriff did not bleed. And that was because the sheriff was already dead. So I ask you, sheriff, why did you order a 'better' Autopsy Report?" summed up Hart St. Clair.

"I don't know nuthin' about no Autopsy report," lied Sheriff Van Der Hoff.

"Really?" said Reno Sweetwater, who stood up, walked over to the center of the courtroom, holding several pieces of paper. Hart St. Clair nodded to Reno and took a seat next to Lindy/Arlene at the Defendant's table.

"According to sworn Affidavits from several of your Deputies and other prominent witnesses including the town mayor, a dozen witnesses have been Deposed, under Oath, and said you, Sheriff Van Der Hoff, were not happy with the coroner's Autopsy report. That the sheriff's body was 'riddled with bullets' and that could be the only cause of death. The coroner only found one bullet. And you said, 'that's all it takes'. You dismissed the poison idea.didn't you?"

Reno Sweetwater walked his documents over to the judge.

"You're full of shit, ya slimy lawyer. You're lying and I can prove it," quipped Sheriff Van Der Hoff.

Hays Randolf came over to look at the statements from the witnesses who testified under oath at a Deposition, that Sheriff Van Der Hoff didn't like the original Autopsy Report and ordered a new, improved Report.

"I'm not lying, sheriff. Nor are the twelve witnesses who said you ordered the coroner to write another Autopsy Report. And therefore neither is the County Coroner lying, who did so because you threatened to kill his adoring wife, their beautiful baby girl, and their family puppy. Why change the report? What did you have to gain? Were you having extra marital relations with Susan Armitage?" accosted Reno Sweetwater.

"Hell no!" screamed Sheriff Van Der Hoff who jumped up, out of his chair.

"Susan Armitage is very beautiful. Very, very attractive. And you were fond of her. You've been seen having luncheon with Mrs Armitage. You would take her for carriage rides on your day off, while her husband, the sheriff, was busy at work. Carriage rides? With a married woman?"

"She asked me!" cried Sheriff Van Der Hoff.

"When Sheriff Armitage was shot in early May, where were you?" asked Reno Sweetwater.

"I was at the station, the Sheriff's Department," said Sheriff Van Der Hoff.

"How did you learn of the sheriff's death?"

"A neighbor kid came running in, soaking wet, saying the sheriff's dead at his house," said Sheriff Van Der Hoff.

"And what did you do?" queried Reno Sweetwater.

"I got on my pony and rode the two blocks to Sheriff Armitage's house."

"What did you see?"

"Well, first off, there was the sheriff, sittin' on his front porch swing. So the first thing I thought was this 'neighbor kid' was pulling a prank. Sheriff looked like he always does sitting on the front porch swing. Only tonight it's raining hard."

"What'd you do next?" asked Reno Sweetwater.

"Well, I knocked on the door and Susan answered it. She was all crying and babbling, I couldn't get an answer out of her, then she said, 'Ross's dead!' So I went to see the sheriff to see if he was dead an' all.   And yep, he was a goner."

"Did you inspect for a cause of death?" asked Reno Sweetwater.

"Well, yeah. There was lightning and maybe he was struck by lightning. So I looked him over and saw a hole in his shirt. I tore open his shirt and he had a hole in his chest."

"Where in his chest?" wondered Reno Sweetwater.

"About here, I believe." lied Sheriff Van Der Hoff.

"There, around his heart?"

"Not exactly in his heart, a little higher maybe." lied Sheriff Van Der Hoff.

"Lot of blood, then," asked Reno Sweetwater.

"I guess. I don't remember," said Sheriff Van Der Hoff.

"The coroner said there was no blood from the bullet wound, which was much higher, by his collar bone. No blood. In fact, you said you were looking for a lightning strike. You found a hole in his shirt you didn't mention any blood. Just a hole. No blood," said Reno closing in.

Reno added, "Have you ever seen a gunshot wound, sheriff?"

"Yeah, lots. This is the 'wild west', so they say," reminded Sheriff Van Der Hoff.

"No further questions of this witness, but we request that Sheriff Van Der Hoff be available for further examination," requested Reno Sweetwater before relinquishing the floor to Hart St Clair.

Hart St. Clair stood and announced, eloquently, "Mrs Susan Armitage to the Witness Chair, please."

Widow Armitage was called from her seat out in the hallway, out of earshot of the testimony and judicial instructions, and warnings, offered by Judge MacMillan.

She entered the court. Suddenly, every head was turned, necks creaking, to get a better look now at a possible murder suspect living right under everyone's nose.

Widow Armitage took her seat in the Witness Chair.

"Mrs Armitage, I remind you, ma'am, you are still under the countenance of your Oath to tell the Truth, the whole Truth and nothing but the Truth so help you God. Do you understand?" asked a smiling Judge MacMillan.

"Yes, your Majesty," said Susan Armitage.

Hart St. Clair approached the Witness Chair and handed Susan Armitage, wife of the decedent, a box of arsenic wafers.

Hart St. Clair asked Widow Armitage what was handed her.

"This is a box of wafers I eat for my beauty regimen," stated Susan Armitage.

"Wafers, something you eat?" wondered Hart St. Clair.

"Yes! I eat several a day. One in the morning, one midway, and one around supper time."

"And what, exactly, are these wafers called?" asked Hart St.Clair.

"Dr Campbell's Safe Arsenic Complexion Wafers. Here, see for yourself," said Susan Armitage, handing Hart St Clair a box of arsenic wafers.

"The instructions on the box of arsenic wafers say to eat one every few hours, to make your skin look like, ah, porcelain. Is this what you do with them?" inquired Hart St. Clair.

"Yes, of course," replied Susan Armitage, smiling, "can't you tell?" she said seductively.

"Did you offer any to your husband?"

"No. Why would I. These are for ladies to keep our skin soft and pure," admitted Susan Armitage, widow.

"Pure? What does that mean?" Hart St. Clair was clueless.

"You know, white as someone who doesn't get out in the harsh sun. Otherwise you turn red like an injun or brown like a nigger from workin' in the sun all day, every day. I want to look pure, pure white, y'know?" So sayeth good christian Susan Armitage.

"Did you ever see your husband eating these wafers?" wondered Hart St. Clair.

"No. But I had boxes go missing from my collection," admitted Susan Armitage, a woman with pasty pure white skin, who avoided the noon day sun as much as possible.

"Did you entice—ask—Sheriff Van Der Hoff to take you for a carriage ride?"

"Why of course. I needed to go to the General Store for items and Sheriff Van Der Hoff rode over on his horse and went in my buckboard," said Susan, clearly spoken with nothing to hide.

"During the day or night. ma'am?" inquired Hart.

"Never noon! Around sundown," said an exuberant Mrs Artmitage.

"Sundown? Where was your husband?" asked Hart.

"At work. Ross said 'trouble starts at sundown and goes into the night,'" reported Susan.

"After you picked up your things from the store, where did you go?" wondered Hart, and the rest of the gallery including judge and jury.

"Sheriff Van Der Hoff took me home—my home—and carried in my things."

".which included how many boxes of arsenic?" wondered Hart.

"Maybe ten boxes." Susan was accurate.

"Ten boxes of arsenic poison." queried Hart.

"Are you saying I had something to do with poisoning my husband!?"

The courtroom exploded with laughter. The judge included. The jury was howling.
Susan felt embarrassed as the courtroom attendees were laughing at her.

When the laughter died down, Hart St. Clair said, "That conclusion came to my mind."

"I don't know what killed Ross, but it weren't me."

"At the general store, what did Sheriff Van Der Hoff—
actually, at the time it was Deputy Sheriff Van Der Hoff—think of
you buying all those boxes of arsenic?" asked Hart/

"He said, 'are you trying to poison your husband?'" stated
Susan, matter-of-factly.

"And you said to Deputy Sheriff Van Der Hoff...?"
wondered Hart St. Clair.

"With my expensive beauty treatments!?"

"Mrs Armitage, your husband, Sheriff Ross Armitage, was
dead while sitting on the porch swing. Did Deputy Sheriff Van Der
Hoff take his body away?" Hart St Clair was closing in.

"Why yes," said Susan.

"Did Deputy Van Der Hoff have help lifting your husband
onto a cart or stretcher?" wondered Hart St. Clair.

"Yes, someone I know from the neighborhood came over to
help, a young man who is rather muscular. He works in the silver
mine. He and the sheriff picked up my husband and put him in my
buckboard," said Susan with a knot in her throat recalling the
incident.

"No, no," insisted Hart St. Clair. "Before that. The coroner
said your husband was already dead sitting on the porch swing. Who
put your dead husband in the porch swing in the first place?"
Hart St. Clair finally asked the question everyone in the courtroom
wanted to hear.

Susan sat stark still like she knew who put her dead 250
pound husband in the swing to make him look alive. She couldn't do
it. So who did?

"Mrs Armitage, what's the name of the man, or men, who
put Ross Armitage in the front porch swing the night that someone
else shot at him? We need an answer, ma'am." Hart St Clair had a
noose around Susan Armitage's neck.

"Was it Deputy Sheriff Van Der Hoff?" asked Hart St. Clair.

"No." That sounded like the truth.

"Was it the neighbor boy, who worked in a silver mine,
someone strong enough to carry your husband to the porch swing?"
concluded Hart St. Clair.

"It could've been. I don't recollect his name," lied Susan
Armitage.

"It was Wilbur Hoagland!" came a thunderous voice from
several of the Rowdy Ladies of the Back Bench.

A tall, strong-looking man-child, about 19, stood up in the center of the courtroom, stepped on toes in the middle of his row, and ran toward the exits.

"That's Wilbur," shouted a second Rowdy Lady.

"Git 'em!" said two or three more Rowdy Ladies.

Not a problem.

The Bailiff's twin brother, Courtroom Security, was 6'8" and 285 pounds of muscle, stepped in front of the double exit doors. Wilbur Hoagland slid on the polished wood floor and slammed into the Bailiff's twin brother's chest. Wilbur fell hard onto the oak plank flooring.

In the Witness Chair right now was the Rowdy Lady who called out Wilbur's name in the first place. Wilbur was getting fixed up by Dr Hardee when he hit his head on the oak floor bouncing off the Bailiff's large brother.

"When Mrs Armitage said she didn't remember the name of Mr Hoagland, why did you call out Wilbur's name like you all knew him?" wondered Reno Sweetwater.

"Cause we've seen Wilbur coming and going from Susan's house for a couple of years."

"**Years**?" questioned Reno Sweetwater.

"**Couple** of years. Wilbur was still in school. He'd bring his tool box over. Susan said she found a handyman who worked cheap." recalled the Rowdy Lady.

"So what? How's that make him a suspect?" wondered Reno Sweetwater.

"Cause Wilbur was telling anyone who'd listen that he was fucking ol Susan pretty good."

"Wasn't he aware of his breach of etiquette?—telling tales out of school?" asked Reno Sweetwater.

"He was a school kid, they brag about anything," started the Rowdy Lady, adding, "after a time, ol' Susan started bragging about the size of Wilbur's manhood. And she weren't talking about his twelve inch ball peen hammer!"

The Rowdy Ladies shrieked and howled with laughter. The gentlemen were embarrassed at this sort of talk. The judge ate more ganache, sipped his afternoon tea. (Coffee in the morning, tea in the afternoon for Judge MacMillan. Everyone in the county knows this.)

The Rowdy Lady in the Witness Chair wondered aloud: "Ask yourself, counselor, what's Wilbur Hoagland doin' in Susan Armitage's house lifting a dead body onto the front porch swing in the first place? How'd the sheriff get dead? Who had the arsenic? And were the two of them in on it—lovers who decided to kill Ross Armitage and take up with themselves!?" wondered the Rowdy Lady looking square at the 12 men on the jury.

"Did you, or your lady acquaintances, ever see Susan Armitage and Wilbur Hoagland out on the town at night while Susan Armitage was married to Ross Armitage?" asked Reno.

"Ever seen them love birds out on the town!?   Tell him ladies." commanded the Rowdy Lady in the Witness Chair.

"You could hear them fucking in Susan's bedroom halfway across town 'cause she was loud and the windows was open.!" mentioned one of the dozen Rowdy Ladies whilst the rest sat in loud agreement.

The judge gently tapped his African walnut gavel and said "thank you, ladies of the court", and okayed the Clerk Recorder to write down their comments as part of the Record.

"Your honor, I would now like to call Wilbur Hoagland to the Witness Chair." said Reno Sweetwater in a firm voice.

Wilbur, now under restraint of leg and wrist shackles, was escorted to the Witness Chair and had his handcuffs removed so he could raise his right hand to Almighty God who wasn't paying attention anyway.   After being sworn in, the handcuffs were affixed to the front, making it easier to sit in a chair. The 6'8" court security and twin brother of the court Bailiff stood next to Wilbur.

"Mr Hoagland, it's come to our attention that you were at the home of Susan Armitage and in the presence of Susan Armitage's dead husband who was also the Sheriff, Ross Armitage, on the night he died, were you not?" wondered Reno.

Wilbur looked around the courtroom nervously. Then at the judge.   Then he went looking for Susan Armitage.   Finally he answered with a soft, "Yes."

"Did you lift the lifeless body of Sheriff Ross Armitage up and carry him to the front porch swing the night of the big rain storm?" asked Reno.

After a short pause, Wilbur said, "Yes."

"What was the weather like that night?" asked Reno.

"Downspout," recalled Wilbur Hoagland.

"You mean a hard rainstorm. Flooding. A foot of mud on the roads, that sort of thing?" wondered Reno Sweetwater.

"Yeah, like that." remarked Wilbur.

"Why were you told to pick up a dead body and put it on the front porch swing?" commanded Reno Sweetwater.

"Susan told me to."

"Did Susan Armitage summon you over to her house in that terrible rainstorm just to pick up her husband's body to display it on the front porch swing?" said Reno.

To people in the court other than Wilbur Hoagland, this sounded like a bizarre, illegal and ridiculous thing to do.

"She put up our flag to signal me that the coast was clear, so I come over," revealed Wilbur.

"Flag? Like a U.S. flag?" queried Reno, "For the sole purpose of alerting you that Ross Armitage was not around, or there was no danger of her husband coming home.that sort of signal?" said Reno with question of clarification.

"It was actually a big ol' white sheet," further clarified Wilbur Hoagland.

"Where was this white flag located on the house?"

"Where I could see it when I looked out my window," said Wilbur.

The courtroom burst into laughter. Reno flushed. Wilbur was nonplussed.

"Of course, Wilbur, I'm sorry for not being more specific. Was the white sheet on a pole on the front porch?   Hanging out back.?" continued Reno.

"Up on the roof. The pole looks like a lightning attractor but the sheet was connected to the pole and ready to go. All she had to do was use the rope that went through the closed rooftop door and lift the sheet up. It was big, white and square!" said Wilbur proudly.

"Square? Did the wind make it square?"

"Yeah. We get wind here every day. Blowing steady all day and night, down from Wyoming. That night the wind was howling something fierce so her all clear flag could be seen for blocks." said Wilbur, again, very proudly, like he might have concocted this arrangement of pole, sheet and rope to pull it up so Wilbur could see the flag some 4 blocks away.

"Any of you back room Ladies ever see this flag waving in the breeze?" asked Reno of the Ladies Gallery.

"Every time the Sheriff was out of town," came the chorus from the back of the courtroom.

Judge MacMillan asked, "Aren't you going to object Mr. Randolf?"

"Tell you the truth, your honor, I'm wondering about Mr Hoagland's testimony myself. Miss Dross did shoot the Sheriff, she may be charged with attempted murder or reckless endangerment." said Hays Randolf, prosecutor.

"Mr Hoagland," wondered Reno Sweetwater, Lindy's lawyer, "You are under oath, which means if you lie, you could go to jail for 5 years per lie. Tell 10 lies and you could be put in prison for 50 years. Okay?"

"That ain't okay!" decried Wilbur Hoagland.

"Well, so Wilbur: have you ever had sexual relations with Susan Armitage?" wondered Reno, and the rest of the courtroom..

"Ain't that a private matter?" wondered Wilbur.

"Answer the question, Wilbur, or I'll send you to jail for Contempt of Court," added the judge.

Wilbur squirmed in his seat. Susan Armitage was out in the hall where witnesses go when they're not testifying.

"Wilbur, the Honorable Judge will throw you in the clink if you don't answer my question. And he could throw you in jail for an additional five years if you lie. So, we're waiting Wilbur." said Reno Sweetwater.

"I, I didn't mean no harm to the sheriff, but Susan, she was." started Wilbur,then the Rowdy Ladies stepped in and shouted: "she's wantin' it bad from you Wilbur."

The judge enjoyed the outburst. As did the jury and even Hays Randolf.

"I need to hear that from the official witness, Ladies. Wilbur, were you and Susan engaged in extramarital relations of sex?" is the best Reno Sweetwater could put it.

"I guess." Wilbur was cunning.

"You guess?" exploded Reno.

"Did you fuck her Wilbur?" came the jolt from the Rowdy Ladies' gallery. "Everyone in town knows you did!"

The courtroom howled for about two minutes before the judge gently tapped his gavel.

"Well, Wilbur? Don't lie, don't hem and haw, don't hesitate. Just spit it out!" demanded Reno Sweetwater.

"Yes!" cried Wilbur.

"Once or more times?" again demanded Reno.

"More," admitted Wilbur.

"How many times 'more', Wilbur?"

"Sometimes we sexed four, five times a day! Sometime in her bed. Sometime in my bed.
I never got a day off! (laughter in the court). My job in the mine is 12 hours a day, 6 days a week. Recently I'd go sleep at a friend's house just to avoid Susan! I couldn't take it no more!" Wilbur was exhausted just saying this.

"Did you kill Sheriff Armitage by poisoning him to death with arsenic?" demanded Reno.

"What?! No! I needed to get away from her. I needed her husband alive.   If I was gonna poison anyone, it'd be Susan!" admitted Wilbur.

Even the jury was laughing out loud.

"On the night you carried Sheriff Armitage to the porch swing, was he dead?"

"I think so," said Wilbur.

"Did Susan Armitage say he was dead?"

"She said he died of a heart attack and to put him on the porch swing. That's all," added Wilbur.

"Why the porch swing? Why not take him to the sheriff's department in her buckboard?"

"He loved to watch the rain! It was his favorite thing to do, sit on his porch, by hisself, and watch it rain. A simple pleasure.." stated Wilbur sadly.

"Thank you Mr. Hoagland. Mr Randolf, your witness," said Reno Sweetweater.

Hays Randolf stood up, walked over to Wilbur Hoagland, took Wilbur's hands and looked at them and said, "You work in a silver mine, about a hundred feet underground?"

"Yeah, it runs deeper in places," said Wilbur matter-of-factly.

"If the sheriff's wife, Susan Artmitage, asked you to kill her husband, and you said 'yes', how would you do it?"

"Probly hit em on his head with an ax, chop em up and throw his body down a part of the mine we ain't digging in no more." said Wilbur, again, matter-of-factly with no emotion.   The gallery, including the jury, was suddenly terrified of Wilbur.

"You ever think about killing anyone?" wondered the prosecutor, Hays Randolf.

"Well, like I said, Susan. She don't let up. Always on me to do something, have sinful relations, pick up her supplies, but not from Dave's Cache Barrel. No! Dave's is one block from her house. That'd be too easy. She wants victuals from the other store, way down on Harmony Road, two miles off.". Wilbur got that off his chest and he was heaving, too.

"So who killed Susan's husband, Wilbur? You know the main suspect, Arlene Dross?" asked Hays Randolf, County Prosecutor.

"I lost forty dollars to her from horse racing'. I ain't never come near her since," said Wilbur as the courtroom laughed.

"Sheriff Armitage is lying dead with a bullet in his chest,"and you don't know anything? What are you hiding? Are you covering for Arlene?" determined Hays Randolf, "You're in love with Arlene Dross and her tight pants, aren't you Wilbur?"

"He's covering for Susan, you jackass!" came Rowdy Lady No. 1 from the Back Bench.

The judge tapped his gavel and said, "The ladies will stop playing lawyer."

"We know what's going on, judge. That lawyer from Denver City don't, and the slick dude from England ain't never been west of London!" incorrectly stated Rowdy Lady No. 4.

"Besides, every man in town wants to fuck Arlene in her tight-ass pants," said Rowdy-Lady No.12.

The judge agreed about wanting to have sex with Lindy but didn't bring it up. The judge, and every man in the courtroom, loved looking at her skin tight leather pants which got Lindy all the attention she could ask for.

"Wilbur, answer the question. What are you hiding, who are you protecting?" demanded Hays Randolf.

"I ain't protecting no one. Widow Susan don't like guns so she didn't shoot him."

"Thank you for your honesty, Wilbur. I have no more questions for this witness, your honor," included Hays Randolf, prosecutor.

"Call your next witness counselor," ordered Judge MacMillan.

"I re-call Widow Armitage," affirmed Hays Randolf.

"Will this be long? Can you do this under 8 minutes? I want to break for luncheon," interjected Judge MacMillan.

"I believe I shall require twenty minutes, your honour," cautioned Hart St. Clair.

"We're feeling faint, your honor," and "We're starved, your honor," quipped the Rowdy Ladies of the Back Bench.

"Luncheon, 60 minutes," said the good judge and slammed his gavel and quickly exited the court like he had a hot luncheon waiting for him in his chambers.

As the Defendant and her lawyers got up and headed to a back door, Hart St Clair's lead private investigator showed up with interesting news:

"We've got some evidence that will finally close this case," declared Danny Maxwell, chief private investigator, who continued, "Oscar's guarding it with his life," concluded Danny. Hart and Reno immediately followed Danny Maxwell out of the court.

Danny nodded at Lindy and said, "You'll go free today little girl." He had no legal right to assume anything. But he saw the new evidence, not Jack, not Hart, not Reno.

Jack and Lindy were enjoying lunch in Jack's hotel suite's dining room. Danny escorted Hart and Reno to the evidence which was secreted away and carefully guarded by Oscar Sullivan.

"What'd they find?" wondered Lindy.

"We'll see in court in about half an hour," assured Jack.

"Why'd he think I'll go free?" countered Lindy.

"He shouldn't have said that," re-countered Jack.

"All rise," requested the Bailiff.

The judge motioned everyone to be seated. He looked over notes he'd made which were strewn over his large desk (the Bench). Then looked at the Defendant's Table and said, "Mr Eberhart St. Clair, if I'm not mistaken, you're up."

"Thank you, your Honour. I have some important evidence to bring to court, with your permission, judge. It is a large wooden crate and this crate was found in the Armitage's out-building—a shed with gardening tools. This box was hidden under a pile of straw. The witness to this discovery is Chief Claremont Tillis, Chief of Police of Fort Collins, Colorado. May my investigators bring in this container and its contents and display them on a table betwixt the Bench and the Juror's Box?" asked a very courteous Hart St. Clair.

[Claremont Tillis is the Chief of Police for the City of Fort Collins, Colorado. Kees Van Der Hoff is the Sheriff of Larimer County, Colorado. Fort Collins is the County Seat where the Sheriff's headquarters are. One block away is the Police Department. The Sheriff's Department and the Police Department are two separate law enforcement agencies.]

"You may," said Judge MacMillan.

Two large men brought up a table the size of the Defandant's Table and placed it between the Judge's bench and the jury box. One of these men used a cotton cloth to wipe the table of any dust or residue. To polish it up.

In the meantime, Danny Maxwell and Oscar Sullivan walked into the Courtroom carrying a large wooden box six feet long, four feet wide and four feet high. It had a lid attached with hinges. The man who cleared off the Evidence Table unfolded a brand new blanket and put it on top of the oak table so the evidence box wouldn't scratch the beautiful walnut table. Very thoughtful.

The table was placed carefully so the six foot long box was placed on the table where it fit precisely, without hanging over the table. The top of the box, with hinges, was opened. Jurors and judge stretched up to see what was inside. One of the Rowdy Ladies of the Back Bench quickly scooted up, looked into the crate and said, without thinking of where she was, or what was at stake (this is a murder trial) yelled out, "Full of packets of something', probably poison!"

The judge thanked that Rowdy Lady for her notification. The Rowdy Lady tip-toed back to her seat at the back of the gallery.

Hart St. Clair reached in and took out several packages of Arsenic from the large box and handed them to the judge. Hart then handed packets of Arsenic,"in hand soap sizes,"to members of the jury.

"Our investigators found this carton with the help from Chief of Police Tillis who got a tip from a neighbor. Chief Tillis met with Reno Sweetwater and the two private investigators and looked into Widow Armitage's shed and found this carton containing 433 packets of Arsenic. The box, according to the information stuck to the outside, said the carton held 525 packets in total. I would like to now call Chief of Police Tillis."

The Chief was sworn in, testified to what he did and what he saw, including counting the packets of Arsenic, holding the big wooden arsenic box in one of his empty jail cells until needed.

Reno Sweetwater interrgated the chief.

Hays Randolf cross-examined the Chief of Police demanding the name of the neighbor—none given. Hays demanded to see the Warrant for the Search and Seizure. The Chief provided one and saw that it was signed and dated by Judge MacMillan who smiled at Hays Randolf. Then Hays dismissed the Chief of Police after his cross examination.

Hart St. Clair next called Professor Harland Fielding, chairman of the Chemistry Department at the Colorado State College of Agriculture and Mechanical Arts, in Fort Collins.

Dr. Fielding, with a PhD from Harvard College, Department of Chemistry, after graduation remained in academia becoming professor of chemistry at the College of New Jersey at Princeton and later as Dean of the Michigan State College of Agriculture in East Lansing. Dr Fielding answered an inquiry while at Michigan State to come west to Fort Collins to become Dean and Chairman of the Agriculture and Mechanical Arts Departments of Colorado State College at a favorable honorarium—twice as much as Michigan State had paid him. Colorado State College had made a commitment to hiring well-qualified professors to train tomorrow's farmers and ranchers in one of the harshest areas of America in which to raise livestock and grow crops.

Harland Fielding loved the romantic notion of the 'wild' west and saw it as a challenge to remove himself to an area of the continent that had very little rain, therefore very little water, hostile Indians and hostile weather. He packed up his wife and three kids then took the transcontinental rail road to Cheyenne, Wyoming Territory, and the train south to Fort Collins. That was one year ago, 1879.

"Doctor Fielding, may I ask what your doctor's degree is in." wondered Hart St.Clair.

"The broad field of chemistry, sir. Applied chemistry, biological chemistry, chemical engineering, agricultural chemistry, quantitative and qualitative analyses." answered Dr Fielding.

"Doctor Fielding, did you examine the body of Sheriff Armitage?"

"Yes, sir," said Dr Fielding.

"When did you examine Sheriff Armitage's body?" wondered Hart St Clair.

"Two days after the sheriff's death, last May. The Coroner, Dr. Hardee, notified me to help him ascertain the clumps of a certain white compound, found all through Sheriff Armitage's body—in his stomach, intestines, liver, throughout his musculature." stated Dr Fielding.

"So the Coroner spotted the arsenic poisoning and looked you up?" asked Hart St. Clair. "Yes, we're friends, sir. Dr Hardee got his medical degree at the University of Michigan.
He was an intern at a hospital in East Lansing, where I was teaching agricultural chemistry at the Michigan State Agriculture college."

"So, together with the Coroner, you examined the body of the late Sheriff Armitage?" re-stated Hart St.Clair.

"We did, sir," replied Dr fielding.

"What did you conclude was the cause of Sheriff Armitage's demise?" asked Hart St. Clair.

"He died from a massive overdose of arsenic poisoning," stated Dr Fielding.

"Dr Fielding," continued Hart St. Clair, "The sheriff's wife, Susan Armitage, eats arsenic wafers as though they were tea sandwiches, and she's alive." taunted Hart St. Clair.

"Yes, the arsenic in Mrs Armitage's wafers is quite minimal. The results are a graying of the skin, loss of appetite and a loss of energy." Dr Fielding sounded like the chemistry professor that he is.

"To what end would Widow Armitage need to eat arsenic, Dr Fielding?" wondered Hart St. Clair and the entire courtroom.

"Purely decorative. It is a contemporary means to announce your elevated standing in the community," concluded Dr Fielding.

"Please explain that in layman's terms, Dr Fielding," suggested Hart St. Clair.

"Modern times favor women who remain in the home, with the drapery closed, so as to not venture out into the bright sun. The only reason for pale skin is vanity. Others—women—assume those who are pale white are well off and are well taken care of." expounded Dr Fielding.

"How much arsenic would it take to kill Sheriff Armitage, Dr Fielding?" inquired Hart St. Clair.

"About half a kilogram," replied Dr Fielding in the language of science.

"And how much does that weigh in everyday American?" chided Hart St. Clair.

"About one point six three six pounds." converted Dr Fielding.

"That's more than one and a half pounds!!!!" exploded Hart St.Clair. "More than one and a half pounds of poison!" repeated Hart St. Clair for juror-swaying effect. "I ate a steak at the High Plains Chop House and that steak covered my platter. And would Sheriff Armitage have eaten that much in arsenic?"

Dr Fielding said, "Yes. That steak which is larger than your plate is a pound and a half."

Hart St.Clair was theatrical—acting—holding his hands far apart getting the jurors to 'see' how much a one-point-six pound steak looked like and added, "How do you get anyone to eat that much arsenic, Dr Fielding?"

"You have to serve it to him in small quantities over a short period of time," offered Dr Fielding.

"How short a time, Dr Fielding?"

"Three days will do it," said Dr Fielding with certainty.

"Do you just offer him a soup spoon of arsenic or do you have to disguise it" wondered Hart St. Clair and everyone in the building.

"I imagine you could bake it in bread, a cake, cookies. Sugar would disguise the unsavory flavor of the arsenic poison."

"Are you sure it was poison baked in a brownie and not a .32 caliber bullet?" stated Hart St Clair.

"The bullet was lodged in the sheriff's left clavicle," reminded Dr Fielding, touching his left collar bone, "and had nothing to do with the sheriff's death."

"Your witness, Mr Randolf," said Hart St Clair to Hays Randolf after nodding to Judge MacMillan that Hart was finished with Dr Fielding.

"Mr. Fielding," began Hays Randolf, failing to call Dr Fielding by any of his academically titled name—doctor, professor, dean or chairman—"How many cases of arsenic poisoning have you studied in your honorable and illustrious career?" cornered Hays Randolf.

"To date, just one, sir," obliged Dr Harland Fielding, PhD.

"How did you ascertain that the late Sheriff Armitage was poisoned by arsenic, and not, say, by poison sumac or poison ivy?" threatened Hays Randolf.

"Qualitative and quantitative analysis, sir," countered Dr Fielding.

"Please, sir, enlighten the jury with your last sentence," pled Hays Randolf, prosecutor.

"The study of unknown substances. If there is blood somewhere, first, is it blood or is it tomato sauce? If you test it and it is blood, whose blood is it? A human? An animal? If you see a substance and it's white powder, is it arsenic, is it baking flour, is it cyanide, are they powdered poisonous mushrooms? Powdered sugar? Quantitative and qualitative analysis tells you." Dr Fielding just educated the courtroom on matters considered by some and unknown by most everyone else. Thank God for Dr Fielding thought Jack, the lawyers, and possibly Lindy.

"If Sheriff Armitge was hit by a bullet, wouldn't he die of lead poisoning?" assumed Hays Randolf.

"In this case, no. The bullet was lodged in his clavicle. It was a small bullet, a .32 caliber, and the subject was dead prior to being hit by the bullet, no matter who shot it."

Dr Fielding laid down the law to everyone in the court room with an authoritative tone of voice and a rigid backbone. Dr Fielding sat straight up in the Witness Chair and looked Hays Randolf right between his eyes.

When Dr Fielding stopped talking there was a stark confident stillness in the air. There was absolute silence in the courtroom. Hays Randolf was stopped dead in his tracks. He was sweating. Finally, Hays Randolf, blinking, said, "Thank you sir. I am finished with this witness, your honor."

"Call your next witness, Mr St. Clair. I'll be interested to see who that would be." uttered Judge MacMillan. Hart St Clair sat down and Reno Sweetwater got up to take on the next witness.

Reno Sweetwater got up and said, "Defense calls Mrs Susan Armitage, please."

Of course, who else?

Piled upon a separate wooden table was the large pile of deadly arsenic in paper packets. This table sat betwixt the judge's bench and the jury box. The arsenic was completely contained in the paper wrappers.

Susan Armitage, waiting out in the hall, came in. It was the end of summer and her skin was as white as any prim, proper and snobbish Victorian lady who hid inside from March through Hallow'd Eve. Then stayed inside all winter due to cold, inclement northern Colorado weather.

Susan was reminded for the fourth time that she was under Oath and that a very angry and vengeful God Himself was caustically watching to make sure she didn't fib.

"All of these packets of arsenic were found in your outbuilding next to your domicile," said Reno Sweetwater. "They were found under a large pile of straw in the outbuilding," continued Reno in a monotone. Reno handed Susan Armitage one of the packages. "Are these more packages for your beauty regimine?" inquired Reno.

"Why of course!" chirped a delighted Susan Armitage, possible killer wife of Ross Armitage.

"Do you bake, Mrs Armitage? Bread, cakes, pies, small edible things called 'cookies' and brownies?" wondered Reno.

"Yes, all except brownies," admitted Susan Armitage.

"Did you bake these foods for yourself and Sheriff Armitage?"

"Yes. And friends, too. We have friends, you know," enlightened Susan.

"Did you add arsenic into anything you baked for your husband?" wondered Reno.

"Why would I do that?" wondered Susan.

"Either to make him more attractive. Or to kill him so you could continue your affair with Wilbur Hoagland," offered Reno Sweetwater.

Susan Armitage didn't like those accusations. She got up from her Witness Chair and stomped out of the courtroom. Well, she got about six steps away when the towering, massive Bailiff picked her up by her bent elbows and gently put her back in the Witness Chair.

"Please answer Mr Sweetwater's question," prompted Judge MacMillan.

"No!" cried Susan.

"Mr Hoagland testified that you signaled him with a white flag to come over and spend time with him," stated Reno Sweetwater.

Susan protested by stomping her leather-soled shoes on the wooden plank flooring.

"We have a laundry list of witnesses, Mrs Armitage. A lot of people were watching you and Wilbur Hoagland come and go like 'star-crossed' lovers," painted the picture by Reno Sweetwater.

"No one saw us, and if they did, so what?"

"I have with me something you made. Brownies," said Reno Sweetwater.

Reno walked over to the Defendant's Table, picked up a plate of brownies and a chocolate cake and walked over to Susan Armitage

"The brownies and the chocolate cake came from your house. The Chief of Police of Fort Collins went with us as a witness. The cake and brownies were examined for arsenic poison by a chemistrry professor at the College of Agriculture. The cake is clean of arsenic. The brownies were forty percent arsenic. This was confirmed by Dr Fielding and his chemical analysis."

Reno took a pause while Susan Armitage glared at the plate of brownies.

"Your husband, the late Ross Armitage, loved brownies," noted Reno Sweetwater, adding, "Recently he was bringing your delicious brownies to work. You knew your husband wouldn't share his brownies because you also sent him with a non-poisonous chocolate cake with dozens of non-poisonous sugar cookies. Your husband ate himself to death. You killed your husband, Ross Armitage, to do away with him and to marry Wilbur Hoagland! Admit it!" scorched Reno Sweetwater.

"You done it, hon, and you done got caught!" sniped a Rowdy Lady of the Back Bench.

Mrs Armitage sat there and took a handkerchief from a pocket of her long sleeve and floor-length daytime dress. She dabbed her tears running down her face. Then, after twenty or so seconds she spoke, "He didn't want me," Susan said softly. "The love of my life told me I was 'too much of a burden' and couldn't be with me. I just got my husband out of the way. I was baking 12 hours a day for that weasel Wilbur, remembering to put the arsenic in the brownie mix and not the cake or pie or bread or pancake mixes. And I had to keep up appearances. Then on that rainy, dreary day, Ross just walked in the living room and dropped dead. Thank God! What a relief. No more baking. No more heating up the kitchen all day—it got up to a hundred and ten degrees in there on those God forsaken hot days! But I was focused. Get rid of Ross, the sooner the better, and get Wilbur over here and settle in with him. Ross couldn't give me a baby. Wilbur and I were cuddling three or four times a day! But still nothing. No baby. Is every man barren.?" Susan Armitage suddenly stopped talking.

Reno Sweetwater looked at Judge MacMillan and said, "No more questions, your honor."

"Mr Reynolds, cross." wondered Judge MacMillan.

Hays Reynolds whispered with his co-counsel and assistants. A couple of minutes went by.

At Lindy's Defendant's Table, Hart St. Clair and Reno Sweetwater looked satisfied. Hart St. Clair looked at sweet and innocent Arlene Dross and said, "Mrs Armitage confessed to killing her husband. If Reynolds agrees that Susan Armitage killed the sheriff with poison, then he will ask Judge MacMillan to…"

"Your Honor," began Hays Randolf as he stood by the Prosecution Table, "The Prosecution wishes to drop all charges against Miss Arlene Dross and to charge Mrs Armitage with the murder of her husband, Ross Armitage. The prosecution further charges Mr Wilbur Hoagland with aiding and abetting Mrs Susan Armitage in the death of her husband."

Judge MacMillan asked Lindy and her counsel to stand. Lindy did without any attitude or consternation. She looked straight ahead at the judge in her everyday outfit of fringed leather pants, silk blouse, leather jacket. Not some sweet, innocent-looking girly in a granny dress and bonnet as Jack wanted to see.

"Miss Dross, I hereby order all charges against you vacated. You are declared Not Guilty by this court of law. You are free to go." So ordered the judge.

The courtroom, especially the Rowdy Ladies of the Back Bench, exploded in hooting, hollering and squealing—as was their custom whenever a verdict was rendered guilty or not.

Hart St.Clair, a crusty Englishman, approached Lindy and nodded affirmatively. Jack looked at Lindy, nodded and smiled.

In the meantime, out in the courthouse's hallway, Susan Armitage had just been taken into custody by the Bailiff. And the Bailiff's brother sought Wilbur Hoagland, sitting far away from Susan, then took him into custody.

Lindy, happy, walked out of the courtroom's back entrance— the same entrance she'd come in since arriving a couple of days ago.

Reno Sweetwater wondered "When's the next train to Denver."

Hart St. Clair approached Edward: "When will we start back to London, sir?"

"I'll arrange to go home as soon as possible," said Jack looking for someone.

News-paper reporters flocked up to Hart St Clair and Reno Sweetwater, stars of the show, pelting them with questions about how they solved the crime by themselves. Jack, believing Lindy had to visit the Ladies Room, and not seeing her after ten or fifteen minutes, went looking for her outside.

The Rowdy Ladies had disbursed outside and went looking for other female friends in order to report their 'eye-witness' account of the Murder Trial of the Century!

Jack, unknown to anyone in town, stood outside the courthouse, scratched his head, looked around and walked over to his private train cars, a couple of blocks down the street next to the Union Pacific train station.

No girl in tight fringed leather pants or jacket was in sight.

"Perchance, would you be searching for the young lady, Edward?" asked Hart St.Clair, walking up carrying his brief case. Two bellhops from the hotel were carrying Hart's luggage.

"Yes."   (Pause) "Perchance, you haven't seen her, Sir Eberhart?" asked Jack.

Hart shook his head and boarded the train with Danny and Oscar.

Jack took one long painful look around to see whether Lindy was walking over to the train—which was easy to spot. The only train with New-York Central RR painted on all its cars and flying both an American flag and the Union Jack of Great Britain. The wind was blowing and so were the flags.

Jack boarded the train and entered the Lounge car where Hart was reading the 'hot off the press' special Murder Trial Edition of the Larimer County *Express,* with the headline **'WIFE GUILTY!'** Kids were running around town carrying armloads of newspapers shouting "Sheriff's wife did it! Read all about it!"

Safely inside Jack's Lounge Car, on the rosewood table next to Hart St Clair, was a bottle of Macallan Scotch. He was also enjoying an H. Upmann Corona Cuban cigar. He was simultaneously sipping a tall glass of lemonade, with cubes of ice, got from the hotel—because it was a hot, dry October day.

Jack took off his jacket and sat down in a wing-back chair and stared out the window.

"Do you love her?" said Hart St. Clair.

There was a pause, then "Yes." followed by, "of course."

"Why don't you marry her?" said Hart St. Clair.

"I was getting around to it. But." admitted Jack, concluding, "Her Majesty won't approve a non-Royal who smokes and drinks and cusses and dresses like a man," admitted Jack.

"That, my good sir, is not an obstacle. You'll marry her in one of the American states and you will live in a smaller home."

"That's part of it," further admitted Jack.

"Goodness. Your mum wouldn't approve?" accused Hart St. Clair.

"No! Lindy doesn't approve. Otherwise, where is she? Home!

The underButler signaled a conductor and the private train chugged out of the Fort Collins, Colorado, station and headed finally for Ashfield Hall.

CHAPTER 31

Return to Ashfield Hall

Jack went to his sleeping compartment, changed into comfortable clothes—comfortable American clothes—not 'comfortable' stiff English clothes.

Jack entered the dining car where post-murder trial pastries and hot tea were available. Also champagne and Macallan Scotch, plus cigars.

The footman said, "And what about her Ladyship?"

"Ladyship?" questioned Edward.

"Yes, sir," said the First Footman.

"She stayed behind, I'm afraid," retorted Edward.

"As you wish." said the Footman, bowing gracefully and looking at the entry door.

Lindy stood in the door wearing her black fringed get-up. No hat. No black leather gloves. No Colt .45. She was smiling.

Jack bolted to his feet in Levi-Strauss denim jeans and bowed gracefully to the non-royal non-guilty, Sheriff-shooting (and not killing) gunslinger. She offered her hand and Jack kissed it with charm, dignity as a 19th Century English gentleman of important Royal standing is trained to do.

"Welcome aboard, Duchess," smiled Jack, suddenly in a spirited mood.

Lindy looked at the First Footman and offered: "You're excused to get us our supper."

As the First Footman walked to the kitchen car Lindy grabbed Jack, pulled him toward her and they embraced, slid their mouths toward each other. They would have blocked the aisle for awhile but an annoying 'Ahem' from an Under Butler, carrying a sterling silver dinner tray, forced the couple to uncouple. This public display of affection was most inappropriate and no one, not even the servants, gave a shit.

CHAPTER 32

Switzerland

With a murder trial going on somewhere in the American wild west, and other minor distractions (Elsie's pregnancy, the Prince of Wales' never-ending philandering, Leopold and Nora's upcoming wedding—designed to veer attention away from Elsie's 'condition' and Alfred's guilt), Prince Arthur and his girlfriend Harriet assuaged their need for adventure when the two escaped to Europe. Without their mommys' permission.

Arthur and Harriet arrived under cover of darkness in Paris and stayed with friends. Then took off by train for Switzerland. Paris to Dijon, leaving at 4pm (except the train left at 4:43pm from Paris, which annoyed the hell out of the punctual Swiss), the couple enjoyed a remarkable dinner in the Upper Accommodation Dining Car. They adjourned to the Saloon Car for after dinner drinks. Harriet was now accustomed to Cognac, Champagne, Chateau Lafite Rothschild wines. And she ordered her own Cuban cigar: "An H. Upmann Corona Corona, sil vous plait." Arthur had been in Jack's Gentleman's Club to witness his future wife enjoy her first Cuban cigar, shots of Jack Daniels and Scotch whisky, thanks to Lindy. Entertainment at the Club was further enhanced by the presence of Princess Red Thunder. Harriet, timid (ladylike) at first, caught on quickly.

Well into the new day, the not yet Mr and Mrs Arthur Royalty slipped off to their Upper Class Sleeper Compartments.

Two impeccably designed, furnished and luxuriated rooms with an adjoining doorway. They were not going to chance becoming burdened with child. Those memories of Elsie and Alfred explaining on bended knee to Her Majesty her condition. But when Alfred and pregnant Elsie got married in the privacy and unnoticed seclusion of Osborne House on the distance Isle of Wight , the Queen, the couple, the Privy Council and Parliament skirted a contretemps, no doubt.

The end of the line for Arthur and Harriet's adventure was the elegant and sophisticated city of Geneva. Prince Arthur and Lady Harriet checked into the Grande Suisse Hotel under the names Mr and Mrs Arthur Hanover, paid cash in Swiss francs and went to bed. They did not have sex. That night.

CHAPTER 33

Victoria has had it with Red Thunder

Her Majesty couldn't get a straight answer out of anyone. Where is Arthur, he hasn't been seen in three weeks. And where is Beatrice? She's running around from the Palace to the house next door, on horseback, three or four times a day. Time to call a halt to all the unsettledness.   Doesn't anyone respect Her Majesty's mourning?

Victoria summoned her Equerry and demanded he find Prince Arthur and what Princess Beatrice was up to. "And if you return without satisfactory responses to my Commands, I shall put you to work in the stables shoveling manure. That's where equerries came from.." huffed Her Majesty. (In latin equus means horse. In the past centuries Equerians were stable boys.)

The Equerry bowed deeply and as he did Her Majesty added, "Find Princess Beatrice and bring her to Me this instant!"

Everybody in London knew that Arthur and Harriet were in Switzerland on their honeymoon. There was no mention of an actual wedding.   But the honeymoon stories were accurate, indecorous and juicy.

After their honeymoon was over, they will get married. Also in Switzerland.

Prince Arthur and Lady Harriet were horrified by the spectacle of Albert's wedding at St George's Chapel, Windsor Castle, seventeen years earlier. They didn't want to be part of any ceremony gawked at by the great unprincipled horde of London.   They were a private couple.   "Let's elope!" said Arthur, because Harriet dropped 20 pounds and looked very hot, which was not a 19th Century word describing sexuality, but should have been. Harriet wanted to show off and be seen walking down the aisle toward her Royal Prince in a drop dead custom made wedding gown designed in Paris.

The weddings of brothers Albert and Leopold were theatrical nightmares, according to Arthur. Time to run.   And that was three weeks ago. Arthur's allowance was laughable, so he came to Jack and pleaded for cash to travel with Harriet. Jack gave Prince Arthur £25,000. A day later, Harriet, fearing her future husband was broke, asked Jack for £10,000. Jack said, "Spend it wisely, travel on a budget, dear sister." However Harriet did not know what a budget was. She spent all £10,000 in Paris. Thank God Arthur had good sense about money.

Happily unchaperoned in French-speaking Switzerland, traveling under the names of Arthur and Harriet Hanover, they portended to be a well-to-do married couple on holiday from Liverpool. And it worked. The Swiss were too busy to be bothered by foreigners. As the English looked down on everyone on earth, the Swiss looked down on the English. So Arthur Hanover could have been an insurance salesman from Liverpool as far as any Swiss citizen was concerned. Which they weren't.

The entire royal staff and all servants at Buckingham Palace followed the travels of Prince Arthur and Lady X, feverishly, in the *Daily Telegraph & Courier, The Globe, the London Morning Post* and the *London Daily News.* All the latest royal gossip, all the time.

HM read *The Times* which never covered scandal or Royal gossip. Beatrice subscribed to the *Daily News* and *The Globe,* following her brother Arthur and also following American news in *The Globe.* Particularly the murder trial in Colorado, and more particularly to see if Lindy were found guilty and hanged. Beatrice would get Crazy Horse. And Jack.

Beatrice at last, walked into the Queen's Reception room like she were the queen. However, due to custom, Beatrice curtseyed deeply before her mum.

"Pleasant day to you, Your Majesty. I was told to see you 'this instant'," replied Princess Beatrice Mary Victoria Feodore.

"Pray be seated," the Queen said with formality.

Beatrice, chipper and smiling, plopped into one of the overstuffed and very comfortable lounge chairs.

"It's been relayed to me that you wish to marry the gentleman who is our next door neighbor," began Her Majesty.

"Who told you that?"

"The gentleman's mother, Lady somebody."

"Yes, I plan to marry Edward. And you met him when he vouched for one of his sisters. The one who married Leo. I think her name is Netty or Nora. She's fun. She smokes cigars and drinks Jack Daniels American whiskey."

"You will not marry. I need you here. If you disobey me, I shall be all alone in this dreadful house. I need you to talk to.." pled Victoria, very seriously. Her tone scared Beatrice.

"Mother, you've got dozens of people to talk to. More experienced in life than me.."

"I do not discuss my feelings with outsiders. I need my daughters, and seeing as they have all run off to have families, you're all I've got!"

"I love Edward and he loves me. And he lives next door! I'll be right over the wall."

"That's what I'm afraid of. If you go, you'll never return. And this Edward's been to America. What if he returns to America, then for sure I'll never see you again!"

"Mother, you've got 8 more children and dozens of grandchildren to comfort you!"

"But you are my favorite!" revealed HM, which startled Beatrice. She always felt that she was her mother's favorite, and now here was proof.

"Isn't this Edward with another young lady? The one who dresses in men's clothes?"

"Yeah, Lindy."

"Where is she?"

"On trial for murder in America," said Beatrice straight out.

"Stop this fibbing." quipped HM, not believing Beatrice's tall tale.

"She is! She shot someone in Colorado. While escaping the murder scene, she jumped onto Edward's train. And that's how she ended up here. A murderess, escaping to England. But Edward and one of his lawyers escorted her back to Colorado for the murder trial."

Victoria didn't believe a word of Beatrice's gibberish. "And why do you love him, because he loves another girl?" HM poured ice cold water on her innocent baby daughter.

"That's not fair!"

"Nothing's fair about love. You have to be lucky. And when you're lucky in love, then one day the floor drops out and your husband is taken from you." reminded HM, dressed in her daily reminder: black.

At that moment, HM's personal assistant, the Equerry, arrived, spotted Beatrice, bowed and backed out of the Queen's Reception. But HM spotted him.

The Equerry stopped, bowed deeply.

"Did you get my information?" demanded the Queen, her blood elevated on account of the precious, endearing special moment with her beloved youngest child.

"Yes Majesty." He was succinct and not about to blabber gossip because the 'queen' of palace gossip was lounging not five feet from the Queen.

"Well? Where's Arthur?" The Queen was in no mood to hear anything but the answer.

The Equerry was hesitant.

"Spit it out, sir!" The Queen would have loved to throw her assistant into the Tower.

"May I speak in private, ma'am?"

"You are in private. Where's Arthur?"

There was a brief pause as the Equerry, a tall man of 24 years, attractive, dressed in a beautiful dress uniform--his eyes darting betwixt HM and Beatrice, sweating, said, "Switzerland. Majesty."

"On a State visit? When did I order that?" wondered HM.

"On Holiday, ma'am," offered the Equerry, giving up very little. He would make an excellent witness for the defense.

"Tell mum who's he with?" blurted out Princess Beatrice.

The Equerry did not answer Beatrice's interrogative.

"Is Arthur with anyone?" asked HM.

"Yes, ma'am." It was clear to all in the room the Equerry wasn't cooperative. Beatrice loved it.

"Tell mum her name, or I will." taunted Beatrice (Red Thunder).

"Her name? She better be Arthur's aging Aunt Penelope," threatened the Queen.

"I'm afraid he is traveling with Lady Harriet, his fiancee, your Majesty." The Equerry gave up the ghost and squealed like a rat.

"So they're married!" exclaimed HM.

The Equerry stifferned, stood mute.

"Arthur and his girlfriend are having a fling, mum. They're on their honeymoon. And if they like each other, *maybe* he'll marry her." smirked Beatrice.

"Why am I informed of this now! Tell me more, sir, or the weight of this Crown shall come crashing down upon you." threatened Her Majesty.

"Stop, stop, mum. I'll tell you more than you want to know. It's really sensational!!" pled   Beatrice, now standing next to the Equerry. Beatrice gave him the once over.

"You better scram," Princess Red Thunder insisted to the Equerry, but he wasn't budging until the real Authority told him to skedaddle.

"Thank you, sir. You are excused." said HM, waving the equerry off and turning authoritatively to her youngest charge.

"You see," snapped HM, "This is why I need you here, at all times. You know all the intrigue."

"Arthur doesn't want to get married in the Church, or Westminster, or even in England. He hates all the attention. So he and his girlfriend took off for Paris a couple of weeks ago and now they're in a run down Swiss hotel acting like a middle class married couple from Liverpool."

"Are they betrothed?" hissed the Queen.

"Not yet."

"Have they engaged in…" the Queen was looking for a phrase that wondered if her third son were banging his girlfriend.

"Yes, mum. They are indeed copulating. Copulating their brains out," smirked Beatrice.

"Oh my heavens." responded HM.

"Yeah, I know. What'll the neighbors think.?" Red Thunder thought she was helping. In fact, she was. The Queen later wondered why she had to stick her nose in her children's private lives. Thank God she was going to protect young, innocent Beatrice Mary Victoria Feodore.

"Do you think they'll be recognized?" worried HM.

"He's traveling as Art Hanover. And they are Art and Harriet Hanover—sounds like a terribly boring couple from Liverpool. He's probably wearing one of his awful checked and striped suits—like those people wear in Derbyshire," assured Beatrice. Arthur was boring and he wore clothing not fit for the royal family. Custom-tailored clothes from Savile Row. Expensive, but the fabric was too colorful, too checked, too striped, too lower class.

"When are they due back?" queried HM.

"After they get married, of course," taunted Beatrice. Hell, if Beatrice can't get married, why should anyone else be happy. Sex before marriage for the royal family was scandalous.

"Why can't they get married here?!" demanded HM.

"They must be married here yet I shan't be married here! I'm tired of this family!" cried Beatrice, being her usual theatrically annoying self.

Her Majesty needed to lie down.

Beatrice had heard that Jack was due back from America this week. She wanted to be at his house when he arrived, without the murderess in tow. And now that Arthur and Harriet had eloped, maybe Beatrice and Jack can do the same thing. Elope and travel the world. A mostly peaceful world in 1880.

CHAPTER 34

Agatha has had it with Jack

Jack and Lindy arrived home at last. As the staff unpacked trunks and suitcases, Jack went to his room and Lindy went to one of hers. She believed Ashfield Hall was a hotel owned by Jack, and any room she wanted was hers. It also kept Jack's snoopy, nosey, untrustworthy mother at bay—not knowing where Lindy was sleeping. Somewhere in a 620,000 square foot house with 150 bedrooms (with attached bathrooms), or at the stables.

The Butler, upon Edward's arrival, handed him an envelope and said, "From Countess Agatha, Your Royal Highness." Edward stuffed it in his jacket and walked upstairs in the opposite direction from his mother's apartment.

"Edward," wrote Countess Agatha, "I must see you immediately.". The note was dated 10 days ago. Maybe she forgot about the note, thought Edward.   He opened his mail and took out rent checks from all his tenants on his land in the City of London. One of the letters in his pile of post was from Beatrice:

'My dearest Eddie! I can't wait to see you. I've missed you dearly. I need to be with you.   We must have dinner and an after dinner cigar with port wine! I told Mum we should be married. See me as soon as you arrive. Heartfelt love, your Red Thunder.'

Jack's response to this missive was, "Eddie!? Nobody calls me Eddie."

Jack unlocked the door to his library, a wonderfully cozy room, intimate, all four walls were lined with his books—sorted by department: (Engineering, Classical, Mathematics, Astronomy, History, America, Europe, Sailing, General Knowledge, French, Technology, Literature, Maps & Cartography).

His library was lit by natural gas lighting. Simple fireplace for affect, to sit next to on cold winter days and read, imagine, work out engineering problems, or stare out the windows. Thanks to Jack and his central heating company, there was a radiator in this room (and every room) to keep it warm.

Jack finally contacted his mother by message delivered by house staff, and arranged for her to visit him in his library. Jack made sure his mother was seated comfortably as he took a seat at his desk chair.

"You must become engaged this month to Beatrice. And before that, possibly next week, you are to convince Beatrice's mother that you're the right man for her daughter," mother was deliberate and pushy.

Jack jumped out of his chair, angry. He was suddenly fuming. This was an unaccustomed and rare event of Jack. Evenhandedness and calm described Jack:

"Beatrice's **mother!?!** Are you mad? If you ever want to regain your royal title and precious style, you would be wise, very wise, to keep a civil tongue in your head. Her Majesty is your Sovereign. As a member of the Royal Family, I demand you demonstrate your subservience at all times," Jack was genuinely upset.

As a Royal, he steadfastly believed in the Monarchy, and especially the current Monarch who had been on the Throne for Jack's entire life and 13 years before he was born.

Countess Agatha let Edward's burst of temper bounce off her and land silently onto the rich, thick woolen Persian carpet.

"This is what's going to happen, Edward," began Countess Agatha, "You will arrange a dinner with Beatrice, she will fall in love with you, then you two will go to 'her majesty', fall on your knees, both of you, and not leave until you have 'her majesty's' blessing. Then let Beatrice plan the wedding with 'her majesty' at one of her better cathedrals. You have a week to accomplish all this. And get rid of that American trash. She's so far beneath you, you'll never see it. And stop pretending you don't want to fuck her. Go fuck her, then marry Beatrice. And if you ever dare to scold me again, I'll take you over my knee and spank you with a leather strap," sayeth the Countess who is also Edward's mother.

Edward's mother, finished, arose, forcing Edward to stand, then stormed out of Edward's library and slammed the solid mahogany door.

CHAPTER 35

The 620,000 Square Foot Hideout.

Dinner this evening, according to the instruction given to Jack, was an hour earlier and in Jack's favorite dining room—his office on the third floor.   "Won't that be inconvenient to the Footmen who must come all the way from the kitchen?" wondered Edward to Mr Harrison.   "Not at all, sir.   We've been using the auxiliary kitchen around the corner from your office," announced the Butler.   Edward had no idea there was another kitchen, and right down from his office, which he could have been using all along.   The sous chef worked this kitchen and cooked up great dinners for Edward and Lindy, served hot in his third floor office.

Dinner was also informal, so no black tie and starched shirt.

Edward, happy to be away from his snooping, demeaning, demanding, unscrupulous, penetrating, ne'er do well mother, relaxed. Until he saw the table set for three. "What now?" he chirped.

Well, instead of terrible news (mother and Aunt Fanny for instance), there was terribly good news: Prince Arthur and Edward's sister Harriet, had returned from their sojourn in Switzerland. Edward shook Arthur's hand and gave his sister a brotherly hug—then smirked.

Harriet saw the smirk and immediately said, "So even you heard?"

"Yes. And worse, so has Her Majesty.   Let alone the rest of England.

"Edwardo, could you go with us tomorrow and help smooth things out with mum?" wondered Prince Arthur.

"You've had, what, three or four weeks, to come up with a story—the one where you desperately needed your privacy seems to work. Only word got back to the Palace that you consummated your marriage <u>before</u> you got married.   That's the hurdle you must overcome.   And, no, this is a husband-wife-Monarch problem," finalized Edwardo.

Arthur had his head in his hands. Jack/Edwardo/Edward got up and slid his index finger across the back of Arthur's neck, "Yes, the blade shall fall right about here. Your head will be next, my dear Harriet," as Edward made a guillotine-chopping noise whilst looking at Harriet.

"Is it that bad?" worried Harriet.

"Yes, Her Majesty is furious. Alfred, a very pregnant Elsie, Leo and Nora are hiding out in my house. Please join us—but everyone wants you to visit Her Majesty as soon as possible. You're her favorite, Arthur. Play on that," were Edward's words of comfort and wisdom, "So we, all of us, can get back to our normal lives."

"Meaning you want everyone out of your cramped little cottage," quipped sister Harriet.

Jack smiled a demeaning smile in agreement with his sister's assessment.

Dinner was served.

"We heard that you and Beatrice were courting," said Harriet, deflecting the conversation.

"Where'd you hear that nonsense?" accused Jack.

"It's all over Switzerland, on the train to Paris, on the boat across the Channel, in *The Globe*" reported Harriet.

"You read *The Globe* now?" interrogated Jack, shocked that his sister would read anything less than *The Times*.

"How'd mum find out about us?" wondered Arthur.

"*The Globe* thanks to Beatrice and Her Majesty's new, gossipy Equarian," remarked Jack.

"The jig is up, Old Girl, we'll make an appointment to see Mum," said Arthur.

"Maybe she won't want to see us for a week or so," queried Harriet, a novice at Court.

Jack and Arthur laughed knowingly. "If the Prime Minister were visiting mum and she got a whiff that you two were back in town, she'd toss him out the window to get her hands on you love birds," remarked Jack, forgetting to say 'Her Majesty' in regards to the most powerful woman on earth.

"What'll you think will happen, Eddie?" wondered Harriet.

"You'll have to get properly married, in a small ceremony, in a quaint church. Or, she'll annul your Swiss marriage—if it isn't already annulled," said Jack with authority.

Letter from the Palace

As Arthur and his wife left Jack's office, heading to their apartments in Jack's 620,000 square foot hideout, Mr Harrison escorted a Royal Messenger, in a Palace uniform, to Jack's office.

The Royal Messenger announced himself to Jack, "Your royal highness, The Palace dispatched me to personally hand you this parcel. I was told it was urgent and I now deliver it to you, sir, by hand."

Jack looked a question at Mr Harrison, who shrugged. The formality of handing someone a letter seemed overly dramatic and theatrical. HM was dramatic, but not threatrical.

Jack thanked the Royal Messenger, and Mr Harrison escorted the messenger out of the house lest he get lost on his way to the servant's (and messenger's) side door.--the Service entrance.

The envelope was 10 inches by 15 inches, made of expensive paper, had Her Majesty's Royal Cypher. The address was to Edward, 3rd Duke of Sussex, Ashfield Hall, Knightsbridge. Jack wondered what this was about—the Queen simply summons a messenger who tells Jack what HM commands and leaves. Why a written note?

The envelope was sealed with Her Majesty's red wax Royal Cypher. Very official. Jack thought, 'what'd I do now? Did Lindy shoot someone at the Palace.?' He broke the seal and took out a two page letter on thick vanilla-colored and perfumed paper.

" *My love*..." began the written note to Jack. ".I can no longer wait as you daly, playing with my heart-strings. Yes, Edward, I shall marry you and you shall make me the Happiest girl in the Realm."

Jack quickly turned to the second page to see who sent this. (Was he that dense?) At the bottom of the page was a drawing of a black cloud with a large red lightning bolt. "All my love, your Red Thunder."

Back to the top of page one. ".girl in the Realm. I will be your loving wife and we shall live in your house and when Mother crowds us and demands attention, you shall whisk me off to your beloved America. We shall have a place in New York and another out in the countryside. I like the sound of Indiana. Lots of Indians I imagine. I'm Red Thunder, so we'll get along famously! I've already come up with names for our four children. There must be an Edward, a George, a Henry and an Elizabeth. Those were great Kings and Queen. Mum shall not interfere in our love and our passion. I won't allow it. I dream of us together, happy, in each other's arms day and night. I do love you, dearest Edward!"

Then the drawing in ink of the black cloud of doom and the overly large red lightning bolt.

Jack's response to this letter was pleasure. Yes, pleasure. Jack had learned, from Alfred, Arthur and even Leopold, that Princess Beatrice was told by Her Majesty that under no circumstances would she be betrothed this year or next. This was exciting. Girls don't write passionate missives to boys. How does Beatrice think she's going to get permission to marry me, thought Jack. He liked being sought after. He loved the attention. And he wallowed in Beatrice's passion. He wanted some of that passion. Children were no problem. They would be raised by nannies and governesses, then off to school until they are 21, educated and civilized. Once civilized they are ready to be around adults, including their parents. A great system. Everyone should try it.

The Duke of Ashfield Hall relaxed and felt relieved. And he liked the fact that attractive and playful Red Thunder loved him and was making wistful plans.

Jack was in such a good mood that he did the unthinkable: he took all the dinner dishes in his office, put them on a sterling silver tray, and found the auxiliary kitchen down the hall from his 3rd floor office. The servants in that kitchen were in shock and took it that Jack was extremely upset that he couldn't get adequate service. Jack smiled and said he thought he'd do a little work around the house. Bowed to the kitchen staff, thanked them for all the work they do, took a piece of cake, a slice of pie on a clean plate, took a fork, and went off, thanking them to excess.

(No, he didn't do the dishes.)

Summoned by Her Majesty

A day later, Mr Harrison found Edward in his cozy library reading Cicero in Latin. The same Royal Messenger was standing next to Mr Harrison. Edward gave Mr Harrison a 'now what do they want?' look. Well, he was about to find out:

"Your royal highness, Her Majesty commands your presence tomorrow morning at 10 ante-meridian. Thank you, sir," reported the Royal Messenger, as he handed Edward an envelope with that exact information on it. The Royal Messenger bowed gently, but not as deeply as he bows to the Queen.

Mr Harrison once again escorted the Royal Messenger out of Ashfield Hall.

Early the next morning, about 9:35, Jack showed up at the Palace as instructed. He followed Her Majesty's Equerry up a long flight of stairs and down a longer hallway to HM's private reception. What could she possibly want?

Jack brought the letter from Red Thunder because after visiting with Her Majesty, Jack was going to see Beatrice and he wanted to discuss Red Thunder's love letter. And possibly have a tiny say in naming their future four children. And why four? Why not a manageable two? Or one?

A Queen's Guard nodded to Jack, knocked thrice on HM's closed door, opened it and announced thusly: "Your Majesty, his royal highness, Edward, third Duke of Sussex, has arrived by your command." The Guard, always at attention, looked straight ahead and never at the Queen, waited for a response.

Her Majesty waved her arm forward. She was playing solitaire.

The Queen's Guard signaled Jack to enter. He entered the room, stopped and bowed deeply, standing about 20 feet from Her Majesty.

There was no comfortable guest chair, nor sofa, only a hard wooden chair with no It looked like a seat for punishment. Edward stood at attention where he was and waited for the Queen to speak.

"We have to talk," announced HM Queen Victoria, "Princess Beatrice tells me that she wrote you a letter in which she proposes marriage to you. Is this correct?"

"Yes, Your Majesty," admitted Jack.

"Hand it over," commanded Her Majesty.

Jack handed the steamy letter to HM who read the letter carefully without making any gestures regarding its steaminess.

Beatrice, as it so happened, was somehow 'just in the neighborhood' and stuck her head in the room, saw Her Majesty reading her letter, and Edward watching the Queen. Beatrice then quietly and gently closed the thick English elm door and smiled victoriously. Wedding bells were ringing for Red Thunder and what's-his-name, Edward.

The Queen tossed the letter onto a sideboard—a nice piece of furniture acquired during the reign of Henry VII from the 15th Century. She was giving Edward, 3rd Duke of Sussex, a careful once over, then spoke:

"I will give you permission, <u>for one week only</u>, to marry without my approval, only if you remain at Ashfield Hall three years after your first child is born. No sneaking off to America. Otherwise I withdraw my permission. Agreed?"

"Agreed, your Majesty. That is very generous..." blathered Jack.

"Of course it's generous, it's who I am," proclaimed one of the most tight-assed Monarchs in the entire history of the monarchy.

"I deeply apologize your Majesty. You are the most generous..."

"Be off with you," said Victoria, cutting Duke Edward off, "before I change my mind."

Jack quickly backed the hell out of there.

CHAPTER 36

The Wedding

Edward, 3rd Duke of Sussex, stood silent at the front of the Chapel of St George. His Best Man was Prince Alfred. His two other Groomsmen were Princes Arthur and Leopold. All three men looked very good in their formal Afternoon wedding attire.

The gallery was packed.

The church organ began playing the processional song, Bridal Chorus by Richard Wagner, written for his 1850 opera Lohengrin.

The gallery rose in unison and turned to the back of St George's.

There stood the bride. She was escorted by Albert, Prince of Wales. The bride wore white silk and Honiton lace. She floated down the aisle, gliding over the black and white diamond shaped checkerboard marble tiles.

Edward smiled. He knew he'd made the right choice. He was actually excited. He also hoped that nothing would go wrong.

A smaller church meant a shorter runway to display the bride. This was good because Edward wanted to get the show on the road.

When Prince of Wales Albert and the bride reached Edward, Albert shook Edward's hand. His future wife stood to Edward's left. The Vicar, in his white robes with gold trim, opened his 1568 Bishop's Bible written in Tudor English, and read several passages, giving relevance to this joining of Man and Woman.

After a few questions and answers and 'does anyone know of any reason why this couple should not be joined in Holie Matrimony?' and the deafening silence, or glorified silence, which followed, the Vicar proclaimed:

"I now pronounce yee Husband and Wyfe,"

"You may kiss your Bride," was his final suggestion.

Edward lifted his bride's lace veil, held her steady and noticed she was happily, joyfully teary-eyed.   "I love you." said Edward. "I love you, too, Jack. Now fuckin' kiss me!"

Jack kissed Lindy Mae Long a little longer than expected. The gallery applauded. They hugged and shook hands with their groomsmen and bridesmaids. Amongst the bridesmaids was Lindy's Maid of Honour, Red Thunder(!)

The organist started the Recessional. It was all of Jack's sisters' favourite song, written by Felix Mendelssohn in 1842—Wedding March.

And now Jack and Lindy were marching out of St George's, getting in their custom built carriage drawn by eight of Jack's majestic Hanoverian black thoroughbreds which went clip-clopping down to Ashfield Hall through London's horse and carriage traffic, on their way to the Grand Ballroom to party.

Then Honeymoon their brains out.

CHAPTER 37

What the Hell Just Happened

Jack's meeting with Her Majesty had an unexpected turn of events. Mainly that the Queen learned that Beatrice wrote Edward an intimate (hot and steamy) letter. The Queen demanded to see this letter. As soon as she read the letter she threw it down on her side table, and summoned Beatrice. Red Thunder was 'captured' just outside the queen's door.

The Queen, Jack and Red Thunder, together heard the letter read aloud by Jack.

Then HM demanded answers.

One of the questions Her Majesty wanted an answer to was directed at Jack:

"Do you wish to marry my daughter?"

"No, Your Majesty."

"Do you wish to be married at all?"

"Yes, Your Majesty."

"To whom?"

"That girl from Wyoming, but I'll never get your permission, Your Majesty."

The Queen paused. She looked at Beatrice, who stood motionless. She looked at Edward, also motionless.

"You have my permission to marry anyone you choose, except Beatrice. And you have one week to ask for that girl to marry you. One week. Then I'll withdraw my generous offer."

"Yes, Your Majesty. That is very generous," replied Jack, suddenly wanting to get the hell out of there.

"Of course it's generous. I'm nothing but generous." scolded Victoria waving Jack away, who quickly backed out of the Queen's Reception, raced down the hall, flew down the long, curved stairway, jumped on Noble Warrior and raced homeward.

Jack stopped at the stables where Lindy was grooming Crazy Horse and who was also pissed that Jack dared take his own horse, Nobel Warrior, for a ride. "Don't run him too hard, Jack."

As Jack dismounted he was overcome with fear! He was as nervous as a teenager about to ask a girl out on a date. He'd never felt so cornered. What if she says no?

Lindy was brushing and talking to Crazy Horse. He stopped to watch. Lindy was happy.   Did she want to ruin her joy by being married to Jack whose mother lived with him? Did she want the burden of raising a family. Did she want anything to do with Her Majesty and the defective Royal Family? Or did she want to get out of England and go back home?   Jack was about to turn around and go back to the house.

"Jack! You spyin' on me?" wondered Lindy.

"Ah, I wanted to talk to you when you're done," said Jack nervously.

"I ain't done for a while. I got to shovel shit and…"

"I just got permission from the Queen to marry you. So, will you marry me?"

He just blurted it out!   Jack had prepared a speech, a meandering speech, but not for now, but over dinner., after half a bottle of good wine. Jack panicked and spit out what he'd wanted to say for months.

Lindy dropped her horse's brush, walked over to Jack, and said, "Say that again, Jack. Only slow the fuck down."

"I said: Lindy, will you please marry me. I'm in love with you. I've felt strongly about you since the night you rode into my camp after you shot the sheriff, and ate most of my chilli."

"Which some fuckin' Paris-trained cook made for you. And had some strong-arms set up your tarp. You're lucky you met me. Damned lucky." said Lindy, drawing closer and closer to Jack's mouth with her mouth.

"I know that, I was just going to say that.."

Lindy shut Jack up with a kiss. A real kiss. Something that would be described as hot, heavy and horny but it was October of 1880. Lindy and Jack kept kissing like this until Noble Warrior got disgusted with this display and kicked his stall's door.

Lindy broke off the kiss, and told Noble Warrior off, "Go over there and leave me alone.   Can't you see I'm kissing my husband."

"So you'll marry me?"

"I've been waiting all fuckin' summer for you to pull your royal head out of your royal ass, wake up and realize what you got. Me!"

In Jack's bed that night Lindy for the first time—wearing a flannel nightie—moved closer to her husband and kissed. "You gonna go limp on me or is it gonna work?" wondered Lindy. Then she appeared to move her arm and said, "Good. Let's git to it."

After initial sex, the first thing Lindy said to Jack was, "Your mother's getting kicked out this weekend."
"Yes ma'am," said Jack.
"Don't call me ma'am. I ain't some old woman. Your mother is a ma'am."
"Yes, your ladyship," said Edward.
"That's more like it. Now, let's get some grub."

Jack enlisted the help of Mr Harrison and the Housekeeper, Mrs Dahlgren, to plan the wedding reception in the Grand Ballroom. Then to find an acceptable church or chapel. Confirm a date, let Her Majesty know that all this was done within the one week time limit for permission to marry a non-royal woman who wore men's clothes.
HM had St George's Chapel booked for a Tuesday, gathered all HM's available children, including Beatrice, and everything was set and the wedding went off without a hitch. That's what the hell happened.

CHAPTER 38

First Married Dinner

Jack gently pushed the chair in for his brand new bride. She thanked him. The Servants in attendance did not roll their eyes. It wasn't allowed. Then Jack pushed the chair in for his mother, Lady Agatha. Still not a reinstated royal Duchess and she didn't know what was taking so long.

All three of her daughters were successfully married to Her Majesty's wayward sons, and two of the three were already pregnant. Elsie, the eldest, was ready to pop. Elsie was also created a Royal Duchess because Prince Alfred was Victoria's favourite son. Now Agatha had to curtsy to her eldest daughter and call Elsie Your Royal Highness. Elsie got used to it immediately.

Harriet was pregnant (from carnal pleasures all through Europe) and she was created a noble duchess, the penalty for running off and eloping. Then returning to get married properly, embarrassing Her Majesty. The style of a noble duchess is 'your grace'. Not 'your royal highness.'
But it's better than 'Lady Harriet.' Harriet is several steps above her mother who has to enter a room after all three daughters—them being married to royal princes. Agatha had to enter tonight's dining room after Jack and Lindy because Lindy is married to a Royal Duke. As a matter of etiquette, no one at table can start eating before the highest ranking member (Jack) and must stop eating when the highest ranking member puts his fork or spoon down. These rules don't affect Lindy because Jack's newly found love life would come to a screeching halt.

Mr Harrison, the Butler, keeps track of Royal protocol and has the power to report any wrong-doing to the Palace. Agatha is aware of this. Agatha is very angry but Agatha has learned how to hold her tongue—until she gets her Royal Duchess title back.

Nora and Leopold were off traveling. They went to America where members of the elite New York 400 Club, organized and ruled by Mrs Caroline Schermerhorn Astor, grabbed them and took them on a whirlwind tour of members of the Gilded Age. The richest of the rich in America.

Prince Leopold, youngest son of Queen Victoria, became a superstar. Young, glamorous and married to a beautiful young woman whose great-grandfather was King George III. She was accidentally called Princess. Nora, and the American press, let that mistake go.

But tonight's dinner at Ashfield Hall was with just the newly married couple plus Jack's mother.

There was no fish course, which annoyed mother. There will never be a fish course, unless Jack and Lindy desire Fish 'n Chips. Which is low class food. Delicious low class food which Jack and Lindy love as much as their Delmonico's steak and jacket potato.

There was not a lot of conversation, which also annoyed mother.

Then, to liven things up: "Why wasn't I invited to your wedding!?" There was a dramatic pause, then mother continued without ever looking at Lindy, "Did she have something to do with it?"

Jack might have said several things to his mother, like, 'Because when the Vicar asked if anyone had a problem with this couple, speak now or forever hold your tongue, that would be your cue to ruin the wedding. I guarantee you, Lindy would have shot you dead a couple of minutes later.' But Jack said something else. He said something that would prove to Lindy that he had something Lindy called 'balls'. Jack wasn't sure what that was: cricket balls? But Jack sure knows what that means now.

"Mother," began Jack, "I want you out of my house by the week-end. Lock, stock and attitude. This was my idea, not Lindy's. Lindy wanted to shoot you and leave you in the cellar for the rats to eat." Jack was not joking. Lindy had drawn up a plan after she saw a rat in the cellar.

"You can't throw me out, where will I go?"

"Your 12 bedroom home in Mayfair. Painters are already sprucing the place up," countered Edward.

"Painters in my home?"

"It's my house. In fact, Mother, it's Lindy's and my house.

"I said 'let the old coot live in a dump down by the river.' Jack says, 'no, there are people in Mayfair she hasn't insulted yet."

"I don't like how I'm being treated," complained Agatha.

"Then get the fuck out now, old woman," clarified Lindy.

"Jack, are you going to let that wild hussy speak to me in that manner?"

"Imagine how much fun we'll have at dinner without mother interjecting her unwanted opinions. Beginning Friday afternoon. The movers are coming Friday morning," reported Jack.

'I'm not budging an inch until I get my title back, so you have to call me your royal highness!" was said to Mrs Bride.

"Kiss my skinny white ass," rejoined Lindy, Duchess of Wyoming.

"If Victoria makes *s* a royal duchess I'll move to America!" threatened Agatha.

"Well, Lindy and I have been invited to dinner at the Palace by Her Majesty. A family dinner! All of her sons and their wives, plus Lindy and myself." reported Jack.

The meat course was cleared and on to the dessert course. Edward did not want a salad course and a fruit course. He wanted pastries because Lindy wanted pastries.

The assortment of French and Viennese pastries arrived. Lindy loaded up her plate.

"When she's as fat as an elephant, you'll wish you married Beatrice," said the always charming and affable Edward's mother.

Lindy put half her pastries back and glared at Agatha. Victory for Agatha.

"I haven't received my invitation," announced Agatha.

"Maybe it was mailed to my Mayview house, mother. Nothing came for you here."

Mother stewed, thinking—which was always dangerous. Then she slapped her hand hard on Edward's highly polished Honduran Mahogany table and said, "That Royal Bitch!"

Now that she was sure that everyone's attention had been got, Agatha continued, "She back-stabbed me on purpose. I was led to believe that if all of my daughters were married to her loser sons, and produced grandchildren, that I'd get my title back. Now I'm not invited to a dinner where all of my children will be gathered! How could that happen?!"

Lindy had an answer: "Maybe if you weren't so scheming, you'd get out more. You're as treacherous as a hungry coyote."

To Jack hissed his mother: "You're the one who fucked me!"
Shocking Jack and titillating Lindy. That was only the second time he
heard his mother swear like Lindy. Like a drunken sailor.

"You're delirious," defended Edward.

"I laid a trap so perfect there's no way you shouldn't be
married to Beatrice this second."

"A trap?" wondered Jack.

"That letter she wrote to you?   I dictated it to her. Made
sure that Royal messenger dragged himself over here. I paid him £5
to deliver it to you. It should have worked."
Agatha was pained that her perfect scheme had failed.

"The Queen wouldn't let Red Thunder get married.
Everyone knew it 'cept you," divulged Lindy.

"But the old woman commanded you to show up. I know
you brought the letter. She was supposed to agree to the wedding,"
said Agatha to Jack.

"Her Majesty called Beatrice into her Reception Room, then
asked me straight out, did I want to marry Beatrice.? And I said 'no',
I want to marry that cowgirl from Wyoming," reported Jack.

Lindy was stunned and pleased. She didn't know this. Jack
had been so nutless and wishy-washy that he should have caved in,
thought Lindy.

That's exactly what his mother had counted on.   His mother
had trained Edward to always defer to women, because that's what
'gentlemen' do. Maybe that's why upper station English 'gentlemen'
go to their private clubs to get away from these same women. Men
only.

Edward's grandfather, Prince Augustus, belonged to Boodle's
Club (founded 1762) and White's Club (founded 1693). His father
and uncle Frederick belonged to those clubs, plus the Oxford and
Cambridge Club (founded 1830). No women members or visitors.

Then Edward's uncle Frederick ordered the construction of
his own Gentlemen's Club, secreted away along a maze of walkways
that led to excellent cigars and superior wines and whiskys. Lindy
found a liquor store in the City of London featuring Jack Daniels
Tennessee Whiskey. The taste of America. This liquor store was on
the ground floor of Harrods.

Jack, without realizing it, had been trained by Lindy from the
second she showed up at his camp in that downpour in Wyoming.
She was a powerful foul-mouthed magnet. She easily got him to take
her to Ashfield Hall.   Then, take her back to Colorado, with high

powered lawyers, to clear her name. And then, to easily choose Lindy over Beatrice in front of Beatrice in the Queen's chambers.   He was wrapped and neatly packaged around Lindy's little finger. And when he went to his private Gentlemen's Club, she was right there waiting seductively for him.   Winning the 100th Running of the Epsom Derby was icing on the cake for both of them. Lindy had escape money and Jack had valuable race horses with the world's finest trainer and jockey.

     "Oh my dear merciless God!   You!!!," shrieked Agatha, pointing her crooked witch finger, "You cursed witch, you've got my boy wrapped around your little scheming finger. You control him!"
     And that was that. Agatha was bested and she picked up her champagne flute, ordered it filled by a footman and drank a deep, refreshing gulp.   Then Agatha got up from the table, as did Jack following etiquette, and escorted his mother out of the room. Forever.
     Jack returned to the table, gestured to Mr Harrison to clear the table and bring in espresso, tea, port and Jack Daniels for Mrs Jack.
     "Exactly which finger am I wrapped around, your Ladyship?"
     "You'll find out tonight.your royal fuckin' highness."

CHAPTER 39

An Enchanted Evening With Her Majesty

Her Majesty had invited Jack and Lindy along with her sons and their wives, to dinner at Buckingham Palace.

At table were Albert and Alix, Prince and Princess of Wales; Prince Alfred and Royal Duchess Elsie; Prince Arthur and Duchess Harriet; Prince Leopold and Duchess Nora; Royal Duke Edward and Lady Lindy.

The Queen was at the head of the table. (Wherever the Queen sat was automatically the Head of the table, especially if the table were round.)

Her Majesty, dressed in black, looked sour. Nice way to start an enchanted evening.

Before the fish course the Queen spoke up. She had been silent for the past 40 minutes.

"Are you four still running off to Edward's to smoke cigars?"

The boys said nothing. They looked down at their plates, about to be served pan seared Scottish wild salmon.

"They're over a couple of times a week. And we all smoke Cuban cigars and drink brandy, wine and whisky," said Lindy with spunk and enthusiasm. "We have a good time, your Majesty."

"I imagine you do."

"Why don't you join us, Your Majesty? You look like you need something to cheer you up!" remarked Lindy very casually, like she were chatting with a familiar dour aunt.

This between-the-eyes outburst shocked, stunned and stupefied the room. Not Jack, of course. He's used to it.

The women, save Lindy, thrust their hands to their mouths. In girly shock.

Alix, Princess of Wales, immediately reacted by jumping up and attempting to mollify or comfort Her Majesty with a hug.

"Ma'am, she doesn't know our history. She's an outsider. She doesn't mean what she said," soothed Princess Alexandra, brought in from Denmark to settle Albert, Prince of Wales, down. (It didn't work.)

The Queen brushed Alix away.   "Edward's wife knows exactly what she's saying."

Now everyone was looking at Lindy, horrified that the American could say such a mean thing to the most powerful woman on earth.

"And she's right. I am a sour old woman. Which is why my sons sneak over to Edward's to drink and be gay. To laugh and delight in their youth. And to get away from sourpuss old me."
The Queen knows. The Queen always knows.

"From now on, whenever I need a straight answer, I shall come to you, Lady Lindy," said HM, straight out.

"You know I abhor smoking, but I like the aroma of a good cigar. My dear husband, Prince Albert, smoked Cuban cigars, too. I have also secreted away some good scotch. Anyone ever heard of Lagavulin?"

The Queen knew how to shut everyone up. The table all looked to Edward, keeper of a lot of Scotch whisky, cognac, brandy, port and claret, for answers. Edward shrugged. Then Lindy opened her beautiful Mark Cross Overnight Case and removed a bottle of Lagavulin single malt Scotch and put the bottle on the table. "This is good shit. Got a smoky, peaty flavor," announced Wyoming Lindy with authority. The table guests, and servants, were shocked because no one cursed in the presence of Her Majesty. No one. Ever. And no one brought a bottle of scotch and put it on the Queen's dining table. Ever.

"Pour me some," commanded Her Majesty brushing off any discourtesy.

More looks of shock by everyone, except Lindy. As the Footmen headed for the table to figure out a proper crystal glass for Her Majesty, Lindy took out some Waterford crystal barware from her beautiful leather overnight bag. A gift to herself from Harrods, obviously. Lindy removed a beautiful hand-blown 12-ounce crystal glass perfect for single-malt scotch.

A Footman opened the bottle and put it on the table in front of Lindy. She got up, took the glass, set it down in front of Her Majesty and poured about 4 ounces of Lagavulin scotch.

"Am I drinking alone?" wondered Her Majesty.

Lindy took another Waterford 12 ounce bar glass out of her beautiful Mark Cross leather Overnight Case and kept it. She poured herself a healthy 4 ounces, then slid the bottle to her husband, then took a second bottle of scotch out of her Mark Cross Leather Overnight Case.

"What's that bottle?" wondered Her Majesty, as she didn't wait for anyone to get liquored up. She sipped, closed her eyes, swallowed, remembering better times.

"Macallan, ma'am," said Lindy, "I favor this stuff."

"I'll have that next," commanded the Queen.

The Macallan (1855) was brought to HM by Lindy. A Footman opened the bottle, getting it ready to pour for HM when she was ready.

"To Her Majesty, for all she does to save the world." toasted Lindy.

The men raised their glasses, mostly wine stem cut crystal glasses. The wives drank champagne or white wine (it was the fish course that was interrupted), and all said, "Hear, hear, Your Majesty!"

"Why'd you bring scotch to my house, young lady?" demanded Her Majesty.

"I was waitin' for you to go to bed, then I'd liven up the party. Ma'am."

Lindy got the exuberant crowd to shut up once again with her truthful, and horrifying, statement.

"Is this when my sons race over to your Den of Iniquity, Edward?" gently asked HM.

"I, ah.". He was stuttering and got cut off (saved) by Mrs Jack.

"Yes ma'am. They run over like greased lightning. And when they was courtin' Jack's sisters, all the sisters came over, too, eager to smoke and drink—they all like to party" said Lindy throwing more kerosene on the fire she'd started.

"And, once again, to be crystal clear, exactly why did my sons race over to Edward's liquor cabinet, Lady Lindy?"

"To get away from you, ma'am. Always gloomy, no fun to be around. I don't blame your boys. When my pa was gunned down in the street before last Christmas, my mom turned ornery as a honey badger. Mean. I couldn't stand to be home. So, I left Wyoming and ended up here. Ma'am."

"Is that right, Albert? As always, speak for your muted brothers," continued HM.

"Yes. There's a point to your darkness. Put on a bright red dress once in awhile. Celebrate Christmas. There are more grandchildren on the way. Pretend to be happy. You mourn from sunup til sunset every day! It drives a man to drink. And drink we shall!" concluded Albert, Prince of Wales, drinking his Lagavulin. (He wanted the Macallan, but he wasn't King yet. He'd have to wait for the Queen to sip her Macallan.)

How does Prince Albert get away with not being cowed by her majesty? Easy. He's the future King Edward VII and can speak with that authority and bluntness. It's called King's X.

"Does anyone wish to add anything to that? Any of my recently married sons' wives?"questioned Her Majesty.

Silence. More silent than outer space. The servants, standing at attention, were especially quiet whilst enjoying every pronouncement, divulgement and anything out of the mouth of Lindy.

"Lady Lindy, thank you for your courage. You shall accompany me to my bed chamber," said Her Majesty with finality.

The Queen rose. "Albert, drink your Macallan.."

"Thank you, Your Majesty," said the Prince of Wales sincerely.

Everyone rose.

Edward whispered to his bride, "walk her to her bedroom."

Lindy walked around the table and the Queen looked at her. Then muttered something no one could hear. Lindy went back to her seat and picked up her beautiful leather Mark Cross Overnight Case and then she and Her Majesty left the room whilst everyone was bowing and curtsying.

A few seconds after the Butler closed the dining room door, Elsie, the very, very, very pregnant wife of Prince Alfred, remarked to Edward, "You better get your wife under control. How embarrassing to us all!"

"Speak for yourself," said Nora, Prince Leopold's new bride, "Lindy said the right thing at the right time."

"Where was Lindy ten years ago to say the exact same thing?" posited Albert, Prince of Wales.

"She was probably four years old" sniped Harriet, wife of Prince Arthur. Also pregnant—having conceived somewhere in Europe—either Paris, Dijon, Lyon or Switzerland.

"I did not marry a 14 year old," defended Edward.

"Well.? How young is she?" hissed Elsie.

"Old enough to ride my three year old to win the Derby. Old enough to shoot a murderous sheriff in Colorado. Old enough to speak up to the most powerful woman on earth," summed up Edward.

"So, she's 15!" chimed in Nora, the youngest of Edward's sisters. The cattiest.

"She's legal," declared Edward.

Albert, Prince of Wales, and a royal who is currently bedding five or six women, some married, some of questionable age, burst out laughing.

"Good show," roared the Prince of Wales and future king. "I approve!"

"How young is your youngest wench, Bertie?" scolded Alix, the Princess of Wales, in a fit of pique.

That comment shut everyone up.

"Any guesses?" demanded Alix.

"If Lindy were here, and not attending mum, she'd tell us flat out," stated Prince Leopold.

"I'm bored," said the Princess of Wales, getting up, throwing her Irish linen napkin down, and huffing out of the room. No one stood.

"You entering Ascot, Bertie?" wondered Edward, changing the subject to horse racing.

"That the name of a girlfriend?" quipped Prince Arthur, looking for trouble.

Laughter by the boys. Sullen darkness by their wives.

"Yes. I've got two four year olds (winking at Prince Arthur) who can go the distance. You?" Said Bertie, perking up because horse racing was his current passion.

"I'm sticking by Noble Warrior. He'll be four. He can go the distance. I'll have my wife ride her again."

"Then, no, my dear Edwardo. I'll not run any of my stable so long as your filly is the jockey," replied Bertie (Tex to Lindy).

Lindy came back in the room wearing a huge smile. The gentlemen stood and applauded Lindy like she did something impossible and good: namely drank very good scotch with HM, thanks to Lindy. A royal first.

"If I were king, I would knight you instantly," remarked Albert, future King Edward VII,   "Knight Commander, Order of the Garter!" stated Bertie, the Order of Chivalry in which he'd invest Dame Lindy, the First Order of Chivalry, founded 1348.

"You were fabulous," said Lindy's husband, Jack, who hugged her.

"What'd Her Majesty say?" wondered Nora, Harriet, Elsie and Alix in unison.

"She told me to come to tea Wednesday to size up some guy named Dizzy, Did, Dis-ailee." answered Lindy.

"Disraeli?!" said all the men in the room, shocked and interested. This was big.

"What's Disraeli up to?" wondered Albert.

"Wants Gladstone out of the way so he can return to Prime," concluded Alfred.

"But what're you supposed to do, pour his tea?" demeaned Elsie of Lindy.

"Are you old enough to pour tea?" wondered Harriet.

"Let's party!" announced Lindy taking two different smaller bottles out of her Mark Cross Overnight Case. Jack Daniels and Boodles Gin.

Prince Leopold promised he'd supply bottles of tonic soda water with quinine for a recent British passion, the gin and tonic. Three servants appeared with a total of six bottles of Schweppes India Tonic Soda Water. And a bucket of ice cubes.

Barware also appeared and drinks were manufactured or poured straight into the glassware.

"I'm 20, born 1860. I just look 14," said Lindy, lying just to shut everyone up. It worked.

"Well, Nora, play the piano, Elsie, you sing and Harriet, sketch us drinking," chirped Lindy and that's what happened until the wee hours (about 11:30pm) when the old married couples headed for home. And that now included Jack and Mrs Jack.

CHAPTER 40

Tea With Benjamin Disraeli

Benjamin Disraeli was Prime Minister of the United Kingdom right before the current Prime Minister, William Ewart Gladstone. Disraeli's last day in office was April 21, 1880. Her Majesty favours Disraeli and wants a solid second opinion: that's Lindy's job. HM requires her subjects to tell her what she wants to know and instead, Her Majesty gets inundated with fiction, tall tales and flat out lies to appease HM, to not upset her with facts. This cowgirl from Wyoming, wherever that is, only reveals the truth, using 'vivid' 'flagrant' 'colorful' 'obscene' language. The result is the Queen gets the information she needs, unvarnished, unpolished yet true. You can't make sound decisions based on fictional stories.

Beatrice tells the truth when she wants to shock her mother, and lies when she wants to appease her mother—to get Beatrice's way. This Wyoming cowgirl only speaks the truth, raw, rough edges, but it's the truth and the truth hurts.

Lindy walked into the Queen's Reception by herself. The Queen's Guard nodded to Lindy. The Queen's Guard opened the private door to Her Majesty's quarters, announcing the cowgirl's arrival.

Her Majesty was happy to see Lindy.

Lindy actually curtsied to the Queen. Both looked a question at the Queen's Guard who 'got the message' and abruptly and politely left, closing the thick soundproof door. Lindy took a bottle of Jack Daniels out of her Mark Cross Overnight Case. Lindy poured some into the Queen's cup of tea. Lindy poured some into her Waterford barware.

"You are about to meet an important man in my government. Tell me what you think of him," said the Queen, which sounded like 'tell me what I want to hear, not the truth.' Lindy was only prepared to tell the truth the way she saw it.

The Queen pressed a button and her Queen's Guard entered and HM commanded, "Bring in Mister Disraeli."

A few seconds later former Prime Minister Benjamin Disraeli entered, bowed to HM then noticed a young woman dressed in black pants, black silk blouse and black leather fringed jacket standing next to HM. A very odd sight indeed.

A table was set for two. For tea.

HM's Equerry seated Her Majesty.

HM's Footman seated Lindy.

Disraeli seated himself. Disraeli was a Conservative and still in Parliament, the House of Commons. He was the head of the Conservative and Unionist Party.

"I will stay for a few moments then leave you two to your discussion," announced Victoria.

"Why'd you lose to Gladstone?" was Lindy's first question to Disraeli, who lost his Prime Minister position to William Gladstone because Disraeli was a conservative and favored the Ruling Class of Great Britain, not the 'servant' class, the people. Disraeli didn't want 'the people' to vote or to enjoy any of the luxuries and freedoms of the Ruling Class (landed gentry, those who owned land.)   Disraeli came to fame during the Irish Potato Famine in the 1840s when he wanted the Irish to starve to death, rather than rescind the Corn Laws which would send needed food to Ireland from all over the world, especially America. The Irish famine caused one million peasants to starve to death. Disraeli wanted to protect incompetent upper class English farmers who weren't very productive with their farmland, Instead of forcing the English farmers to compete with good farmers and welcome grains from all over the world, the Corn Laws said Ireland can only buy grains from England.

But that's not how Disraeli told his story.

That's why HM invited Lindy—a girl from farm and ranch land—to see what Disraeli was up to. And why he lost an important election to William Gladstone, a liberal and man of the people.

The Queen did not favor anyone not holding land to be able to vote and voice an opinion in government through their representatives. The Queen was very much in favor of the Ruling Class and not allowing the Servant Class any power. That's why the Queen favored Disraeli and not Gladstone. The people, who didn't own much, were given the right to vote by Gladstone through his series of Reform Acts. It was these new voters who threw Disraeli out because of how he allowed millions to starve. The Corn Laws were overturned and massive amounts of food went to Ireland.

CHAPTER 41

Lindy Brings The Empire to its Knees

Not ten minutes after former Prime Minister Benjamin Disraeli left and the servants removed all the remnants of Tea, did HM return to the room where Disraeli sat alone with Lindy the Interrogator.

HM entered, smiling and confronting Lindy Mae Long, to provide instructive and constructive analysis of this critical event.

"What did you think of my friend Sir Right Honourable Lord Benjamin Disraeli?"

"Honorable? That piece of shit. I'd kick his ass down the stairs!"

"What? How dare you?" commanded Her Majesty.

"The guy has it in for poor people. Jack told me he was against lowering the price of bread, something about corn laws, so poor Irish can afford to feed their families. What Dizzy did was criminal. You get hanged for something like gat where I come from."

"Look," continued Lindy "If you don't feed the poor, then the poor will find ways to feed themselves. And that's what my daddy did. Robbed banks. You've never been hungry. You'll never be hungry. That's good. You can't imagine how terrible it is to go hungry and not know when your next meal is—that's what it's like been' poor."

The Queen was flummoxed. How did Tea with a former Prime Minister turn into being hungry, robbing banks and not knowing when your next meal was coming from? Your meal came from the kitchen prepared to perfection by your Paris-trained executive chefs, and brought to you by servants!

"Disraeli made me Empress of India!" declared a perplexed Queen.

Lindy looked startled. Confused. "You mean that jackass is your boss?"

"No! That's preposterous.   He's just a member of my Parliament. The lower house."

"But he has to be your boss to make you Empress. Otherwise you make yourself the Empress. That's what I'd do if I was Queen. Make myself Empress." Lindy was adamant. There was no other way.

The Queen now looked confused, as in the foul-mouthed kid from America has a point.

"Jack once told me he needs your permission to marry me. I told Jack that he needs **my** permission to marry me. No one else. But that ain't the point—you think it's better to be some empress of some place no one's heard of than it is for your own people to afford to eat?   Let your own people—your own family—starve to death? And not give a whip! That's what Diz-really wants. Is that what you want?"

Lindy was fuming.   She put her hands on her hips, challenging the most powerful woman on earth, glaring at HM.

The Queen didn't blink.

Lindy turned and walked out, knowing that no one turns her back on the Queen. No one.

Lindy pushed the thick soundproof door open, walked out and went home.

CHAPTER 42

The Investiture

Lindy Mae Long was seated on a velvet covered chair out in a long marble hallway. The ceilings were high, the hallway was empty of humanity. Lindy was dressed differently. In a dark sapphire blue dress that went from her neck to the floor. This dress was custom tailored from Harrods. But on her it looked plain. Her hair was no longer 'blowing in the wind' wild but pinned up and contained. She looked subdued as though she had been royally scolded.

She sat by herself, fidgeting, looking around as if to be saved from whatever it is she's waiting for.

Shortly, the 20 foot tall mahogany door near her chair opened. Out stepped an elderly gentleman in a dashing red and gold tunic. He was the Lord Great Chamberlain. He stood tall and looked down upon Lindy and said, simply and clearly, "Step inside Lady Sussex." No 'please', no 'thank you', just a cold, unfeeling command.

Lindy's fate awaited her behind the 20 foot tall mahogany door. She stood and flattened her dress. This was the second time she'd worn a dress. Ever. The first time you'll remember she wore a white dress to her wedding. And now this dark blue silk and satin number. It shimmered in the dreary gas lighting inside the Palace. Both times she'd worn a dress were for occasions that had to do with royal affairs. Lindy's stomach was churning. She ached to be riding Crazy Horse out on the wide open range of Wyoming, where she and Crazy Horse were at home.

She silently walked past the Lord Great Chamberlain who stood motionless at attention.

Inside the large room with very high ceilings, and very large paintings of former kings and queens (Elizabeth, Mary I, Mary II, Anne and Victoria), were a small gathering of dignified upper class individuals. Amongst them were Jack, her loving, patient, *very* patient husband. He was dressed in a black tuxedo with a white bowtie. Harriet and pregnant Nora. (Obscenely pregnant Elsie was home loudly complaining.) Prince Alfred, Elsie's husband, came over and shook Lady Lindy's hand, mentioning how his pregnant wife was loud and annoying. Jack mentioned that Elsie was loud and annoying thirty years before she was 9 months pregnant.

Jack's mother was present. Lady Agatha sniffed out an Investiture at the Palace, and seeing as she was 'owed' her royal duchess title, with amenities, barged in just incase Her Majesty felt generous, or guilty about reinstating Lady Agatha's royal title and style.

There was a band. Yes, a band of musicians. And there were soldiers in dress uniforms.

Lindy was led to a space in the front of the room. There was a tall mahogany rostrum. The Lord Great Chamberlain led Lindy to this tall, thin rostrum, also called a dais. On top of the dais was a red leather Royal Investiture Container. Upon the Container was the Royal Cypher of Queen Victoria.

Before Lindy could focus on anything, a double set of doors opened and an announcement was made for all to hear. It was loud and enthusiastic: "Her Majesty, Victoria, Queen of the British Empire and Empress of India."

Queen Victoria, wearing her small crown, dressed in her usual black, swept into the room accompanied by two Gurkha Orderly Officers (Nepalese soldiers who are integral to the British Royal Army). Following Her Majesty were the Yeoman of the Guard (Queen's body guards).

The Queen stopped at the center of the room. The band played the National Anthem. Lindy perked up because she thought the band was playing My Country Tis of Thee (Sweet Land of Liberty). They were not. They were playing God Save The Queen. Same music as My Country Tis of Thee, far different lyrics.

The Queen's Equerry, whom we've seen earlier, escorted HM to the tall dais (but not too tall as HM was under 5 feet.) where Lindy was standing.

The Queen stutter-stepped when she saw Lindy in a dress, squinted to make sure she was the same girl in the tight leather fringed pants and jacket.

Lindy curtsied and did not look HM in the eye. She kept her head bowed, not knowing what to expect. Lindy did not know the exact reason she was there. Jack, a royal who grew up with customs and ceremony somehow expected his wife to know what an Investiture was.

The Queen motioned to the small audience and said, "Pray, be seated."

Everyone sat quietly. The Lord Great Chamberlain approached the dais, looked at the crowd and announced, "Her Majesty has chosen to Honour a new member of the Royal Family. Lady Lindy Sussex from America, recently Betrothed to Edward, 3rd Duke of Sussex."

The Lord Great Chamberlain stepped away leaving HM on one side of the dais facing Lindy on the other side, just a couple of feet apart.

HM's Equerry stepped in and opened the red leather Royal Investiture Container on top of the dais. Her Majesty removed an elegant, ancient gold and diamond necklace and placed it over Lindy's head.

The Equerry then handed HM a small crown, a Coronet, made of gold, silver, platinum and diamonds. Lindy's eyes bulged. The Queen placed the Coronet on Lindy's head. "I hope it isn't too heavy for you," added Her Majesty. Lindy looked HM in her green-blue eyes. HM looked confident and relatively happy.

The coronet fit perfectly. The Equerry spent a minute with hair pins making sure Lindy's coronet didn't slide off her head.

Lindy had a rehearsal a couple of hours ago with the Equerry and Jack, making sure her hair was ready to accept a small crown and her dress—sapphire blue—would surely show off the gold and diamond necklace.

The Queen looked over Lindy and said, "By all rights and honours of my Kingdom, from this day forth, I create you, Her Royal Highness, Lindy Mae, Third Duchess of Sussex."

There was a pause, then The Queen looked at Lindy and said, "Now fix me a drink."

Jack rushed over to Lindy and said, "Your royal highness, you are now a true royal duchess, part of the British Royal Family."

"Boy, they'll regret that," said Lindy, "Now outta my way, HM needs her scotch."

Lindy took off toward an area in the Palace (the cozy room next door), known to Lindy where the 'good stuff' was stashed.

Lindy opened a 'hidden' doorway and disappeared.

Her Majesty and Lindy quickly returned to the Investiture Ballroom, took a seat at the head of a small round table, with seating for only one more. Everyone else stood and mingled and let Lindy and HM chit-chat and sip their scotch.

A footman arrived at HM's small table and presented Her Majesty and Her Royal Highness, Lindy, 3rd Duchess of Sussex, with a bottle of Macallan which he put on the table.

Peace at last. The Equarry approached carrying a beautifully carved African walnut chair with a thick padded seat and placed it betwixt Her Majesty and Her Royal Highness.

"Baby, you know Lindy.?"

"She named me Red Thunder," said Princess Red Thunder, adding, "we're old drinking and smoking buddies, Mum," reminded Beatrice, "And I was Lindy's Maid of Honour."

"When're you gonna let Red Thunder get married and sprinkle the floor with more grandchildren for you to play with?" wondered Royal Duchess, Mrs Sussex.

"I'll tell you what, Mrs Sussex, every time Baby finds a man, you interview him the way you do a horse or Disraeli. If you kind a keeper, bring him to me immediately," commanded Her Majesty.

Baby lit up like an over-candled Christmas tree. "Really, Mum?"

"But you still must live in this God--forsaken house until your first child is off to school!"

"I'll do it! Can I have a drink to celebrate?"wondered Red Thunder.

"Most certainly not. You're not old enough," said HM.

"I'm 26 years old!"

"And I'm the Queen."

You can't argue with that. You can, but where will it get you? Over to Jack and Lindy's drinking and smoking club.

Victoria saw someone look her way, then pretended not to notice and turn around. Victoria summoned her Equerry, whispered something inaudible and sent him on his way.

"I assure you Lindy, my people, my family, even the Irish, are well fed," was Victoria's only reference to last month's contretemps regarding Disraeli's failure to rescind the Corn Laws. Parliament rejected Disraeli's attitude, got rid of the Corn Laws which brought shipments of foods into Ireland and prevented the starvation of more Irish, due to their potato famine. Lindy nodded in agreement with the Queen.

Approaching with the Equerry was Edward's mother, Lady Agatha. She was dutiful. This was Investiture Day and there was a possibility that she might regain her title, style, position and seat at the royal table. However, she showed up uninvited. She mentioned that all three of her daughters were married to the queen's sons, which got her in.

Lady Agatha came over to the table where Her Majesty, and two Royal Highnesses sat. Agatha curtsied deeply, one knee scraping the thick Persian carpeted Ballroom floor. Agatha did not look at, or seem to notice Lindy, seated not 3 feet away.

"I wanted to speak with you Lady Agatha," began HM.

Agatha gasped. Could this be it? My title reinstated? My royal highness style recognized? I certainly deserve it was the look on Agatha's face.

Her Majesty continued, "I've someone important for you to acknowledge. Her Royal Highness, Lindy, Third Duchess of Sussex, is my right hand man. She gives me readings on anyone I wish to learn about. I trust my royal duchess implicitly. I believe you two have met," said Victoria with a smirk in her voice.

"Yes, your Majesty, we have met," said Agatha with limp hesitation.

"Is that how you show respect to the most important person in the Palace after me?" demanded the queen with an acid tongue.

"Please, your Royal Highness, Duchess Lindy, I sincerely beg your forgiveness for my inexcusable rudeness," cowered Agatha, former royal duchess, to Lindy, cowgirl and brand new royal duchess, who shot a sheriff and is now married to her son who should be married to Beatrice.

"You weren't being rude, Lady Agatha," replied Lindy, Third Duchess of Sussex, member in excellent standing of the Royal Victorian Family, "You were acting, as always, in your best interests," smiled Lindy, then turned to HM and said, "I want you to have a big Christmas this year. I'll find Red Thunder a good husband who will keep her here, near you, ma'am."

HM's Equerry escorted Lady Agatha away from the area and out the door.

Her Majesty went to bed early, happy that all was well in her Kingdom. A happy queen meant the party in the Investiture Room (the Grand Ballroom, the largest room in the Palace) heated up. A young man, a recent Oxford graduate who couldn't take his eyes off Red Thunder, was overjoyed when she grabbed him and made him dance with her. Lindy looked pleased.

Jack watched Lindy look at them and said, "She playing with him?"

"I think she could go for him in a big way, Jack," remarked Her royal highness, Mrs Lindy.

"Will she court him?" wondered Jack.

"I got a feeling she'll fuck him all night long startin' in about half an hour," replied Lindy matter-of-factly.

"I see." is all Jack could utter. Still shocked at Lindy's view of the world which was, according to Her Majesty the Queen, an extremely accurate view.

CHAPTER 43

1899

It was a dark and stormy late afternoon, raining very hard. In the family dining room, the family was gathered: Jack, his lovely bride of 19 years (Lindy), and their three children. The kitchen had a simple dinner prepared: chili con carne and fresh baked cornbread for the main meal. Apple pie for dessert.

Today was May 3rd, 1899, the 19th anniversary of the day Lindy shot the sheriff in a terrible downpour, rode north and bumped into her future husband a few miles south of Cheyenne, Wyoming Territory.

Jack's traveling chef had made chili con carne, cornbread and an apple pie as other staff set up camp, built a fire, parked his carriage, made sure his horses were fed and watered, erected a large water-proof tarp because a big storm was headed Jack's way. Jack was excited to be camping so far from home out in the wild, wild west. His servants were excited to get the hell out of there and back to their rooms in the swankiest hotel in Wyoming.

The three children of Jack and Lindy, seated at table, recognized the chili and apple pie dinner. Once a year they got to hear how their mother, a Royal Duchess and prominent member of the British Royal Family, grew up in Wyoming Territory, took the law into her own hands and gunned down an outlaw sheriff who murdered Lindy's father. The kids loved the fact that her father robbed banks.

The children weren't sure whether they wanted their mother shooting anyone. Well, one child, the middle child, liked her mother taking the law into her own hands.

Jack and Lindy's first child was born in 1882. A bouncy baby boy named Jack. His Christened name was Jack. His full name was Jack Edwardo. He is currently 17 years old and will graduate St Paul's School in two weeks. Edward (Jack) went to St Paul's as did his father. St Paul's was founded in 1509 (when Henry VIII was king) and prepared students for colleges at Cambridge or Oxford University.

Their second child, a girl, was born in 1884. Her name is Arlene. Her full name is Arlene Lindy Mae Sussex. Arlene is 16 and sassy, rides ponies like a man, is confrontational like a man and swears like her mother. **And yes, Arlene loves the fact that her mother gunned down the sheriff and got away with it. And ended up with a royal duke who lives next door to Queen Victoria. And the queen and Lindy are 'drinking buddies'—according to Arlene, middle child of Jack and Lindy.**

The baby of the family, another girl, was born several years later in 1888. Presenting Victoria, whose full name is Victoria Cheyenne Crazy Horse America Sussex. After that naming outburst, the lovely married couple decided to stop breeding. Victoria is now going on 12.

Lindy didn't stop racing in the Epsom Derby. Lindy won the 1883 Derby on her 3-year old named Wyoming Renegade, then she won the 1884 Derby, while 2 months pregnant, riding Sheriff Shooter, and she won the 1886 Derby honoring Princess Beatrice by riding Red Thunder II. Lindy retired as a Jockey to take care of her kids. The job of nannies to upper class English. Lindy's attitude was 'no nanny is gonna screw up my kids. That's my job.' All three kids learned the ways and customs of the Lakota, and who Crazy Horse the warrior was. They learned to ride with Western saddles, how to rope, how to shoot, but not how to smoke, drink and cuss. Arlene, the middle child, excelled in her lessons, especially smoking, drinking and cussing. Lindy's daughter Arlene was mini-Lindy. Mother Lindy was not amused, especially at social gatherings.

Tonight's dinner presentation was different. Instead of their mother's Colt .44 Peacemaker—empty of bullets—holstered, and on the dining room table for Show & Tell purposes, there was a model of a transAtlantic Ocean liner, as the centerpiece on the dining room table.

The boy, Jack, called Jack Junior by Lindy, and Jackie by Arlene and Victoria, was riveted on the ship.

"Yes, son, we're going to America on the RMS Oceanic. Its maiden voyage will be September 6th," alerted Jack (Edward) to his son and everyone else within earshot.

Jubilation!

"No school! Thank you, father!" jubilated Arlene, the one child who, like her mother, liked to play all day and sleep all night. Distractions like school, then homework, were displeasing to Arlene. Jack, on the other hand had this to say: "Unfortunately, father, I cannot go on your 'adventure'. University begins Monday the 11th."

"Okay. Victoria, what about you? You going to America with us?"

"Well, father, how long will we be gone? I am expecting another grand birthday celebration on the 15th, and this year it's a Friday, as you should know," reminded Victoria Cheyenne Crazy Horse America Sussex.

"The Oceanic takes 8 days to get to America. We will then board our own train and head to the wild west to see where your mother grew up and where the murder trial took place. We should be back here before Guy Fawkes Day, November 5th. Jackie will be at Cambridge and you shall stay with grandmother Agatha at her house. I'm sure she will figure out a smashing birthday party for you." said her father with an evil smirk slathered across his face.

"I'm going with you!" shrieked Victoria. Of course she is. Ten minutes in Agatha's clutches will send any child screaming, running for her life.

The good news for the entire family was Lindy's royal duchess title. It was Agatha-repellant. Agatha, still no longer a royal duchess, had to curtsy and call Lindy 'Your Royal Highness' when in Lindy's presence. That has never happened since Lindy's investiture when the Queen made sure Agatha bowed and scraped to the mischievous Wyoming renegade. Agatha returned home and vowed never to cross Lindy's path again.

"So son, we have purchased your ticket. You may give it to a trusted fellow who isn't up to the tasks of school just yet. But remember, the consequences of going with us are dealing with Arlene and Victoria on a daily basis for several months."

Halfway through apple pie and ice cream, Jackie, sipping his sparkling water concluded, "I shall be joining you on the Oceanic." He then put two more scoops of ice cream on top of his third piece of apple pie.

"Junior eats like the Prince of Wales." remarked Jack senior.

All Aboard the Oceanic

Jack and Lindy's family, along with their luggage, six servants which included three kitchen, under butler and two footmen. boarded the RMS Oceanic at Southhampton.

The children were excited. The Atlantic Ocean was cooperative, only a few minor storms with minimal rocking of the steam ship.

They arrived safely in New Jersey, and immediately wobbled (sea legs) across the pier and were greeted by one of the Vanderbilt children (Henry, age 27) who leased Edward, 3rd Duke of Sussex, his 14 car train. Jack, traveling by himself needed 9 cars. Having a family required more food, more sleeping space, more space for storing gifts, presents and just plain stuff picked up in America.

TheVanderbilts provided Edward with Rights of Way, two engineers, two firemen, and two conductors. Plus Water and Coal Rights along the way.   Edward gave Henry Vanderbilt a Certified Bank Cheque from the J.P. Morgan & Company, in the amount of $30,000.

Henry bowed gracefully then shook hands with Edward, 3rd Duke of Sussex, and said to Edward, "Thank you, your Majesty." Edward replied, "You're quite welcome, sir."

Lindy was itching to get to Wyoming. First of all, Wyoming was now the 44th State. Wyoming had its own star on the U.S. flag. Lindy's mother, Irdine, was alive and well.   And that's all the information she had. If Irdine had a husband, thought Lindy, he was probably in jail, or about to go to jail. Or about to be hanged or shot dead for robbing banks, in jail or not.

After taking the train along New York Central Rail Road rights of way along the 'water route', they arrived in Chicago. The Windy City had a population of 1,099,000 citizens and was the second largest city in the United States in 1899. The trip took four days and made stops along the scenic Hudson River; Albany, New York; Lake Erie; Cleveland; Detroit; along the southern rim of Lake Michigan, to Chicago.

From Chicago, their private train headed south to St Louis, then west to Kansas City, and up to the Union Pacific tracks that headed straight to Cheyenne.

Their train arrived in Cheyenne near sundown. Their enclosed Clarence Carriage was removed (carefully) from its box car. The family then clip-clopped in the hand built Clarence Carriage, pulled by six horses, over to the same hotel Jack stayed in 19 years ago, in 1880.

"You stayed here?" said a saddened Victoria Cheyenne Crazy Horse America Sussex.

"Yes!" said Jack senior with enthusiasm.

"Don't act like a snob or I'll wollop the shit out of y'all," said Lindy in a time when a parent was expected to wollop a mouthy kid.

"This is where you lived, mother?" wondered Arlene, the mouthy one.

"Yes. But a couple miles yonder (south)," pointed out Lindy.

Arlene hugged her father and said, "Thank you daddy for taking mother from this wretched place."

"Maybe we shouldn't take them to the house where I growed up. It'll scar them for the rest of their lives." feared Lindy.

"Maybe we'll stay in the carriage whilst you go inside," suggested Jack senior.

Their beautiful hand-built enclosed Clarence Carriage, pulled by six Hanoverian black Thoroughbreds, rode south for a couple of miles. Lindy instructed the driver, who sat outside, up on the top of the carriage (like every stagecoach you've ever seen), to turn right down a dirt road and stop at the first 'house' along the road.

"This's it! Stop driver," ordered Lindy.

"What's wrong? Are we lost?" wondered Jack Junior.

Arlene looked around disapprovingly and got even more disappointed when Lindy walked briskly up to a ramshackle building. A small house with a roof that needed repair. In fact, the whole place needed to be scraped to the ground and something useful built in its place.

"Father, we're lost, aren't we?" wondered Arlene. Victoria took her father's hand.

"America is a very large place, children. Very large. You can fit England, Scotland and Wales comfortably inside the state of Wyoming. And still have room for another Scotland.".

Edward had conveniently forgotten to answer the question, but his calm demeanor relaxed his children.

Lindy walked boldly up to the front door and knocked on it. "Open up mom, it's me, Arlene!"

Arlene, their middle child, reacted by stating, "Why's mom using my name?"

"Because that's your mother's original name before she shot the sheriff."

"Rleen quit your tom foolery and git in here. R-leen!"

"Coming mother," said Lindy, pushing hard on the door and finally opening it.

Inside the house, which was an open living/family/kitchen area, hasn't changed much in 19 years.

At the same time as Lindy walked in the front door and saw her mother, a young girl walked in the back door and saw Lindy.

Both girls—Lindy and the young girl—looked at each other and said, "Who the fuck are you?"

"Rleen?!?!" squeaked Irdine, "That you?"

"Yes, mama, I brought my family from England!" said, obviously, Lindy.

"What the fuck's goin' on" said the young girl standing in the living room.

"Rleen, meet your little sister!"

"Sister?!" said both girls, stunned.

"My name's Arlene," said Lindy.

"My name's Rleen," said Lindy's half sister.

"So Rleen, where's your daddy? In jail or shot dead?" wondered Lindy.

"You are my sister!" said 18 year old Rleen.

"Jail. But he's due out Tuesday week," said Irdine.

"Where you from again?" said little sister Rleen.

"I grew up in this house, then I shot a sheriff and escaped to England. I married a royal duke and he and my kids are outside right now."

Rleen opened the front door and looked. Sure as shit there was a carriage and standing outside, looking in horror, were Jack, Jack junior, Arlene and Victoria

That night

Lindy sat at the head of the table in their Cheyenne hotel's dining room. To her right was Irdine. To Lindy's left was Rleen, little sister. Lindy's family took up the rest of the table.

Arlene, Lindy's middle child, said, "I'm changing my name! Too many fuckin' Arlene's."

"Change it to Henrietta," suggested Jack senior.

"No! I like Beatrice!"

Lindy and Jack senior screamed "No!"

"Mama, I'm buying y'all a new house. I got cash-money.

"I'm gettin' my own house?" said Irdine.

"Yes!" said Lindy. "Brand new, big as you want!" Jack senior nodded and smiled.

"Take me to California," demanded Rleen, in a manner reminiscent of Lindy at that age.

"Hell yeah!" said Lindy to her new-found sister Rleen.

Two Days Later

A pretty good sized brand new house in Cheyenne, Wyoming. The house was in a section of other brand new homes. Their home was painted white with a brand new roof. Out back was a barn for carriages and horses (also called a carriage house).   Men were moving brand new furniture into Irdine's new home.

Inside the house, in the kitchen, was an ice box--an oak refrigerator.   On top was a 75 pound block of ice which cooled everything inside the ice box. Irdine had beer bottles and victuals inside her brand new ice box. The ice man cometh once a week on Friday.

A new oval kitchen table sat on polished oak plank floors.

Irdine had a brand new bed in her bedroom. There was also a privy. Jack arranged for a flushing toilet from New York City which would arrive, with plumbers, in five days.

"You stayin' Rleen or goin?" wondered Irdine, not caring one way or the other if her latest child went to California or stayed in Wyoming. Eighteen year olds need to vamoose.

"I gotta see where Lindy lives. I hear'd their house is bigger than yourn."

"You got a bank account now, mama. Don't tell no one about it especially how much you got. Git me?. You give your husband an allowance. Ten dollars a week. No more bank robbin'."

"You packed?" threatened Lindy to Rleen.

"I could use some duds."

"We'll stop in Salt Lake, git you some Mormon clothes," quipped Lindy.

"I ain't wearing' no fuckin' Mormon clothes," salted Rleen.

"The hell you ain't." smirked Lindy, Big Sister.

Onward to California

Jack's private train pulled out of Cheyenne heading west on Union Pacific owned railroad track. Lindy's mother was not tearful. She was flirting with one of the moving men who picked up Irdine by her thin (and mean) waist and set her gently down on the top step of the train that would take her south to Denver City and the Daniels & Fisher Department Store. More furniture. Irdine now had $40,000 in her bank account in Cheyenne.

Jack's Family Train

Their new family was in the dining car enjoying dinner: Jack and Lindy, Jack junior, Arlene and Victoria Cheyenne Crazy Horse America. And New Rleen. The UnderButler was serving the soup course whilst the First Footman poured Perrier Sparkling Water for everyone. No more heavy spirits, no more Cuban cigars, and rarely some after dinner port. Lindy put the kaibosh on frivolity once the kids showed up.

The talk was royal family gossip and how Queen Victoria was healthier than ever which was driving Albert, Prince of Wales, mad. He should have been king by now, but wasn't. Other Rleen wondered, "This Albert fellow. Is he really a whale? Can someone harpoon him?"

The royal family members loved it.

"He's as big as a whale, Rleen," quipped Jack junior and 16 year old Arlene added, "The Prince of Wales--called Bertie--is fucking five or six mistresses. His wife doesn't mind because she doesn't want a 400 pound whale lying on top of her!"

Jack senior watched his family, plus Rleen, and thought, 'they're all the same! Each one is more intolerant than the next! They're all like backward Americans. I love it!'

Their train clickety-clacked westward toward the Golden State and the quiet dark blue majesty of the Pacific Ocean, where more adventures were waiting to unfold before this entire family headed back to Ashfield Hall in about a month.

The End